THE ETERNAL QUEEN

Cover Design by: Beautiful Book Covers

THE
ETERNAL
QUEEN

For my husband, who was so angry I killed Malin,
I had to bring her back… sort of.

In him we have redemption through his blood, the forgiveness of sins, in accordance with the riches of God's grace.

Ephesians 1:7

I am crucified with Christ: nevertheless I live; yet not I, but Christ liveth in me: and the life which I now live in the flesh I live by the faith of the Son of God, who loved me, and gave himself for me.

Galatians 2:20

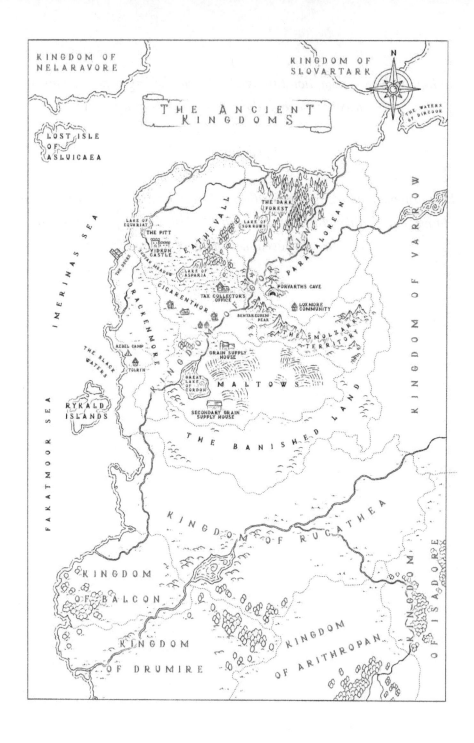

ONE

Eiagan Allurigard

Light. Flames danced over the remnants of a felled tree, licking the darkness with its orange tongues as the Winter Queen stared into its depths. It would be so easy to let go, to allow the darkness within her to catch fire and burn through her heart and soul and mind until all that remained was the hollowed-out shell of who she had become — caught between the person she wanted to be and the burden of what she used to be. But it was too easy to let the anger take her to dark places, for it to fill the shell until all she felt was that white-hot, all-consuming flame that fueled her through every battle, every war, and every moment of self-doubt she had ever experienced. There was no having one without the other. She could not be a warrior without the anger.

Eiagan closed her eyes and inhaled the world around her — the pine, the burning corzaloan, the crispness of the snow, and the spices that wafted from the bakery across the market from where she stood. Those things were real. They existed, just as Reven, Darby, and Violet existed somewhere in the world, somewhere Eiagan would find them and free them from Nessa's grip.

"It is not your fault."

A stick broke under the weight of a boot as a shadow passed over the fire pit, blocking the moonlight for a moment before settling beside Eiagan. She did not need to look at him to know him. Eiagan knew all her people, her *friends,* simply by their presence. She knew their emotions, health, desires... everything by intuition.

"You do not need to make excuses for me, Ari. I know what I did, and it was foolish."

Ari cleared his throat and stamped his feet. "This cold. How did you ever come to love it so much?"

Eiagan ignored his question. It only served to ease the tension between them before Ari dove into his speech.

"Is Emora well?" Eiagan let her eyes drift toward him, to his face. Hard lines with dark shadows beneath his eyes, stubble over his chin and jaw, and the mark. The blasted mark. She wished she might erase it, but her own heated temper had caused it, and nothing would ever change it. Save magic, but Ari had refused magical treatment to rid himself of the red line of death carved by Eiagan's own hand. Likely he did not wish to see Emora use her ability after... *everything.*

"She is recovering from our last journey, as you should be." Ari released his arms and turned to face Eiagan. "This was an accident. We are in a war, Eiagan. Perhaps we do not see a battle every day, but we are in a war all the same. I know you, and I know your heart.

8

Your fire and intensity are the *only* things that have kept us alive thus far, and if you —"

"I almost killed you, Ari. I did not see your face but my father's. Do you understand what I might have done if Porvarth and Emora had not stopped me?"

"I surprised you, and after everything you have lived through, it is no wonder you reacted so violently. I forgave you the moment it happened, Eiagan. Do not do this to yourself. Do not do this to *me*."

Eiagan swallowed a stone that lodged in her throat. It had been there since the incident and refused to ease even a fraction. She allowed her eyes to drift upward again, taking in the man as he stood, waiting for her to accept that the wound he bore was not her fault. She could not.

"I must learn control. I cannot chastise Emora for her weaknesses if I cannot even control my own. This," Eiagan said, grazing her fingers over the scar that traveled from Ari's ear to his collarbone, "will never be acceptable to me. Porvarth is the only reason you did not die, and Emora cannot even look at me without flinching."

"She's afraid for you and for herself. This darkness that pushes you both into solitary confinement is not healthy."

Eiagan shook her head. "You are as close as a brother to me. You are the man my sister adores, and I almost stole you from her. Just as I stole —"

"Stop. Stop, no more. You did not steal Reeve from her. Your father did, and the sooner you realize he was the *only* monster in this story, the sooner these outbursts might contain themselves. I love you, Eiagan. You *are* my family. *You* are the reason I never gave up when Nessa imprisoned Tend and me. It was only a sliver of hope, Eiagan, just a speck that the rumors might be true. And it gave me what I needed to survive it all. So no, I will hear no more of this.

9

It has been five days since the incident, and I have been patient. Now it is time to do what we promised."

"Ari, I cannot simply turn it on and off. It is ingrained in me, in my blood, and in my mind." Eiagan took a step back, suddenly claustrophobic as Ari closed in on her.

"You feel it now, don't you? You feel caged, cornered like a cat." He stepped closer still, taunting Eiagan with that smirk Emora loved so well. Blast it all, Eiagan did not appreciate it the way her sister did, especially when he used it against her as he did then, pushing her to prove she could control herself if she tried hard enough.

"Ari…" Eiagan's raven hair billowed in the breeze as the flames swallowed the last of the logs, casting long shadows over Ari's face. Still, he advanced.

"Work through it, Eiagan. Your blood is, as you said, no excuse for your behavior. So, stop making excuses for your temper and control it. You have conquered every obstacle presented to you since the day of your birth, yet this," he motioned between them, the distance wrought with tension and heat and violence Eiagan fought to control, "will be what conquers the Winter Queen?"

"Stop, Ari. Please don't come any closer." Eiagan's jaw tightened, every muscle tensed, prepared for defense.

"Why? It is *me*, Eiagan. You know, deep in that stony heart of yours, that I would never harm a hair upon your head. Understand. Believe. Trust."

"It's not that simple, fish gutter!" she spat, grinding her teeth. The rage boiled beneath her skin, threatening to darken her vision as he pushed her farther into that corner. "I trust you, but I cannot see that it is you when the rage takes over."

"I don't believe that. I believe you can, and I know you will overcome this hurdle. When you do, it will show Emora that she might overcome it as well."

Ah, there it was. The fish gutter always had a plan, a motive that wound its way back to Eiagan's sister. The man was a fool in love with a woman equally as volatile as Eiagan, but to his credit, he never shied away from a good fight—not since his days gutting fish in Drackenmore. Eiagan inhaled again, focused on Ari's voice and the ease of his motions. He would not stop his advance, so she was forced to do what he asked.

He is your friend. He is not a threat. He is good and kind, and he loves Emora.

Eiagan swallowed and let her gaze drift toward the fire. She closed her eyes and nodded, giving in to the trust that had built between them since they had escaped Nessa's prison together with Tend and Borgard. She focused on the smells, the sounds, and the feel of him as he walked closer to her. Her senses engaged, allowing Ari's signature to wash over her, to remind her he was not a threat. His scent, his gait, his touch—she knew it well enough to keep the picture of his face in her mind.

Ari's fingertips grazed Eiagan's shoulder, then traveled down her arm to her elbow. There, he paused and allowed her time to focus. A breath passed, then his fingers followed her arm to the wrist, then to her sword. She tensed. Ari paused long enough for Eiagan to center herself again, then gripped the sword and tugged. The rage tickled Eiagan's throat, burned, and licked her esophagus like the fire that swallowed the night, but she resisted. She held on to the fury until it felt common and usual, until Ari removing her prized sword from its sheath did not bother her.

"There now, was that so difficult?"

Eiagan opened her eyes. Ari held her sword with a grin on his face that would make her sister swoon. She accepted her sword and replaced it in its sheath.

"It won't always be so easy, Ari. I remind you of what I did to you when you snuck up on me in the forest."

Ari shook his head and sighed. "Anyone might have done the same, Eiagan. It was a mistake, but you are the only one who blames yourself. You are the only one who believes you are cursed by your blood, except Emora, who grows more worried by the day."

Another presence caught Eiagan's attention. Porvarth stood in the shadows, his blue eyes settled on the scene before him. Ari glanced toward the loxmore-turned-dragon, then back to Eiagan.

"I will leave you to be with him, but please stop blaming yourself for this. It was a mistake we both made, but I am alive, and I bear you no ill will. Please. Please, for all our sakes, move on from this so we might continue with our mission." Ari's tone, firm yet kind, settled on Eiagan's heavy heart only a moment before he turned on his heel and headed toward the inn. His muscular frame disappeared in the shadows for several paces before the torchlight at the inn's door illuminated him again. He did not look back, did not hesitate to keep his back to the Winter Queen, and did not offer even a breath of fear in her presence.

"He's not wrong, you know." Porvarth stepped from the shadows.

Eiagan shook her head. "I know, and yet my mind and heart are still at war."

"They cannot be, Eiagan. They must come together if we are to find Nessa and save the children from her clutches. What happened was unfortunate, but we must trudge along as we always do. It's been months, and we are no closer to finding them."

"Will it ever end? Will we ever find peace, or am I a fool to believe we will win this war?" Eiagan's tone left much to be desired, but she could not control even that.

"All questions I have asked repeatedly for centuries, my love. I do not know the answer, but I do know that you need rest. Gael will not be held off another day, and if we refuse to continue our journey, the treaty with Asantaval will become strained, possibly..." Porvarth didn't dare say it aloud—that Eiagan's actions might doom them all if she did not move past her darkness, that lonely place that swallowed her each morning before she even set foot out of bed.

There was so much to hope for, so much potential for her people only a few months ago. But now, after following rabbit trails that led nowhere, after weeks with little sleep and even less food, all seemed dim and hopeless. Save Porvarth's eternal hope, of course. The man had enough hope for the lot of them, but even his had diminished. The darkness. What tricks the mind played when it was angry with the world.

"Come to bed, Eiagan. Tomorrow, we rise and begin again. It's time."

Eiagan's chest caved under the weight of her duties, though she did not carry them alone. Perhaps that was the root of it all, that she needed these people she had grown to love, and in that need, she found weakness she had not known in centuries. Fear for them, fear of what might come, fear of what had already happened... it sat upon her chest like a boulder and would not budge. She thought of a time when she feared nothing, but it was a ruse. Fear looked different then, but it existed, and now it seized her heart until her chest ached.

"I cannot."

"Shh. Eiagan, stop. This is normal. It is *mortal,* and though it hurts, it is good. Your fear is your heart telling you there is something worth fighting for. This darkness in us can be brightened if we only try. Do not spiral into that hole alone, for I cannot live without you. I cannot bear this burden without you by my side."

Eiagan licked her lips and remembered, if only because Porvarth's words brought the memory to her, that she had made promises. She had sworn on her life she would return Hazel's daughter to her father, that she would protect Reven and Darby. *Promises.* She must keep her word, for it might be all she had left by the time she saw Nessa again.

Porvarth's outstretched hand guided Eiagan back toward the light.

Splinters of sunlight pierced the seams of Eiagan's makeshift tent as Porvarth's steady breaths ticked away the moments before the camp woke, before the sounds of bartering, wood-chopping, gossip, and idle chit-chat invaded her peace. It was why Eiagan and Porvarth had chosen to camp along the outskirts of town rather than stay at the inn where it seemed no one slept.

The light danced over Porvarth's face, illuminating the curve of his cheeks, his jawline, the slope of his nose, and the faint grin that always tugged at his lips when he slept. It was a stolen moment, one Eiagan welcomed each morning before reality claimed her again and took her to the dark place.

Soon Gael, the Asantavalian soldier, would enter their quarters in the same fashion he had entered Goranin eight months prior, brimming with energy and tales of Eiagan's destiny to fulfill the prophecy his people had awaited for centuries—the very prophecy that initiated Eiagan's spiral into a darkened hole where her worst thoughts and memories plagued her. Gael was a kind man, but his peculiar ways and abundant energy wore Eiagan's nerves thin and bristled Porvarth in a manner Eiagan had not thought possible.

Eiagan pulled her gaze from Porvarth and sighed, longing for days when the world would not end if she chose to stay in her bed. The sunlight danced over the tent walls, flittering among the dust motes that floated just out of Eiagan's reach, not that she cared whether there was dust in her quarters, but it served to distract her from what truly pained her. Again, the queen and her men had been tricked by the mage Nessa. Again, they had followed the wrong path and endangered her people. And again, Eiagan had lost her way and allowed the darkness to consume her, which nearly cost Ari his life.

Eiagan squeezed her eyes shut, clamping out the daylight that exhibited her failures as well as it did the dirt and grime inside her tent. She rolled to her side and brushed Porvarth's hair from his forehead. He stirred and opened his eyes.

Porvarth blinked and yawned, then took her hand so that she might feel grounded. It had been their way for several weeks to steal a moment together before the camp and its people's demands began, before pain and fear hit her like a hammer. Searching for Reven and the others that had been taken from their camp on Rynkald had occupied every hour since Gael arrived, but no bit of information seemed to bring them any closer to finding the young prince. There had been no time for anything else except minimal sleep and that stolen moment each morning. No time to search for Nessa's hiding places, no time to understand Porvarth's unique abilities, no time to soothe the wounds inflicted by the last battle… just… *no time.*

"Good morning," Porvarth said, his voice low so that they might steal a few more moments before reality demanded their attention.

"It is morning, but whether it is good will remain a mystery." Eiagan squeezed his hand and sighed. "Shall we rise or wait for Gael to interrupt us?"

"Mmm… or perhaps we should run away and never return?" Porvarth stretched and yawned again, then settled his head closer to hers.

"We cannot run from our problems, but I do wish we could. I'm tired," she admitted.

"Beautiful morning, my campmates!" Gael yanked the tent closure open and stepped inside without requesting permission, prompting Porvarth to growl and throw a bowl at the man. Gael caught it, though the remnants of Eiagan's half-eaten supper sloshed onto his clothing.

Porvarth scowled and assessed Gael, who was already prepared for a day of perilous adventure. There had been a time when Eiagan longed for such adventure, but as the days crept into years, her longings also shifted toward something else, something different — a promise made to a man that she wanted to keep. Marriage, children, peace, and quiet… all things that she might never have if she did not find and kill Nessa.

"Shall we send word to Noxious of our plans for the day?" Gael asked as he placed the bowl upon a stack of unread books. Eiagan's eyes settled on them, but they only served to churn her stomach and remind her she still had much to learn, so she shifted her attention back to Gael.

"Send a squawk. I've no time to find a messenger." Eiagan took in his clothing. A deep red fabric draped his gray tunic, gathered at the shoulder, and was secured by a pin. The pin's craftsmanship was

16

extraordinary — intricate woven knots that seemed to loop endlessly amongst themselves — but it was plain in comparison to the carvings upon his bow, which he kept at his side always. Gael appeared every bit a soldier, a prince, a leader… all that he was and was not depending on his chosen position, which he established each morning when they began their trek.

"Must you wear such garish clothing? We just survived a war, you know, and people want necessities like food and clean water," Porvarth said with a sneer that was not lost on Gael. "You are ostentatious beyond belief."

"There is no love lost in your heart where I am concerned, is there, my friend?" Gael asked with a smirk upon his lips.

"Ah, but you see, we are not friends, and as such, there is no love to lose. Perhaps you should prepare the squawk as Eiagan requested?" Porvarth ushered Gael out of the tent so that Eiagan could prepare for the day.

"Fetch some breakfast, please," Eiagan said. Porvarth nodded and left Eiagan to dress.

From the moment Gael arrived, his jovial way disturbed Porvarth. However, Eiagan suspected it had more to do with worry he might be replaced as the camp jester than any real dislike for the Asantavalian. There was much to be learned about the underground kingdom that was to be Goranin's new partner and ally.

A shrill call pierced the morning din, indicating the squawk had been sent on its way. Noxious would not be pleased, and Eiagan could envision his response even before it had been sent. Making camp in the middle of the Market Square of Parazalorian had not been part of the plan. No, they were supposed to be in Drackenmore, but as usual, their plan had been altered when Nessa attacked a small village in Parazalorian. Still, Eiagan was pleased to

17

see the people welcomed her with open arms, fed her men, and treated Emora cordially though they did stare at her as if they could not be sure she would not take their heads any moment.

"My queen, may I enter?" Ari's voice hardly rose above the morning clatter.

Eiagan pulled a fresh tunic over her head and cinched it around her waist with a leather cord given to her by Gael — another slight in Porvarth's eyes but merely a peace offering from Gael's kingdom to her.

"You may," Eiagan said, then stepped aside so he and Emora might enter. "Is there news this morning?"

"Yes, sister. A loyalist, one from Zanaka's group, has verified an account presented by an elderly mage who resides in a small village just south of the Docks. She swears she has seen a woman fitting Nessa's description but that she was unable to use her magic against her," Emora said, her tone bitter. "Of course, it is not the first such report and is likely a ruse put on by Nessa."

"Probably wise she did not attempt such foolery if it were Nessa," Ari added, his eyes cut toward Emora. When she saw he watched her, her features softened.

"You are right. The mage might have died, and then we would not have any information to guide us," Emora said.

"Or that she might have *died* should be our primary concern," Eiagan said.

Emora pursed her lips. "I said that Ari was right. Must *you* chastise me as well?"

"It was not meant to be, Emora, but we *all* must remember the promises we made to our people. We promised as little death as possible as we searched for our nephew. Neither Reven nor Princess Darby of Nelaravore would want death and destruction among the kingdoms for their benefit, and imagine poor Violet learning of such things." Eiagan pressed to find the right tone to take with Emora, but it seemed no way of speaking fell kindly on her sister's ears. Sadly, Eiagan knew Emora felt the same way when speaking to her.

Emora sighed and clenched her cloak with ever-whitening knuckles. She grunted and stormed from the tent in a flurry of grumbles and angry words. Ari watched her go, then ran his hands over his face before facing his queen again. His tired eyes settled on Eiagan's face, a silent understanding that they had failed, once again, to convince Emora that a rampage through the kingdoms was not the way to find their lost loved ones.

"I will speak to her again. Before I go, I wondered if I might have a word about Gael and Porvarth?" Ari's frankness was refreshing to Eiagan, as he was one of only a few offering it to her since Emora's return. Eiagan swallowed, but Ari cut her off before she could utter a syllable. "And about last night, I was wrong to force you to —"

"No. No... wait." Eiagan's nerves rattled but not because she was angry or afraid. He had been right, and to deny that she and Emora both suffered for all the trauma they had endured was foolish. "I have thought about what you said, and I have decided what I might do. If you are willing, I would like to... to..." Eiagan was not often at a loss for words, but it seemed since she rose from the dead, her words failed to encompass her thoughts and emotions.

She sighed and dropped her hands to her side. "I would like to work with you to dispel this darkness. It is of no use to anyone, least of all to me or our mission. You seem to understand it, and you do not fear me even after the incident in the forest."

"You mean the incident that was partially my fault?" he asked, his eyebrows raised.

19

"Why you insist on taking half of the blame, I will never understand, but yes. I *do* trust you, but after the Bleak, I cannot say what is up and what is down even after all these months. And Emora, I cannot imagine what it was like to lose total control of her own body for years before my return."

Ari's shoulders relaxed, and he smiled. It was soft and understanding, two things Eiagan had not thought the fish gutter capable of when they first met.

"Porvarth has been good for Emora, and I think he might reach her. I am happy to do the same for you, my queen. Though it is strange, don't you think? That Porvarth helps her, and I help you?"

Eiagan knew his thoughts, for they were her own. "I do not question what works, Ari. I only wish to move past this so that I might do what needs to be done without losing my soul. Though since you seem concerned, I will say this... I think Porvarth and Emora's hearts are cut from the same cloth, whereas ours are harder and sharper. They are alike, while we are alike."

Ari chuckled. "I never thought I would take such a statement as a compliment, but I do. Now, about Porvarth and Gael. Might we discuss their... *issue?*"

Eiagan gathered her sword and a crust of bread, then nodded toward the tent exit. "We might, but I am quite sure I agree with you on the matter, and I will speak with Porvarth about Gael. You speak with Emora and pray she can control her heated temper. Perhaps between the two of us, we might establish some sense of comradery amongst the camp once more."

"How did it break down in a matter of days?"

Eiagan tethered the Sword of Vidkun to her waist, pulled a cloak tight over her shoulders, raised the hood, and then placed her hand on Ari's shoulders. "Pain and loss, my friend. We always begin new things with ardor and hope, but when they do not go as we planned, we lose faith, and our hope fades. We must maintain our tenacity as the Asantavalian does, and then we might find our family and end the mage who took all from us."

"Repeat those words in your mind until we can speak again, my queen. They will help you live in the light and dispel the darkness." Ari offered his hand. "We do it for Hazel."

"Always for Hazel," Eiagan said, took his hand, and grasped him with the other in an embrace that had become their custom in a few short days. When the camp split to follow two options, Ari insisted on remaining with Eiagan and Emora, though Porvarth and Gael were both capable men. It was more than love for Emora that kept Ari at their side, but a sense of duty to the prosperity of Goranin that had taken his heart as well. The fish-gutter had, it seemed, learned to care about something more than his rough way of life.

Outside, the world had risen from its restless slumber, and the usual activities had begun. A weaver startled when Eiagan passed and admired his wares, but when the queen smiled at him, he relaxed. It would take time for the people to realize she meant them no harm and that Emora would soon come to her senses and treat them amiably as well. Emora's anger stemmed from the same place Eiagan's had in many ways. It was failure, sorrow, regret, and anxiety all bundled into a neat package that settled in the pit of the princess's stomach, exhibiting itself with outbursts and grumbles. Eiagan knew too well, though the incident with Ari had been the first time in a long while that Eiagan's paranoia had manifested into action.

"Eiagan?" Porvarth approached with his bundle prepared, breakfast included, ready to begin the journey to Drackenmore. The smell there would not compare to the heavenly aroma of spiced

21

bread that emanated from the baker just three shops down from the weaver, but if the battered sea docks held promise, then there they would go despite its fishlike smell.

"I'm ready," Eiagan said, but her stomach churned. Another mislead would only harden Emora further, and if anything was true of an Allurigard, it was that hardening came naturally to them.

"Here, Your Highness," the weaver said. "A few strands of my finest." He offered Eiagan deep purple strands of yarn, which likely took much patience to prepare and dye, for they were smooth and tightly woven, and so richly colored she was sure any tapestry made with it would be a glorious sight. "It is not much, I am afraid, but it would be a lovely adornment for your hair."

Eiagan smiled at the weaver once more, nodded, then stowed the gift so that she might use it on a day she did not intend to be covered with fish scales and sludge. "It is a pleasing gift, and I thank you."

Porvarth had wandered apart from Eiagan while she gathered her strength. Days with little rest had taken their toll on her mortal body, but it was her myriad emotions that weighed her heart most. Just as Eiagan prepared to call Porvarth back to leave, a squawk swooped low overhead, shrieking its fool head off as it ruffled Eiagan's hair. The queen clenched her teeth and followed the bird until it landed near Gael's feet.

"Those birds will never warm to you, I'm afraid," Porvarth said, stepping beside her. "What a pity for them." Porvarth's grin said more about what he thought of the blasted birds than his words, but Eiagan ignored his impish way in favor of discovering what Noxious had to say.

Gael unraveled the correspondence and looked it over, then handed it to Eiagan. Gray-white eyes scanned the haphazard penmanship, which only heightened Eiagan's worry that the news was not good. It was not.

"Seven?" Eiagan asked. "Seven more children missing from our kingdom?"

"It seems so, Your Highness," Gael said. "Shall we move to the Docks to see what the mage has to say, or shall we meet with Zanaka, Ballan, and Borgard first?"

"Why should we meet them?" Eiagan crumpled the message and clenched it in her fist so that she would not strike out at anyone to alleviate her frustration.

"I am not convinced following these scraps will lead us to Nessa. Our people are cunning, and though Nessa is not a glowing specimen of our ways, she is still Asantavalian at heart. We are patient. We plan, and we mislead, as you well know," Gael said. "It would not be a surprise if that is her long-term plan, to tease you along for years if it pleased her."

Emora and Ari joined them and pieced together bits of the conversation they had missed.

"What would you suggest we do, then? Sit around while Nessa steals our children from under our noses? What might she do with hordes of children, not just from Goranin but also from every neighboring kingdom?" Eiagan asked.

"I believe you know what she will do with them," Gael said, his green eyes narrowed. "She is unafraid of you, nor does she have a modicum of nobleness left in her blood. Those children will be her army, no matter their age or their ability."

"She would know we would not fight children," Porvarth said, his jaw clenched as tightly as Eiagan held the message. Her knuckles blanched, but it kept her temper in its place.

23

"That, I would say, is the point. She has time on her side given her perpetual life and would not bat an eyelash at waiting until her army of children has grown stronger and older and solidified allegiance with her."

"Reven would *never* align himself with such a creature!" Emora drew too close to Gael for his comfort, exhibited by how his fingers toyed with the strap of his quiver.

"Emora!" Eiagan scolded, then grasped her arm. "You must control your anger and focus only on what must be done."

"A fine one to talk! Look at your hand, sister. It is dripping blood as your nails dig into the palm. Look at Ari's face! It is scarred where you lashed out in fear that he was an enemy." Emora thrust Eiagan's own hand toward her face, smearing the crimson liquid over her own fingers.

Eiagan relaxed her hand and her grip on Emora's arm. "I do not wish for you to be like me."

"I already am, Eiagan." Emora released Eiagan's hand and wiped the blood on her pants. "I have been since the day of my birth, but my deepest desire is to make our kingdom whole again. I will try to keep my temper and remember that it is also your wish and that of all those who aid us."

"I only seek to find the truth," Gael said, releasing his grip on the quiver. "If I see the truth, I must state it, for your children are also my children. If our kingdoms are to thrive, we must see one another as more than allies, but also as friends."

"Family," Ari said, his tone firm and decisive.

"Yes, family." Gael turned his attention back to Eiagan. "I would suggest we take a moment to plan our advancements both here and in the other search camps before we follow another false trail."

Rather than voice her agreement, Eiagan pivoted on her heel and headed toward the only secure building such a meeting might be held. The village seamstress was a spitfire of the highest order with flaming hair and knobby knuckles and a slightly hunched back from a decade of years spent over her work, but she also had the keenest sight and sensed danger from a martick away. Beneath her shop was a storage cellar with one entrance well-hidden behind a false bookcase. Eiagan pretended the hideaway had not been built during her reign, if only so that it did not seem ironic that it was now *her* hideaway.

Porvarth pushed the front door in, revealing a dusty workspace filled to bursting with clothing that required mending, bolts of fabric, and one flea-bitten dog that growled at everyone *but* Eiagan. The seamstress, Catia, lifted her head from her task for only a moment, moaned a quick greeting, then jerked her head toward the meeting area.

"Open," she said, then lowered her head to the cloak she mended.

But there would be no meeting that morning, for Nessa had other plans.

"Fire!" Villagers everywhere shouted as the usual bustle in Market Square shifted to screams and shouts. Screeching echoed through the square, which meant only one thing — the village was under attack.

Eiagan burst through the door and back into the open square. Behind her, Gael and Ari readied their weapons while Emora's hands itched to strike at the first sign of trouble. The trouble landed in the middle of the market and raised its head high, squealed so loudly its noise sent a shiver down Eiagan's spine, then lowered its gaze to her. A forked tongue flicked between scaled lips as black eyes took her in.

By all accounts, Nessa's prized messenger was as grand a dragon as Porvarth or Noxious or any number of dragons among Eiagan's allies, but this dragon had killed the mighty Ellaro — Darby of Nelaravore's guardian and friend — and as such, there was nothing about it that pleased the Winter Queen.

"Bracken, to what do I owe this disruption?" Eiagan asked.

The dragon spat at her feet and released a burst of flame that nearly scorched the queen's cloak before dropping its correspondence. The caustic spit sizzled near her, but Eiagan did not flinch, nor did she yield a mixlin to the dragon. It snorted, then lifted into the sky before disappearing in a fog that settled heavily over the village.

"I grow tired of her games," Emora said. "If only I could get my hands around that pretty neck of hers, why I would..." She paused when Ari shoved the message in her hands. Emora gasped and handed the paper to Eiagan.

Porvarth's gaze settled where Bracken had disappeared into the fog, sure he would return any moment. It was not the first time Nessa had sent the despicable creature to hound them, but soon enough, Eiagan would have its heart for a meal, and its head mounted as a statue.

"Eiagan," Emora urged her sister to read the message. "You prepare, and we will aid the villagers. Once the fires are extinguished, we will send word to Nox. He will send the builders to help them repair what was damaged today."

For a change, Emora was level-headed while Eiagan read Nessa's latest taunt. "Turn the kingdom over, indeed," Eiagan said, tossing the letter aside. "I will turn over nothing but her head."

"She will not stop these taunts, and I fear they will only increase so long as Nessa can find us. We must go underground. As little as you prefer it, I fear it is the only way we might turn this fight in our favor," Gael said.

"I do hate to agree with the man, but… I do. Let us trust Nox fully with the kingdom and do what we must to end this reign of terror in our lands," Porvarth said. "Or you might let me kill her dragon and draw her out. I am fine with either option."

Eiagan cut her eyes toward the former loxmore. "That dragon killed Ellaro with ease, which was the only reason Nessa was able to steal my nephew away, to begin with. Even my immortal grandmother feared it, and you believe you are some match for such a creature?"

Porvarth's blush filled his cheeks, but it was not embarrassment that colored them. "When will you accept that I am capable and —"

Eiagan held up her hands to silence him. "No. That is that. You will dismiss any and all ideas of attacking Bracken this instant. I will not lose you, Porvarth. Have I made myself clear?"

"Am I to be your pet, then?" he asked, his own eyes narrowed as he waved his hands about.

"You are to be my husband, are you not? Might I have *something* to look forward to in this life that constantly teases me with happiness only to steal it from me at every turn?"

Porvarth's eyes widened, and his frame relaxed. Once Eiagan was sure his ears were open, and his temper was controlled, she said, "I do not wish to stifle you, but to wait until the moment is right. I am confident in your ability, but I will not waste it with foolish actions that do not serve our purpose. Do you understand?"

Embarrassment flickered in his eyes, but he nodded. "I do. Let us speak no more of it and hurry to send word to Nox again. He must grow weary of these incidents."

"Four in only three days," Gael said, his own cheeks pink. "I will ready the squawk, then I will live up to my duty as your guide and lead you into my kingdom. It is glorious. You will see, Winter Queen."

As Gael left to aid Emora and Ari, Catia peered from her window. The crooked curve of her lips and her grip on the draperies struck Eiagan as peculiar, so she shifted her focus to the seamstress and stepped back inside. The aroma of burning wood permeated the little shop, but it was not from the meager fire in the fireplace.

"You seem to care very little about the homes that burn in your name," Catia said as she dropped her draperies and turned around.

"I care very much, but it is my position to start fires, not to put them out. Your interim king will send aid by the setting sun, I swear it. Possessions lost will be replaced tenfold for those who aid our cause, so tell me, Catia, why do you support it?"

"Bah," she said, then sat at her worktable. "Why should I turn my back on a good fight? A flame-haired woman is not the sort to turn her back on a little mischief, but if the truth is what you ask, then I will say. It is because I prefer the new king over... *you.*"

"Now, you bite your tongue for just a—"

"Porvarth," Eiagan said. "I asked for the truth, and she offered that which I sought. I am not offended by her honesty, but I am curious."

"Curious?" Catia gripped the edge of the table, her back rigid.

"You prefer Nox. Why?"

She swallowed and pushed her body back into the chair but remained stiff. "He is not an Allurigard, and as such, I believe he is unclouded by the blood that stains your vision."

Eiagan's heart twinged, but the truth was what she asked of the woman, so she swallowed her wounded pride and moved to another line of questioning. "What did you see a moment ago that concerned you?"

"I don't know what you mean," she said, her tone clipped.

"Do not lie now, Catia. What did you see?"

"It was not what I saw but what I heard. The guide is eager to drag you beneath the land where Nessa cannot see you, but neither can your people. When you are out of sight, what shall become of you if it is all a trick?"

"The agreement with Asantaval?"

"Indeed," she said, her red curls bobbing as she nodded. "What is to say they are not playing you for a fool? Nessa is royalty, or she was, and why not take their land back now that they can? It would be impossible to stop an invasion even with the aid of the neighboring kingdoms, would it not?"

"It would be," Eiagan admitted, but what Catia said was not a new concept to the queen. More than once, she considered Gael's intention, his loyalty, and his heart. Each time she decided she could trust the man, but a woman as keen as Catia could not be ignored. "What would you say if I asked you to join me?"

Catia's eyes went wide as her mouth fell open. "Are you a madwoman? I tell you I mistrust the man, and you offer to drag me into the likes of Hell with you?"

Porvarth chuckled but bit his lip when the seamstress grumbled.

"One might say I am mad, of course, but I accept only the most reliable souls into my advisory, and I wish for you to be among

29

them. I have observed you these past two days, and it is with your eyes that I might see an attack coming."

"I am no prognosticator, woman." Catia shook her head, but there was a spark in those gray eyes that betrayed her.

"I do not seek one who can read the future, but one who can see the present in a way that I cannot. Join us, Catia. Aid me and help us to reclaim our children."

"I will be richly rewarded, I assume?" she asked, her tone light.

"Your reward will be a good night's sleep knowing you did all you could to save your countrymen from the purest evil the land has ever known," Eiagan said.

Catia chuckled. "I would say you killed that evil when you took your father's crown, but I will do as you ask, if only to ensure you do not walk right into a trap you cannot escape. Besides, there might be a bit of mischief found beneath the ground that I haven't discovered up here where the birds sing."

"You mean to say you will join us to see what sort of trouble you might cause?" Porvarth asked.

Catia shrugged, but there was something in her heart Eiagan sensed with each beat. There was a fighter in her, a story that Eiagan longed to hear, and having the seamstress on the journey might prove to be the wisest choice Eiagan had made in some time — at least since she had risen from the grave. The woman rose to pack her bag while Eiagan moved to the window.

The fires had been contained, and soon Nox would send people to aid in reconstruction so the villagers would not be left in the cold. Gray clouds descended, bringing bone-chilling rain that aided in dampening the last of the smoldering homes. Eiagan swallowed, for fear rose in her heart like she had never known. Fear had never been a friend to the queen, and now it lodged in her throat and told her the worst was yet to come.

Gael and the others gathered outside the door once again, just as Catia entered the room with a bag of meager necessities. Eiagan forced the fear from her body and cloaked herself in a shroud of strength she only gained through the belief that God would guide her, that He might help her to choose the right path. Her relationship with Him was new, but it hadn't failed her yet.

TWO

Noxious "The Savage" Skjoldsson

The obnoxious squawk kicked rubble from the window edge when it pushed off, headed back to Eiagan with the sad news—more children had been taken from their beds during the night, lost to Nessa and her ultimate plan. The chatter of workers below drifted toward Noxious, but he couldn't make out what they said. Most likely, it was a flurry of complaints about the way he tended the kingdom in Eiagan's absence.

Noxious sat atop a plush chair of deep blue, elbows upon his knees, staring at his boots. To sit upon the throne of Goranin was unthinkable despite Eiagan's command that he lead their kingdom while she searched for his daughter and the others. It took all his strength every morning to ignore the fatherly—nay, the *beastly*— urge to tear the same kingdom apart looking for his little Violet. Of

32

all the people he knew, it was Eiagan who would undoubtedly find Violet, but his instinct as a father was stronger than anything he had ever felt in all his years.

Seven children… Seven more had gone missing during the night. So many children lost, that the echoes of their mother's cries haunted him whenever he lay his head upon his bed. Though sleep was no comfort either, not when his dreams haunted him.

"You called for me?" Tend's sturdy voice fell upon Nox's ears, bringing a moment of peace. There was some comfort in knowing Tend understood Nox's pain. After all, Tend had been married to Freesia, Hazel's sister. The men shared the loss, knowing the sort of women they had loved and seen die at the hands of Nessa. Directly or indirectly, she had killed them both. The difference between the men, though, was that Tend handled his grief well while Nox wanted to kill everything in sight.

Nox lifted his head and found Tend covered with mud.

"What have you been doing, friend?" Nox stood and crossed the room, taking in Tend's dirty and haggard appearance.

"I was helping an assembly of men dig a new well. The work is distracting," Tend said. He wiped his hands on his pants and took Nox's hand in a shake. "Are you well, brother?"

"As well as any man thrust upon a throne he does not want while his daughter is in the clutches of a madwoman might be. Are you well?"

Tend snickered. "As well as any man who has lost his entire family to the same mad woman might be. You were thinking of Hazel just now?"

Nox sighed. "She would know what to do. I am nothing more than a brainless lizard, just holding on by threads each day."

33

Tend scoffed and sidestepped Nox so that he could sit on the bench along the far wall, just close enough to the fire that he might be warm but without being drawn to stare at the flames. It was a fascination among dragons, and one that often led to hours spent in idle contemplation of its existence, and how a simple man might shift into an abomination that created such a hungry element.

"You are no brainless lizard, my friend. The villages are growing each day, and we are rebuilding faster than anticipated. The people adore you, and where you falter, they have patience. *Abundant* patience because you do try, and that matters."

"Do you ever wonder when it ends? This slaughter and destruction, does it have an end or do humans continue to destroy themselves forever? It has been that way for as long as Eiagan has lived, or so she says, but I dare to hope there is more."

"You saw more with Hazel. She changed you, and for the better. You were an insufferable, narcissistic man before you fell in love with her." Tend bit back a smile, but his cheeks bulged.

"And now?" Nox teased.

"Now you are only mildly frustrating and egotistical, not nearly as insufferable." Tend stood. "I must help with the well, but I suggest a flight. You have not shifted since you took possession of the throne months ago. Go out, spread your wings, and let the dragon free for a while. You might find a clearer mind when you return."

"You are probably right." Nox stood and walked out with Tend, not daring to look at the throne as he did. There was something different about it since Eiagan had left it seven years prior. Perhaps it was because Nessa had sat upon it, or because Eiagan had changed so much since she last ruled. He could not say, but to even go close to it set his stomach upside down.

34

"I will return to check on you tonight and to give you an update on the progress of rebuilding here in Eathevall. We should have updates from the other regions by morning. Or would you like company?" Tend, though taller than Nox by nearly a foot and a few years older, had always been like a little brother to Nox. It was a strange twist that he kept watch over Nox rather than the other way around.

"I will be fine. I think you are right. A nice flight around the lands would be good for the dragon. Besides, I'm not used to being locked in a room all day."

Nox followed Tend outside where they parted ways with a nod. Nox got a running start and jumped, shifting midway through before taking to the sky. The sunshine warmed his aching wings and rejuvenated his shadowed soul. Too much time inside pondering how he was supposed to rule a kingdom while his child was missing made the dragon restless, but letting it take over was risky while he was in such a sour, vengeful mood.

He flew over the area where men dug the new well, then east toward the Banished Lands border. The winter chill cleared his lungs and his mind, but he did not dare go over the border. The Asantavalians were a breed he did not wish to cross, not that he particularly feared them, but they were unknown. As such, they warranted caution on his part — especially when one of them had his daughter.

The scent of winter invaded his nostrils — the crispness of the snow coupled with chimney smoke and baking bread — and reminded him of a time when there was nothing *but* winter. This winter, this season, would change into spring one day, and then summer and autumn and winter again. But sometimes, if only for a moment, Nox wondered if Eiagan's perpetual winter had been better. Those days before he cared about anything but himself and his blind desire to possess an unpossessable woman, they were difficult but they did not leave this aching hole in his heart.

The dragon shook his body, releasing the memories that haunted him. His love for Eiagan had evolved, grown into something more appropriate, and their bond was stronger for it. Nox thought of all his family, those who had been chosen through shared trauma, through war, through… *everything*. They would help him through this time, this wretched grieving and depression that snuck up on him when he least expected it. After the kingdom was secure, that was when he might properly grieve his wife and learn how to move on.

Hazel.

Nox squeezed his eyes shut and pictured her — the curve of her cheeks, her smile that always grew when she saw him, even early in their travels before Eiagan was killed. Her golden hair that always tickled his nose when they slept. He missed her. He *needed* her.

Cheers and shouting distracted him from his musings, leading him back toward Vidkun. The well had finally sprung, bringing with it renewed hope for the people. Fresh water was a commodity since Nessa had destroyed many of the wells, forcing dependence on her crown for basic needs. She provided meager essentials, enough for the people to survive, but they had been forced to grovel for scraps.

Nox smiled, though as a dragon he imagined it looked a bit more like a snarl, then flew toward the castle. At the balcony to his quarters, he shifted and landed on his feet as he peered out over the kingdom. He sighed as he took it all in. The people, despite all they had lost, despite all they *continued* to lose, still cheered. They still fought and pushed on with the hope that one day they might see peace, and that peace might exist for generations. They reminded him of Porvarth and his uncanny ability to hold out hope even when there was no evidence such a thing would be rewarded.

The loxmore had known more about Eiagan than any of them, and as such he was the perfect partner for their queen and a proper fit as the next King of Goranin. Nox, though, wondered if he was enough to fill her boots while she was gone. He had not known his father well before his death, but there was one thing he did remember. He could not forget it if he tried.

Men are not made for great responsibility, but great responsibility makes a man. Whether he wanted to or not, filling her position was his and his alone. He would have to become more a man than he already was, and that was all there was to it.

Nox wandered into his quarters, dressed, and went back to the throne room. With a ragged breath, he stared at the throne that, truly, had intimidated him even more than the position. He saw Eiagan there the way she was years ago, cold and aloof, but always with the faintest of smiles when he entered her presence. It was that sly quirk of her lips that had always given him hope — misguided, of course, but hope nonetheless.

He sat upon the throne and rested his arms on the armrests. The chair was hard, rigid, not meant for comfort by any means, but the longer he sat, the more it felt like a place he might accomplish great things. And so, with his dearest friend's blessing, Noxious finally accepted his place in the world. For now, he would rule Goranin as if it were his destiny, as if it were *his* kingdom.

The unfortunate thing, though, about finding oneself is that life often chooses another path. That path was thrust upon Nox when the door burst open, and a great gust extinguished the fire and candlelight. Preceded by a hiss that made even The Savage shudder, a red snake slipped around the doorframe and slithered toward the middle of the room, eyeing him as it did. It coiled there, poised to spring, but instead it grew into a slender, elegant figure with blonde hair tumbling in waves over her shoulders, a braid down one side that kept the locks from her face. Almond shaped eyes, pouted lips, and prominent cheekbones defined the face of the woman Nox hated most in the world. Though she was beautiful on the surface, what hid beneath her face was as ugly as Hell upon earth and equally as dangerous.

"Noxious, my love, have you finally remembered you are a beast?" Nessa's taunt, still carrying the slight lisp of a hiss, enraged the beast. Its talons stroked at his mind, begging him to release chaos upon their mutual enemy.

Nox bit back his anger, scolded the dragon, and stood from the throne. "What do you want, woman? Have you come to steal more children from my people?"

Nessa's eyebrows arched as she leaned against the doorframe. *"Your people?* Surely, you cannot think Eiagan has enough faith in your ability, that she would leave the kingdom to you indefinitely? Besides, if we are to be factual, I would think Reven would be the appropriate seat upon that dreadfully ugly throne." Nessa peered at her nails, then flicked an imaginary bit of dirt from her shirt sleeve.

"Mine, hers, Reven's... It does not matter so long as it is never in your hands again, you wretched, filthy monster." Nox took two steps toward Nessa.

She stood straighter, her lithe muscles outlined well by the deerskin pants and blouse she wore. The curiosity of her clothing piqued Nox's interest, but not enough to outwardly question how *she* maintained clothing when she shifted between her various forms, while others could not. Magic, likely.

"Ah, ah. Stand where you are, beast, or I will call Bracken to dispose of you. What would little Violet do then?"

A rumble grew into a growl that escaped Nox's lips. His eyes flamed, the golden irises darkening until the blackness of the dragon took them. Still, he held the monster at bay. His chest rose and fell, rose and fell as his breaths lengthened. She was not wrong. If he killed Nessa where she stood, he might never find his daughter. If Bracken came it would be a fight he would likely lose. Who knew where the woman had found *that* dreadful beast.

"I only came to offer you an olive branch. Hand over the throne, and I will set the children free. It is as simple as that." Nessa smiled, exhibiting a row of perfectly aligned, pristine white teeth. Magic, Nox decided, was not only deceiving but also conniving. It painted a pretty picture, but beneath it all was never anything good.

"You know I will not," he said.

Nessa heaved a sigh, then pursed her lips as she shook her head, her honey hair billowing around her face. "Such a stubborn man, much like your distant uncle, Zero."

"What would you know of my lineage, you slummie?"

Nessa's cackle cracked through the room like a hammer to rock, disrupting the quiet with an all-consuming echo that drilled in Nox's ears.

"I have had men, yes, but none so many as that." Nessa's lips spread into a wicked grin, one that cut into those sharp, high cheekbones, painting her as more a lunatic than Nox thought possible. But that grin, oh how telling it was. Whatever words slipped from those wretched lips were sure to be the truth, and they

39

would leave a heavy, dark mark on him. Only someone like her could use stone cold truth as a weapon.

She chuckled. "You might have had Eiagan as your own, you know? If you had another face, she would have marked you as her prized king, kept you young and handsome for centuries alongside her. But oh..." Nessa raised her hand into the air and dragged her fingers through the open space in front of her. Though she did not touch Nox, he still felt the cool stroke of her fingers over his face, forehead to cheek to chin, caressing him. "... what a beautiful face."

Nox jerked his head, dismissing her touch. To endure such a thing was maddening torture.

"Leave here. Your offer is declined." Nox turned his back, his nerves rattled. He would never show his fear, but the man did tremble inside. The things she might do to his daughter if he lashed out... He could not even *think* of them.

"You should ask your beloved Eiagan why she did not choose you though she loved you."

Nox ground his teeth and took the bait, if only to prove her wrong. "She did tell me, and I accepted it long ago. I fell in love with another woman who bore me a child before *you* killed her."

For a moment, just a blink of time, Nox thought he saw a shadow of remorse cross Nessa's features. And then it was gone.

"An unfortunate casualty of war." Nessa stepped closer to Nox, her grin on full display again. "But I wonder, if the loxmore were to... *disappear*... would she turn to you as she did Zero? Would she then accept your affections as she did his? Would she *steal* you as she did him?"

Nox clenched his fists at his sides, once again forcing those talons down, back into a corner before the dragon ravaged the castle for only a taste of her blood. "You stay away from Porvarth, do you

40

hear me? With or without your dragon to protect you, I will rip your spine from your back and stuff it down your throat if you so much as scratch him!"

Nessa took a step back, her eyes wide — but her grin remained. "Well, I had no idea you were so fond of the loxmore. Consider myself well warned where he is concerned. Nevertheless, I have only just begun to torment you, Noxious Skjoldsson. When you finally put all the pieces together, it will be too late."

A gale forced through the room again, forcing Nox's eyes shut. His clothing whipped and tore as he fought to keep his body erect. All at once, the gale stopped, and Nox opened his eyes. Nessa was gone.

Nox screamed his agitation, tore at his hair and clothing, then kicked the table. One leg gave and the whole thing tumbled onto its side, covering the floor with water, bread, and meat. He heaved and choked back the beast, determined to keep Nessa's intrusion and taunting from goading him into shifting again, into chasing her down and dying at her hands.

...why she did not choose you though she loved you... Nessa's words teased the dragon that had always adored Eiagan, and angered easily when she rejected him.

"No." Nox shook his head, refusing to allow dark thoughts to invade his mind. He had a kingdom to rule, friends and family to serve, and a daughter to find. There was no time for darkness, no time for grief, and he would not succumb to her mental torture.

...would she turn to you as she did Zero...

He growled and smashed his fists into the wall, tearing flesh over stone as he fought the beast. Its claws thrashed at his mind, wings pushed against his back, and scales penetrated his face. Still, he bit his tongue and distracted himself with the pain.

...would she steal you as she did him...

Nox clenched his jaw and ground his teeth again, spit out a flurry of curses that would have made even his father blush, then pounded the wall again. If he could control the beast when his anger and pain and sadness had pushed him this far, then he could — *would* — control anything... *everything.* In and out, his breaths finally eased into something measured and controlled. The scales receded, and the wings stopped pressing against his back. The talons that scraped against his consciousness dove back into their resting place.

He pushed off the wall and wiped the sweat from his brow.

Nox squeezed his eyes shut and dismissed those wretched thoughts — the distraction Nessa had planted to pull Nox's attention from what mattered most. Eiagan's relationship with Zero was her matter, not his. Whatever happened between them, *however* it happened was also none of his concern. So Nox marched from the room, from the castle until he reached the courtyard, then he jogged to where the men celebrated their small victory — a new well for Eathevall. There, Nox joined them as their temporary king, their comrade, their friend. He would spend his time among them, replacing the distraction with one suitable for a king, however transient his position was.

But Nessa had planted a seed. Despite Nox's insistence that it was not his concern, despite the unbridled joy of the men around him, he could not let go of it. It rooted, and soon it would sprout until it consumed him. What if... what if... what if...

What if she had chosen me? What if Porvarth had not been Dardire? What if he had not stolen her heart?

Tend caught Nox's eye, his own narrowed as if he had never seen Nox before in his life. It made Nox pause and study his friend. But

42

as swiftly as it had come on, Tend's curiosity faded, and he smiled. Together, they celebrated this small victory.

THREE

Reven Allurigard

Reven stared out the window a moment longer, longing to leave this prison and return to his family, but that was impossible. Even if he managed to escape the narrow window, the drop would kill him. And what about Darby and Violet and the other children? No, he would remain where he was until his aunts retrieved him. It was the only option that did not risk the lives of the children.

Darby's dainty hand settled on his shoulder. She had cried herself to sleep every night since Ellaro was killed, months of grief that never seemed to heal. The emptiness had bothered her most, no longer hearing her dragon or feeling the connection she had with him. It was, Reven assumed, much like losing part of oneself — perhaps a bit like losing one's mind into permanent darkness.

"They will find us. I am sure of it." She sighed, then said, "Seven more children arrived. We should get them settled in and try to reassure them." Darby smiled, but they both knew her heart was not with the task. She would rather eat dirt than explain the situation to one more child, but as the only adults locked in the tower with them, the small ones often looked to Darby and Reven for solace.

"When will this end? What will she do with these children?" he asked, motioning over the room.

Darby pursed her lips. Reven hated when she did that because it almost always meant she had thoughts on the matter but was not ready to share them. He felt his face droop, his shoulders following, and so on until his entire body sagged with dread.

"I wish you would not do that. I have thoughts, yes, but I fear sharing them with you might make them... *real*. As if speaking them into existence, and then I only have myself to blame for the awful consequences," she said.

Reven closed his eyes and sighed. Locked in a prison together for more weeks than he could count, the two had nothing better to do than to talk. Their bond had grown, intensified until they both knew... they just *knew* they were meant to share forever together, assuming they survived what Nessa had planned for them. He opened his eyes and pulled her closer so that he could kiss her forehead. She melted against him, wrapping her arms around his waist as she settled her head on his chest. That way, they felt almost normal, as if nothing around them was real and they were simply two young royals in love... though perhaps his eternal youth was less natural than hers.

"I know. I only want to help but being locked in this dreadful tower makes me feel useless." Reven's eyes settled on something he had not given much attention to since their arrival. An armoire of sorts was nestled in the far corner, partially hidden by a tapestry that hung from the ceiling.

"What? What is it?" Darby followed his gaze until hers settled on the same bulky piece of furniture.

"When she put us here, she said we might understand if we only knew her. When she said it, her eyes darted toward that armoire," Reven said, pointing toward it. "I thought nothing of it at the time, all things considered. For some reason, though, my gaze keeps falling on it today."

"I thought very little of it myself, given the rate at which the children arrive. I have had little time to consider anything else." Darby furrowed her brow, concentrating on the bulky closet.

"It is the only piece of furniture in the room save the dining table and chairs." Reven looked around the room as if something might have changed in the past months.

"You think there might be something inside she wants us to discover?" Darby asked, releasing Reven so that she could pick up a small child who had tugged on her sleeve.

"I cannot say, but it does warrant investigation. Have you seen any other furniture or personal items on your trips to the washrooms?"

Darby snickered. "The washrooms, indeed. You mean where she sends us with a bucket of dirty water and a prickly brush?" Darby looked at her skin, pink and raw from cleaning with the uncomfortable brush.

"Well, have you seen anything on your way to the torture room then?" he asked, mustering a smile.

"No, nothing. Not even a bed where she might sleep. Where do you suppose she goes when she's not here?"

"Who knows? Where do you suppose *we* are? I have stared out this window for months, and I cannot fathom where we might be. What is this land? It is like nothing I have ever seen before, and I have seen more castles and kingdoms than I can mention." Reven looked out the window again, taking in the rolling hills and the forest beyond that seemed to scream its pain and hate through the wind that rushed through the trees. Reven had never seen anything so dark. Even if he were to escape the castle, the forest held its own promise of death and destruction.

Darby shook her head. "I wish I knew. It gives me chills to even consider it. Shall we open the armoire?"

Reven shrugged and crossed the room. Violet and her little friend, among other children, watched them. The children were thin and losing weight. So were Darby and Reven, but it wasn't because Nessa did not offer enough food. There was plenty, but plentiful provisions were of no need when one could hardly swallow from worry. No matter how much food the mage brought them, no one could eat more than a few bites a day.

The armoire was made of heavy hardwood, something dark and haunting — likely wood from that dreaded forest. Reven's fingers settled on the handle, but a cool breeze washed over him, forcing him to release the handle and step backward. Darby took his arm at the elbow and hid half her body behind his.

"Did you feel that?" he asked. Darby nodded, but she urged him forward all the same. She put the child down, whispered to her to join her friends, then turned back to Reven once the child was safely huddled amongst several other children.

Reven's fingers trembled as he grasped the handle. This time, he turned it and pulled the door open wide before he lost his nerve. Inside, the armoire was inlaid with a lighter-colored wood, and the

47

shelves were lined with silk, well padded, and still shined as if newly upholstered. The cabinet was filled to bursting with all manner of items — books, maps, drawings, and even a small jewelry box.

Darby pulled the jewelry box from the armoire and opened it. The lined box held a single item, a pendant carved from the same dark wood, shaped as a heart with initials engraved on either side... *NC* on one side and *ZS* on the other.

"Who do you suppose it belonged to?"

"Nessa Callanan, most likely," Reven said. "But whose initials might those be?"

"Someone who loved her, I would assume, since it is engraved on a heart. I suppose there is someone for everyone. What is the rest of this?" Darby returned the jewelry box and pulled out a rolled paper. "A map. It looks like Asantaval. At least, it encompasses The Banished Lands and then some." She handed the map to Reven, but he was already distracted by something else entirely.

A book seemed to call out to him, that same echo he heard emanating from the forest outside. It was dark and cold and unfeeling, yet he could not deny the pull it had over him. Reven pulled the book, a deep purple volume with gilded lettering, from its place on the shelf and cracked its spine. There, on the worn pages of an ancient journal, was everything the young prince had hoped to find — a detailed account of Nessa's life.

"What did you find, Reven?" Darby ran a slender finger over the text, then yanked her finger away. "Ouch! It burned me. What a sneaky..."

Reven gasped and grabbed Darby's arm moments before the two were transported to another place, another time... somewhere where Nessa's story began.

Darby gasped when they stopped moving, though they had not really moved at all. "I… I think this is the same thing that happened to Eiagan with the letter Emora left with me for her."

"Where are we?" Reven asked, his eyes darting around the small room, working to pinpoint a location. They were in a wooden shack, sparsely furnished, with a meager fire in a cracked stone fireplace. A ferrous scent filled the air, crinkling his nose. A scream shattered the quiet, and a door to their left whipped open, revealing a woman strapped to a bed, wailing in the throes of childbirth.

FOUR

The History of the Callanan Royal Family

Screams echoed through the community, but this was not an uncommon occurrence among the loxmore's small village. After all, their gifts were often sought by those in pain or trouble of some sort, but that did not stop Analia from wishing the woman would bite her tongue, if only a little. As loud as she was, Analia was sure the king would hear her and dispatch his army to eliminate them all for disrupting his solitude. It was just the thing Icluedian Allurigard would do—punish a woman in the throes of labor simply for being in pain.

"Analia, gather more water from the basin. I fear this child will kill its mother," Inga said as she wiped the woman's brow once more. Even with Inga's superior healing ability, there was no guarantee the child's mother would live.

50

"I will fetch some. Shall I also call upon—"

"No, Analia. The water will be all, please." Inga's stern tone was, as always, final.

Analia wandered from the birthing room into the only other room of their home. Just outside the door was a basin that was filled with water daily. By nightfall, it was usually bone-dry or stained with the blood of those who'd already visited the community. Analia dipped her bucket into the basin while she hummed if only to distract her from the mother's wailing.

A baby, Analia decided, was nothing short of a miracle so long as it did not kill its mother in its venture into the world. How a small child managed to inflict such pain upon the one who loved it most was beyond her reasoning, so she accepted it as one of many things she would never comprehend and occupied her days cleaning up the mess left behind by her Aunt Inga and her patients.

Another scream splintered the cool evening's peace, but this one was not the mother. Analia hurried inside with the water in time to see the mother smile, then roll her head to one side as she lost consciousness. Inga noted Analia's wide eyes and frozen frame as she wrapped the child in a cloth swaddle, then bundled it in a blanket of wool.

"She will live. Worry not. She is only exhausted. But I do have a task for you, my little Analia."

Analia placed the bucket near the child's mother, where Inga could reach to clean her, then pointed to her own chest. "For me? What shall I do to aid you, Aunt Inga?"

"The child must be taken away from here. You are tasked with seeing that it is removed from the kingdom and swiftly."

"What? What shall I do with a baby?" Analia's eyes drifted toward the child's mother, who might have another opinion on the matter once she woke from her exhaustion. Her face was disguised by a sheer cover, which did not strike Analia as odd. Many ladies who birthed fatherless children did not wish for their faces to be known, but there was something familiar about the woman Analia could not quite place. It was as if she had seen the woman before but given only the silhouette of her face to judge, she decided she likely imagined the familiarity.

"Analia, it is of the utmost importance. You must do as I say. Take the baby to The Banished Land and leave it there," Inga said. "It is... best that way."

A surge of panic rose in Analia's chest, burning every mixlin of the way until bile tickled the back of her throat. "The Banished Land? But Aunt, you have told me time and again to never go near the border. And now you wish for me to enter that horrid place?"

"No. I wish for you to go to the border, toss the baby across it, then hurry home. Do not stay and wonder what happened to the child, my darling, but return to me as quickly as you can."

Analia's jaw fell, and her shoulders slouched. "I'm to *kill* the baby?"

Inga peered into the semi-closed eyes of the pink-skinned baby and pursed her lips into a line so thin it erased any sign she had lips at all. "I do not wish to, but to freeze to death would be a more fitting death than what surely awaits this child in the future. It is kinder."

"To freeze to death is not kind, Aunt! What has come over you? Are you mad? I will not kill an innocent baby, and you cannot force me to." Analia crossed her arms even as her guardian prepared her things for the arduous journey.

"You must, Analia. For if you do not, then I fear the wrath this child might bring upon our kingdom. Nay, *all* the kingdoms of our ancient lands. Now, do as I say and know that you are saving many from death by sacrificing this one." Inga held the swaddled baby out as if it might bite her given the opportunity, but all Analia saw was a sweet child with a swollen face and skin the color of an underripe nobwood fruit.

"Yes, Aunt Inga. I understand," she said, then tucked the baby close to her as she drew on her cloak. She would not kill a baby, but she would decide on some alternative on her journey toward The Banished Lands. Perhaps an elderly mage or a childless woman might take it in? Analia could not be sure, but to kill an innocent child simply for being born was not a task the apprentice was willing to perform.

Once her loxmore wings were tucked neatly beneath her cloak, Analia pulled the hood over her head, grasped the basket of supplies her aunt offered, then hurried out the front door before her aunt decided to eliminate the child right there.

Outside, the air was crisper than it had been. The season would soon change and bring with it the usual turns of color that glorified the landscape before it was doused with snow. The mule was not pleased with her for pulling him from his stable, but Analia could not make the trip on foot with a newborn baby. The child, though, made no noise which struck the apprentice as an odd thing for a newly birthed child considering it had not eaten, nor had it been coddled by its mother. The baby was content tucked inside Analia's cloak and did not fuss.

The panic in her throat cleared as Analia mulled over the options her predicament presented to her — a baby with no mother or father, an aunt who wished to see the child killed, and no means of providing for the child herself. Her options were limited to finding another newly made mother who might nurse two infants or finding some other kind soul to aid her search—preferably the second so Inga would not realize how long she had been gone.

As the marticks passed, the night grew darker as if even it knew the solemn mood that had fallen upon Analia. With each footfall, the mule grew tired, and yet the child still had not made a sound. She peered into her own cloak and smiled when the baby peeked out at her, her eyes sparkling in the moonlight. She cooed, but that was all.

"You are quite sweet though you did nearly kill your mother," Analia said. "What shall your name be?"

The baby cooed again and closed its eyes as its fragile head bobbed each time the mule clambered over the rockier bits of the trail. Analia's heart clenched, and her throat constricted. If she could care for a child on her own, she might have considered running away with the baby. What had happened to turn her aunt so cold? Just that morning, she had been a joy, but the very thought of killing an innocent child—surely, her aunt would not turn so cold over one fatherless child who pained its mother?

"I do not know what will become of you, little one, but I swear I will not see you killed. Not tonight, and not under my watch. In fact, I shall name you so that you will always know who you are. What shall it be?"

The child gave no sign she cared what she was named, and so Analia examined each name that occurred to her before rejecting it in favor of another. "Hmm... I believe I shall name you after my mother. She is gone now. Thanks to Icluedian Allurigard, but surely, she would not mind if you took up her name. She was a good woman, and I trust she would agree with my decision."

Analia continued her journey toward The Banished Land with a full heart, though her guilt also tugged at her. Lying to her aunt would pain her, but she simply could not do what was asked of her.

When the wind increased, and a chill took her entire body, Analia knew she had arrived at the border of The Banished Land. That, coupled with the mule's resistance to travel even a single footfall more. Intelligent mule, Analia decided, for there were things in the Lands that would eat them both alive.

Her red eyes scanned the Lands just ahead, but what they searched for Analia could not be sure. Perhaps it was fate or blind luck, but she did not question her senses when a man covered head to foot in furs crossed her path. It did startle her just a bit to find another soul in the ravaged land, but her start quickly morphed into desperation and hope.

"You, there!" Analia called.

The man froze, caught in his tracks under the moonlight. Had he taken a few more steps before Analia turned her gaze in his direction, she would have missed him altogether. His thick furs surrounded his head as a cloak, bundled around his body, and tapered just above his boots. That was all she could see in the dim moonlight, but it was enough to know there *was* another human in her presence.

"I said, you, there!"

He pivoted on one heel to face Analia, but he advanced no more. Analia gathered her skirts and cloak in one hand while pressing the child against her chest with the other. The mule remained in its place, but she did not wish to leave it for long. The blasted thing would probably run off as soon as she was out of sight.

"Who goes there?" she called again.

"A stranger," he replied. "Turn and go back to your home, lass. There are beasts among us." His accent was decidedly *not* Goraninite, not even similar to those in the northernmost parts of Parazalorean where the Varrowans had some influence on culture and language. Where he was from, she could not say but she also did not care. If he would take the child to his people, it might survive.

"I need only a moment of your time, please." Analia did not have a fearful bone in her body where people were concerned, but if she had, instinct might have told her to run from the bulky man who, Analia realized with each step, was a full head and shoulders above her — perhaps more.

"Lass, I tell you for your own good, you best head home before the Lands wolves pick you apart for supper," he said, then scanned the snow for any sign of danger.

"I wish only to ask for your aid, then I will return home as swiftly as my mule will take me. You see, I am an apprentice to a — "

The baby screamed beneath her cloak, but the man did not startle. Instead, he peered over Analia as she peeked into the cloak. The child had finally grown too hungry to keep quiet.

"Fine time for your baby to squeal like the hogs," he said. "Offering it up as bait, are you?"

"What?" Analia asked as her head whipped up to face the man.

"If you stay here much longer, the baby will be nothing more than a morsel for the wolves."

"Were you hunting?" Analia asked.

"I was, but it seems my plans have changed. What are a young lass and her baby doing in the Lands?"

"You see, as I was saying, I am an apprentice to a healer in Parazalorean — "

"A loxmore girl?"

Analia nodded. "My aunt is the Birthing Mother there, and she insisted I bring this baby here and… *leave* it." The words burned Analia's throat, her mouth, even her lips as they passed.

Warm brown eyes settled on her face, but in them Analia saw the same shock she had experienced when Inga first told her to dispose of the child. They drifted from Analia back to the baby, then up again. "Will you do as your aunt instructed?"

"I do not wish to. I… I had hoped to find some other way."

"Yet here you are, standing ten steps inside the border of this barren land."

Analia had not considered where her path had taken her. She followed her instinct, though it was unfathomable that anyone would dare enter the Lands at all, let alone in the dark of night. Why she had even traveled so far was beyond her, but as he said, there she was.

"Perhaps it is fate that we have met this way?" Analia said. "Can you take her? Would you care for her and find her a mother?"

The man gasped and stepped back. "You wish for me to take this child? Are you out of your senses?"

"I wish for her to live and grow. How it happens is of no concern to me. Do you know a woman who might take her?"

He sighed and pushed his hood back revealing hair the color of a sunset. His thick beard had covered half of his face while the cloak shadowed the other, but now that he had removed the covering, Analia could see more of him. His features were sharp and cutting, but in a way that made him more handsome than most men she had met. Her appreciation of his features was interrupted by a groan. He ran broad hands over his face and sighed.

"I know of one. It is not a favorable situation, but I will try," he said.

"What is your name?" Analia asked, struck with the need to not only understand his kindness but to attach a name to it so that she might always remember him.

"I am a humble servant, that is all. Give me the child, then take your mule and hurry home."

Analia hesitated, but there was no turning back, and if there was, she would not know what to try next. She handed the child to the servant and swiped a tear from her cheek. A bitterness toward her aunt settled in her heart, but it was more than that. It was anger toward her aunt, her community, her kingdom — with the King of Goranin himself, for it was his fault that no child in the land knew what it meant to live with two parents and a full belly.

"Please, ensure she grows and lives happily, for I... I cannot bear to imagine what else might come of her."

The man tucked the child under his furs, quieting her whimpers. "I swear on my mother's resting place, I will not let any harm come to the child. She will be cared for whether my plan succeeds or fails."

Analia nodded once, twirled on her heel, and stepped toward her mule. "Oh, one more thing," she said. "Her name."

"You have named her?" he asked, a smile tugging at the corners of his lips as he studied her face.

Analia felt a blush prickle her cheeks — foolish to name and grow attached to a child she knew she might never see again, but she could not help herself.

"Indeed, and a worthy name it is. It was my mother's."

The man, whose chiseled features had not offered any indication of his emotion until then, let his lips turn up more, offering a full smile. "And it is?"

"Ellenessia."

"Ellenessia. A name for a princess. Go now, lass, get home."

Analia hurried back over the border and grasped her mule by the reins, then turned her head to offer a goodbye to the servant man — but he was already gone. All that remained was snow and darkness. No man, no baby… and no footprints.

Bribadge Callanan rapped on the heavy wooden door that separated him from his brother's court. With a groan that gave way to a creak, the door opened to reveal Argor, the king's personal guard. Bribadge bade him a good evening, then squeezed through the narrow doorway that opened into the near-abandoned Grand Room. He followed a winding staircase to the second level where he would, if granted entry, deliver a gift to his brother's wife.

At the top of the stairs, Bribadge paused. His brother's wife still wailed as she mourned the loss of her child, born still as death only hours before Bribadge left the safety of the village to go to the surface. There, he buried the deformed infant where no one would find it, then said a prayer that the kingdom might forgive their queen once again. Three failed pregnancies and no heir to the throne meant his elder brother's position as king might become threatened.

The prince had not expected a miracle at the surface, but the moment the loxmore girl called out to him, Bribadge had decided God had heard his prayers and saw fit to reply. The bundle the girl handed to him, a little baby girl, was more than he had hoped for but there she was smiling up at him from her swaddling. Her fair hair would not give away her true heritage, nor would her pale skin. For any who looked upon the baby Ellenessia, would never believe her anything but an Asantavalian princess — she even *looked* like the queen.

Bribadge inhaled and followed the hall toward the Queen's Chambers. Once there, he took another moment to prepare his argument. The child was no replacement for those lost, of course, but it would preserve their claim to the throne. There was no other way, and Bribadge would not see his brother dethroned for something the queen could not control.

"Let us pray Queen Lureah finds favor with you, little one," he said as he patted the baby's head, then knocked on the ebony door intricately carved with knots and flowers.

"Leave us be," Bribadge's brother growled, his voice laced with agony. He'd lost a third child, a pain Bribadge could only imagine.

"It is only your brother," he said.

Footfalls echoed through the hall as they grew closer. King Illaric Callanan opened the door and allowed his younger brother entry, though Bribadge saw little patience in his brother's eyes even for him. He would only be welcome for so long.

"To what do I owe this visit?" Illaric asked, his eyes trained on the bundle in Bribadge's arms.

"Is the queen... How... How is Lureah?" Bribadge let his eyes wander toward his dearest friend, besides his own flesh and blood brother. Lureah had been their friend since childhood, had been a good wife, an amiable queen, and a shoulder for Bribadge when his own wife passed away from a cough.

"She is distraught still, but she will be ready for the proclamation by tomorrow morning, if that is what you —" Bribadge stepped forward and pressed his hand on Illaric's chest. He shook his head, his eyes wide with hope and... perhaps fear Illaric might see his offer as an insult.

"Brother, no. I am here with a solution if you would be so kind as to hear me. Come nearer the fire before she catches a chill." Bribadge took four long strides until he was beside Lureah, who had drawn so far into herself, the chair nearly swallowed her whole. Her face was swollen, her eyes rimmed with red that never seemed to fade, and her cheeks were slick with newly fallen tears. There would be many tears to come, but perhaps some might be of joy — assuming she chose to adopt the girl Bribadge brought for her.

"Brother, what have you done?" Illaric asked, his eyes shifting between Lureah and the bundle.

"It is not what I have done, but what has been divinely bestowed upon us. I took your direction now as I did before and buried the child where he might rest well, but while on the surface, a miracle happened."

"A miracle? My baby, he is alive?" Lureah asked, perking up enough to offer her attention to Bribadge.

"No, sister, I am afraid that is not possible. The lad has gone to his maker, but there was a young woman at the border. I was startled by her, but she was there on her own task."

"A task, you say? Of what sort? Is our kingdom exposed?" Illaric, ever the dutiful king, switched his concern from one family to the whole of the kingdom — another family he never took for granted.

"I do not believe so. The girl was so relieved to have been absolved of her mission, I dare say she might have forgotten I existed at all. Nevertheless, she was a loxmore midwife's apprentice with a difficult mission, one she could not complete."

"Why? What was her... Was she to *kill* this child?" Lureah asked, her shoulders slouched but eyes still grasping on to hope.

"She was tasked with the elimination of the child, yes. This child, but she could not. She entrusted the babe's life to me," Bribadge said, offering the bundle to Lureah.

Lureah's eyes widened as she accepted the baby. She pulled back the covering to see the child's face and cooed. "How lovely," she said. "How could anyone wish to harm you?"

"She is not a replacement, of course, but I believe the kingdom will be pleased an heir has been born, and this little one deserves a happy home despite her beginnings. Perhaps you might grow to love her in some way?" Bribadge held his breath while Illaric and Lureah observed the child, then, when both smiled, he added, "The midwife had given her a name. She called her Ellenessia."

"Oh, how beautiful. Little Ellenessia. Princess Nessa," Lureah said. Illaric placed his hand on his wife's shoulder and grinned. "Shall we... Would it be too much for you to bear, my love?" she asked.

"You are a mother without a child, and she is a child without a mother. We will love our children we have lost, but we might love this one as well. If it is not too much for you to bear, then I might bear it as well," Illaric said, then motioned toward the door.

Bribadge exited to leave Lureah alone to nurse the child, followed by Illaric.

"Come, let us meet in my private chamber for a moment," Illaric said, then passed Bribadge and headed toward the only room in the castle that was designed so that no sound might exit the room. Previously used as a war room, it now heard the secrets of the kingdom reserved only for those who were not only highly trusted but born of Callanan blood.

Once secured in the room, Illaric turned and embraced Bribadge. It was hearty and bear-like, and Bribadge reveled in the joy of having pleased his brother.

"Your gift will not go unpaid, brother. You have given Lureah what she wanted most, and in doing so, you have ensured the Callanan rule will continue," Illaric said.

"Do you believe the kingdom will accept the child as yours? Will they be fooled?" Bribadge asked.

"I see no reason why it cannot be so. You are the only soul that knows the truth, and Lureah's wails might easily be attributed to the pains of labor."

"I am pleased to have been useful, dear brother. I cannot say what might have become of the child had I not crossed paths with the midwife's assistant."

"And you are certain our secrecy has been maintained?"

"I am. I entered the tunnel when her back was turned. She saw nothing but a burly man walking in the snow. She assumed I was hunting."

"Good. That is good. Now, I have another matter to discuss, Prince Bribadge. There was a lady in court today that is one year out of grieving. She is pleasant and agreeable, quite beautiful, and has three sons in desperate need of a father's guidance."

"Are you insinuating I need another wife? I had a wife, and she took my heart to the grave with her." Bribadge scowled and crossed his arms. They'd had this discussion before, but Bribadge refused to take another wife. He had hoped Illaric would grow tired of forcing the issue.

"As our third stillborn child has taken our hearts to the grave with him, brother. Yet, we still accepted this new child."

"For the sake of the kingdom and for your throne," Bribadge said, tightening his crossed arms. "I need no wife to secure the throne."

"No, but you do need a wife, Bribadge. Your Hall of Taliskar is an abomination, brother. What sort of prince lives among that sort of filth? Would you at least *see* the woman?"

Bribadge groaned, knowing well he could not deny his brother's request. It was, after all, only a kind gesture meant to make him happy, but it seemed Illaric never quite understood the hold his beloved Mildora had over him—heart, mind, and soul entwined together forever.

"I will meet her, but I will not like her," he said, then lowered his hands. "Shall we check on Lureah and the babe?"

"Your ability to direct a change in subject is still unparalleled, but I agree. Let us check on our queen and the new princess, shall we?" Illaric opened his arms wide, motioning toward the door. Before they reached it, Illaric grasped his brother's elbow and pulled him close for another bone-crushing embrace.

"You will break my bones, brother," Bribadge said, but he could not deny the pride that surged through him knowing he had pleased his remaining brother—the last of seven he'd had.

"This child will change everything, Bribadge. I feel it in my soul. She will change the future for Asantaval."

FIVE

Eiagan Allurigard

The journey ahead was long and not without risks even though the throne now sat in capable hands, but Emora had insisted she could manage her magic well enough to allay any mishap that might befall them. Eiagan, though, could not shirk Catia's warning. If Gael and his kingdom's decision was to lure Eiagan and her people into the depths of Asantaval to destroy them, surely, they would know that Noxious the Savage would make good use of his name. No man would survive his rage if the remainder of Nox's chosen family was eliminated.

"You seem unsettled still, sister. Can I help?" Emora asked. Her gray-white eyes that matched Eiagan's were far less worried, but Eiagan still saw the slightest bit of concern.

"I'm not sure I will ever fully relax and let trust rule over me, but that is nothing that you might change. I fear centuries of mistrust can only breed more of the same," Eiagan said.

Emora shifted the weight of her satchel and mounted her horse, but her gaze never left Eiagan. Eiagan, the last to mount, did so with the same hesitation she reserved for only the most daunting of missions. Each detail of the trek down to the last was catalogued and processed countless times in the queen's mind, but each time she evaluated the situation she felt the same — confused, uncertain.

Only hours before, she trusted Gael, but the seamstress had offered her a worthy point. What if the Asantavalians played the long game alongside Nessa? The woman had patience that knew no end — centuries of it, to be exact. Could Eiagan dutifully walk her comrades into death without pausing for a moment to evaluate further? To consider this might be one more move in a centuries-long battle dance?

"Eiagan, let us lag behind and talk," Emora said, allowing Gael, Ari, and Porvarth to move ahead, directing the way across Parazalorean to the Smolzark Territory, where they would navigate the steep terrain and unrelenting mountain landscape before slipping into Asantavalian territory — The Banished Land.

Catia fell in beside the princess and the queen but kept her thoughts to herself. Instead, she kept a keen watch around them, her focus on the conversation between Gael and Ari.

It had been less than a year since Eiagan last spilled blood on purpose, since they had begun chasing their own tails searching for Reven and the others, yet Eiagan felt a chill in her bones that only meant one thing. Dread, something worse than the usual pit in her stomach, ate up her body like a starving wolf, pushing her into an internal frenzy she could hardly control. Butterflies danced in her stomach, but they were not gentle and did not care that she could hardly hold her food. This was not the darkness of her depression speaking. No, it was the old Eiagan, the one who suffered no fools. She was still in there, screaming that this was not right. Going underground into a mysterious kingdom was all wrong.

When the men had sufficiently taken the lead, leaving the women well enough behind that their hushed conversation could not be heard, Emora lowered her hood and cleared her throat. When she did not speak, Catia chuckled.

"What?" Emora asked.

"Speak your mind, princess. Do not hide your thoughts behind useless grunts and groans," Catia said, waving her hand as she did.

"Do remember that while you are a guest invited by me, you will address my sister with the proper amount of respect due a princess," Eiagan said, though she did not disagree with Catia. Stuttering, throat clearing... all wastes of time much better spent speaking one's mind.

"Eiagan, I know that your mind is unsettled the same as mine. Mine is because of that infernal woman rattling around in it for six years, but you are another story. I did not want to mention, but perhaps it is because you have hardly had a moment to rest since your return," Emora said.

"You mean since she dug herself out of that fancy coffin?" Catia asked with another chuckle. "I cannot say that I blame her for not resting. She's already had a bit more of it than any one woman needs."

"Oh, would you clamp your mouth before I sew it closed?" Emora said.

"Sew it all you want. My opinion will be the same," Catia said. "Your sister's worry is right. It would not be the first time an Allurigard walked into an Asantavalian trap, would it?"

Eiagan glared at her, which achieved its intended purpose and then some. Both women voiced their apologies, then Emora said, "We should hear from Nox long before we arrive in Asantaval. Might we wait to hear his opinion before we choose one way or another to abandon our alliance with Gael? I fear…" Emora glanced forward, her eyes landing on the guide. "I fear if Gael knows of our concern, then the Asantavalians might believe we intend to back out on our agreement to return their lands."

"Would make no sense to keep The Banished Land," Catia said. "Nothing more than ice and snow, save what is under it all. Seems like no one wants it but the Underdwellers anyway."

"Underdwellers?" Eiagan asked.

"Mmm, yes. The people have taken to calling the Asantavalian people the Underdwellers. A silly name if you ask me, but no one does."

"Eiagan, what are your chief concerns?" Emora asked, ignoring Catia.

Eiagan sorted through the details again, then said, "How does Nessa always know where we are? The kingdom is large, and when one considers the agreements we have with the surrounding kingdoms, I cannot see how she might find us without the aid of spies or magic of some kind."

"Locator spells are not difficult, Eiagan," Emora said. "Surely, after so much time spent in Vidkun, Nessa has many personal objects belonging to you that she might use to find you."

"Fair, but would she not also discover us underground?"

Emora bit her lip and stared at her horse's mane. Catia clenched her reins, relaxed then clenched them again as she also thought through the scenario.

"It does seem a bit odd," Emora said. "Unless Asantaval is cloaked or protected in some way against such magic, it would stand to reason Nessa would find us there as well."

"Asantaval does not, as far as is known to me, have a tunnel system that traverses beneath any other kingdoms..." Eiagan paused. Her back stiffened and her teeth ground.

"What? You believe Nessa might have an elaborate system of tunnels that we never discovered?" Emora's frame matched her sister's.

Catia only laughed.

"We built the entire underground system right under your nose," Emora admitted. "It wasn't until you lost your immortality that you discovered them, and even then, it was because Hazel showed you."

"I do not like this," Catia said. "You brought me as a beacon for danger, and I tell you I feel it all around me. Ever since I was a child, I have had a sense for these things. I feel it now as surely as I feel this saddle beneath me and these reins in my hands. Something is coming."

"Are you magical?" Emora asked.

"No, but I have feelings about things. I cannot explain what it is or how it works. I cannot control it in any way." Catia's eyes darted left to right and back.

"You might have some magic. Perhaps it is a gift that has been left unpolished? Come close and let me grasp your hand. I can detect latent magic. The technique was taught to me by my mother," Emora said, then, "I mean... by... by Simorana, the mage."

Eiagan did not comment on Emora's claim, for it was fair. Simorana had been her mother—she had raised her, protected her, loved her—and so Eiagan would not fault her for calling her by the title. Serecala's abandonment had taken many forms, not the least of which was leaving Emora with the mage for safekeeping.

"What do you feel, Catia?" Eiagan asked.

"I cannot say, but we should be cautious." Catia directed her draft to the opposite side of Eiagan and took Emora's outstretched hand. However, it seemed Catia's sense was as accurate as any could be in that instance, for before their hands grasped, the earth quarreled within itself, shifting and sliding until everything upon it shook with it.

Since the warriors from Asantaval rose from the depths during the fight with Nessa, the land had been displeased. It rippled and groaned, shook and shivered, and forced many to relocate their villages—but it had never cracked beneath them, threatening to swallow them whole.

Catia's horse whinnied and reared, tossing her from its back with ease before darting into the forest. The moss-covered dirt beside Catia pulled apart as the earth groaned its displeasure. The part widened as violent rocking pushed the forest into a frenzy. Wild animals called out and darted this way and that, but there was no escape. The ground cracked wide and sucked them in, felled trees and absorbed them into the abyss, and stretched closer to Eiagan with each moment.

"Grab her!" Eiagan shouted to Emora whose horse was a far sight braver than Catia's. Even so, it constantly reset its footing and grunted, his eyes wide and darting.

"I've got her! Go, hurry!" Emora pointed toward a field where they would be much safer than huddled under falling trees.

70

Ahead, Gael and Ari dodged trees but were in no hurry to leave the women.

"Go! We're coming!" Eiagan ordered.

Porvarth had shifted, but his horse was nowhere to be found, likely swallowed by the ever-widening crack in the land. His discontented calls distracted Eiagan for a moment too long, and her horse, now fearing for its life, lurched forward against her command. The queen wound her hands in its mane, but its footfalls were constantly jostled by shifting rock and slick moss.

Gael reached the clearing ahead of Ari, but only by a few lengths. Eiagan heard Emora's horse's steady footfalls behind her and could only pray she had Catia with her. Now in an uncontrolled gallop, all Eiagan could do was hold on.

Porvarth circled but could not fit between the trees to offer any aid to the women. Instead, he fussed about it and circled himself into a frenzy. This, Eiagan decided, was wholly unacceptable, especially since his screeches only pushed her horse into a harder gallop. Her teeth rattled and her tailbone ached as the horse tossed her like a plaything on its back.

Wave after wave of land shifted beneath the horse, forcing him into a slide every few paces. Emora gained on them, and when her horse fell in line beside Eiagan, it only startled hers further. Eiagan did not believe her horse could run so fast, but it seemed the fear of God had bitten it on the rump, and nothing could slow its advance. Once Emora reached the clearing with Catia, Gael and Ari checked them over. Eiagan's bulky draft burst from the tree line and dug his hooves deep into the soft earth of the field.

"Whoa!" she called and pulled on his mane, but he would not slow. The horse would not stop until he dropped dead, or the ground swallowed them up.

Porvarth circled overhead and dipped low, so Eiagan prepared to leap from the horse. Better to have Porvarth's talons in her shoulders than stay seated on a runaway horse, so she steadied herself. When he was within range, Eiagan shifted her weight to push from the horse. This was a mistake.

The movement startled the already terrified horse, and he lost his footing. The soft ground slid beneath him as he fought to stay upright. Eiagan, ready to jump, fell from the horse when it tipped toward its left, but before she could scramble to safety, the draft fell atop her.

"Eiagan!" Ari screamed, but Eiagan could not see him.

A crack preceded a shock of pain that shot up Eiagan's leg. Her own scream was muffled by the sounds of trees splitting and ground shifting. The horse tried to get up, but only succeeded in rolling further back onto Eiagan. Her fists pounded the horse's neck, but it did no good. The horse was unconcerned with her well-being, it seemed, but Eiagan bore him no ill will despite her pain.

The horse crushed her leg, but it had not killed her. Not yet. The horse rolled again.

"Ah!" Eiagan's cry was cut short by a stabbing pain in her chest followed by a whoosh of air that exited her lungs so quickly, it stole her voice. The pommel of her saddle — a wretched thing she despised using — pressed into her sternum where it dug until bone gave way beneath.

All at once, the weight lifted, but Eiagan could not breathe. Short, shallow gasps pained her, and even that was punctuated by a whistling that should have worried the queen, but the pain was too immense to concern herself with anything more.

"Eiagan!" Emora slid onto her knees beside Eiagan and took her hand. "Oh, no. No. What will we do?"

Catia pushed her way between Emora and Ari until she could reach Eiagan. She quickly assessed the wounds and decided for them all. "There is a village nearby, just across the border in Smolzark. There, we can find a healer for her."

"How will we *get* her to the village. I would think moving her would be excruciating," Ari said, his eyes wild. They darted as Emora's horse had, but it was not fear in his eyes. It was worry.

"The quaking has ceased. There is a hatchet in my bag. Here," Catia said, handing her bag to Ari. "Make quick work of a tree. Fashion a bed."

Ari took the hatchet and ran toward the fallen trees while Gael pulled a spare tunic from his pack. Eiagan focused on the clouds, watched as the puffs of white floated in a sea of blue just like she had when she was a child. She imagined Reeve sitting beside her, laughing at his own jokes as he teased her relentlessly. It offered some peace and calm, but it did not ease her pain.

With each breath, Eiagan grew more tired. Her leg was numb, and her chest was heavy as if the horse was still there, putting its weight on every inch of her body. Where the horse was, she could not say, but she ventured to guess that Porvarth had disposed of it — a matter to discuss later if she survived.

Gael ripped the tunic into strips and bound Eiagan's leg, which she had not realized was bleeding. A pool surrounded her thigh, but it was the bone protruding from it that reminded her that her mortality came with a high price.

Porvarth shifted and ran toward them. He settled beside Emora and looked over at Eiagan. "I'll try to take the pain, at least. Perhaps it will be enough to get you swiftly to the village. I do not know if it will work. I have not tried since I healed Erdravac."

Eiagan tried to nod, but even that shot ribbons of pain through her chest. It burned. Oh, how it burned.

"This will hurt, but I think it must be done. I have seen injuries such as this before on the battlefields," Catia said as she took the remaining strips of cloth from Gael. "If we can wrap your chest, we might make it easier to breathe."

"But... Are you sure?" Emora asked, tears slipping from her eyes.

"I am not sure of anything, but her chest is flailed open, and the sternum is cracked. If we do not try, then it might become dirty and infected before we arrive in the village."

Porvarth whispered over her, but no one could be sure his ability would work. No longer a loxmore, yet not like any dragon seen before, Porvarth's abilities had yet to be fully discovered or understood. Even so, a warmth spread over her body, easing her pain enough that each breath did not feel as if it were splitting her in two.

Between Catia and Gael, a bandage was wrapped around Eiagan's chest while she lay helpless as a child. The queen could not say why she was so easily subdued, but to know her family would not betray her or forsake her in her weakest moments offered her peace.

"Here, will this suffice?" Ari asked. He had tied the thick branches of a tree together into a bed that could be carried by the men.

"It should. Help me get her onto it. I will roll her toward me, and you place it beneath her," Catia said.

When she was rolled, Eiagan felt no stabbing or pain, not even an ache that indicated she had any injury at all. Porvarth's plan had worked, at least, for now. Eiagan was sure Porvarth would blame himself for her injury. It was his way, after all, and her mind was so distracted with thoughts of comforting him that she did not feel the jostling of the bed when Ari and Gael lifted it, nor did she feel Porvarth release her hand and shift so that it might be fastened to his back for faster transport.

Emora climbed upon Porvarth just behind the bed. Eiagan assumed the others would ride the remaining horses into the village, but her mind slipped in and out of consciousness—too much to formulate any full thought.

"Travel..." Eiagan mumbled, her mind drifting toward the time they would lose in their search for the children.

"Travel? What do you mean?" Emora asked as Porvarth lifted them. Her words were swallowed and did not reach Eiagan's ears, but it mattered little. Eiagan's head rolled to the side, and her eyes closed, losing their fight to stay open.

"Shh... Sleep, sister. We will have you healed and be on our way to retrieve our nephew and the others before you know it. I assure you." Emora stroked Eiagan's forehead and ran her hand through her hair, such a motherly thing to do, and Eiagan allowed herself to drift deeper and deeper into sleep knowing well her sister would protect her.

SIX

Noxious "The Savage" Skjoldsson

Nox had just swallowed the last bite of his food when the ebony bird landed on his table with a message clutched in its beak. He hadn't heard it arrive, but they had been sneakier as of late, always shifting from the massive bird into the smaller messengers and spies long before approaching him. He wondered if there was any reason for their behavior, or if they simply enjoyed annoying him.

He pushed his plate away and opened his hand. The bird warbled, then hopped toward him before dropping the correspondence in his palm. He still had not responded to Eiagan's request for his opinion—should they go to Asantaval or continue their journey toward Drackenmore? Something about his queen going underground did not settle with Nox, nor with the dragon

76

which had been angrier since Nessa's visit. In truth, he had not solidified his opinion well enough to offer it.

Golden eyes scanned the penmanship—Gael's—and with each word, Nox's stomach twisted further. Eiagan had been injured, nearly killed.

"Tend!" Nox pushed away from his table and gathered his things, not that a dragon had many things to gather before going on a murderous rampage. Eiagan's injuries were by Nessa's design, he was sure, and as such he would not simply sit on his haunches and wait to see if she improved.

Tend pushed through the door with his usual expression—cautious awareness that never seemed to ease. It was no wonder.

"Eiagan has been gravely injured. I must go to her bedside to check on her."

Tend grasped his shoulder and shoved him into his seat, eliciting a snarl from Nox. "What you must do is what she entrusted you to do, Noxious. You will rule this kingdom and aid its people in her absence, and you will trust the others to care for her."

Nox shoved Tend's hand from his shoulder. "I must go to her. She needs me!"

Tend's jaw tensed, and his shoulders squared. He pointed at Nox with such intensity in a single finger, that Nox paused long enough to hear what he had to say. "She *needs* you to rule this kingdom before it falls apart entirely. Everything else she requires will be supplied by those with her, or have you forgotten your place?" Tend leaned close. "Porvarth will ensure *his* future wife's care is acceptable."

Nox was no fool. He should never have told Tend what Nessa said, what she did—that she had ignited a small flicker of desire that Nox still harbored for Eiagan despite his vast and endless love for

77

Hazel. It was a familiar love, and as such it was the only thing that kept him from going insane.

Tend sighed and stood erect. "I know how your heart aches, brother, but you will destroy Porvarth if you pursue this ridiculous thread of affection you still carry for our queen. It is imagined, and I think you know that is true. Focus your mind, and do not let the mage trick you."

Nox ran a calloused hand over his face, his gaze taking in everything in the room if only so he could avoid looking Tend in the eyes. A sigh, and then, "You are right. What have I done? I allowed the one who took everything from me to blur my vision."

Tend sat at the table across from him and rapped his knuckles on the dark wood. After a few moments of melodic tapping, he paused. "Eiagan is a woman unlike any other, and her charisma and dedication are what draw people to her. Her beauty, indeed, is captivating, but it is her undeniable focus on that which she deems right that keeps us in her circle. What you, my friend, fail to see is that you are alike. You, too, carry that same essence."

Nox chuckled. "I thought I was egotistical."

"You are, to be sure," Tend said with nary a smile. "But your compass points north, my friend. Keep it there. Do not let Nessa turn you against those who mean the most to you, or put you in a position that pits you in competition with them."

Tend kept Nox's gaze for some time, the two reading one another as only brothers in arms might. Eventually, Tend flattened his palms on the table and spoke again.

"I miss her every moment, and there are times I consider seeking another woman for comfort. Then I remember that there is no one like Freesia, and my heart breaks again. Perhaps one day we might find women who can see past our scars and into our hearts again, but until then we should focus on what is most important in this time."

"I am not a fool in love, Tend. I am only —"

"Aching for what is familiar, and you loved Eiagan for many years. The mage only opened an old wound that *Hazel* healed. She gave you a daughter, born to you through the love you shared, and that sort of love is not so easily snuffed by old wounds."

Nox licked his lips, forcing both the bile and the dragon back into their place. To realize he had been so close — *so close* — to defying Eiagan's order and tearing across the kingdom to sit by her bedside was, admittedly, embarrassing. Why had he been so quick to fall back into those old feelings, that routine that had brought nothing but pain? Nox's eyes widened.

"You have discovered something," Tend said. "There is a flicker in your eyes."

"The mage is clever. Though she knew I loved Eiagan, she also knew the pain it brought upon me. The *darkness*. She is playing me for a fool, pushing me into that darkness so that I will be easily overcome."

"So do not fall. Do not allow her to force you backward when Hazel worked so hard to bring you here to the man you are today." Tend stood and nodded toward the door. "There was some trouble in a nearby village during the earthshaking. Come along with me to inspect it. Have a presence among your people. See them. Know them and who you sit upon the throne for."

Noxious nodded, knowing well that Tend was right. The man was *always* right, and likely the only reason Ari did not lose his mind when he was locked in the dungeon. If any man could read Nox's position accurately, it was Tend. He would follow his brother in arms to the village, see the people, offer his aid, and when Eiagan returned and married Porvarth, he would hold no grudge or ill will because he loved them both. He loved them as family, and he would not ruin such a thing for an evil mage.

"I am no one's puppet. I will go with you and aid the people. I must send communication first, a response to Eiagan's earlier request, then we will be on our way."

"I will ready the horses."

"We will not fly?" Nox asked.

Tend shook his head. "Let the dragons rest tonight."

Nox watched Tend's back as he exited the room. *Let the dragons rest?* There was more to it than that, Nox was sure, but prying would only ensure Tend would tell him no more, so he penned his responses. Once complete, he leaned out the window and whistled.

The squawks were never more than a shout or whistle away, which was odd to Nox but there was no other way to communicate with Eiagan unless he sent a messenger. There was danger in sending a human messenger, so Nox offered the correspondence to the squawk that landed on the table.

"This one you deliver only into our queen's hands once she is capable. You give it to no one else, and once she has inspected it, you ensure its destruction. Am I clear?"

In response, the raven bird leaned forward and screeched in Nox's face.

Nox grumbled his displeasure and released the paper. "And give this one to the Asantavalian."

The squawk cheeped again and disappeared into the clouds, leaving Nox with nothing but his prayers and an unsettled gut. The mage was cunning and mischievous, but above all, she was deadly. If she desired Noxious in a state of desperation and pain—two things that surely awaited him if he pursued those old feelings—

80

then it stood to reason she had other plans for the dragon shifter. He would not succumb. He would never give in, would never allow such weakness to destroy him or Hazel's memory.

With renewed determination, Nox joined Tend and set out on their journey.

SEVEN

Eiagan Allurigard

"Focus everything on your task just as you did as a loxmore, and your ability will increase. An unfocused mind will wreak havoc upon you and your gift." The gentle tone of a woman's voice roused Eiagan, but it was Porvarth's touch that forced her eyes open.

His lean fingers pressed against her sternum, an action that should have caused a shock of pain, at the very least. At worst, it should have forced her mind back into unconsciousness, but instead, his cool fingers brought comfort. There was no pain at all, not even a sliver, which meant she was either dead or his healing ability had worked better than expected.

"There now. Once more should heal her entirely, but a good meal and a night of rest would do her well. I'll put on some gruel and fetch some meat from the basement." The voice faded as it exited the room, but Eiagan could not focus well enough to see the face it belonged to.

By the scent that lingered in the air even indoors, Eiagan knew they were in the Smolzark Territory, most definitely in the Miner's Village. She let her eyes take in the room. Dark wooden floors, dark walls, dark stone... everything covered with a permanent layer of soot the town could never scrub clean. The blanket that covered her from mid-chest down, was poorly woven but warm.

"You are awake," Porvarth said. "I thought I lost you again." He pressed his forehead against hers and closed his eyes, then released a breath. "How do you feel?"

When Porvarth lifted his head, Eiagan tried to sit, but pain reverberated through her leg. She hissed.

"Wait, not yet. One more healing session and you should be good as new. I only have the focus to heal one broken part at a time, and the chest wound was my priority."

"It is healed?" Eiagan asked, peering inside her tunic. There was no bruising to mention, not even the yellowed skin that remained on a body weeks after the black and purple marks had gone. She knew traumatic bruising well, given her early life under Icluedian's rule. But what she found most remarkable was that even the scars from Moriarian's magic were gone.

"It is. We flew many marticks here to the Miner's Village where the mage, Thyre, heals the sick and mortally wounded," he said.

"Thyre? How did you know of this woman?"

"I remembered meeting her once about ten or so years ago. I took a chance that she was still alive and still living amongst the miners. They are often the most in need of healing given the danger of their occupation, and my memory served me well."

"She has taught you how to heal again?" Eiagan's mind swam, but the confusion was most likely attributed to the throbbing in her temples. She had pounded her head on the ground many times during the tussle with the horse.

"Not taught, reminded. It seems I never lost my ability, but I must focus my energy on healing. Dragons do not care much for focusing on tasks that require patience and quiet, it seems, and so I must fight my own instinct to *cause* destruction. I must repurpose it to heal."

"So... you are still a loxmore who might die from your healing?" Eiagan's heart held its breath while she searched Porvarth's eyes for any sign he might lie to her.

"No, I don't believe so. I don't feel weakness after healing, and since I am not *fully* a loxmore, I would say there is little need for concern. Perhaps becoming a dragon was the right thing after all? First, the wolves in The Banished Lands, and now this," he said motioning over Eiagan's broken but healing body. "I think I might be the only one of my kind in existence, so discovering all I can do will likely take years, decades even."

"Thank you," Eiagan whispered and relaxed deeper into the bedding. Considering all that he might be took more energy than she had to expend, so she sighed. "When can we expect to head out on our journey again?"

Porvarth grimaced as if his reply pained him physically. "I am afraid the rumbling of the earth caused much devastation here and in neighboring villages. Gael sent word to Nox that you were injured, and of course, Tend had to reason with and fight Nox to keep him on the throne. He wanted to come, but he knows his place."

84

"We will be delayed in finding his daughter again," Eiagan said, her teeth grinding.

"I believe Reven and Darby will protect Violet and the other children. I cannot say why, but I feel it in my heart. Your nephew is the son of Astrid and Reeve, and as such, I cannot imagine there lives a cowardly bone in his body." Porvarth shrugged and swiped Eiagan's hair from her face.

"That is what I am afraid of, Porvarth. He will get himself killed as sure as the sun takes the sky each morning if he has even an ounce of Allurigard blood in his veins. Tell me about the people here and in the villages affected by the quakes. What can be done while we are stuck here?"

"They do not begrudge you time to heal or a bed to do it in, but they would like to see us on our way the moment you can walk. They are not unkind, but they do not wish for more trouble. They have enough of it."

"I understand their position. We will not overstay our welcome. Was anyone else injured?"

"Catia's wrist required a light healing, but no one else took a tumble under a horse. Only you, my love, prefer to scare me out of my wits ten times a day."

Eiagan bit back a smile and pulled the bedside curtain back. Outside, the sky was dismal, and gray clouds rolled in from the west. The pressure in the air indicated a storm, but it would not clean the blackness that stained the village. Across the dirt road in front of Thyre's shop, an inn, a bakery, a butcher, and an ale house slumped under the weight of centuries of oppression. Well worn, the roofs sagged and longed for new clay shingles. The windows were blackened and boasted broken panes, one shop door was cracked, and two shops had crumbling chimneys.

"What are you now, Porvarth?" she murmured.

"I don't know. Something unlike any other."

Eiagan dropped the curtain and focused her gaze on the man. "Did the mage know anything about your strange iridescence or your blue fire?"

"She is unsure, but she did say it is not unusual for those made dragons to exhibit signs of latent magical abilities. Perhaps I had some ability even before I was made a loxmore? As such, she believes only time will show what I am, truly, but in my heart, I still feel that I have not changed in centuries. Maybe I am a new species of half-loxmore and half-dragon." He took her hand with delicate fingers and squeezed them. "But I do know I am the man who loves you, and for whatever reason I have become what I am, it is only so that we may help our people together."

Eiagan's heart relaxed. "I am pleased you have peace with what you have become, and if you are not worried, then I am not. Will you fetch my sister, please?"

"Of course. Emora is quite beside herself," Porvarth said, released her hand, and eased from the bed as if it were the most difficult decision he had made in his lifetime.

"I am fine, Porvarth, thanks to you. I will remain so, I swear."

Porvarth swallowed and glanced toward the door, then back to Eiagan. "Might I speak out of turn for a moment?"

"It is a characteristic common to you, Porvarth. Speak your mind." Eiagan brushed her dark hair from her shoulder to examine a tender place over her collarbone. It had been broken, too, but was healed. It, though, was red unlike her chest.

"I know that you believe my frustration toward Gael stems from... Well, truth be told, I am unsure where you believe it comes from, but the truth is that I simply do not trust the man. I cannot offer a valid reason, only to say that something about him does not settle well on my stomach. He is brave and kind, of course, but there is something in his heart that feels wrong, Eiagan. Everything about him feels like a lie to me, but I have no evidence to support such a feeling."

Eiagan swallowed the bile that rose in her throat. "I know. Catia said as much herself. I cannot say much but know that I am choosing my path and my words carefully near the man, and I will continue to do so until I have decided what is best."

"That is enough for me to know. I will retrieve Emora. She and Ari went for a walk around the village to restore our supplies and to buy new horses."

Eiagan nodded and let her gaze follow Porvarth from the room. Before he reached the door, an aching in her heart urged rarely spoken words from her mouth.

"Porvarth?"

"Hmm?" He pivoted on his heel, his beautiful blue eyes trained on her with such anticipation, she smiled at its boyishness.

"I love you. That's all I wanted to say."

His grin warmed her further, including her cheeks. "I love you, too. I'll be back soon."

Her heart swelled as he left the room, filled with love for the family she trusted and longed to see happy before her final days — not those spent in the Bleak, but those after she finally closed her eyes for the last time. Until then, she would fight with everything she had to ensure they and her kingdom's people prospered. The first order of business, to restore the Mining Village to something livable and thriving again.

When Emora entered the room, Eiagan had just drifted to sleep again. The creaking door startled her, and she grasped her sword.

"It is only me," Emora whispered. "I was so worried. How are you?"

"Well enough. Porvarth's healing has improved. I am told one more session and we might be on our way."

"The sooner the better. Reven and the others have been on my mind all day, and we even received a message from King Alekzan of Nelaravore. There was a false sighting in Nelaravore, but he is sending teams of men to scour the countryside to be sure."

"Would Nessa travel so far?" Eiagan tried to reason why she might do such a thing but could find no good reason except that it might throw them from her trail — a good enough reason for anyone, Eiagan believed.

"Who knows? I cannot determine anything while in this frame of mind. We have lost so much, and I was sure I had lost you, too." Emora bit her trembling lip and turned her head away from her sister's intense stare. Even so, she could not contain her gasp. "I am sorry for such weakness, but all my life I watched you from afar. I only wanted to be in your life, to be by your side through everything, and I thought... Oh, Eiagan, I thought you were good as dead, forever this time."

Eiagan's hand settled on Emora's forearm. "You have not lost me, and you will not."

"You shouldn't say such things. You cannot see what will come. Eiagan, I missed you desperately all my life, and to lose you now would devastate me equally as losing Astrid and Reeve. And now we share this... this darkness that occupies our minds. I wonder if we will ever find peace?"

Eiagan's heart softened further toward her sister. "I *needed* you all my life, and now I have you. Let us not waste time thinking of what we did not have or lost and focus on what we might gain. As for finding peace… I know we will. We will make sure of it. I was taken by surprise because I allowed myself to trust a stranger too much. It will not happen again."

"Gael?"

"Indeed. Porvarth mistrusts him as Catia does."

"And Ari. He admitted his curiosities about the man during our walk."

"His curiosities? What are Ari's thoughts?"

Emora drew closer to Eiagan's bedside and leaned toward her. "He says the man puts off the stink of a month-dead carp, so to speak." Eiagan chuckled and leaned closer. "Gael is a prince, a guide, a—oh, whatever. He claims to be many things, but what proof do we have?"

"None," Eiagan admitted. Foolishness had never been a part of Eiagan's character, but it seemed she had let it get the better of her this time. "Did Nox's correspondence include his thoughts on the matter?"

Emora shook her head. "No. I believe he will reserve that for you alone."

Her sister spoke the truth. Nox would not offer his evaluation of Gael to anyone but the woman he trusted most, aside from his deceased wife, of course. "You and Ari are well, then?"

"A change of subject is not like you, sister, but yes. We are moving past what was done. He's already forgiven me for imprisoning him—for Nessa imprisoning him. I know he bears no ill will for the things she used my body for, but… but I fear he cannot *unknow* them just as I cannot." Emora said, shivering at the thought of Keirnor and Nessa's intimate moments while Nessa inhabited her body.

"It was an intrusion and a crime and if Keirnor were still alive, I would skin him mixlin by mixlin until—"

Emora placed her hand on Eiagan's forearm, bringing her temper back under control. Eiagan could not imagine what her sister felt—the filth of knowing a man had intruded upon her without her consent, all while a woman had controlled her mind in the same way.

"I must not remind myself of it too much, or I slip into the same darkness that you do. I am… *managing,* I suppose, with Porvarth's help. Ari said you wish to work with him to recover from your own depression and paranoia. Do you think they can help us?"

Eiagan took a few breaths while the remnants of anger left her body. "I hope so. I think Ari can see those broken parts of me more clearly than Porvarth, just as Porvarth sees yours."

Emora smirked. "They both love us too much to see it in us, don't they?"

Eiagan smiled, knowing that wasn't *exactly* the truth, but perhaps there was a small bit of truth in it. "Perhaps. Or at least, they will deny what they see because of their love. Will you marry him?"

Emora shrugged. "He has not asked directly, but I do not expect him to do such things while we are under the present circumstances. He has alluded to a future where we might have children, so I would assume that he will ask. Will you marry Porvarth?"

Eiagan chuckled. "It is my hope, but the world must stop falling apart around us first."

Emora's pale gray eyes settled on the woolen blanket as her dainty fingers pulled at its threads. "Do you think we will ever be happy, to have that peace, or are we cursed with our father's blood *and* misfortune all our lives?"

"I do not know, but I will never stop fighting for those we love to find happiness. And, if we are so lucky, their happiness will include our presence and we might revel in it with them." Eiagan was drawn to the window again, and she pulled the threadbare drapery back. "Will you send a request to Nox? Please ask him to spare a few workers to aid the village here. Over there, the buildings are in dire need of repair."

"I will. I am sure he would be pleased to do something for the people."

Eiagan dropped the drapery again. "Might I inquire your opinion, perhaps an assessment?"

Emora's eyebrows met and her head nodded forward. "You may, but I doubt there is anything you might ask of me that you have not already considered at length. Even so, I will hear your request. What is it, sister?"

"Catia said she prefers Noxious as the king. Is that the sentiment of all the land?" Eiagan asked.

Emora waved her hand and pursed her lips, then said, "Nonsense. You died for them and then rescued them from me… from *Nessa* as me. The people have sought you out for a second chance, and when we find Reven, you will sit upon the throne again, and so you will remain until you choose to pass it on to our nephew."

"It is rightfully his now as Reeve was the heir in his day."

"But Reven is too inexperienced to rule a kingdom," Emora argued, but Eiagan did not bother to correct her. Eiagan commanded an army at an age less than Reven's, but those memories only brought forth those of Zero, complicating and muddying Eiagan's present focus.

"Perhaps," Eiagan whispered, but her mind was elsewhere.

91

Emora tilted her head so that she was in Eiagan's line of sight, but the queen was too focused on Catia's earlier statement and the way it settled in her heart to notice she had left her sister with unanswered questions.

"I will fetch you a meal, then you should rest," Emora said, then gathered the mess Porvarth and Thyre had left behind — bandages and ointments — then exited and closed the door behind her.

Eiagan watched the door for some time, expecting another of her people to enter, but when no one did, she eased deeper into the bed. It was uncomfortable, but she could not decide if it was the fault of the bedding or the horse that had rolled over her. Her mind, though, was filled with thoughts that muddled it. Would there ever come a time when her mind could rest without the constant threat of war or devastation taking her by surprise?

Just when Eiagan had settled on one image to set her focus upon, a scraping sound at the window opposite her bed pulled her attention. One of the dreadful squawks had slipped through the open shutters. The giant bird burst apart into many, most of which exited the way they came, but one remained. It held a roll of paper in its beak but did not appear interested in relinquishing it to Eiagan. Its talons scraped along the stained wood floor as it paced and eyed Eiagan.

"Be gone with you, nuisance," Eiagan said, then let her head rest upon the musty bedding.

The scraping of talons grew nearer, close enough that Eiagan thought the bird might attack her or… *something* undesirable, so she opened her eyes and lifted herself enough to see the bird clearly. The large bird flapped twice and settled on the foot of the bed, digging its sharp claws into the soft wood frame.

"If you seek a friend, you are in the wrong room," Eiagan said, motioning around. "Go, find your friend elsewhere and leave me —"

The squawk dropped the roll of paper at her feet and looked up at her with worried, beady eyes. Had anyone told Eiagan before that the birds possessed any sort of emotion besides a strong desire to frustrate her, she might not have believed it. But there it was, clear as day looking back at her. The bird was scared, yes, but not of her. Its back relaxed as it took a small step onto the bed, then it took several small, cautious steps toward Eiagan, nudging the letter a little with each step.

"You wish for me to receive the letter?"

The bird warbled a bit and released a low-pitched squawk before nudging her hand with its razor-sharp beak. The size of a cat when in its separated form, Eiagan preferred this one bird over the dozens that melded together into one.

Eiagan retrieved the correspondence and unrolled it. Her tired eyes absorbed the familiar handwriting that was written in a hurry. Noxious often let his penmanship slip when he was angered or, in this case, unsettled.

"I see why you have brought this to me. Noxious does not trust the Asantavalian either." Eiagan folded the paper and prepared to slip it underneath her until it could be destroyed, but the bird snatched it from her hand and leaped from the bed.

"Stop!" she scolded, but the bird had a mind of its own. It dropped the letter into the fire and hopped back a few steps. "I appreciate your loyalty, but the next time you shall do as I say. Am I clear?"

The bird cocked its head and ruffled its feathers, but it made no sound.

93

"I do not care for taking orders either, but it is a necessary evil, I am afraid. Might I take this action to say that you also do not trust Gael?" Talking to a bird. What had gotten into her?

The bird's ruffled feathers stood on end as it lowered its head. A low rumble escaped its beak, but it was not like any rumbling Eiagan had heard before. Then the squawk flapped its wings, lifted itself over her bed, and landed at her side.

"Are we amiable now?" When the bird made no motion to leave, she sighed. "Then do be quiet. I would like a moment to rest before I decide what to do next. It seems we are all in agreement. We do not trust the Asantavalian until we have gained more evidence."

The Winter Queen laid her head down again. The squawk settled beside her and watched the door like a faithful companion — one Eiagan had not known she had.

EIGHT

Noxious "The Savage" Skjoldsson

It was an agitated and disturbed sleep, but Nox finally found some rest after sending a group of men on assignment to the Miner's Village in Smolzark at Emora's request. Their buildings, he assumed, would suffer more damage before the war was over but if he could alleviate some of their want, if only for a short while, then he was pleased to do so. Fires of some sort sprouted in every territory, but there was an adequate supply of materials and willing men to do the work. The women, too, had been invaluable to the cause — becoming physicians, tending the crops in Maltows, aiding the search parties across the kingdom. Goranin was healing but for how long?

Another chill pulled him from sleep, and so the temporary king rose from his bed to fetch another blanket. The fire burned low, so

95

Nox added three logs and stoked the remnants until they caught, then warmed his hands near the flames.

That chill… it surrounded him despite sitting at the hearth, but with it came a scent. A mix of death and beauty and mystery, it flowed over him as a gentle breeze chilled the nape of his neck. Nox clenched his jaw and stood.

"It is uncouth to enter a man's quarters without permission. Wholly unladylike but I suppose you are no lady."

That dreadful red snake coiled in the corner and stood on end, stretching until Nessa's full form was revealed. Nessa's laughter chilled him to the bone as her magic enveloped him. "I have been called many things, but never a lady. Tell me, do you tire of sleeping all alone?"

"What do you want here?"

"To have an answer to my question. Are you lonely, Noxious the *Savage?*" His name dripped from her lips like honey, but the sting was deadlier than any he'd ever known. She tapped her finger on her chin, her other arm crossed over her chest.

"The woman who killed my wife should know how lonely I am, but I suppose you do not consider those things. How pleasant for you that you might sleep with a guilt-free conscience while the rest of us are forced to see your brutality played out in our nightmares each time we close our eyes."

Nessa's stare bored into his, yet a flicker of remorse flashed over her face before the stoic hardness returned. "Your assumptions know no bounds, dragon."

"It is no assumption. You murdered my wife and many others I loved, and you seem to lose no sleep over your deeds."

The tapping of her chin ceased as she crossed both arms, her expression oddly... *sorrowful.* "Would you believe me if I admitted that I did not intend to kill your Hazel?"

Nox's shoulders rolled forward as he stepped back, taken by surprise that Nessa not only confessed her mistake, but that he *believed* her. He shook his head. Whatever enchantment she used against him, he would fight through it. He could not, not even for a moment, believe a single thing that fell from her mouth.

"No. You kill with glee, so forgive me if I — "

"As did you, or have you forgotten why they call you the Savage?" Nessa's eyes narrowed, closing in on him, prepared to strike at the first wrong step.

Nox swallowed as his fingers found the cool metal of his dagger, one Hazel had gifted him on their third anniversary, and wrapped them around to the hilt. Though her eyes never left his, there was no doubt she had seen him do it. Even so, she allowed him to prepare himself, to plan out his attack as she watched. There was no fear or doubt in her gaze, only that wretched sorrow. It could only mean one thing.

"You are not here in the flesh," he said, releasing the dagger.

This brought a wicked smile. "Do you wish that I were? What would you do to me with that dagger if I were here in flesh and blood and bone?"

Nox groaned and kicked the end of one log, spitting embers all over the hearth. "Why did you come here, Nessa?"

Another smile more wicked than the last. "I do enjoy the way my name sounds upon your lips."

Nox growled and gripped the dagger again, if only to keep himself anchored, to keep the dragon under control. Shadows encircled his shoulders, crept over them until they caressed his face in fingerlike tendrils. He closed his eyes, breathing in the scent of his departed wife. They trailed over his cheeks, his jaw, his browbone, over his lips before his eyes snapped open and he stepped backward.

"Stop it!" he roared. "This is evil magic, and I want no part of it."

"You miss her." Nessa's hands dropped to her sides as she strode closer. "And despite your belief that I take joy in seeing you suffer, I am truly sorry. She was not meant to suffer, not even meant to see a scratch much less..." Her statement trailed, leaving her staring at the floor.

Nox inhaled, prepared to issue his order that she leave his presence when she spoke again.

"I know your pain in many ways."

"You know nothing of this pain. You cannot know how it feels to have your love die, then to have your child taken from you by the same evil being that destroyed the only good thing you'd ever had." Nox felt the dragon stir to life, its talons clawing on the back of his consciousness. *Release me... Let me kill her.* He squeezed his eyes shut again and breathed.

When he opened them again, Nessa had moved closer. She stood an arm's length from him, her eyes focused on his face. Stars above, she was as exquisite as Eiagan and equally as lethal. There was none of Hazel's softness, her kindness, or her unbridled passion for good in this woman. Not even a shred.

"I know pain and loss and suffering the likes of which you could never, *never* understand, and yet I find myself *wanting* to ease the burden of such harsh emotion from your shoulders. Tell me why, though I know you are not *him,* do I see him in you with every blink? Why must you look the way you do and tear my heart to pieces with every breath? And why... *why* did I ever ruin what was yours?"

Nessa's gaze burned every inch of Nox's skin, unsettling him more than the dragon when it would not yield to his authority. He raised a hand between them, creating a barrier that snapped her mind back to reality. Nessa's eyes widened and she gasped, then stepped back.

"Even your intensity is the same as Zero's." Nessa stepped back again, nearly tripping over the bearskin rug.

"My ancestor? How would you know?" Nox asked, his eyes narrowed on the fair-haired woman whose features were twisted in some painful, angry expression, though he could not pinpoint exactly what had caused it.

Nessa's back stiffened and she wiped her palms over her leather pants. Her usual wickedness returned and drew her lips into another smile. "I have a new offer for you to ponder. I swear to stop taking children from Goranin, perhaps even return those I have already taken to their guardians, in exchange for one simple thing."

Nox snickered, unsurprised that there were conditions to her offer to do what was right. "And what, stars above, could I possibly give you in return for our children? For *my* child?" Violet's sweet face flashed in his mind, testing the dragon inside him further. It adored Violet, and the very thought she could be in some danger, infuriated it to the point of frenzy.

"Come with me. Join me, and I will release the children of Goranin."

Nox roared, his laughter echoing through the sparsely furnished quarters and through the empty halls of Vidkun Castle.

Nessa's jaw clenched and she inhaled. "I do not jest. It is an offer I will make only once, and I will give you a day to choose."

"And if I deny you?" Nox forced the smile from his face and turned his back to the woman. She had lost her mind entirely, and as such, he did not fear her. He let his gaze settle on the fire. His question was met with silence for a long while, so he glanced over his shoulder to find her staring into the same fire. The serenity in her existence was unexpected. "Why do you even want me? A man whose life you've destroyed?"

Her gaze lifted to his again. "It was an accident. I never meant to hurt you." Her whisper barely carried to his ears before she stiffened again. "I will return tomorrow to hear your reply."

She started from the room, but a flicker of anxiety moved Nox into action. He crossed the room and pressed her further.

"I want to know. Why? Why would you want me?"

Her eyes flamed and brow furrowed in anger. "Because you are her *lap dog*. You are nothing more than her errand boy, just like *he* was. She does not appreciate you, but I would. I *do!* Your loyalty, your strength, your ferocity, and your... your *face* are all things I desire in a man and a mate to conquer this world beside me."

Nox stumbled backward. Her words attacked his mind like a hammer, shattering the illusion that Nessa was a madwoman. No, the woman was far from mad. Nessa was... heartbroken... lost... *needing.* Even so, Nox was not the man to offer anything to the homicidal woman, especially after her cruelty toward his people, his family, his *wife.*

"I will return tomorrow night. I suggest you choose your path before it is too late." Nessa's projection vanished, leaving Nox wholly unstable, ruined, confused.

He stumbled through the door, ignoring the chill that swept over him as he slid down the hallway, creeping in the shadows like a bandit. Eventually, through no intent of his own, he ended up at Tend's door—a guest quarters where he had taken residence to be near the king should anyone choose to attempt regicide.

A broad fist knocked upon the door until it opened, revealing a man ready for battle.

"Nox? What is it? It is the middle of —"

"Nessa. She was here, in my room. I..." Nox shook his head, reminding the dragon he had things quite under control, and refocused on his friend's face. "I think I know how we can find the children."

Tend opened the door fully and allowed the king entry, then sealed it tightly behind them.

"She was in your quarters? As a projection?" he asked, running a hand over his face. Shoulders slumped and eyes half-closed, it was a sure sign he was not in the mood for the mage's antics, but he inhaled and stiffened his posture, ready for a fight.

"Always a projection, of course, but she offered me a choice. If I go with her, she will return the children." Nox almost laughed at himself when he repeated her words, knowing well there was some trick behind them. Tend did laugh.

"You cannot possibly think she will hold true to her word. What word does she even have? None. She's a monster, and as such, we cannot trust a thing she says. You cannot be considering this?" Tend's eyes narrowed almost as if to say *I forbid it.*

Nox snickered and shook his head, then scanned the room. That dreadful snake could hide anywhere, and letting Nessa in on his intended ruse before it even began could create more problems than he already had.

"Of course not. But if I go with her, perhaps I will figure out where they are and can send word back here. Then you can ready the armies and save the children." How foolish he sounded, but it was the closest they had come to a plan since Nessa took the children.

Tend's narrowed eyes widened, then softened as his entire body eased. "I hate to admit, it is a lunatic plan but it just might work. The only problem I foresee is how on earth you plan to communicate with me once she takes you." Tend paced the room, forcing Nox to follow.

"If she takes me where she keeps the children, then one might assume Darby of Nelaravore would also be there with Reven. Perhaps she can teach me how to mind speak as she did with her dragon?"

Tend scoffed. "And then what? You'll speak with her while you are both locked in a dungeon somewhere? How does that help the cause?" Tend asked, pausing his pacing long enough to ensure Nox knew what he thought of his plan. Tend was impressively intense when he chose to prove his point with little more than a glare.

"No, but if I can ensure her release—"

Tend held up his hand, stopping Nox short. "We need to think this through. No stone must be left unturned. We cannot make assumptions about Nessa's behavior or actions, least of all that she left Darby and Reven alive." He said what everyone failed to say before—that there was every reason to believe Nessa had already killed the two adults she had abducted.

Nox swallowed while his head swam. Heaven help them if Nessa had killed Reven. Eiagan would scorch the whole earth searching for the woman, her advancements where her temper was concerned be damned.

"What do you suggest?" Nox asked.

"Come, sit at the table. Let's walk through this possibility and see what we might discover." Tend motioned toward a small table that sat by his fireplace. He wasn't wrong. Leaping in head first wouldn't help anyone, but for the first time since Violet had been taken, Nox saw a way out. At least, he saw a way for his daughter to be saved, and that sparked a light of hope in him he hadn't had in a long time.

Hours passed as they plotted and planned, closer than ever to finding not only the children of Goranin, but of all the kingdoms. When the last piece of the puzzle was craftily placed, Tend wiped a hand over his face and stood.

"I believe we might have one problem left."

"What is that?" Nox asked, glancing up while Tend began pacing again.

"Once that woman gets you in her clutches, I fear she will never let you leave alive." Tend's blonde-brown hair stuck up in all directions, a disheveled mess much like Nox's mind, but of one thing Nox was sure.

"I would suffer the fate ten times over for Violet's freedom."

Tend's kind eyes searched Nox's face. Finding truth there, he nodded. "Then we have our plan."

NINE

Reven Allurigard

Reven's body shook while a little voice beckoned, pulling him from the remnants of a dream. Not a dream, but a vision of the past. With a groan, he opened his eyes and stared at the beams above his head. Flat on his back, Darby whimpered and rolled onto her side, bumping into him. She held her head at the temples and blinked to focus.

Violet's little hand pressed against Reven's shoulder, her fingertips digging into the flesh. "You fell down and went to sleep," she said. "We've been trying to wake you for ages."

Reven sat, careful not to do so quickly lest he lose what little water he had consumed. He offered a pathetic smile, but it seemed to soothe Violet's concern. Darby, though, was less amused.

"That woman is dreadful." Darby sat fully and rested her arms upon her knees.

"Do you suppose she intended for us to see her birth and who she really is?" Reven asked, his black hair falling into his eyes. He swiped it away and offered a soothing pat to a child's head. He nodded toward the corner where the others played. "You two go back with the others while the adults speak. There's no need to worry. Princess Darby and I are fine."

Darby watched while they dragged their feet along the boards, reluctant and fearful. "I cannot be sure, but of this I *am* sure… it was definitely the same magic Emora used to correspond with Eiagan after she arose. Eiagan fell when she touched the words, then was unconscious for some time. Only she spoke to Emora through their… their meeting. I don't understand this magic, especially since I have trained my entire life to heal with mine."

Reven rubbed the back of his neck and glanced around the room. Nothing had changed while they were unconscious. "Do you think what we saw was true?"

Darby glanced sideways at Reven, a glint in her eyes. "God help us if it is. Reven, what will we do?"

"Surely, my aunts would not change their course because of this information. As ironic as it is, they cannot allow Nessa to live." Reven shook his head. "No, not after everything she has done. There is no redemption for this." He waved his hand toward the children, most of them orphaned by the woman who now held them captive.

"I would not make any assumptions where redemption is concerned. Things tend to look a bit different when —"

Darby's comment was interrupted by a slamming door, one down the hallway where Reven assumed Nessa kept her own quarters. She shifted her focus to the only point of entry, a thick, tall wooden door with iron bars at the top that kept them secure inside their tower. Through the bars was nothing but a long hallway that turned right at one end, and dead-ended at the other just past a second door.

The door creaked open. Nessa entered with a basket filled to the brim with fruit and freshly baked bread. She placed the basket on the floor and then shifted her attention to the opened armoire. "You were rummaging through my things, were you? And what, might I ask, made you believe that I would allow such an invasion?"

A taunt. There was no edge to her tone, none of the icy sharpness that laced Nessa's voice when she was truly angered or frustrated. No, this was an invitation, one that Reven had anticipated from the moment he opened the book.

"If you did not wish for us to rummage, then perhaps you should have stowed your property elsewhere, Ellenessia." Reven's lips curled to mimic his captor's.

"You are an intelligent lad. So much like your father. It is a shame your beloved aunt murdered him, is it not?" Even her grin was taunting, begging him to fall into her world if only so she might use his newly gained knowledge against him.

Darby gripped Reven's knee, keeping him seated on the dingy floor. His muscles tensed, and that anger, the heated blood his guardian Ima had warned him to contain, boiled in his veins. Only Darby's hand kept him connected to this reality, this time and place, and reminded him the mage could tear him limb from limb without a second thought. There wasn't enough Allurigard blood in him to take on such a beast.

Nessa chuckled and slid the basket closer to the children. "We will have a guest tomorrow. One I am sure you will be glad to see.

Eat, gain your strength, and perhaps you might find a special treat at the bottom of the basket."

With her final words resting heavily on the children — their little cherub-like faces wary that whatever lie at the bottom of the basket might swallow them up — Nessa strode across the room and slammed the door shut. The book was still there resting on the table where Nessa had stood.

"She didn't take the book. She looked right at it before she taunted you," Darby said.

"I think she *wants* us to see it." Reven shuffled and stood. "I think… I think we are approaching her final act, and she wants us to see what brought her here."

Darby snickered and rolled her eyes. "I think she adores drama as much as she favors herself, but I will humor you if only to see what comes next in her story. Heaven only knows what went wrong to make her this way." Darby stood beside Reven, then searched the group of children. "Daniel, kindly keep a keen eye over the others. Ensure they eat and rest while Reven and I complete our mission."

Daniel's eyes went wide. "But… the book made you fall asleep. What shall we do without you if she returns?"

Darby shook her head, her blonde hair swishing over her shoulders. "You will be safe until we wake again."

Reven pursed his lips. There was no way to be sure the children would be safe while they ventured through the stories in the book, so Reven pulled her aside. As if reading his mind, she shook her head more vehemently than before.

"You cannot do it alone, Reven. What if… what if you need me?"

"No one can hear us in the visions. I am safe and secure, and if anything confuses me, then I will…" He couldn't do it, couldn't look into her eyes and leave her behind. She knew it to, blasted woman, so she softened her features until he melted in her gaze. With a sigh, he offered his hand. "You had better pray those children are safe while we are gone."

Her narrowed eyes were proof enough she was annoyed. "I would never leave them here alone if I did not think they were safe. If Nessa planned to harm them, she would have done it already. Her plans for us are long-term, Reven. And if we can only see more, we might know what they are and why."

With another deep sigh, Reven focused on the page and skimmed the pads of his fingers over the enchanted words. In a blink, they were back in Asantaval.

TEN

The History of the Callanan Royal Family

Illaric had not been wrong about the widow Portia, nor had he been wrong about her sons. The three boys needed guidance and purpose, lest they end up in jail or as beggars. Portia did her best to ensure they kept their manners, but it would take more than that to bring them up as men of Asantavalian blood. But the boys alone were not what drew Bribadge to Portia. It was her heart, her sharp mind, and that smile that lit up a room whenever she entered no matter how deep in darkness and despair it had been.

And so, one year after their introduction, Bribadge offered marriage to Portia. She was agreeable, though she requested a quiet ceremony over the traditional merriment of a royal wedding. Since it was the second union for both, Illaric agreed. Lureah, though, had been disappointed, which was why Bribadge and his new wife and sons were gathered in the ballroom, pretending they were not annoyed with the formal wear and attention bestowed upon them.

"It is merely Lureah's way of showing she cares," Bribadge said as his hand found his wife's.

Portia smiled. "I know, and I do adore her, but I feel so out of place. I'm no young swan, and this is entirely too much pomp and circumstance for a second union. We don't even have a claim to the throne."

"No, but she was not wrong when she said Asantaval needs a reason to be joyous." Bribadge thought of the food stores that had dwindled through the winter, and with another just around the corner, no one could be sure they would not starve to death beneath the earth.

"You did all you could, darling," Portia said, reading her new husband like a book. "You hunted, we found new ways to grow crops, and even the fish haul was larger this summer. What else can we do?"

"Illaric is considering a scouting mission to the surface, one that might lead to a trade agreement."

Portia gasped. "He cannot possibly — "

"He can." Bribadge's eyes lowered to his wife's. "He has. There are spies among Goranin, Varrow, and even a few of the southern kingdoms."

Portia gasped again, but this time she kept quiet. It was a matter to discuss in private when prying eyes and ears weren't watching their every move. The husband and wife shared a look, something dark and worried that didn't match the merriment around them.

The boys — Arden, the eldest at fifteen, Caston at twelve, and Fritz at ten — watched their mother like a hawk hunting a rabbit. Always circling, always scenting the air, they would not even let

Bribadge court her without supervision. In hindsight, Bribadge thought it was a wise thing they did, for the life of a royal was wrought with worry and danger. Now, they stood in a row watching ladies dancing, but with little interest given their distaste for the aristocratic girls.

Bribadge scratched his chin, ruffling his red-hued beard, then he smoothed it and offered his other hand to his wife. "Shall we pretend this is a good time?"

Portia giggled, then let him twirl her around and onto the dance floor. They'd hardly made it when four guards burst through the double-doored entrance to the ballroom. Ladies squealed as gentlemen gawked at the unruly behavior.

Bribadge glanced once more at Portia, then disengaged from her embrace to address the disruption. The guards had already found the king, which was highly improper. Bribadge was their commander, and as such, they were to report directly to him. The first guard — Quenten by name and Bribadge's most trusted man — waved his hands around, then leaned in to whisper to Illaric.

Illaric's gaze drifted upwards when Bribadge approached. There, in those familiar eyes, was a terror unlike any Bribadge had ever seen in all his years. The king licked his lips.

"Dismiss the crowd. Tell them… I don't care what you tell them, just get them out of here," Illaric said.

Quenten nodded once, then turned to his men, dispensing orders in Bribadge's place. Affronted, Bribadge raised a hand to make a point to his brother, but he was dismissed by Illaric's frantic grasp. His fingers trembled as they dug into Bribadge's arm, and his skin blanched a shade too pale even for a king who ruled an underground kingdom.

"We have a situation," Illaric said. "Take your family home, then meet with me. You know where."

"Brother, what is—"

"Now, Bribadge." Illaric's tone left nothing to question.

Bribadge strode back to his family and took Arden by the arm. The boy obliged, obedient since he came to trust Bribadge, and followed him to a darkened corner. "There's been some disturbance. Kindly take your mother and brothers home, convince her there is no worry, and keep watch until I return."

"Yes, sir. Shall I expect you late?" Arden asked, half a man yet still half a boy who worried more than anyone should.

"Likely, but all will be well my boy. Go on now, take some food with you and keep your mother in good spirits."

Arden swallowed and eyed his new father, then nodded once more and did as he was told. Bribadge watched as he returned to their family, smiled, and offered his mother his arm to escort her home. They paused to gather a basket of food, then Arden insisted they hurry home so they might play a game before turning in for the night. Arden's gaze drifted to Bribadge for a moment, a silent agreement between them—he would do as he was told, but Bribadge had better bring home a good excuse.

Bribadge darted to the soundproof chamber to meet Illaric. Each footfall felt as if he were wading through mud, pushing himself toward a meeting he felt sure would not end well. Had they already found food shortages? Had one of Illaric's scouts been discovered? Upon arrival at the door, newly polished and shiny, he paused. Before even opening the door, Bribadge knew what he would find— Illaric pacing, the sound echoing over the stone floor in a room devoid of furniture, tapestries, windows... devoid of anything but worry and fear.

He pushed the door open and closed it behind him. Illaric's head snapped up, then his shoulders relaxed.

"Brother. Brother, little Nessa, we have discovered who her parents are, and I fear it is worse than we imagined."

"What? How?" Bribadge ran his hands through his hair and began pacing alongside his brother. "If anyone in Asantaval discovers her identity —"

"How would they? Only those who are trusted know she was taken in," Illaric said, but his tone said he knew it was possible. If the people discovered Nessa was not of Callanan blood, they would be removed from the castle and hanged for treason — king or not.

Bribadge ignored his brother's inquiry and asked, "What do you know? Whose child is little Nessa?"

Illaric glanced around the room as if there might be invisible forces who had infiltrated the walls of their meeting space, then leaned in to whisper his secrets to the only man Illaric would never lie to. When the names flittered from Illaric's mouth to Bribadge's ear, he nearly came out of his skin. Every cell burned, every muscle twitched knowing he'd held the baby daughter of such inimical souls — one a far sight worse than the other, of course.

Illaric swallowed and leaned against the wall. "What will we do? Have we any reason to believe Nessa might grow up to be... like them?"

"We won't know if she's magical until she's older, but I've heard tales that such things are hereditary in that bloodline." Bribadge leaned beside his brother and stroked his short beard. His eyes fixed on the opposite wall, he cursed the day he'd met the loxmore girl in the Lands. He should have ignored her, left well enough alone, but he hadn't, and now must face the consequence of his ruse against the people.

"What shall we do?" Illaric deferred to his younger brother, though Bribadge had very few thoughts on the matter, all things considered.

"What is there to do? We ensure the people never discover her true lineage, pray she does not develop any magical ability, and do our best to remain hidden. If her parents discover she was not killed, I fear they might try a location spell."

Illaric pushed off the wall and cursed. "I had not considered such things. This baby could be the death of us all."

Bribadge shook his head. "She is your daughter, and we love her. We still have time to perfect a story should she develop abilities. As for the location spell, I would suggest we end the exploration missions. If one of our scouts is discovered among the people—"

"There is no reason to think that would incite an inquiry into the whereabouts of a supposedly dead baby, Bribadge. We must scout. If we cannot determine the status of the surrounding kingdoms, how will we know if it is safe to return to the surface?"

Bribadge pursed his lips. It was the same beginning to the same argument they'd had every day since Illaric first suggested the scout above. "All things are connected, brother. Perhaps one question might lead to another and another until suddenly, our scout has given away our location to the enemy."

"I still fail to see what that has to do with Nessa. Her parents believe her dead."

Bribadge would not win this argument, he never did, so he changed tactics with only a sliver of chance he might reach his brother before he'd made his mind up entirely. "Tell me, what have you discovered in the other lands?"

Illaric swept his hair back from his forehead, smearing sweat across it in a sheen that reflected the false lighting in the room.

114

Admittedly, Bribadge had wished to return to the surface again. He hadn't been since the end of hunting season, and he longed to feel the sun upon his face and to watch the moon take its place among the stars. The magical lighting in Asantaval was depressing.

"Varrow rumbles. They dislike their king, but they despise Icluedian Allurigard even more. King Allurigard has no hesitation when it comes to Varrow. If there is opportunity, he will strike against them. Queen Serecala is pregnant."

Bribadge stood straight. "Pregnant? But... why? After everything... why?"

Illaric snickered. "I haven't a clue."

"Should we fear a war between the kingdoms? What of the southern lands?"

"War between Goranin and Varrow is always possible, but in the south, they keep to themselves. Arithropan and Drumire always tussle, but it should not invade our land. For now, I see no reason to believe we might resurface, but that can all change with the tides."

"So, we continue as we have been? Nessa is the crowned princess, and we speak no more of her true lineage?" Bribadge believed Illaric was mad if he thought this discovery changed nothing, but he would follow his orders.

Illaric's weary gaze settled on Bribadge again. "What we do is pray, brother. We pray."

ELEVEN

Eiagan Allurigard

The clamor of pickaxes and buckets woke Eiagan from her rest, but only after Porvarth had woken her for a final healing, then Catia to ensure the loxmore-dragon had not injured her further. The squawk had gone but left behind its warning, one that Eiagan did not quickly dismiss. If Noxious mistrusted Gael, then there was a good reason to worry.

Eiagan shifted and set her feet on the floor, groaning with the stretch of each muscle. Though no longer broken, her body still refused to allow her a day without pain. This, though, she had grown accustomed to and would soon be able to ignore. Once outside, she would have other matters to focus her attention on rather than the stiffness that seized her muscles and the dull ache of stretched-tight scars on her chest.

116

Along the far wall was a clean change of clothing. As usual, there would be no time for a full bath, so Eiagan settled for cleaning her face and body with the floral-scented water and rags Thyre had left beside the clothing. The mage, though kind to Porvarth, was quite uppity with Eiagan. Even so, Eiagan gave her no second thought after she helped Porvarth with his still-present loxmore abilities. What she thought of Eiagan was no matter and did not change her position or her mission.

Once dressed, Eiagan secured her sword and stepped from the sleeping quarters into the main room. It was empty but the fire roared as if expecting someone any moment. The remnants of breakfast littered the table, and one chair had been toppled. Eiagan searched her mind, wondering if she had dismissed a racket in the kitchen for a dream but could think of nothing. A bit of blood stained the main room floor just in front of her boots, but it was impossible to tell how long it had stained the dry floorboards. Upon further inspection, she noted a wash basin had been overturned and water flooded the kitchen area.

Eiagan pushed the front door open to find the sun had not yet risen, leaving her to navigate by the shadows cast along the main road by torchlight. Each shop boasted several, but they did little to light her way between the buildings. The noise that had woken her was not the usual clamor of miners returning home from work, but those returning from a cave-in.

A dark plume of dust rose above the village, blocking the sun — it *was* daylight — as people darted around her, some coated with blood while others searched frantically for a familiar face. Apprehension filled Eiagan's whole body as she began her own search for the faces she knew — faces who would stop at nothing to save the lives of the innocent, likely putting their own in mortal danger.

Ahead, the glint of light against iridescent scales sent a wave of relief over her, but not for long. Finding Porvarth only meant he was safe, but what about the others? Eiagan ran toward the dragon.

How could she have slept through a cave in? Why had her senses failed her when danger was around every corner? Her questions would remain unanswered until she had done her duty to her people. A final call toward Porvarth earned his attention. The beast maneuvered around people and lowered himself so she could easily step upon a wing to mount. Once settled, he lifted her over the devastation so that she might formulate a plan—or, at least, know how ruined the village was.

The horizon was changed. The peak that once offered a pristine backdrop had collapsed on one side, leaving a crater in the ground beneath. Villagers both in the mines and in the fields had been swallowed by the mountain, but how? The men in Smolzark were expert miners and had never had a collapse for as long as Eiagan had reigned.

"How did this happen?" Eiagan's thoughts swirled. She had not heard the collapse, not even a shudder. Had the pain medication Thyre given her caused such a deep sleep that she had been lost in her dreams?

Porvarth dipped low over the mountain, offering Eiagan a better view of the pit created by the collapse. If anyone beneath the rubble lived, it would take days to find them. Village elders gathered near Thyre's shop, so Eiagan directed Porvarth toward them.

"There, land so I might formulate a plan with their village leaders. I have to do something." Though what could be done was a mystery to her. Once again, it was likely the best she could do was request Nox send additional men and aid to the town.

Porvarth complied, dropping her just shy of the shop where the elders paused their discussion only long enough to pull her into their confusion. The elders, all covered head to foot in coal-stained vermillion cloaks, eyed her up and down before offering curt bows.

"Queen Eiagan, a visitor has come with devastating news. Come. Hurry, we shall take you to him straightaway." The Chief Elder with his single green eye — a story Eiagan wanted to hear but likely never would — scanned her face while his hand tugged at her arm.

"A visitor? Before or after the collapse?" she asked.

"A moment before, but too late to warn us, I am afraid. You know him well. He comes to — "

"Eiagan? Is… is that you?"

Eiagan spun on her heel. Erdravac's deep, melodic voice sent a shiver of fear through her entire body. Though pleasant and welcome, it meant something had gone wrong in Varrow. Porvarth tensed beside her as he dressed, no longer in need of his dragon form.

"Erdravac? Why are you here? Why are you not seated on the throne of Varrow?" Eiagan asked, huffs of breath escaping her mouth as she tried to contain her anxiety.

Erdravac's black hair was tousled and his face wounded — a laceration from forehead to nose — but he was otherwise well. He dipped his head then said, "I am ashamed to admit that the mage fooled us again. There were many in Varrow who saw this time as an opportunity to take more, and so they disregarded my reign and the peace agreements. The revolt killed many, and they seated their own king, one sympathetic to Nessa. They mean to take Goranin,

Eiagan. I came to warn you, and this," he said, motioning around, "is all my fault."

"She sent her men after him," an elder said, his hand upon Erdravac's shoulder. "But we do not blame him."

"She did, and it was those men who blew up half the mountain and killed your people. I am sorry, Eiagan. Truly, I thought I had escaped unseen, but it appears —"

"Make no more excuses. Where are her men? I will kill them myself for all they have done." Eiagan's Allurigard blood bubbled, blinding her to the truth of the situation. There was nothing she could do in revenge that would help her people, not now, probably not ever.

"Eiagan, we should send word to Nox first," Porvarth said, reminding the queen she was not, in fact, the queen any longer — at least, not until the mage Nessa was good and dead.

"I will send one of the birds," Gael said, joining them. He was sneaky when he desired, which forced a prickle of annoyance under Eiagan's skin. She ignored him.

"What of the other kingdoms? Are they upholding their treaties?" Eiagan asked.

"So far as I can know. Once I was attacked in my own castle, I escaped and ran here." Erdravac grasped Eiagan's elbow and pulled her toward Thyre's shop, but Gael and Porvarth followed. "Wait, I need to speak to Eiagan. It is... a matter between... I have no need of extra ears."

Erdravac pushed open the wooden door and dragged Eiagan into the dimly lit shop, leaving Porvarth with a scowl upon his lips. Once inside, he released Eiagan and lowered his hood entirely.

"You wish to keep a secret?" Eiagan asked.

120

"I do not trust the Asantavalian. Porvarth might join us but not him."

Eiagan ducked her head out the door, spied Porvarth, and waved him over. He nodded, made a quick exit from the remaining elders, and slipped inside the dimly lit shop with them.

"Erdravac, what has happened?" Porvarth asked.

"All Hell has come upon Varrow, and it is not a curse I can control. My people—I should say, the people Nessa infected with her drivel and nonsense—have run me off the throne. It was a ruse from the beginning. Slovartark has threatened to end their treaty if Varrow is not controlled, and if they break the terms..." Erdravac faded, his eyes settled on Porvarth.

"Then it is all lost. Everything we have sacrificed and everything we have worked for will have been for nothing," Eiagan said. "Enough of this sitting around. I am well enough to do what must be done. Noxious does not trust Gael either, at least not for now."

"I cannot say that Gael is not an honorable man, but given his blood, I also cannot say that I will ever trust him," Erdravac said.

"He wishes for us to go to Asantaval. We had considered it before the last land shift." Porvarth glanced at Eiagan as if assessing her wellness before going on. "A horse rolled over on Eiagan, crushing her, but she is as she says. She is well enough to move on."

"Crushed?" Worry flashed in Erdravac's eyes, and he reached for her, but before his fingers caressed her arm, he dropped his hand back to his side.

"Porvarth's ability to heal strengthens each day, and the mage, Thyre, has helped him. This is a matter we can discuss another time. For now, I have begun formulating a plan, but I must speak with Emora first." Eiagan swallowed a bit of worry that her sister and Ari might not be well after the cavern collapse.

"I saw her enter the inn with Catia and Ari on my way in here. Should I retrieve them, or — "

"That will not be necessary, Porvarth. I will go to them. For now, you and Erdravac observe Gael in secret. Gather what you can for the next hour, then prepare to leave."

"Where to, my love?" Porvarth asked, his eyes slanted toward Erdravac.

"Vidkun Castle. We're going home." Eiagan turned her back to the men then paused. Over her shoulder, she said, "Someone send a squawk in secret to Nox. Tell him to ready the army for an attack from Varrow."

With her final word, Eiagan pushed open the door and strode across the path toward the inn. She nearly made it all the way without interruption, but as her fingers brushed against the iron door handle, Gael placed a firm hand on her shoulder.

"I would say now is the time to be on our way to Asantaval. With Nessa on the rampage, I cannot imagine my people having much patience." Gael's beard glinted red in the dim light, but it did not hide the smile on his face — always cheerful, even in miserable times.

"We will go when I say it is time to go. Have you not noticed anything around you?" Eiagan motioned around the area. "My people need me, and though I want nothing more than to find my nephew and the others, I will not simply abandon the people after such a tragedy."

"But, if I might — "

Eiagan shoved Gael backward, forcing him to remove his hand from her shoulder. "You might not. Do not touch me again or suffer the same fate many men who have put ill hands upon me have suffered."

Gael lifted his hands in front of him. "I did not seek to offend you. I only meant to imply that time is of the utmost importance. If Nessa has unseated the young Prince Erdravac, I can imagine she might come for Goranin next. Varrow is a great army."

"I appreciate your suggestion but do remember that you are a guest in my kingdom. Your land was returned to you without a fight, but there will be a battle unlike anything you have ever seen if you should cross me, *Prince Gael.*"

Gael's eyes narrowed as he lowered his hands. "Am I to believe you mistrust me now? After everything my kingdom has offered to you?"

"What, exactly, has been offered? I see no army searching for my nephew, for Violet, for the Princess of Nelaravore among others. Where are the search parties promised? Where are the armies raised in the name of peace between Goranin and Asantaval?"

"They exist. Just because you do not see them, does not mean that they are a figment of my imagination."

Eiagan's senses heightened as they always did when faced by someone of equal intelligence, but it was more than that. It was a sense that she missed not only one piece of information, but perhaps an entire volume of facts that Gael did not seem overly willing to share.

"We will go when I am ready. Until then, send word to your king that circumstances have changed. I will not leave my people to suffer. They have done so long enough."

Eiagan pulled open the inn door and entered, nodded toward the attendant, then inquired as to the whereabouts of her sister.

"The main room, Highness," he said, then went about balancing his books. Eiagan wondered how often they entertained guests given the village was not a highly sought-after place to travel, let alone a comfortable accommodation unless one was, as she had been, in a dire situation.

Eiagan dismissed her thoughts when she knocked on the closed door to her sister's current quarters.

"Come in."

Eiagan entered to find Emora and Catia seated on a bench beside the window while Ari paced the floor. She shut the door firmly behind her, then motioned for them to crowd in the far corner.

"Erdravac is here," Eiagan said, then promptly covered Emora's mouth when she gasped. Eiagan pressed her finger to her sister's lips, silencing them. "Gael stopped me on the way in. He might overhear. Listen, don't speak yet."

Emora nodded while Catia wrung her hands. Ari clenched his teeth so hard, Eiagan heard the scrape of his teeth over one another.

"Porvarth is sending word to Nox. Nessa had people in Varrow, and they overthrew Erdravac. They mean to take Goranin, and if they do, Slovartark will pull out of our agreement. Peace hangs in the balance, but I have a plan."

Emora lifted her hands over them, then brought them down in an arcing motion. The charge in the room changed, grew thicker and heavy. "Gael cannot hear through my barrier, but I cannot keep it for long. Speak freely but quickly."

"We will not go to Astantaval. We will return to Vidkun and prepare for war with Varrow," Eiagan said.

"But what about Reven and the others?" Emora asked.

"We will never find them like this. I see Nessa's plan now, and it has worked so far. We are occupied with searching for our loved ones, solving problems all over the kingdom, and distracted from the real threat—an invasion by Varrow, who support Nessa." Eiagan pressed her lips together, frustrated she did not see the plan for what it was. Brilliant in some ways, but thoroughly predictable if Eiagan had been in her right mind.

"When shall we leave?" Ari asked.

"We will aid the people here while we wait for a reply from Nox. Then we will return to Vidkun and prepare. As for Gael, I will determine his worth on our way, and if need arises, I will put him in the prison."

A movement outside the window caught Eiagan's attention. It was the flapping of a squawk's wings, then a flutter as they broke apart. Eiagan moved to the window and opened it, allowing the single bird to enter. It was the same bird that had visited her bedside. It held correspondence in its beak, which it dutifully dropped at Eiagan's feet before squalling its discontent.

Eiagan glanced toward Emora. "The barrier?"

Emora waved her hands again, recreating the silent space so Eiagan might relay Nox's correspondence with her allies.

Eiagan read the paper. "Nox is furious over the cave-in and quite ready to turn the throne back over to me. He expects us soon and has recalled Zanaka's ranks back to Vidkun. Borgard will meet us here, and he is sending Quix and Vey for additional support." Eiagan scanned the remainder of the message but could not make out the lines Noxious had scratched out. It was unlike him to hesitate, but there was not time to worry over it. She couldn't decipher it anyway.

Catia listened to each word that fell from Eiagan's lips, the newcomer who had leaped into the fire to see what mischief she might cause. Now was the time to offer her a way out if she was not prepared to go deeper into the fray.

"Catia, you are welcome to return home if you would prefer," Eiagan said. "I can arrange transport for—"

"No. No, I did not come this far and see what I have seen to do nothing," Catia said, then upon realizing she interrupted Eiagan, she lowered her head. "My apologies. I am, as they say, too big for my own dress skirts at times, but I should not have spoken out of turn."

"You are forgiven, but I must warn you that it will only become more dangerous as we proceed." Eiagan crinkled the letter and allowed the squawk to drop it into the fire.

"I know," Catia said. "I'm prepared. Tell me, who is coming to aid us? Bring me into the fold so that I might prepare and help." She tied her red hair into a knot and pushed her sleeves up as if she were ready to get to work. In a sense, she was, and Eiagan was pleased to find another soul as heated for the cause as hers.

"Borgard is a Balconian brute," Ari said. "But one who is like family. Vey and Quix are dragon shifters, both skilled in battle. We will be well protected with them and Porvarth. We should return to Vidkun within a day once we leave."

Catia, after a short time away from her sewing, stood straighter and seemed younger. Eiagan noticed a spark in her eyes, and estimated she was, in fact, younger than she had originally assumed. This observation brought additional thoughts and questions she had all but forgotten while she had been healing.

"Catia, how old are you?" Eiagan asked.

Catia narrowed her eyes but responded. "Twenty-eight years, give or take one I might have forgotten."

Eiagan glanced at her sister who seemed to suspect the same thing—that Catia *might* possess magic she was not aware of. Emora had not been able to test for latent magic before the earth caved beneath them, and after the disaster, such things were not thought of again.

"First things first," Eiagan said. "We will aid our people, then tonight, under cover of darkness, we will test Catia for magical ability."

Catia sighed. "I will submit to it, but I've told you already, I have no magic."

"Your senses might be a sign you do, something you haven't discovered. In terms of people with magical ability, you are a bit old to discover such things, but it's not unheard of," Emora said.

"And if I do have magic? What then? I am raw as a babe!"

"Calm yourself, Catia. I would not expect more from you than you might handle. And if you have no magic, then so be it. You will be valuable to our cause no matter your magical ability," Eiagan said.

The squawk had finished watching its message burn and indicated so by warbling as it wandered closer to Eiagan. At her feet, it peered up at her with wide, black eyes, tilting its head this way and that. Then it rubbed it's face over her pantleg at the knee.

"This one seems to like you," Ari said just as the bird alighted, then settled itself upon Eiagan's shoulder.

Though its talons were long and sharp, it did not puncture Eiagan's skin. It did bristle her nerves. She tried to shirk the bird, but it would not be dissuaded from riding perched on her shoulder.

"What are you doing, beast?" Eiagan asked, then shook again. The bird stayed in place. Eiagan groaned. "Is this how it will be? Will you never leave my side now?"

The sleek black head twisted to stare into Eiagan's eyes. Those eyes, they were familiar in ways Eiagan could not pinpoint or explain, except to say that she *knew* them. A contest of wills ensued while Emora, Ari, and Catia watched them. After several breaths with neither Eiagan nor the bird blinking, the squawk leaned forward and pressed its small forehead against Eiagan's. A surge of emotion rocked Eiagan's body, but she still could not place this bird and its familiar eyes. It did not give her time to contemplate it longer but leaped from her shoulder and darted out the window to rejoin with its brethren.

Eiagan watched it go, watched it morph with the others and disappear into the distance before she finally tore her eyes from the creature. She shook her head.

"We should move and help our people," she said, all the while her conscience told her she had been in the presence of a loyal friend... but who?

TWELVE

Noxious "The Savage" Skjoldsson

Nox groaned while he tapped his fingers on the armrest of the Allurigard throne. The woman had come to him during the night, practically begged him to join her, then sent people to destroy the mountain in the Mining Village, all because of Erdravac. Surely, Nessa knew this would anger Nox. How could she not? Despite her atrocious behavior, she wasn't an unintelligent person. With a louder groan, he rose and went to the window where Tend stood peering out over the kingdom.

"I am having second thoughts about our plan," Nox admitted. "I do not like leaving the kingdom unattended, not after what she did to the miners and this new threat from Varrow. Erdravac is one man. It's true he has much support, but it is significantly less than one would have hoped, so there was no reason for her to chase after him in such a manner. Surely, she could not think attacking our people would convince me to go with her."

Tend glanced toward him, then back out the window. "She's testing you."

Nox huffed his displeasure, ignoring the dragon that wanted to peek out for a while. "I am likely to fail."

"I doubt it. She is merely testing to see how far she might push you, among others, and still have you bend to her will. You will go with her despite what she's done, and she knows that."

Nox hated when Tend made sense, but he was right. Even after causing a cave in that killed many, he would still go with her even for a sliver of hope that the children would be spared.

"Incoming," Tend said just before a bird landed on the sill. "Likely more information about the status of Varrow. We can decide your next steps after we have read it."

The bird dropped the message in Nox's palm and disappeared out the window, exhausted from its work after several messages across the kingdom in only a few days. It was the same bird each time, and Nox wondered if it ever slept. Once the message was unrolled and Nox found it written in Porvarth's impeccable penmanship, he relaxed.

"They are returning to Vidkun as I suspected they would. We will mount a defense and counter-attack if necessary to defend Goranin against Varrow and any others that attempt to overthrow our kingdom." Nox folded the paper and gave his attention back to Tend. "Zanaka will return by sunset assuming they do not come upon trouble, so that does offer some peace of mind where leaving the kingdom is concerned." Nox rolled the message and tossed it into the fire. "Though I do still worry what might happen between my exit and their arrival."

"Zanaka is always battle-ready and a capable general, and once Eiagan returns there will be no need for worry at all. Zanaka has Ballan with him, and he has become quite the soldier and adviser. You were right when you said this might be our only chance to find the children, the prince, and the princess." Tend shrugged, then said, "Perhaps playing into her hand for a short time might offer long term gain despite how unpleasant it is to swallow."

Nox considered all they had done already, thought of what Nessa might do if he refused her, and weighed each outcome carefully just as Eiagan had taught him. When all choices were thoroughly examined, he sighed and pushed off the windowsill. "I suppose I will prepare so I can leave this evening, perhaps sooner if Nessa is as impatient as I assume she is."

Tend chuckled. "You make me glad I am not a handsome man whose face makes women swoon."

Nox shoved Tend, then said, "Your face is plenty enough to earn you stares in the market. And Freesia loved it so, at least, that was what Hazel told me."

Tend swallowed and closed his eyes. "I pray this will be enough, that once Nessa is dead our wives might rest in peace knowing they have been avenged."

Nox clasped a hand over Tend's shoulder. "I pray with you, brother."

A knowing glance was shared, one that said everything they could not say to one another aloud — be careful, do not die, I will miss you, I love you — and swallowed their fear over what might come. Tend, though, was not satisfied with the sentimental stare alone and said, "If I do not see you again for any reason, know that I love you as well as I did Gregor and Aryneza before their deaths, as a sibling in blood and not just circumstance."

131

Nox swallowed and nodded. "And I, you, brother. Tell no one of our plan except Eiagan and do so in secret. She is the only one who will understand why I have done this. Leave it to her to choose who shares the knowledge. She will be angry at first that we did not tell her before her arrival, but we both know she won't allow me to go if we wait."

Tend nodded and turned his back.

With the thickness of emotion hanging in the air, Nox strode from the room, blinking back his tears. The mage had taken more than she deserved, more than anyone deserved, but there was one thing she had done that made him a better man — she forced him to trust and depend on others, and in doing so, he found a family. He found a brother in Tend that filled the empty places his own siblings had never filled. Rarely thought of these days, Nox wondered if his sister might have changed given enough time. It was a useless wonder since she had shown her traitorous ways and found her death sentence at the end of Eiagan's sword, but where were his brothers? Gone, he assumed, since even while he sat on the throne, none had come to see him.

He did not want to go with Nessa, not truly, but he would.

With each step through the quiet castle, Nox's anger grew. Of course, she would find another way to twist his mind, to tear out his heart, to force suffering upon him all in the name of seeking vengeance against Eiagan... but why? *Why* did Nessa hate Eiagan so? Why was her focus, which she claimed was conquering every land in the Ancient Kingdoms in the name of Asantaval, a kingdom that despised her, seemingly secondary to taunting and torturing Eiagan? And Emora? Taking Emora captive had nearly killed both women.

He shook his head and pushed open the heavy wooden door that led to his quarters. Nox had not been wrong regarding Nessa's patience, for she sat upon a chaise — one that had not existed in the room until then — staring into the fire, entirely too comfortable in his quarters. A sigh earned her attention, but it was fleeting. She turned back to the fire, solemn as she watched it eat up the last log.

"Sit with me," she said — more a request than an order, so enough curiosity took Nox that he did as she asked.

He closed the door and crossed the room. She seemed less lethal this way, comfortable in a chair meant for relaxation, something he hadn't done in ages. Her ease made him second-guess her intentions, so he stopped halfway across the room. The moment of hesitation earned him a glare, so Nox sat quietly at the opposite end of the chaise.

"Do you ever wonder what this land might have been like if someone else had ruled?" she asked.

"You mean, like you?" he asked with a bitter tone, staring into the fire so as not to accidentally admire her. Annoyance set him on edge. How could he think her beautiful even after all she'd done? She was the ugliest person he'd ever met on the inside, perhaps darker than Icluedian, but Nox had never had the displeasure of knowing the former king personally.

"Anyone. Anyone but an Allurigard. Or perhaps even one of Icluedian's children he murdered?"

Nox peered sideways at her, took in her expression, and decided it was a question asked in earnest. Not once in all his years had Nox ever considered anyone but Eiagan ruling Goranin, but it was a fair enough question. Reeve was, for all intents and purposes, the heir to the throne before Eiagan killed him. It was, according to Nox's father, a turning point in the relationship between Eiagan and Zero — one that had benefitted his family for centuries.

"I have not considered it, no," he admitted.

"Of course not. Your family has been in a position of power since she married Zero. Why would you consider another way?"

"Last night, you claimed I was her lap dog." Nox relaxed in the seat. If Nessa wanted to discuss history, then so be it. Perhaps she would slip and reveal where Violet and the others were, then he could avoid the unpleasantness of spending another moment in her presence.

Nessa's gaze shifted toward him, wholly unreadable, but Nox knew what it meant. "*You* were her lap dog, not the others. Not your father or grandfather. Why? Because you pushed her, you forced her to her limits, and she did not appreciate your face as a reminder of all she had lost. And when you pushed her too far, she banished you to the mines." She shifted in her seat and turned to face him. "Did you know she is the reason Zero was killed? That her inability to properly rule gave the people too much confidence and they murdered him just to spite her."

"Emora told us the story, yes. She was there when it happened."

Nessa scoffed. "She did nothing to aid him."

Nox turned toward her. "How would you know such things? Were you there, Nessa?"

A flash of heat in her irises indicated a soft spot, one Nox thought might offer him an advantage if utilized. She pursed her lips and lifted her chin, defiant. "I am everywhere and nowhere, learning all things that aid me in my pursuits."

"That means nothing. Were you there when my ancestor was murdered?"

She pushed from the chaise, took two steps, and leaned over Nox, her blonde hair framing a fiery red face, flared nostrils, and a stare so monstrous even Nox shivered. "If I had been there, he would not have died. If I had been there, I would have ripped them apart one by one until all that remained was a bloodbath, and no one would have dared to lay a finger upon him again."

Her reaction was more than anticipated, so Nox filed it away for future examination, swallowed his heart back down, and stood to meet her, forcing her back. "I have made my decision."

Nessa's expression morphed as she stood erect, waiting for him to vocalize his choice.

"I will go with you, provided you release the children."

Nessa snickered and shook her head. "Make no mistake, dragon, if you cross me, you will not live to regret it. If you go with me, you will stay with me forever — forsake your Eiagan and your kingdom and stay with me."

"My daughter?"

"Will remain with you if it is what you wish. I am not a monster without feeling, Noxious."

"And yet, you stole her from me." He dared to watch her when he accused her, curious.

Again, that flicker of remorse took her. "I did not know she was your daughter then, and when I learned her identity, I took great care to ensure her safety. She has been well cared for, I swear."

There it was again, that subtle demureness... the flashes of regret... the way she *flirted* with him... Why? Why him?

Nox squeezed his eyes shut and shook his head, then opened them, his mind a bit clearer. "Tell me, please, why me? Why do you wish to take me from Eiagan? To torture her, or to torture me?"

Nessa's eyes hazed, her shoulders slumped, and her entire body pulled away from him. "One day, when I am sure you can be trusted, I will tell you the truth, Noxious. And when you learn it, when you know every detail of my life, perhaps you will not look at me as the only monster in the story."

For a moment, just a lightning flash, Nessa's eyes shifted from green to grey-white. It was enough to stop him cold. He knew those eyes well, but before he could comment—between blinks—he fell unconscious at her feet.

THIRTEEN

Reven Allurigard

There was still enough food to feed an army when Reven and Darby returned to their prison, so they both swallowed their worry about Nessa's history and ate. Silence fell over them for a long time, so long that the children had eaten then gone to sleep before Darby lifted her head to discuss what they had seen.

"Do you think we will see your family in one of these visions?" she asked, holding a turkey leg so tightly, Reven thought she might snap the bone. At least she was eating now.

He inhaled slowly, then let it out before he said, "I both hope I do and pray I don't see them. I often wonder about my father and what he was like. My guardians told me stories, but hearing and seeing are two things. But if I see him die, I worry I might grow bitter. I do not wish for my relationship with Eiagan to suffer."

137

"You would blame her if you saw it, you believe?"

Reven shrugged. "I cannot say one way or another. I pray that I would not, but who can know how one would react to such a thing? I know she was in a blind rage and that it was his choice to push her there, but what if it seems different from what I was told? What if…" He shook his head. "No, she loved my father. She wouldn't have done it if she were in her right mind, but that does not mean it would be easy to watch."

"And… and your mother?"

Reven's pale eyes studied Darby. "I do not want to see it, but if I must in order to save the kingdoms, then so be it." He swallowed and dropped his bread onto the table. "I have been thinking about the visions, though, and I wonder if showing some sympathy toward Nessa might reveal more information?"

Darby chuckled and fidgeted with the turkey leg. "You think you can show such a thing to that evil woman? You would choke on your own words, Reven."

"Not if you help me. Your magic is soothing. It might help."

"I can try. You might be right. After all, who is to say we might *not* have some sympathy for her? We know Icluedian killed her adoptive parents, and with what we have already discovered so far, I would say she has reason to be a bit vindictive."

Reven leaned forward and rested his elbows on the table. "I might understand why she did what she did, but I doubt it will bring meaningful sympathy. I wonder what it was, exactly, that drove her to be so vengeful? Was there a single event, or was it simply a lifetime of pain and suffering?"

Darby snickered. "I think it is just in the blood if you want my honest opinion. It is foul and vengeful in itself." She crossed her arms, not noticing the shadow of hurt that passed over Reven's face.

She glanced up, making eye contact with him when he did not reply. When his pursed lips and heated gaze registered, she uncrossed her arms and leaned forward. "I did not mean—"

"You did, but it is to be expected. People like to blame the bloodlines for everything, yes? Far be it from me to attempt to be a better person." Reven snapped and withdrew from her, wholly annoyed with the constant reminder that he hailed from a heated bloodline, a murderous ancestry that brought pain and chaos and suffering to the world. "Always lovely when someone can remind me of my origin story."

Darby leaned forward and let her fingers brush over his arm. "Reven," she whispered. "Reven, I should not have said that. You are right, and I'm sorry. You are the purest heart I have ever known, and that was an unfair thing to say. Regardless of her bloodline, Nessa made her own decisions, and you can, too."

"I wish that I knew what you saw when you first gazed upon my face in Nelaravore," he said, uncrossing his arms so that she could take his hand. "You were probably disgusted with my very presence once you knew who I was... who I am."

Her lips curled into a smile, and the twinkle returned to her eyes. "My heart fluttered, maybe even skipped a beat or two. I saw kind eyes and a roguish smile, and then I heard your voice, and I think that is when I lost my heart, Reven. I care not who you are in name, but who you are here." She pressed her hand against his chest, then leaned closer to kiss him.

The door clicked open, but instead of Nessa entering, Noxious the Savage pushed through it and scanned the room. Darby gasped, but Nox did not notice. His eyes had fixed on his daughter, curled up and sleeping along the wall with dozens of other children.

Reven stood and went to Nox. "She is well. How... What are you doing here?"

Nox relaxed, and though Reven saw it in his eyes — an unyielding desire to scoop his daughter into his arms, to hold her and kiss her brow — he instead relaxed and ran his hands over his face before offering Reven his full attention. Still, he couldn't speak.

Reven glanced at Violet, then back to Nox. "She was upset for a while, but we have done all we can to ensure they are all comfortable. She misses you, but she has eaten some and slept." Reven assured Nox as best he could, but deep down, he knew there were no words that would ease Nox's worry. No, he would not stop until he'd heard Violet tell him herself that she was alright.

"How did you find us?" Darby asked. "Is Nessa dead?" The princess's voice rose to something almost joyous, but her eyes did not meet the same excitement.

"Not dead. She brought me here as a bargain." Nox's mouth twisted into a gruesome expression that exhibited his disgust, an entire story Reven wanted to know but would not dare ask. "I am not here to rescue you, not today, but I do have some plan. Nessa has gone to rally her soldiers in Varrow, and I cannot be sure she does not have some way to spy on us, so..." Nox studied Darby, then leaned to her ear and whispered, "Might you see into my mind as you did with Ellaro?"

Darby blinked a few times and shook her head. "No, I... maybe? I have never tried to enter a dragon shifter's mind."

"I have much to share, but I cannot take the risk." His voice faded, already saying more than any wise man should given his predicament.

"We have much to share as well, all things we should probably discuss in the privacy of mind to mind communication. It warrants an attempt, at least," Darby said, then motioned toward the empty chair. "I cannot say whether it will be painful given your human side, so you should sit."

"Now?" Reven asked.

Darby pushed her blonde hair behind her shoulders and shrugged. "Will there be a better time? What else have we to do?"

"Will it hurt him too much?" Reven asked.

"I have survived pain the likes of which you will never know. Just do it, quickly, before she returns." Nox's impatience didn't seem to bother Darby, so Reven ignored it. "What should I do?"

"Just sit still and see if you can hear me," Darby said, then focused on the dragon shifter. Reven watched as the two stared at each other for some time, neither uttering a word, hardly blinking. Nox flinched occasionally, and Darby pursed her lips and closed her eyes. After long moments of silence, moments marked with Reven's own impatient tapping on the table, Darby opened her eyes.

"Did you just ask me what my favorite food is?" Darby asked with arched brows.

Nox chuckled, then glanced toward the children when one groaned in her sleep. "I... I did. A test to see if it would work."

"And was it painful?"

"Bearable. In my bargain with Nessa, she promised to release the children. I can't be sure that includes you and Reven, so I want a secondary plan. Let us share our knowledge, and then I pray you can teach me how to communicate with my brethren over a long distance, so they might find us if she goes back on her word."

"Do you even know where we are?" Reven asked.

"No, I was unconscious when she brought me here. I only roused a little while before she sent me in here. But if the others can hear me in their minds, then perhaps we can figure out a way to draw

141

them here?" Nox's plan was not without complication, but it was worthy an attempt. "We should not say anymore aloud."

"I agree. We can work out the particulars while you continue with the history lessons, Reven," Darby said, waving him away.

Reven chuckled, though he was unsure whether it was amusement or irritation that brought the sound to his lips. "Am I dismissed, then?"

Darby slouched and stepped away from Nox. "You know that is not what I meant. Will my thoughtless statement about your bloodline come between us forever?"

Reven swallowed the lump in his throat when he saw the shimmer in her eyes, true and honest regret that brought her to tears. He brushed them away and kissed her again. "No. It is forgotten. But you said you did not want me to go alone on these trips through her past."

She licked her lips and looked back at Nox, who was staring at his daughter, hardly containing the urge to go to her. But sleep was valuable, especially when war was on the brink, and little Violet needed rest. "I can communicate with him, and that is something we must work on if he is to reach the other dragons. I want to go with you, but if you wait for me then it might be days before we know the entire story. Go ahead, and if you need me for the hard parts, I will be here for you."

Reven nodded, then grabbed the book from the table and settled on the floor. The book seemed to know where he'd left off, flipping page after page on its own until it reached the next part of Nessa's story. Just before his fingers grazed over the words that would transport him to another time, Darby brushed her fingers over his cheek.

"I love you. Be careful," she said, then smiled as Reven drifted back to Asantaval.

FOURTEEN

3215, THE YEAR OF LOSS
WAR ROOM, TALISKAR CASTLE
GILGRAMAGH, ASANTAVAL

The History of the Callanan Royal Family

Nessa danced around Illaric as he studied his maps, lost in the world above. Illaric was concerned. The Goranin Princess Klara had gone missing, presumed dead given Queen Serecala's claims, but he was not convinced. Where had the queen taken her child, and what was her plan? Why lie and say the child had been killed?

Bribadge and Queen Lureah entered the only door to the room, but their expressions left little hope that the latest news from the surface was encouraging. Lureah picked up little Nessa, offered Illaric a curt smile, then left the room to entertain their child. Bribadge waited until the door was secure before revealing what they had learned.

"The Princess Klara is alive, living with the mage Simorana in Sudyak Meadow. I know not her reason for taking the girl in, but we cannot rule out that it was because she has magical ability like her mother. Perhaps Serecala worried Icluedian would kill the girl rather than bind her magic as he did hers."

Illaric sighed and sat, his elbows perched upon the ever-changing map. More often than not, the borders swayed between kingdoms as battles and war raged on the surface. It seemed no one could keep peace, save the Isadorians, who were still forced to take up arms to defend themselves.

"Brother," Bribadge said, "we do not know that anything will go wrong. Our spies have been careful, and the information has not pointed toward our lands. In fact, some say the people have all but forgotten Asantaval ever existed."

"I worry war between Varrow and Goranin might uncover our lands. They are equally matched, and the last time two kingdoms of equal matching with power as great as theirs went against one another—"

"I know our history, brother. I've lived it all my life." Bribadge sat across from Illaric. "The question is whose side will we join if our kingdom is revealed? Or will we seek that moment to take back what is ours?"

Illaric faced Bribadge, his eyes cast in shadows from lack of sleep, and sighed. "I do not know, and that is what worries me most. For now, we continue as we have been. We study, observe, make notes, train our warriors. But I fear…"

Bribadge waited, but Illaric never finished his thought. Instead, his gaze settled on the map and his shoulders slumped.

"What is it?"

Illaric traced the border of his kingdom, the Banished Lands incorporated into Goranin, and let the tears slip from his eyes onto the page. Bribadge did not taunt or tease him for this action. Instead, he let the weight of their love for Asantaval fill his heart until he, too, shed tears for their loss. No longer a kingdom proud and strong among the rest, but a silent survivor hidden beneath the dirt, its people always worried they might perish.

"I fear someone might come to unseat Icluedian Allurigard, and though it should be of some comfort, I cannot help but worry that his usurper might be worse," Illaric said. "Anyone who could kill him should be feared."

Bribadge did chuckle at this. "Or he might be our savior. We cannot fear that. A usurper might free us, lead us back to our former glory, and make a union with our people that will stand the test of time."

"Then let us pray such a savior comes soon, for I cannot say how much longer our people will survive underground. Our food stores are always short, and our medicines are scarce." Illaric stood and resumed his usual pacing. His boots scraped along the floor, echoing in the near-empty room.

"Will you allow me a trip to the surface? I would like to see for myself," Bribadge said. "Let me make regular trips as a scout. Let me judge for us whether there is need for concern."

Illaric sighed again but nodded. "Yes. I agree. I trust you above all others, and my conscience won't let me rest until I am sure of our path. Go up today, return tomorrow with some news, and then we shall decide a more regular schedule from there."

"Good. That is good." Bribadge stood but Illaric grasped his shoulder and squeezed before he rose fully.

"Be careful. I cannot lose you, and your family needs you. Congratulations are in order."

Bribadge smiled. "Thank you, brother. I never thought I would be a father, but here I am with three boys and a babe on the way. I'm blessed as any man might be."

Bribadge Callanan left the confines of the war room, the stuffy and worry-ridden hideaway where the king kept most of his hours. Deep and unwavering love and loyalty to Illaric kept Bribadge from relaying his own fears — that there was nothing they could do to stop the inevitable, and any notion they might was foolish.

With a heart full of lead, Bribadge prepared for his scouting mission to the surface. His goal — discover why the Princess Klara had been given away to one of the most powerful mages in any land, and what Queen Serecala's lie was meant to cover.

Goranin hadn't changed much since Bribadge saw it last, though where the mage Simorana's home was supposed to be, there was nothing but a field surrounded by trees. Bribadge assumed, with a mage as powerful as Simorana in residence, it was simply hidden behind layers of magic so strong, he might stand there for the rest of his life and never see so much as a glimmer of it.

Bribadge moved on to inspect more of the kingdom, doing what he could to blend into the background. It was easy, given that most people never bothered to look up when he passed, let alone question where he came from or where he was going. The land's soul was half-dead, hardly surviving under the Allurigard rule. If Varrow was a threat to the people of Goranin, they might welcome such a war if only to ease the suffering Icluedian inflicted upon them daily — nay, *hourly*.

Just north of the fields, in the heart of Eathevall, Vidkun Castle boasted. As grand as the king wished himself to be, it soared toward the sky with nary a worry that it might blot out the sun. Bribadge strolled through the fields until he neared the outskirts of the royal grounds. Young voices drifted toward his ears, grasping hold of his attention the moment Princess Klara's name was mentioned. He slipped into a thick patch of trees where he might overhear their conversation.

"Brother, you must not speak her name again. If he hears and suspects she lives, he will drop us all in the Pit." The girl, about four or five years old with raven hair and pale skin, stood with her hands upon her hips, scolding an identical boy.

The boy with matching hair and roughly five inches of height over her, slouched and sighed. "I know, but it is hard to forget our sister, Eiagan."

Bribadge held his breath. There they were, the two remaining Allurigard children, out in the open for anyone to whisk away. That would be a horrible mistake, though, for despite Icluedian's apparent dislike for his own offspring, there was no doubt he would slaughter his way through five kingdoms just to have them back, if only because they were *his*.

"I cannot bear to lose you, too, Reeve. Please, for me will you be careful?" Eiagan, her white-gray eyes focused on her brother, grit her teeth. Already hardened at such a young age, Bribadge wondered what the poor girl had already seen.

Reeve stiffened his back and nodded. "Yes. Yes, I will be more careful. We're all we have now."

"Good. That is good," Eiagan said and lowered her hands to her sides. Even so, she was not relaxed. As Reeve passed her and headed toward his pony, Eiagan shifted her gaze to Vidkun Castle. Those icicle eyes narrowed, and her jaw clenched tighter. There was a fire in those eyes, a paradox of nature to be sure given their snowy color, but fire in them all the same.

A chill passed down Bribadge's spine. That look, he had only seen it on the faces of grown men — grown men in the throes of homicidal rage on the battlefield. For a moment, he almost ran into the field and offered to take them away from their pain, to offer them a different life safe and secure from the evils of an Allurigard father, but he pushed the thought from his head as soon as it entered. He could not bring such danger into his homeland.

Eiagan and Reeve left on their ponies, and Bribadge left the security of the trees. The sun was low, time for him to return with what he'd already learned. It seemed like very little, but he knew, deep in his gut, that he had found the usurper — the savior that would devour every darkness in the land of Goranin and more. Icluedian Allurigard harbored his future murderer in his own castle, but with a heart already hardened at such a young age, would Eiagan become the savior... or would she destroy everything Icluedian had already broken?

FIFTEEN

3731, THE YEAR OF RECKONING
THE MINER'S VILLAGE
SMOLZARK TERRITORY, GORANIN

Eiagan Allurigard

Ari had resumed his usual pacing. There had been no time for him or Porvarth to help Eiagan and Emora with their respective situations, but Eiagan felt more clear-headed than she had in days. Her old intuition slowly but surely crept closer to the forefront, but without the heat and anger of her former self. Erdravac stared at Eiagan, but when she looked his way, he turned away every time. Porvarth merely stared out the window in silence, but it wasn't contentment. Rather, it was unspoken opinions and unasked questions that kept his lips pursed and gaze narrowed.

"Well, will you share your opinion or simply stare out the window and avoid my gaze?" Eiagan asked Porvarth.

Porvarth chewed his lower lip for a moment, then turned to face her. "Are you sure it is what you want? To abandon the search for Reven and the others?"

"I am not abandoning the search, not truly. We have no hope of finding them this way, not with Nessa pulling the strings to distract us from her plans. If we continue down this path, all we will do is hand the kingdom over to her with no hope of finding our missing loved ones."

"I agree with Eiagan," Ari said. "Each time we think we have advanced she turns us down another path. A sighting at the Docks and another in Nelaravore in the same day? Impossible given the timeline. At least one must be a projection if not both."

"I will follow Eiagan's wishes, but I would be remiss if I did not illuminate every possible pitfall." Porvarth stood and crossed the room. "If she has considered them all, then I am in full agreement."

"Is it settled, then? Will we all go to Vidkun?" Erdravac settled his gaze on Porvarth as if asking his permission to encroach on his home.

Porvarth shrugged. "There are plenty of rooms, and I hear the food service is to die for."

Eiagan rolled her eyes and pinched the bridge of her nose. "Must you, Porvarth?"

He shrugged. "No, but it does serve to lighten the sour mood from time to time. Besides, we should expect our company any moment—"

"Eiagan, woman, what a sight you are for sore eyes!" Borgard had slammed the door shut and crossed the room before Eiagan had even registered someone had opened the door, reminding her that while her mind was finally catching up, her body was still in recovery. Her hand settled her sword, then relaxed when Borgard paused a fraction before touching her.

"If I touch you, will you have my head?" he asked, his lips turned into a grin. With his red hair and beard, he resembled Gael, but Borgard was—Heaven help them—a trusted ally, where Gael was not.

"I will allow it this once," Eiagan said, then prepared herself for a bone-crushing embrace. Borgard lifted her from her feet, squeezed her, then set her right again.

The door opened again. Quix and Vey wandered in with scowls on their faces. Quix slammed the door. "You are a cheat and a liar!" he said, jabbing a finger toward Borgard.

"And you smell like a pig pen!" Vey added.

Quix turned his gaze to Eiagan, bowed, then said, "Your Highness, we have come to aid your trip home under Nox's command."

Eiagan had no desire to learn what antics Borgard had been up to before their arrival, so she dismissed the outburst and moved on to the pressing situation.

"Will additional aid arrive for rebuilding?" she asked.

"Indeed," Quix said, "but the materials will take time, and so Noxious asked that we inform you that it would be tomorrow at the earliest."

It was not pleasing to hear, but Eiagan swiped her black hair away from her face and prepared to dive into the disaster again. They had already readied a makeshift infirmary in the center of the village as well as temporary quarters for those displaced when their homes were swallowed. They would need time to bury the dead, take a count of those who remained, and quantify their needs. Eiagan was anxious to test Catia's ability, but there was much to be done before nightfall—including hunting. Eiagan would not let a cave-in that destroyed the food supply house starve her people.

"Borgard and Ari, please continue building the temporary quarters. Porvarth, assist Thyre with any healing and medical help she might require, but be careful. We can't be sure your healing is completely safe for you, not yet. Vey and Quix, keep watch over Gael. Assume the position of his aids while he continues with the rescue mission. There are still some alive and trapped beneath smaller pockets of rubble. Report to me if you have any suspicions."

A round of agreements followed, save Erdravac who stared at Eiagan awaiting his task. "You and I shall hunt. We have much to discuss," she said.

Porvarth kissed Eiagan's cheek on the way out, then nodded toward Erdravac. Before leaving, Porvarth glanced over his shoulder. "I've another change of clothing should you desire something clean. You are quite disheveled, King Erdravac."

Erdravac looked over his attire, ripped and blood-stained, covered with soot and grime. "Thank you, Porvarth. I appreciate your accommodation." There was a subtle, underlying meaning to his words that was not lost on Porvarth *or* Eiagan. Rather than address it fully, Porvarth simply nodded and exited Eiagan's quarters.

"He bears no grudge, even now," Erdravac said. "He is a good man. Are you happy?" His tone indicated that he was not, given the circumstances, but that he desired to be equally as accommodating as Porvarth.

"I am pleased to be with him, if that is what you ask." Eiagan braced, prepared for a discussion about everything that had happened on the Rynkald Islands not long ago.

Instead, all Erdravac said was, "He is a lucky man, but after getting to know him, the real Porvarth and not the man riddled with pain and desperation, I believe you are equally as lucky to have him."

Feelings had never been a part of Eiagan's composition, at least, not a part she spoke of freely. But more recently, it seemed those things had taken up more of her mind and heart, and so she offered Erdravac some small morsel of hope.

"It took more than five centuries for me to find peace with another human. Do not wait that long to seek someone who might stand by your side while you rule, through the happy moments and through those that make you cry and scream."

Erdravac stood and stretched. "Perhaps I might find someone with such tenacity during this war, for there is no one in all of Varrow I would ever trust with my heart. Not after they turned their backs on me so easily to side with a homicidal maniac." His eyes connected with hers for a blink before he let his shoulders slump. "I did not... that was not..."

Eiagan smirked. "I dare say Nessa's homicidal tendencies are a far sight worse than mine, so no offense is taken. Do you wish to change before we hunt, or wait until we have provided food for my people?"

Erdravac shook his head, releasing hold of something — perhaps memories of losing his throne after only a few months, or that he had swiftly lost the battle for Eiagan's affections, or any number of stresses — and pointed toward the door. "Let us go hunt. Perhaps it will help my mood."

"It often improves mine." Eiagan chuckled and secured her sword, then headed for the door. With what remained in food stores, Eiagan estimated two large animals would suffice until Nox could replenish the village's supply.

Outside, the noise and confusion made way for organized work. Longing to help those who were still trapped tore at Eiagan's soul, but there were plenty of able-bodied villagers doing what they could. If she contributed, each deceased body pulled from the wreckage would only increase her anger, perhaps beyond her control. So, she would hunt for the living instead.

On the outskirts of the village, the trees were close, and the underbrush was thick. Finding large animals in the forest would be difficult, but if she could not bring back two beasts, then she would gather fowl and woodland creatures to feed them. Eiagan did not care what she killed, so long as her people did not go hungry before Nox's supplies arrived.

"The last time we went hunting, things did not end well," Erdravac whispered.

"They won't go well this time if you scare off the food." Eiagan narrowed her eyes and glared at him as she stepped over a small stream.

"There are fish if we need them," he said, then quieted.

His silence was more unsettling than his attempt at conversation, so Eiagan paused and turned to face him. She found what she had expected — the face of a lost soul, a king without a throne, a man so turned around by his own life, that he could hardly see the opportunity in front of him. He froze when Eiagan stared at him, having been on the receiving end of her fury more than once, but Eiagan had no plans to reprimand him.

"What unsettles you the most?" Eiagan asked, noting that for once, it was not her mind slipping into the darkness but someone else's.

Erdravac stood straight and stretched his neck before offering any reply. "I cannot say one thing, for each plays off another until everything is so convoluted, I cannot make up from down. But I suppose, if I had to choose, I would say my people turning on me in favor of Nessa is not good for my ego."

Eiagan chuckled. "Your ego does require constant stroking, but I assure you, their ignorance is no indication of your ability to rule a grand kingdom, Erdravac. You cannot know what the mage promised them, and those who have not seen good days in ages, perhaps ever, are usually willing to take the first offer of something different, *anything* different, no matter what it is."

"You speak from experience," he said, a statement, not a question.

"In a sense, yes. My people accepted your father without question but look where it left them."

"My worry exactly. I was to be the *something different*, but they turned me away despite all I did for them."

"You are the son of their enemy. Of course, they did. I did more for the people of Goranin than they will ever know, certainly more than my father. I kept evils from their doorsteps that no man should have to face, but I did it for them without recognition or appreciation. They did not see that, and that is my fault."

Erdravac snickered and shook his head. "Even if they had, would they have seen you any differently?"

Eiagan inhaled and relaxed. "Likely not. I was marked by my name, just as you are, my friend."

Erdravac's eyes darted to the left, then he drew his knife. Eiagan barely sidestepped him before he raised it over his head and flung it away from them with little more than a flick. Eiagan spun in time to see the blade sink into the meaty chest of a doe — one who was either deaf or did not fear human conversation. Erdravac's gaze shifted to Eiagan.

"Sorry. I didn't want it to escape before we concluded our conversation."

Eiagan chuckled. "It makes no difference. We are who we are, the children of tyrants, and as such we must work harder to prove ourselves worthy of leading our kingdoms. Now come, let us dress this deer and find another before we return. Everything else will work itself out in time."

Eiagan slipped from her quarters after her bath and knocked on Emora and Ari's door. Emora cracked it open, spied Eiagan waiting, then allowed her access. Ari sat in front of the fire finishing his dinner, enjoying a quiet moment before setting out for home the next morning. The scar Eiagan left on his neck, illuminated by fire, screamed at Eiagan. She shook her head and gave her attention to Emora.

"Are you prepared?" Eiagan nodded toward the door, urging her sister to make haste before the sun set. She was quite sure, by the tingle her limbs, that she would want to set out toward Vidkun before first light.

"I am. Though I must say, I think my suspicion is correct. I think Catia is an undiscovered prognosticator. If she is gifted but no one else in her family is or was, then she would not learn to identify and hone her skill. It's a shame, really."

Eiagan chuckled. "Perhaps not. Magic has many pitfalls, and I believe I have experienced them all."

Emora's sigh was more than agreement. It was a pressure release, a resetting, and a mind-clearing all at once. "Well, let us see if we shall bestow both a blessing and a curse upon our new friend."

The women exited Emora's room and crossed the hallway leading toward another section of the inn. Eiagan was not overly pleased her people were separated in the inn. It was not the people of Smolzark that concerned her, but how little secrecy it afforded her having them spread across the building. Though the inn was not large, it still took some time to maneuver the narrow hallways to Catia's room.

Eiagan knocked, then pushed the door open when Catia invited her inside. The room was the mirror opposite of Emora's and boasted a different color palette, though the bedding and tapestries were equally as worn as those in every other room. Catia wrung her hands.

"I'm nervous," she admitted, stroking the red hair tied at the nape of her neck.

"There is nothing to be concerned about. It is painless, and if you do have latent ability, it will be up to you whether you utilize it or not," Emora said, offering Catia her hand. "You won't feel a thing, save your hand in mine."

Catia licked her lips, her eyes etched with worry, darting between Eiagan and Emora's outstretched hand.

"However," Eiagan said, "should you wish to decline before Emora begins, that is permitted."

"You mean to say you won't force me?" Catia asked.

Eiagan shrugged. "Have I forced you to do anything since you have joined us?"

Catia's posture softened, and she placed her hand in Emora's. Within moments, Emora smiled.

"I feel it. It's a faint buzz, but it's there. You are magical, Catia. I would suspect, given your propensity to sense when disaster strikes, that you are a prognosticator of sorts. You might sense rather than see, but if you choose to, I think I can help you see as well."

"See the future?" Catia asked, then went to wringing her hands again. "I'm not so sure that's any sort of future at all, not if I can see it." She dropped her hands to her sides and shook her head, seemingly dispelling every argument she had prepared against accessing her magic, then said, "But this is not about me alone. This is about the future of a kingdom and its people. Yes, teach me to see."

Eiagan's heart swelled with pride, not because the woman had chosen to use her magic, but because she did so for unselfish reasons. Requesting Catia's presence on the journey had been a wise decision, and it was one Eiagan was glad to have made. Perhaps she was not as far gone as she had believed. Perhaps her abilities were still there, just under the surface should she choose to focus herself on her tasks rather than her pain and anxiety-riddled mind.

"It will take some time to learn and perfect, but with my help you might see here, right now," Emora said. "Take my hands. You'll feel a mild hum, like a buzzing through your skin as my magic flows into you. It will amplify yours, letting you slip into a vision."

"Slip into a vision, you say. Will I slip back out, or be left a drooling buffoon on the floor?" Catia blew a strand of her red hair from her face, then settled her hands on Emora's.

"You'll be fine. With our magic linked, I can see the vision too." Emora licked her lips and closed her eyes. Catia did the same, leaving Eiagan to consider whether to sacrifice Catia's mind to magic was worth the return.

"I feel it," Catia said. "But I don't see anything. What do I do?"

"Patience. Just let the image come to you. Try to empty your mind of everything else except the hum of magic passing through your body." Emora's tone was gentle, soothing, and encouraging. Eiagan wondered if it was put on, or if using her magic for something good was like a balm for her soul. Having used it for murder and mayhem for years, Eiagan assumed it was the latter.

"I see something. Do you see it?" Catia asked.

"I do. It's… it's a place I've never seen. A darkened room with a fireplace carved with a lion's head," Emora said. "Eiagan, you are there. It's an odd sort of library with maps and walls lined with drawings on one side."

Eiagan's skin prickled as impatience bit at her.

"And Nessa. Eiagan… no. No. This can't happen." Emora grasped Catia's hands tighter, but Catia did not flinch. Instead, she ground her teeth and leaned closer, as if she were trying to step into the image before her.

Then she gasped and the link was broken. Both women opened their eyes and shifted their gaze to Eiagan. Emora's, horror stricken and rattled, said everything Eiagan needed to know.

"I will die again." Eiagan sat on Catia's bed, unprepared for such news though she *had* considered it many times.

"In the library. She will sneak up on you and stab you to death and then…" Emora paused and glanced at Catia.

Catia groaned. "Well, go on and tell her." Her tone, clipped and frustrated, encouraged Emora to relay the rest of the vision.

"Nessa will kill… *everyone*, Eiagan. Everyone you love will perish. Me. Porvarth. Ari. Our nephew. Everyone, Eiagan." Emora's entire body shook, and darkness passed over her face. She drew into herself, visibly shrinking away from Eiagan and Catia.

"Emora, stop," Eiagan said. "We will get through this as we have everything else."

"You will die!" Emora screamed.

Catia hushed her and grasped her arm, then turned back to Eiagan. "What she said is true. I saw the same thing, but what if it's not accurate? It is the first vision I have —"

"No, that makes no difference. Your ability does not affect the vision, only how much of it you see," Emora said. "If you saw it, it will happen."

"What if we didn't see enough? Perhaps she's not dead, but…" Catia pursed her lips, thinking.

Eiagan chewed her lip. She was not prone to such nervous habits, but given the darkness that plagued her own mind, she gave in to it if only to see if it would help her focus. Catia and Emora bickered for a moment, but it fell into the background as Eiagan weighed her options. A flicker of an idea, just a glimmer of hope that took hold, caught Eiagan's attention. She worried over it, molded it, worked through the details of it until everything fell into place — until *she* fell into place. She had approached the entire situation as an aunt, as a sister, as a friend, and a wife — but not as a warrior. Not as a *queen*.

"I have a plan," Eiagan said. "We will need to see Iditania first, but I believe it will work. If it does, we will not only save the lives of everyone we love, but we will take Nessa by surprise. Catia's vision will become reality, but not."

"What is your plan?" Emora asked, her pale eyes focused on Eiagan. "We can't change the future, Eiagan."

"Ah, but we did. I was meant to die, but instead Simorana sent me to the Bleak." Eiagan held up a finger, pulling Emora's focus back to her rather than her worry about the future.

"We can't all go to the Bleak. Besides —"

"I never said that was the plan, but rather another sort of ruse. I do not wish to speak of it here, not when so many ears can hear." Eiagan glanced around the room. "I must send word to our grandmother so she might be prepared for such an endeavor as I have planned, but if she is strong enough, I believe this will end the war entirely. It's been under my nose this whole time."

"When will you bring us into your grand plan?" Emora asked, visibly irked by Eiagan's shun.

"You will read the letter before it is sent to Iditania. Someone find me a—"

Cawing and the heavy flapping of wings interrupted Eiagan as the familiar squawk, now evidently her personal assistant dove through the cracked open window and settled at her feet. It fluttered its wings several times, then inclined its head toward Eiagan. She bent and patted its head, still unnerved by the clarity of its eyes, the familiarity that niggled at her.

"Such a strange bird," Catia said, peering at it.

"And to have taken such a personal interest in Eiagan though the others seem to despise her," Emora added, staring at the bird. "It does look a bit familiar, though, doesn't it sister?"

Eiagan was already writing the letter to Iditania, but to know her sister also felt drawn to the bird pleased her — partially. Why did the blasted squawk feel like a friend, though it was only a messenger bird?

Catia leaned over her shoulder, watching as Eiagan crafted her perfect penmanship onto the paper. Once the details of the plan had been written — at least, enough for Catia to grasp the idea — she gasped.

"It could work, provided Iditania can manage such a feat," Catia said. "It is brilliant."

"She has done similar work in the past. I think she can manage it," Emora said, now leaning over Eiagan's other shoulder. "It is brilliant, sister. Save one detail, of course."

"Indeed. How to find Nessa's body should she choose astral projection or inhabiting another as she did to you. I am working through those details myself, and once I have figured out how we might find her hiding place, I will let you know. Until then, let us work through any issues we find with this portion of the plan. I will send it now and await Iditania's reply."

"I pray it works. If it does not, Goranin will fall, and its people will all die." Emora wrung her hands until they blanched, but Eiagan was in no position to tell her how to feel. She, too, felt every bit of fear her sister felt, perhaps elevated, for she had already been dead once and had no plan to be again in a matter of days.

"We should rest if we will leave early." Catia smiled, then added, "This will be recorded in the history books if we succeed. A grand event, and I am glad I came along."

Emora scoffed, but Eiagan understood Catia's thoughts. To be on the side of good, to fight against a foe as wicked as Nessa and win, that was a feat few had accomplished. Eiagan longed for such a victory, especially if it meant her people would live in peace, a life free from tyranny and oppression.

Emora was already at the door when Eiagan refocused her thoughts. She rolled the paper and tied it with a string, then handed it to the squawk. The bird darted toward the window and disappeared into the night without so much as a peep.

SIXTEEN

Noxious "The Savage" Skjoldsson

"What you say is impossible to believe, yet I find myself believing anyway." Nox paced the floor. To say Darby's revelation about Nessa's history was shocking would be an understatement, yet he also found himself connecting all the puzzle pieces together. The picture was clear. At least, it was less muddled than it had been, though there was still plenty to question.

"I suppose it could be lies, but it makes too much sense to dismiss," Darby admitted. "Reven will wake once the vision has ended. I hope. Until then, we should try to bond more, ensure we can clearly hear one another."

Nox dragged his eyes away from Reven, unconscious on the floor, and settled them on Darby. He had never submitted his dragon to anyone's command but Eiagan's, and so the idea of allowing this princess to rifle through his mind already unsettled him. Even so, it was necessary.

"How does your shift work?" she asked.

"Do you mean to ask if I am still in full control while a dragon?" Nox raised his eyebrows, but it was not an unusual question. Darby nodded. "I am, but the dragon instinct is strong and difficult to control. I can't promise it will take kindly to your intrusion."

Darby shrugged. "Can you... *summon it?*"

"It is always there. I only need to allow it access. Think of it as a dual personality occupying the same mind." Nox let the beast slip into his presence, but only enough for the instinct to rise. To shift *inside* their room would be disastrous with so many children sprawled about. Once the dragon tickled his mind, he nodded. "Do what you do, and I'll try to listen."

"It's not that easy. I need to get a feel for it, to know what sort of dragon it is, and what drives it."

Nox narrowed his eyes at the princess and smirked. "I think we both know what drives my dragon, princess."

"Well, we haven't anyone here to kill, so there must be something else it connects with, something a bit less bloodthirsty." She tucked her blonde hair behind her ear just like Hazel used to.

Nox's eyes immediately went to his daughter and the dragon calmed. "My daughter. It's fiercely protective but gentle with her. I do not work as hard to control it in her presence."

"She soothes you, then? So, think of her while I slip in, for lack of a better description." Darby licked her lips and focused while he thought of his daughter.

Nox watched Violet's steady breathing as she slept, the gentle rise and fall of her shoulders and the sweet, angelic face that was so much like her mother's it took Nox's breath sometimes. The dragon doted over Violet, but the young girl had never shown any signs of inheriting the dragon-shifting ability. She was much like her mother, but with no one left to share her prognosticating ability, it was useless to her.

Can you hear me?

The dragon snapped back into Nox's subconscious with a snarl. His golden eyes shifted to Darby. "I heard you, but the beast didn't like it."

"So, how do I make him tolerate it?"

A deep laugh echoed through the room while Nox sat against the wall, arms resting on his knees. There was a lot Nox could do but forcing the dragon to comply by force was not only unnatural, but cruel.

"You cannot, but we keep trying until it is used to your voice in my head."

Darby sat across from him with a grunt, likely not used to not getting her way immediately. "What about this? Tell me what your fears are right now. Perhaps the dragon knows them and protects you both?"

Nox laughed again, his heart so full of pain there was no way to convey it all. He wouldn't know where to begin, in truth. But his most recent fears were at the forefront of his mind, and the dragon was never more than a slip in thought away from full rage. Those were the worries he suspected blocked it from accepting Darby as an ally.

He sighed. "What does Nessa want with me? Surely, she knows I won't turn on Eiagan or Goranin. Will she expect me to sit here and do nothing forever?"

Darby leaned beside him, her lips pursed in sympathy.

"Will she make me prove allegiance with her under threat? Shall I kill in her name? Or will she torture me with reminders of my past?" Nox shifted his weight and leaned his head on the wall. "I will never regret coming here for Violet, but I fear what she will do to me. Would she use my daughter against me to force me to bend to her will?"

Darby exhaled slowly. "I would say nothing is beyond her. Given her history, I cannot say she has a rational bone in her body."

"Irrational as she might be, it is not without understanding." He scoffed and swallowed the lump in his throat. It ached so much he couldn't be sure he wasn't biting back his own flames. "I never thought I would say that."

"What?" Darby's eyes glistened in the dim lighting, but she was inquisitive as ever.

"Admit that I understand Nessa in some way. I probably never would if I had not known Eiagan for so long. And Emora."

"You cannot have sympathy for her?" Darby's head jerked back a bit, her brow furrowed, and eyes narrowed on him. "She's hurt you most of all."

"No, not sympathy. Perhaps a little empathy. I do realize that her upbringing and her blood would turn anyone into a madman." Nox had seen what such things had done to his friend, to the woman he used to love, and how it tore at her still.

"Might I offer a suggestion? Something that might aid us in connecting?"

Nox slanted his gaze toward her, reluctant to agree to a magical cure for his ails.

"It will only last a short time, I swear it." She held her hands up, but he would never be convinced magic lasted a short time. He had seen it tear people apart, and he truly wanted no part of it, but once again, there was little room for bargaining when those he loved and their kingdoms were at risk.

He pushed off the wall and stood, brushed dirt from his seat, and offered Darby his hand. "I will submit to your magic this once, but let us not make a habit of solving our problems with it. Magic only compounds the tragedy in the end."

"Understood perfectly." Darby took his hand and stood before him, undeterred by his fierce gaze upon her. Nox found it wholly odd that she seemed undaunted by... *anything*. He had never met a princess save Eiagan, who was as hard as iron in the face of adversity. Though Darby was beautiful, dainty, and feminine, she was undeniably a force to be reckoned with, which only made Nox reconsider his opinion of nearly every woman he had ever met. Had those lacy, frilly women been as deadly as this one?

"What shall I do?" Nox looked around, but for what he could not say.

"Nothing. I have it all under control. Just stand there. Close your eyes if you wish but try not to wiggle too much." Darby smiled and tossed an invisible magic in the air. From it, a little pink spark glowed to life and danced around the dust motes drifting in the air. It swirled a moment, then shot toward him... around him... kissing his skin every few moments.

Nox closed his eyes and let her magic do its work. Calm took him, a kind he had never known before. The dragon had always been there, lurking in the shadows waiting to pounce. It was hungry... savage... and controlling it had always taken Nox's full strength. So much he hardly noticed he hadn't relaxed in his entire life. Until now. Now, Darby's magic soothed him, relaxed his muscles, and allowed him to rest.

Can you hear me?

His eyes snapped open. "Yes."

Darby held her finger to her lips, so Nox closed his eyes again and focused.

Try to answer me without speaking.

What did he want to say? Would she hear his thoughts with the dragon's, or must he project it in some way? Images, ideas, and feelings shifted through his mind in myriad colors until he focused on one thing. *Violet.*

Darby giggled, so he opened his eyes again. She shook her head. "Well, I expected this to work the same as it did with Ellaro, but it seems you are a visual speaker, Nox."

He blinked. "What do you mean?"

"I didn't hear your thoughts. I *saw* them. I know how we can do this even over long distances. Let's try again. Ensure we can sense one another and the dragon is in agreement."

"What about when your magic wears off? How will I hear you then, princess? What if the dragon's instinct is too loud?"

Darby smirked. "It already wore off, Nox. I think your dragon needed a moment to see I meant no harm."

Nox shook his head and rubbed his eyes with his thumb and forefinger. "Wait, you mean to say you saw what I thought, and the dragon... *allowed it?*"

"Nox..." Darby gasped, seeming in possession of some information he did not possess. "Nox, I saw your thoughts *and* the desires of the dragon." She pointed to Violet, still sleeping. "The moment you thought of Violet, I was *flooded* by images from you and the dragon."

He couldn't help but chuckle. All his years, he'd thought of the dragon as his strength, the core of his existence that kept him not only alive but thriving. Though he struggled with it for dominance

169

at times, it was still his lifeblood. But it seemed even bloodthirsty monsters were tamed by sweet children.

"Let us work on this bond until it's as solid as rock. I want out of this nightmare so I can take my child home."

SEVENTEEN

3731, THE YEAR OF RECKONING
UNKNOWN LOCATION
SOMEWHERE IN THE ANCIENT KINGDOMS

Reven Allurigard

Reven was prepared to wake inside his prison with Darby, but instead he slipped into darkness. Fear tugged at his heart, but he forced it away with a calming breath. The visions couldn't harm him, and the information gleaned from each one would only help them escape and save Goranin... save the *world*. Soon enough, the darkness faded and Reven blinked in the dim lighting. Instead of going back to their prison, he'd been sent into another memory.

"A library?" He spun in place, finding nothing but rows and stacks of books all around. Soon, his gaze landed on a head full of blonde waves. Nessa browsed the books, periodically interrupting her mother.

Like this, she seemed like a harmless, sweet child. Beneath that, though, was the heart of a tyrant, a madwoman ready to pounce when the timing was right. Reven swallowed and stepped closer so he might overhear any conversation between the child and her adoptive mother. Surely, if he listened and paid attention, he might see it. The moment it all changed. The moment the seemingly kind soul cracked, bled, and rusted until all that was left was a hollowed-out shell of a human.

Queen Lureah was stern and strict, but also thoughtful and kind. Reven couldn't imagine she was the cause of Nessa's dramatic turn, but one could never be too sure. After all, he had been raised by the kindest guardians in all the world, but deep inside, he knew the Allurigard blood bubbled at his core. His father might have been honorable, an innocent soul among bloodied ones, but if given time, Reven suspected even Reeve would have had questionable moments.

Reven stepped still closer to Nessa, hoping to hear every word. The girl paused and looked up, straight into is eyes. Chills pushed up on his skin. Could she see him? Deadly as she was, Nessa's eyes were still beautiful, and they pinned him to the wall as well as any dagger. His lips parted, prepared to speak when she raised on her toes, her slender fingers gently brushing along the spine of a book. She pushed it even with the others and smiled. Her gaze shifted to another, leaving Reven with a sigh.

For a moment, just a blink, Reven wondered if his presence could somehow change the future. If Nessa *could* hear him, see him... would she listen? Believe him? He squeezed his eyes shut and pushed that thought from his mind. Tampering with the past was worse than any magic, and the consequences of such things would likely be worse than the original course of history. She didn't seem to notice him anyway. Besides, was he truly *in* the past or pilfering her memories like a street thief?

Nessa wiped a smudge of dust from the shelf. Her lips parted, and a small whimper escaped, something that almost made Reven's heart crack. She was lonely, troubled already. Any number of small changes might have changed her future at this point, even this moment in the library with her mother, but as Reven discovered... it was *that* moment in the library when Nessa's life *had* changed. Her path had been chosen for her, and Reven spied it firsthand.

EIGHTEEN

3217, THE YEAR OF CORRUPTION
THE QUEEN'S LIBRARY, TALISKAR CASTLE
GILGRAMACH, ASANTAVAL

The History of the Callanan Royal Family

Queen Lureah's eyes darted left to right as they absorbed the ancient text which, it seemed, interested her more than Nessa's quiet whimpers. With little to occupy her time, the child often found herself counting the books on the shelves, but often had to begin counting again when she forgot her numbers. She knew, though, there were forty-eight sections of books all categorized by the region and year of their origin. That was all she knew of the library. That, and her mother's obsession with the books inside.

"Mother, will you play with me?" Nessa asked.

"In a moment, darling. Let me finish this page first, and then we shall go for a walk." Lureah pulled the book closer to her face to read the final lines in the magic light.

It was always dark in Asantaval. The light the mages created was harsh and bothered Nessa's eyes, but she was forbidden to go to the surface. There were armies of men who would steal her away and she might never see her mother and father again. That was what her nanny had told her, and since she loved her nanny, Nessa was inclined to believe every word that slipped from her sweet lips. Even so, Nessa did wonder what it might look like above their buried kingdom.

"Mother, what does the sun look like?" Nessa's slender finger fiddled with the binding of one book, the only one with purple binding and gilded lettering. It was where she always stopped herself to ask the same question.

"As I said before, my love, it is a burning ball of fire in the sky. Nothing for you to worry over, of course, but that is, I am afraid, all it is." Lureah closed her book and placed it on the small side table beside her beloved reading chair.

"Can I see it? Just one time? Please?" Nessa's blonde curls bobbed around her head, and she puckered her lips. It never hurt to *try* tugging on her mother's heart strings. Unfortunately, the queen's determination was stronger than Nessa's, and the child had not won a fit since the day of her birth.

"No." Lureah's command was so final, Nessa flinched.

"The moon, then? It comes out when the sun sleeps, yes?"

"Nessa, I have said no and so it will remain. You will never see the surface while you are a child, and that is that. Am I clear, or must I reprimand you more harshly?"

Nessa shook her head, bobbing those soft curls frantically. She crossed her arms, pressed her lips, and grit her teeth—but said nothing.

175

"Come, let us go for a walk, and I will tell you the history of our kingdom.

"I know it well already, mother. You tell me every chance you find." The princess rolled her eyes and stared at the purple bound book — the one with a sun emblazoned on the bottom just above a title she could not read, for the words were not Asantavalian.

"I will tell you why we remain underground, and before you protest against me again, I will add that I think you are old enough to hear what my plan and your father's might be for you."

This was new, her mother's admission that there was more planned for her than decades spent muddling through dusty books longing for something more, but Nessa was still guarded. It was not often Lureah shared anything with the princess other than her constant reminders to eat her meals, not dirty her dresses, and to stand straighter. When Lureah offered her hand, Nessa took it, intrigued by the way her mother's eyes darted around the library as if someone might hear her explaining the history of Asantaval and Nessa's purpose as the future queen.

"Mother?"

"Shh... Keep your tongue and I will take you somewhere new. Your father and I believed we should wait until you are older but... but I think the time is growing near."

"Time for what, Mother?" Nessa's fingers tingled but she dared not shake her mother's grip.

"Come, follow me." Lureah tugged her daughter's arm and led her to a part of the library she had not explored. It was not allowed for children, not even the princess, because the books were filled with things that proper women and children did not tamper with — dark magic.

Once Lureah was sure no one had seen them, she pulled one book from the shelf, replaced it with a near-perfect replica, then pushed on the wall beside the bookcase. To Nessa's surprise, the wall shuddered then opened. She gasped but hardly had time to understand what had happened before she was dragged into a dank, dark space.

Nessa coughed. "Mother? What is this place?"

"Hold tight, dear." Lureah's shuffling gave nothing away, but soon there was light. It emanated from a fireplace in the far corner.

"Is that... fire?" Nessa crossed the room and reached toward the flickering light as it bit at the darkness. Each flash seemed to antagonize the dark, tease it until it was convinced it could not swallow the light.

"Do not touch it!" Lureah snatched Nessa's hand just as the flame tickled the tip of her finger. She hissed. "It burns, darling. Fire is all consuming, and if you touch it, you will be eaten up alive."

"Like the sun?"

"Mmm, I suppose so, but to reach the sun is an impossible feat. Come, sit with me."

While Nessa's curious mind wondered where the smoke from the fire led—it *did* spiral upward, somewhere toward the surface, but where?—her mother settled in a chair similar to her favorite in the library. She placed the book on her lap and crossed her hands over it.

"Nessa, what I am about to tell you must stay between us for now. I will tell you when it is the appropriate time to... bring your father into our secret, so to speak."

"Keep a secret from Father? Mother, you always say—"

"I know what I say, Nessa. I say it because it is important for us to trust one another, but in this instance, I think it is necessary to keep our adventure here a secret from him so that he can honestly deny his knowledge if the need should arise."

"So... we are protecting Father by keeping this adventure secret?"

"In a sense, yes. Come, sit." Lureah motioned toward the stool beside her chair. The moment Nessa's rear hit the padded stool, Lureah dove headlong into her confession.

"When I tell you that you will never see the surface, it is to convince myself that this plan your father and I have is foolish, that it will not likely work, and even if it does, we will probably perish before we see it to fruition."

"Mother —"

"Do not interrupt, darling. What I want to tell you requires patience, a calm mind, and... I pray you will understand, but it also requires that you know the truth. The whole truth."

Lureah shifted in her chair and swallowed. "You see, I was unable to have children for a long time, and when I did birth children, they all died soon after birth. When your uncle went to the surface to hide one of —"

"Uncle Bribadge has gone to the —" Nessa cut her own words short when Lureah glared at her.

"While there, he came across a midwife who was tasked with disposing of a child. The child was an inconvenience to the father, something he abhorred, and so the mother begged the midwife to take it away. She did not have the heart to abandon the child in the cold, so when she came upon your uncle, she asked that he take it to a new home. That home was Taliskar Castle."

Nessa's stomach pitched, threatening to release her morning porridge. She did her best to question with her eyes alone, but she was never any good at expression. Fortunately, Lureah needed no question to provide an answer.

"That child was you, my love. I hope that you do not feel put aside by this admission, for I love you as if I bore you of my own womb, and I will love you fiercely until the day I die." Lureah toyed with Nessa's hair then pressed her palm against her cheek. "Do not ever fear that our love for you is forced or that you were unwanted. We wanted you, and you have been thoroughly loved since the first moment I nursed you."

Nessa only nodded, but the ocean in her stomach churned. Perhaps Lureah and Illaric *did* love her, that was true, but someone did not—someone on the surface who could not be bothered to shirk an abominable husband to love and care for her own flesh and blood born of her own womb.

"Do not feel hate toward your mother, child. I see it burning in your eyes, but you should know that she loved you."

"How can you know such a thing?" Nessa's tone was clipped but unintentionally so.

Lureah did not chastise her. Instead, she said, "I know who she is, Nessa." When Nessa gasped, Lureah held up her hand, staving off an onslaught of questions. "Her husband is a discontented and angry man, and if he had learned you were born a female, he might have ordered you killed. Your mother ran to the midwife in the loxmore community in Parazalorean—you know of the place from your history studies—and there, she begged the midwife to hide you."

"But I thought... she was told to kill me?"

"The midwife ordered you abandoned in The Banished Land, but her apprentice could not bear it. It was she who met your uncle. If

179

you swear not to speak of this to anyone, Nessa, I will show you an image of your birth mother. Your father, too, if you wish."

"You can… do that? How?"

"They are here, in this book." Lureah tapped the cover of the tattered book. "But promise me, my darling, that you will always look to me as your mother, and that you will not attempt to go to the surface to find another. It would end in your death."

Nessa regarded Lureah as if she were a fool. Of course, she would not look to anyone else. For her entire life, Nessa knew no mother but Lureah. She was the one who held her when her dreams scared her, who snuck her favorite sweets past the nanny even when she did not eat all of her meal, and the only woman who made Nessa feel loved — not only cared for but loved beyond reason.

"I love you, Mama. No woman in a book will change that."

Lureah smiled and opened the book to a marked page, then handed the book to Nessa. When her eyes fell upon the image of the woman, everything fell into place. She knew why she was abandoned in the land above their kingdom, and she knew the woman's story as well as she knew her own kingdom's history. She knew her father, too, without looking at his illustration. She did not want to. Her eyes fluttered up to her mother with a lingering question.

"Tell no one." Lureah gripped Nessa's upper arm gently but insistently. "Not even your father until the time is right. And there will be a time, my love, that you will set our kingdom free. I know it."

"What do you mean, Mama?" Nessa asked, her eyes absorbing the image of her birth mother again.

"You will be the one, Nessa. You will be the queen who brings our people out of their slumber and into the light again. You will rescue our kingdom, and when you do, all those on the surface will know their place."

"Mother?" Nessa's chest grew heavy as she listened to the change in tone of her mother's voice. Gone was the sweet, gentle tone, and in its place was the voice of a calculating warrior.

"Asantaval will rise and take back what was taken by force, and when it does, you my love, will be queen over all nations. *All nations.* By my dying breath, I swear it will be so."

NINETEEN

Eiagan Allurigard

When the sun kissed Catia's face early the next morning, Eiagan smiled. The woman stood taller, no longer hunched like a seamstress who'd spent too many years over her work. She strode with purpose, with some unseen drive that Eiagan knew all too well. Catia's determination and moral compass reminded her of Hazel, the prognosticator who'd taken a bit of Eiagan's heart with her when she died. Thinking of Hazel also brought memories of Astrid to her mind, which led to Emora's losses. Everyone had lost someone, and Eiagan prayed no one else would feel the deep ache in their chest, the ache of loss and a certain guilt that came with surviving while they did not.

Catia packed a horse while the men loaded their supplies into the wagons. Emora had gone to the baker's — the only shop open at such

182

a dastardly hour — to secure breakfast for the trip. Gael spied Eiagan, though she had tried to avoid the Astantavalian until she was prepared to let him in on the bad news. She would not be his savior, nor would she entertain any ideas of going beneath the ground. The plan had changed, and Eiagan would lead from that point onward.

Gael closed the distance between them, crossing over the worn and broken stone pathway that led from the inn to the stables. It had cost Eiagan half a bag of coins to buy the horses necessary to transport their supplies, but it was money well spent. The horses were pristine specimens and had many years of work left in them, provided they did not encounter another earth shake, of course.

Just as Gael reached Eiagan, a squawk dove between them, then shot back into the sky.

"Blasted — you miserable fowl!" Gael said, shaking his fist at the sky.

Eiagan bit her smile and fastened a bag to her mount's saddle. The squawk broke apart as they always did, and a single bird — *Eiagan's* bird, as she had taken to thinking of it — landed at her feet with a letter, likely a response from Iditania. The bird shook its head then craned its neck toward Eiagan. She bent and retrieved the letter, patting the bird as she did.

Emora approached with her basket of bread and jams, her eyes trained on Gael who said nothing while the women read the correspondence. Emora leaned closer. "He stares at you with that look," she whispered.

"What look?"

"The look of a man determined to have his way, even if it means subjugating a woman to achieve it. A brute, you might say."

Eiagan snickered and rolled the letter. "If Icluedian did not succeed in such things, I do not see *him* doing so."

183

"Doing what?" Porvarth asked, popping up from nowhere as was his way. "Becoming a homicidal maniac hellbent on destroying everything in his path simply because he could not control the sun?"

Eiagan sucked in a breath—not out of frustration, but because Porvarth was right. Icluedian had been a ridiculous man, all things considered. But Gael grew impatient and expressed as much with his constant fidgeting and movement. The time had come for him to know his place, and the prince would not like it.

"My grandmother is prepared," Eiagan said, though none but Catia and Emora knew her plan. Fortunately, the men did not question their leader in this manner. Instead, they mounted their horses and readied themselves for the long trip back to Vidkun Castle. Eathevall would be a two-day ride with so many people and wagons—a day longer than she had originally hoped—but the trip would give Eiagan time to evaluate the rest of the kingdom and what it needed.

"Prepared for what, may I ask?" Gael's tone had a hard edge that Eiagan assumed meant he would not be easily deterred from *his* plan.

"Our return to Eathevall," Eiagan said, then pulled herself up on her horse. Everyone else, save Borgard and Ari—the muscle—were ready to leave.

Gael tensed. Borgard and Ari stepped closer behind him, which only further stressed Gael.

"Am I to believe you intend to kill me?" he asked.

"That depends," Eiagan said, turning her horse west. "Do you intend to fight against us, or return peacefully with us to Eathevall? I would prefer the second but will dispatch of you with full animosity if you so much as split a hair on my men's heads."

"Your men? A Balconian thief and a fish-gutter from your slums?"

Ari shoved Gael from behind, but Gael only stumbled, then regained his footing. To his credit, he did not strike out against Ari.

"I might come from the slums, but I'd bet my last coin I can filet you faster than you can blink," Ari said.

Borgard chuckled. "I'd bet mine, too. Even so, let us follow the lady's orders, shall we?"

Eiagan suppressed a laugh. Borgard doing as she had asked, what a change from when they first met. He'd tried to abduct her for sale to the sawbones before they'd both been captured by Nessa's Ghost Riders and General Maelveidr.

"What will it be, Gael?" Eiagan asked. "I wish to be on my way."

"Might I at least ask why you have chosen to abandon our pact?" Gael's red hair glistened in the early-morning sunlight as his eyes locked on hers. He had secrets, plenty of them, but if he wanted to know Eiagan's then he'd have to share his own first.

"I have not abandoned the pact with Asantaval. I will honor the land reversal and remain an ally, but as for defeating Nessa and retrieving my kingdom's children, I will do what I see fit. I have never taken kindly to anyone forcing my hand, and I will not allow you to do so any longer."

"That was not my intention. I will come willingly, but know this will not be seen fitting by our—"

"Your king is not our king, Gael. Do remember that before it gets you killed," Eiagan said, then clicked to her horse. The single squawk decided to ignore its brethren in favor of riding atop Eiagan's horse with her. It settled behind her, just over the horse's romp.

Ari and Borgard flanked Gael as he mounted his horse, then settled on their own. The caravan moved forward with Eiagan at the rear, Erdravac at the front. Emora nodded at Eiagan, then rounded the caravan to ride beside the King of Varrow, unseated or not. Catia rode alongside Quix in one wagon, while Vey and Porvarth each maintained another. It would be slow moving with the three wagons over the narrow roads, but once they reached Sudyak Meadow, the pace would increase. If they did not run into trouble, they might make the trip in a day and a half rather than two.

Hardly five marticks into the trip, Gael started his mumbling and grunting, his usual way when faced with doing that which he had not chosen to do. Eiagan ignored his whining until she could no longer focus on her task—watching the forests on either side of the trail for signs of danger, while her people made their way toward Eathevall.

"What is your concern, Gael?" Eiagan asked.

"This was not our arrangement, and I feel like a prisoner," he said, regripping his reins.

"You are no prisoner. If you would like to leave, be my guest." Eiagan closed the short distance and put herself between Gael and Ari. "However, should you choose to stay, perhaps I might suggest telling the truth regarding your intentions."

"I've told you my intentions." Gael's tone said otherwise but Eiagan would beg no one for information, so she let her horse slow and fell back into her position.

After another half-martick, Gael glanced over his shoulder and nodded forward, urging Eiagan to return to his side. Eiagan nudged the horse and bit back her smile. A man with secrets as deep as Gael's could only survive so long without them eating him alive. Gael was near bursting, finally unable to maintain the lies he'd kept

186

for so long. Eiagan swallowed the anticipation that bit at her throat so that she might put on a stoic front, but she could not deny that she was elated the man had finally reached his capacity.

"What do you wish to say?" Eiagan asked.

Gael stopped his horse, forcing Borgard and Ari to do the same. The entire caravan stopped.

The Asantavalian's mouth opened and closed several times as he stared at his own hands, clenching and releasing the reins. What a paradox he must feel—torn between keeping the secrets that had kept his kingdom safe for so many centuries, versus sharing them and saving his kingdom once and for all.

He inhaled slowly, then released a measured, calculating breath as he made eye contact with Eiagan. "It is true. I have lied to you, but when I explain everything, I believe you will understand why I lied."

This was no surprise to Eiagan, for she had suspected him for some time—perhaps not as long as Porvarth had, but for a while all the same. "Go on."

"My given name is not Gael. I took the name after my second wife died so that I might move through the kingdoms without anyone recognizing my true identity." Gael shifted his weight to something more comfortable for a long story. "My name is Bribadge Callanan, the once dead Prince of Asantaval."

Porvarth locked his wagon in place and jumped from the side, his boots landing with a thunk in the mud. Each step squelched through the thickness of it until he reached Eiagan's horse. Eiagan, though, was too taken aback to question Porvarth's actions.

"You say you are the once dead prince? King Illaric was your elder brother, the one who raised Nessa?" Porvarth asked. "And am I right in assuming that *you* are the current king?"

"Indeed, he was. And I am. You see, I was the one who brought Nessa from the surface and down into our world, and so it is my fault. Everything that has happened, I say, is my fault." Gael — Bribadge — swallowed hard and regripped his reins for the hundredth time. "The story is long and painful to remember, but you deserve the truth after everything your people have given for the cause. I shall tell you everything from the beginning as we make our journey, should that satisfy you."

Porvarth gazed up at Eiagan, questioning her. His navy-blue eyes held so many thoughts, but the one that screamed loudest was *be careful*. Eiagan stared back at him, her gray-white eyes focused on his alone. Every emotion she knew swirled in her mind, but his steadfast loyalty, coupled with his ever-present worry forced her to heed his warning. She would be careful. This connection between them, the intensity with which they felt each other's emotions, was easily conveyed through that short exchange of eye-contact. Porvarth nodded and returned to the wagon, while Eiagan fixed her gaze back to Gael.

"Ari, take up the rear while I discuss the truth with our guest, please."

Ari took his order and settled in the back of the caravan. Borgard inched closer to Gael, so close, that if as much as a light breeze blew Gael's hair toward Eiagan, Borgard could cut it off before it reached her.

The caravan began again. Gael's gaze settled ahead but his mind was far, far away. In such a short time, he had morphed from a joyful man to one whose mind was as plagued as Eiagan's. That familiar darkness shadowed his features, and a heavy silence fell over the caravan as his story began.

"We were running out of food, so my brother decided it was reasonable to make short trips farther from our usual hunting and fishing grounds. It was always dangerous to leave our caverns, but necessary to obtain food. But traveling beyond the Lands was madness. Even so, it was travel or watch our people starve.

"I had become a bit of an expert in navigation, better than anyone else at finding my way around the surface—the area you named the Banished Lands. And so, when Queen Lureah birthed another dead child, I was tasked with bringing it to the surface to bury. While there, a loxmore girl approached me. I nearly wet my leathers when she called out to me, but she was in the Lands for her own reasons.

"The girl had a babe, the child of a Goraninite woman who could not keep the child. She had a hard husband, and he would not take kindly to a female offspring. But the loxmore could not dispose of the child, it seemed, so she asked if I might know someone willing to nurse the child and keep her. It felt like a miracle. Our kingdom would maintain its royal line, and this tiny child would not have to die. I brought her underground and convinced my brother and his wife to raise her. We were unaware of her lineage at that time, only that she was Goraninite."

"What lineage?" Eiagan asked.

"I will get to that in time, but for now you must understand the position my brother was in, or the remainder of the story will not be so easily understood." Gael glanced toward Eiagan. There was something in the connection, a spark that set Eiagan's mind ablaze.

Gael faced back toward the front of the caravan a moment before the earth shook. This time, it did not crack, but there was no controlling the horses. They screamed and bolted, leaving their riders holding on for their lives. Only Porvarth's horse maintained

189

any sensibility, fortunate since his was the wagon with their food supply for the trip.

Catia and Vey leaped from their wagon before it slammed into a thick tree, splintering into thousands of pieces as the horse plowed through the forest with half of it still attached to his harness. Trees fell around them as the earth shook harder. With no clearing in sight, the most anyone could hope for was an end to the quake.

Erdravac helped Catia onto his horse, who had gathered its wits along with Emora's horse. Vey shifted and took flight, circling over the forest while Borgard cursed his draft until it bent under his will. Gael's, though, had no desire to be shaken clean out of its skin, so it bolted through the trees with little regard for its rider. Eiagan's horse reared, tossing her to the muddy forest floor before disappearing.

"Curse the stars, I will never ride another horse!" Eiagan screamed, then pushed herself onto all fours before she was stomped by Ari's horse. He dismounted and smacked the beast's romp, sending it away before it did more harm than good.

Vey ducked between the trees, corralling Gael's horse. Darting left to right and back, he managed to convince the horse that a spiked dragon was far worse than any earth shaking.

Just as quickly as it began, the earth stopped moving. Everything stilled and was quiet for several breaths while Eiagan counted her people. Everyone was accounted for, but two wagons had been destroyed and three horses were gone. Their two day trip to Eathevall had just doubled.

The squawk landed on Eiagan's shoulder and screeched. Eiagan winced. "Blasted bird. Why would you do such a thing?"

It jumped from her shoulder and landed beside her, still screeching its fool head off.

190

"Are you alright?" Porvarth asked, brushing mud from Eiagan's face as the bird danced around them like a court jester.

"Fine. Are there any injured?" Eiagan called, but no one answered save a few shaking heads. Dazed and short of breath, they awaited their leader's orders.

"Gael and Borgard will ride with me in the remaining wagon. Catia and Erdravac can share a horse, as can Emora and Ari. Quix and Vey can fly ahead to the next town. It is only ten marticks, so we should arrive within the next two hours, save additional interruptions."

Without question, Quix and Vey took flight and headed toward the next village, a small collection of homes that surrounded a physician's office. The rest of the caravan settled in their positions — except for the squawk. It chattered and pranced, then flapped and squawked until Eiagan gave the bird her attention.

"Get on the wagon or do not, it is your choice, but make it soon so that we might be on our way," she said, standing by the wagon.

The squawk screeched once more, then darted toward Eiagan. But before it reached her, it grew and morphed into something wholly different. It was no longer a bird, not even one as large as it was when it joined with its companions. Instead, the squawk stretched and widened until it sprouted four long legs, a muscular rump, a lean and long back that stretched into an arched neck, finally giving way to a full head covered with sleek, black fur. The squawk had become a horse. The horse whinnied and stomped several times, then wings erupted from its back. After a final whinny, it leaned forward and settled its forehead on Eiagan's, finally calm. It huffed a few times, then stood still.

Trembling fingers rested on the horse's cheek as Eiagan stared into its deep brown eyes. She *had* known them very well after everything the horse had been through with her. Eiagan released a slow breath, for if the horse was alive, then perhaps its former owner might be as well?

Another hand pressed against the horse's cheek. Emora's eyes were wide as she petted down its neck and let her fingers tangle in its mane.

"Lucifer," Emora whispered, then buried her face in his mane.

TWENTY

Noxious "The Savage" Skjoldsson

Within an hour, Nox communicated with Darby as if it were the most natural relationship ever formed, though most of that time was spent convincing his dragon her intrusion was welcome. Violet had woken midway through their practicing, which only intensified the beast's urge to reject Darby's advances. However, once Violet snuggled up with Nox, the dragon was content to sit still and listen.

"I must admit, that took less time than originally anticipated," Darby said.

Violet played with her hair while the other children played with toys found in a basket near the armoire. When Nessa had distributed them, no one knew, but they seemed content for the time being. As soon as Nessa returned, Nox would insist they be returned to their homes.

"You still seem unsettled. I think our plan will work, Nox," Darby said.

Nox chewed his lip, debating the whole situation. It was entirely possible that it would, that Darby could return to Goranin with the others as Nessa promised, and their connection would help her relocate him. She could bring Eiagan and all Goranin's army right to Nessa's door, wherever they were.

"I admit, I still wonder why she wants me here."

"To spite Eiagan, I'm sure."

"She seemed to know my ancestor Zero well. Almost as if she cared about him, but he married Eiagan, and they had a child. I can't imagine Nessa allowing that to happen if she had been in love with him. From what I have been told about my ancestor, I cannot fathom a world in which he might return such love if she did. He was a good and honorable man, not a lunatic."

Darby shrugged. "I never question love. It is, by all standards, unmeasurable, unexplainable, and impatient as anything in this world. It plays by no rules, does not care who it offends, and often hurts its bearer more than a sword."

Nox chuckled. He knew she spoke the truth. "Yet you fell in love with Reven despite love's unbearable ways."

She shrugged again and grinned. "I never said it was unworthy of the effort. But whether Zero loved Nessa or she loved him is hardly the problem now. What she wants with you seems impossible. Would she have you as her husband? A companion? Surely, she would not expect such things."

"Perhaps she believes time is on her side. If she keeps me here long enough, she believes I will change toward her." Nox huffed and crossed his arms. "I might grow *some* empathy given her past, but she killed my friends, caused my wife's death, and kidnapped my child. There is no amount of time that would make me care what happens to her."

Across the room, Reven roused. His black hair was plastered to his forehead with sweat and he groaned. He'd been, according to Darby, unconscious far longer than they had been before. Nox crossed the room and helped the prince to his feet, but he swayed and leaned against the stone wall. His face was pale and slick, but he offered a small smile and a nod.

"Thank you. I'm exhausted." Reven accepted Darby's coddling as she wiped his face and kissed his cheek.

"What did you learn?" Nox asked, his voice low so the children would not be disturbed.

Reven's eyes widened and rolled. "More than I ever cared to know, but useful information. Nessa knew at a young age who her birth parents were. Her adoptive mother was a power-hungry woman but managed to keep her desires a secret from even her husband. I believe I witnessed the first shift in Nessa, the one that set her up for a lifetime of poor choices and questionable behavior."

"That is a mild way to phrase her actions," Darby said, brushing her hair from her face.

"Yes, well, I never said —"

The door swung open, and Nessa strode into the room with a basket of bread and clean clothing. Her hair was disheveled, and her cheeks smudged with soot, clothing wrinkled and mud covered as well. Nox bit the urge to ask the woman what she had been doing.

"I will bring dinner in an hour," she said, then turned her heel and exited. She paused just outside the door. "Prince Reven, follow me, please."

195

Reven glanced between Darby and Nox, but Nox was unwilling to allow the boy from his sight. As Eiagan's nephew, he had a duty to ensure his health and well-being, especially in the presence of the woman who sought to ruin every drop of Allurigard blood in the land.

"Whatever you wish to discuss with the boy can be done here in my presence," he said.

Nessa chuckled. "It was no request. He comes with me, or he leaves here in a coffin."

"I will go." Reven pushed off the wall and nodded toward the children. "They need clean clothing and food."

He gave them no time to discuss his decision and strode across the room. Nessa shut the door behind them, leaving Nox as unsettled as he had been when the boy was unconscious.

TWENTY-ONE

Reven Allurigard

Chills covered Reven's neck and crept down his spine with each footfall. Knowing the depth of Nessa's magical power didn't necessarily inspire confidence in his ability to protect himself should she choose to end his life rather than keep her promise to Noxious, but not following her commands would not encourage her to keep it either. So, the young prince followed her into the darkened hallway until they reached the end of it, then tried not to gasp when she smoothed her hand over the stone wall and a door appeared. How many hidden pathways did the castle have?

Nessa opened the door and allowed Reven to enter, then closed it behind them. Would Nox hear if he called? Would he even see the door if Reven needed rescuing? Even the thought forced a stone in

Reven's throat. He felt like a child playing a man's game with Nessa, but what choice did he have?

She crossed the room and snapped her fingers, igniting a fire that immediately warmed the room and revealed its contents. Practically bare, it held only a plush chair and a shelf of books beside a small table. Nessa faced him, her light blonde hair slipping over her shoulder as she did. Knowing what he knew... who she was... he saw the key features in her face, primarily in her eyes, that confirmed what he had seen in the visions.

"You needn't fear me, Reven. I intend to return you to your aunts tomorrow, as I promised. In fact, I have an offer for you." Her eyes danced over his face, absorbing every curve and line into memory.

"An offer?" he croaked. Oh, how he hated the way his voice sounded when he spoke to her. Perhaps he would never be as strong as Nox, or any of the dragon shifters for that matter, but he did wish his voice didn't waver so much when he was nervous. Fear he accepted as reality, but he had worked so hard to overcome it despite little exposure to things like war.

"I know you used my journals. That you saw the visions of my childhood, but you must stop." Nessa sat in the chair and snapped her fingers again. Another chair appeared. "Sit. Rest, and I'll explain."

Reven wiped sweaty palms on his pants and closed the distance between them with long, hesitant strides. His black hair dipped into his eyes, so he swiped it away. This brought a smile to Nessa's face and a frown to Reven's.

"You look exactly like your father. It's as uncanny as Noxious and his ancestor." Nessa studied his face again before reclining and staring into the flames. "Here is my offer. Allow me to tell you from my own mouth what happened next. Let me show you I am not entirely what you think I am, and then I will reward your patience with that which you most desire."

Reven scoffed. How could this abominable woman know what he wanted most? *He* didn't even know exactly what he desired most, save a simple, quiet life with the woman he loved. Perhaps a few children and no more war. Those were things this woman had no knowledge of, no real understanding of, nor did she *care* about them. Nessa's blood was worse than anyone he knew, but he could not deny her story was also as intriguing as any he'd ever heard.

"Do you doubt I know your deepest desires, young prince?" Nessa tilted her head, her eyes focused on him.

This way... the way her eyes were now... it shot more chills down his spine. They matched his. "You know nothing of me or what I might want. In fact, you've taken more from me than you could ever return."

"Your mother?" she asked, shifting so she did not tilt her head to look at him.

"To begin with, yes."

"Yet, you forgive Eiagan for taking your father. Curious." She crossed her legs and tapped her fingers on the armrest of her chair. "What is the difference between us? Why forgive her and condemn me?"

Reven's jaw clenched, and his teeth ground, forcing a headache into his temples. He knew what she saw — a boy playing the role of a man, one who knew nothing about this game she played with Eiagan — and that incited the Allurigard rage inside him. It gurgled and heated his skin until he could hardly stand it, but one thought of Darby cooled him entirely. He must endure this for her, for their future. She loved him. He loved her, and he would not allow Nessa to draw him into a battle that he would surely lose.

He licked his lips. "She seeks forgiveness. She seeks repentance. She has regret in her heart for the things she has done. All of that combined with the circumstances surrounding my father's death allow me to have room in my heart to forgive her. *You* have no regret. No *feeling* about what you have done. You do not seek my forgiveness, and as such, I see no reason to offer it."

"I am a monster, then?" she asked, her gaze fluttering over his face, watching each emotion that crossed his .it

He narrowed his eyes. "Are you?"

Silence fell over them while they stared at one another. Myriad emotions crossed her face, but Reven could not identify a single one. Not for lack of trying, of course, but because they were so misplaced upon the woman's face. Regret? Sorrow? Were they true feelings or put on for his benefit, to pull him in before devastating him further in this game of cat and mouse?

Mercifully, she tore her gaze from his and settled back in her chair.

"I am," she admitted. "I'll tell you the next part of the story to save your mind from turning to mush with the visions. When I finish, I'll give you what you desire with no consequence. You may leave in the morning with your princess and the children."

"And Noxious?"

"He and I have a different arrangement," she said, clipped and cold before moving on to her story.

Reven stifled the urge to push her further, to delve into her reason for taking Nox as her prisoner, but he quite liked his head on his shoulders, so he bit his tongue and settled in for a story, just like the child he felt he was.

TWENTY-TWO

Nessa Callanan

Reven feared her, that was certain, but he kept her gaze as well as any battle-hardened warrior. It was the blood, to be sure, but he controlled it better than any Allurigard before him, save his father, perhaps. That face, so identical to his father's it was as if she was staring into Reeve's gray-white eyes and not his son's. For a moment... a blink in time... Nessa considered stopping herself from destroying everything she had left. But that was foolish, and so, she conjured a memory... the one when everything started to go wrong.

"Secret walks through the hidden part of the library had become a sort of bonding time with my mother, Queen Lureah. During that time, we discussed her hopes for me and our kingdom — time when we plotted while my father was blissfully unaware the women in his life aspired to much higher positions than a queen and princess of a single, underground kingdom. Time when my mother showed me the truth—that she had kept a dark little secret from her husband, a magic so lethal, it gave even me a chill."

Reven swallowed and opened his mouth but bit his tongue. A wise boy.

"You may speak. This is a conversation," Nessa said, desiring some small thread of connection with him. *Why?* That voice, the bloodthirsty whisper deep in her soul that never truly went to sleep, asked... screamed... why? Why do you care for this boy? No. He was a man, though his features would not age beyond that of nineteen, perhaps twenty without intervention to remove his curse of perpetual life... something they shared in common. She blinked and clenched her jaw while Reven swallowed again.

"Queen Lureah had magical ability? Dark magic?" he asked.

"Indeed. Powerful as the sun. However, as interesting as Lureah's power was, I was particularly absorbed in the history of my birth mother. Her abilities had been cruelly bound by her husband, and their kingdom lived in misery just like mine. So close, and yet I never saw her face, not in person. Once, Lureah almost caught me admiring an illustration of my birth mother, so I hid the book in my dress skirts to take back to my quarters. There, I could read without suspicion."

"So, you wished to know her?"

"Would you not wish to know yours?" Nessa's chest squeezed. She had not meant to remind the boy of what he lost.

He said nothing for a moment, simply stared back at her with vacant, pale eyes. He cleared his throat. "I suppose I would, yes. But that is not the point of your story is it?"

"No, not particularly, but it does provide a foundation. My mother had magic, and so I knew mine might be equally as powerful and *unbound*. If I could harness it, then I might free my birth mother from her husband's clutches. As I was saying, I took the book to study, but my father wanted my company on a trip. When he knocked on my door to request that I accompany him to the Meat Storehouse in Mearhaven, I sighed and shoved the book between my bedding, then wiped my face of all emotion. At ten-years-old, I was required to attend meetings with my father to prepare me for my future role as queen. Of course, I didn't have the heart to tell him my role would change drastically after Asantaval's rise, so I put on my best princess smile and followed him to the wagon.

"Mearhaven was small, and consisted of the meat processing, drying, and storage houses, a few homes where the butchers resided, and a tunnel system that stretched for many marticks before it rose into the so-called Banished Lands. It was the only opening the hunters were permitted to use when leaving Astantaval to surface and hunt.

"Of all the regions in the kingdom, I liked Mearhaven the least. It always smelled of blood and rotting meat, and the people there were rough and hard. I *liked* the people, but it always took a moment to adjust to their ways. By the time I did, it was time to return to Taliskar Castle.

"Along the way, my father listed our tasks which included collecting an updated census recently completed by one of the record-keepers. It seemed the population of Mearhaven dwindled, and this was of great concern to Illaric Callanan, especially since no one else in Astantaval held a candle to the skill and bravery of the hunters Mearhaven produced."

Nessa paused and swallowed. There would be no turning back if she told him this, the first time her people saw her magical ability. Why did this matter? For what reason did she desire this boy to *feel* something for her other than burning hatred and resentment? She licked her lips.

"And?" Reven asked, on the edge of his chair waiting for her to continue.

"I cannot..." Emotion gripped her throat, stinging like she'd swallowed a hive of bees.

"Nessa?" His eyebrows knit together, and he moved to stand, thought better of it, and firmly planted himself in his chair. "Go on, please. I'm listening."

She cleared her throat and her mind, pushed aside all thoughts of this being anything more than an educational conversation, and continued. "I asked if we could take dried meat home to my mother as I took in the sights along the way to Mearhaven—primarily tunnels with a few open spaces for homes built into the rock, a smattering of shops and storage houses, and darkness filled with false, magical lighting. He agreed there was no reason we should not. Then my eyes landed on the weaver's shop. Along a wall, she had displayed several rugs and blankets all crafted with beautiful workmanship, but it was a simple doll that caught my attention. Though I was a bit old for such things, I couldn't help longing for it. My father saw me staring at it from the corner of his eye and slowed the carriage."

Nessa fought the tear that threatened to show her emotion.

"He got the doll for you?"

Nessa covered her pain with a smirk. "Of course. He wandered to the weaver's and knocked on her door, bartered for a moment, then filled the woman's hands with coins and took the doll. We left the exchange with smiles upon our faces. 'A doll befitting a princess,' he said. He dropped the cherub-faced doll with blonde hair and freckles on my lap. I adored it and cradled it as if it were alive, grinning so wide my cheeks ached. By then, we had reached the Narrows—a section of Asantavalian infrastructure that skirted the shore, making it prone to leaks, caving, and flooding. My father had been assured the narrow tunnel had been assessed and safe for his travels, but the unpredictable portion of the passage was just that—as untrustworthy as a hog. The wagon creaked along the tunnel, scraping its sides along the walls as it went. I drew close to my father and clutched the doll tighter."

"I fear how this story ends," Reven said, staring into the fire.

"I felt something in my stomach. It felt wrong, but he assured me it would be alright. The words hardly left his mouth when the magical lighting flickered, then failed. A whoosh echoed through the tunnel moments before my feet felt wet and cold. I screamed and grasped my father's arm, but still he soothed me and encouraged me to hold tight and be his brave girl. The horse bucked and groaned as he worked to convince the beast to back up, but even the most obedient mares reacted poorly when trapped in the Narrows. This one was no different. She balked and thrashed, then smacked her own head on the tunnel wall. I could not see it, of course, but the sickening crack followed by silence was all I needed to know the horse had either broken its neck or knocked itself unconscious."

Nessa paused for a breath. Only thinking of the Narrows and the cave in made her lungs heavy and tight. She focused on the flames licking the back of the fireplace and pressed on. "Fear gurgled in my chest as my stomach knotted further. Father took my hand and tugged, bringing me to the back of the wagon. The water was high now, up to my neck. If we didn't swim fast, we would drown in the miserable passageway, the only way to travel to Mearhaven. I kicked my legs, but my dress skirts slowed me and tangled around my legs as frigid salt water tickled my ear lobes. Father dragged me along, but the freezing water slowed him, too. I knew we would die. I knew it, but the fire in my belly raged. If only I could force the water back out into the sea, even just enough so that we could manage a slow walk back to the widened tunnel where the water drained before reaching the village."

"Your magic was strong even then?" Reven asked.

"Yes, but raw and untested. By then, the water stung my nose, and each breath was stolen as I bobbed above the surface, still too far from the outlet to hope we might reach it before drowning. I would never see the surface, never breathe fresh air—how fitting to drown having never even inhaled a breath of air outside of the caves of Asantaval." Nessa chuckled, half-choked and angry at the memory. "But no. No, I would not have that. I kicked harder, defying my dress but my father's hand went limp. I tugged his hand. He had gone under, likely blacked out. That fire burned hotter until my insides threatened to boil while my skin froze under the sea water. It gurgled in my throat, forcing its way over my tongue and out of my mouth in a silent scream. Vibrations cut through the water, forcing it back and back and back as I screamed. It flowed over me, and my scream echoed in the tunnel. The water receded until there was not a drop left in sight, revealing my unconscious father beside me."

"You pushed the water back into the ocean by screaming at it? How fitting," Reven taunted, but Nessa did not take his bait.

"I pushed my wet dress skirts aside and kneeled beside him, pounding on his chest. I screamed at him to wake up, just open his eyes. Then light splintered from my fingertips, slicing through the darkness. His body seized and thrashed as the light cut through him, surrounded him, and shoved his body around. I cried out, sobbing until his body finally stilled and the light dimmed, leaving me cold and alone. 'Stars above, what was that?' someone said, then I heard the clammer of boots on the rock floor. 'It was the princess. I saw it with my own eyes,' another said."

"They had seen your magic. And now what? Did they fear you immediately?"

"They were confused. My father, woozy and disoriented, sat beside me with his hand over his forehead. I stared down at my hands, unsure whether touching my own father might harm him. People milled around, surveying the area but staying clear of me. He finally stood and took my hand, but I jerked it away. I was afraid I would kill him." Nessa smiled and huffed, remembering her father's soft, kind expression. "'It is alright, my darling. You saved my life,' he said. But the people had oriented themselves. They spoke amongst themselves, claiming I had magic, wondering how it was possible when neither of my parents were magical. Rather than have patience and ensure their royal family was safe, they speculated."

"Did they attack you?" Reven's tone spoke to the color of his soul. Despite her hardened, blackened heart, he still worried she had somehow been treated unkindly and unfairly by her people when she was young. His soul was too kind for this world, which meant he would probably leave it in a most painful and horrific way, but it would not be at her hands.

"No, not then. The people had grown hard and cold over time, yes, but that was to be expected when they lived beneath the ground, never breathing the fresh air, soaking in the sunshine. My father was no longer a favored king, not like he had been when I

207

was first born, and each day he sat on the throne was a gift. I knew this as well as I knew anything, but I kept my mouth shut and let my father spin his lies. He said they had researched the matter thoroughly and had not expected me to show magical ability, but that my mother had gifted family members far back in her bloodlines."

"And they believed him?"

"They were angry he had not admitted it was possible before then, but it was a lie. He could not have told them a thing he had not even known. He assured them it was nothing to be concerned over and agreed to meet with the elders. He promised to have me evaluated before any rash decisions were made. My pulse sped faster every second. What decisions? Would I be forced to leave my home? Would Father be dethroned all because I saved his life with the magic I did not know how to wield? People grumbled all around, but all I heard was the blood rushing in my ears. How could the people, those for whom my family had sacrificed so much to keep alive, hate my father? Anger boiled under my skin, but I swallowed my frustration if only so I did not create a more significant concern for my father. No, to lash out at the simpletons who took my father for granted would not help, so I bit my tongue and towed my anger for another day."

"I have no doubt your anger only mounted from that day on. Magic does that to a soul." Reven whispered the last sentence, likely remembering his beloved Princess Darby was also magical. Her magic could never be cruel, though. This much Nessa learned about the dainty princess. It healed, loved, cured. But it was never devastating. Though it sliced her like a blade to admit it, Nessa admired the princess's abilities.

"It did, some, but my father urged me to head back home with him. His face was strong, stoic even, but the waver in his voice did not match his expression. Father was afraid — of his *people*. To see it, to feel it in the way he grasped my hand, marked me in a way I did not quite understand at only ten years of age, but I knew I would never forget it. I would never forget the way the people looked at me, the way they cleared a path — not because I was their princess, but because they feared me. I asked my father why they were so afraid. I hadn't hurt anyone. 'They fear what they do not understand, Nessa. Your magic is different from the mages here, and as such, it strikes fear in them,' he said. I thought they should at least try to understand but he only pursed his lips and trudged on. He feared an uprising we could not control, and it terrified him.

"Everything fell into place then. I would hone my magic, prove to the people that I might use it for good, to aid them, and to provide for them. If they learned to love me *and* my magic, perhaps it would improve relations between them and my father."

"And did it?" Reven asked, his tone hopeful.

"Where do you sit now, prince? Do you think they accepted me? That they realized my magic might help them rather than harm them?"

He swallowed.

Nessa relaxed. The difficult part was over now, and the boy did not run away or flinch in her presence. He engaged in the conversation, truly connecting with her past. It was more than most, and so she would keep her promise to him. She would give him what he desired most. His mother.

"Now that you know where it turned, leave me, outside the door, to your left. You will find another door. Behind it is what you need most." With that, Nessa let her projection fade, leaving Reven

209

Allurigard alone in the room with a chill and his confusion. There was so much more to tell, but remaining with him in that room would only make her feel... and she couldn't afford such a luxury.

TWENTY-THREE

Eiagan Allurigard

"Lucifer? You said he died, that he was consumed by Nessa's fire," Eiagan said, stroking the horse's neck. Everything about him fell into place then—the way he guarded her door when she was injured, that he only trusted her, the long stares that reached Eiagan's soul. This horse knew her, always had, and once again he stared into the depths of her soul, soothing it, and wrapping it in a sort of understanding that only a loyal horse might.

"He did. I saw it with my—" Emora cut herself short and glanced toward Eiagan with wide eyes. "Do you think it was a ruse?"

Emora's wide eyes meant only one thing, held only one real question. Could Astrid be alive?

Eiagan pursed her lips and fought to control the elation and hope that surged through her body. Hope was one thing, but to wish for

211

something such as that was insanity. "I cannot say. I pray it is so, but we should not assume without further evidence. Our course should remain the same."

Lucifer neighed his content and nuzzled Eiagan and Emora.

"What shall we do now?" Porvarth asked, eyeing Lucifer as if he were not wholly sure of what his eyes saw, despite having seen much grander, much more confusing things.

"We continue with the plan, only now we have a truly brave horse to aid us," Emora said. "You ride him, Eiagan."

Emora kissed Lucifer's neck and patted him, then returned to her horse with Ari. Adrenaline surged through Eiagan's body now, a certain excitement she had not felt in some time. To have even Lucifer back was a blessing, and one she would not take for granted. He nudged her, and so she took that as permission to do as Emora suggested—no saddle, no blanket, nothing between them to diminish the connection between horse and rider. Lucifer did not need a bridle or reins to guide him. He read Eiagan as if his soul was connected to hers.

"What a connection you have with him," Gael said. "I've never seen anything like it."

"Lucifer is more than a horse," Emora said. "He is very nearly human, if you ask me."

The caravan moved several marticks before anyone spoke again, leaving Eiagan with her musings. To hope that Astrid might also be alive *was* foolish, but had they not died on the same day? Did Nessa steal Astrid to inhabit as she had Emora?

Eiagan's thoughts were interrupted when Gael cleared his throat.

"Shall I tell you more or are you sufficiently annoyed so that your ears are closed?" he asked.

"Keep your tales for now. When we make camp, you shall share them."

Gael honored her command and continued toward Vidkun. They would travel a long way before stopping again, or so Eiagan hoped, but there were so many dangers between them and the castle, anything might happen. She longed for a time her kingdom might come together, to be more than it had been over the thousands of years Allurigards held the throne. Once again, her thoughts drifted to what Catia had said about the people preferring Nox over her on the throne. Her musings entertained her for so long, they had covered more land than she realized by the time they reached their stopping point.

"My love, the horses are exhausted." Porvarth's gentle reminder encouraged her to glance down at Lucifer. He would go on forever, but the others drooped, and their riders hardly stayed upon their backs. Eiagan nodded and held Lucifer back.

"We will make camp here for the night as planned, then push through Maltows at first light. With any luck, we will arrive at Vidkun by nightfall tomorrow."

"You heard the lady," Borgard grumbled. "Everyone out, prepare a camp."

Eiagan did not remember putting Borgard in charge of making demands, but she let it go since the people did as he suggested with minimal grumbling. Ari, though, had other plans. He approached her from the right side with a bit of twinkle in his eye.

"Shall we do a bit of training? We can talk if you wish," he said, playfully punching at her arm like the prize fighters in Cicarenthor. Eiagan narrowed her eyes, then punched him with a grin upon her face. Ari's head snapped back, then he grasped his jaw. "Oh, you are a wicked woman. I'll take that back on you in just a moment."

"Find a clearing and I shall join you." Eiagan motioned toward the left side of camp, then surveyed the progress. Two tents had already been pitched, and Borgard grumbled about the quality of the third in progress while Emora and Catia threatened him with all sorts of painful deaths if he did not help them. Erdravac sorted the supplies and began setting out food for dinner. Porvarth stood by Eiagan, watching Gael watch everyone else. Vey and Quix were nowhere in sight, but she assumed they would soon realize the remainder of their group had arrived and join them.

"Do you think he's telling the truth, that Nessa was a Goraninite baby?" Porvarth asked.

"I see no reason to lie about it. I am curious to hear the story, but we will wait until tonight when we've eaten and our minds are focused. I don't want to miss a word thanks to hunger and frustration."

"That is why you quieted him earlier today?" he asked.

"Mmm, yes. I was lost in thought about Lucifer, but after training with Ari, I should be more focused. Would you try to speak to Emora once the camp is prepared?"

"Of course." Porvarth pecked her cheek and wandered away, making his usual jokes.

Once the camp was settled, Eiagan and Ari separated from the rest and found a clearing wide enough to train. He tossed her a heel of bread, something to sustain her until dinner was complete. She gulped it down in a few bites, ready to spar until her muscles wouldn't move. Eiagan had not, though, anticipated Ari taunting her into rage for their training.

"The trust between us is more than that of friends, Eiagan. You are a sister to me in almost every sense, and I do hope that you see me as a brother." Ari was no fool. He knew well that suggesting he

214

was Eiagan's brother, if only by impending marriage, would rouse emotions she still had not fully resolved. *Reeve.* And thinking of Reeve only made her think of Reven and how she could not fail. This was more than reclaiming her kingdom, protecting it from a psychotic mage. It was about restoring her family and creating one that would never break again. She would not rise to the occasion, though, and taunted him in return.

"Should I take that to mean you finally intend to propose to my sister?" Eiagan asked, turning slowly toward her right so that she might strike another way. This was good. It was Ari's plan, but Eiagan had to admit that there was great merit in sparring with him. She held her focus, reminded herself that she did not have to *kill* to protect herself. When her opponent picked at the scabs from her past, she could use them to center herself rather than fuel that instinctual desire to murder her enemies.

"Should I take that to mean you would approve?" he asked, dancing away from Eiagan's swipe. Quick on his feet though muscular and tall, Eiagan found it difficult to find his weak point— though, admittedly, she truly had not put everything she had into the fight. Doing so might ruin any advancement she had made in controlling the darkness, the anger that made her so paranoid she could hardly keep her focus on any single thing.

"I would, and I do wish you would ease her worry that you might not ask her," she said, then dodged his jab. A fist that size to her face would knock her out.

"The truth?" Ari flung a series of jabs at Eiagan, but she dodged each one like a trained dancer.

"I expect it." Eiagan ducked low and swiped her leg out, but not fast enough. Ari jumped it, then countered with a shove that almost knocked her off balance—almost. Eiagan rammed her shoulder into

215

his gut, forcing a sputter before he bent at the waist. "I forgot you fight dirty. Give me a breath."

Eiagan eased back and shook her arms, forcing them to relax while Ari caught his breath.

Once he did, he leaned against a tree and stared up into the canopy. Eiagan allowed him to collect his thoughts, knowing well how hard everything had become. Nothing was easy. *Nothing.* And where love was concerned, nothing ever *had* been easy.

"The truth is that I love her. I would die for her, kill for her... I *have* killed for her. But my time in the dungeons changed me, Eiagan. Knowing that Keirnor has touched her sickens me, but I cannot, no matter how hard I want to, stop seeing him with her."

Eiagan let out a forced breath. *That* was not a problem with an easy solution either. "What about the dungeon changed you?"

Ari swiped his dark hair from his face and the sweat from his brow. "I cannot pinpoint an exact thing, but it's more... it's everything. I am tired. I am hardened in more ways than I was before. And why should she suffer with a husband who cannot touch her without growing sick thinking of another man—"

"Stop. Just... stop for one moment." Eiagan's own stomach had lost its fortitude merely thinking of the things Keirnor and Nessa had done to Emora. To put herself in Ari's position, or worse, in Emora's, was more than she could bear in addition to the atrocities she had already endured.

"I did not mean to anger you," Ari said, his comforting gaze settled on Eiagan's face.

"You did not. I was merely sick at the thought myself. Have you said this to her? Have you asked her to talk about it with you?"

Ari shook his head. "It seems Porvarth is the only one who can reach her where that is concerned. I think it is his kind heart and soft tone that lull her into telling him her innermost thoughts."

"You sound as if you wish it were you." Eiagan could not deny the pang of jealousy that Porvarth had a connection with anyone other than her, but to keep him from doing what he did best — healing the hearts and minds and souls of others — would be akin to putting him in a cage. And that was something Eiagan would never do.

"I do. Don't think I haven't noticed the same between us. This connection we have is as undeniable as theirs, but I think that is acceptable. I think that is what family does, is it not?"

Eiagan chuckled. "How would I know?"

Ari joined her laughter and pushed off the tree. "How indeed. I wouldn't know either." Ari gazed toward the wagon where Emora and Porvarth conversed. "Do you ever doubt your love for the loxmore?"

Eiagan followed his gaze and caught Porvarth's smile just moments before he shifted his gaze to search for her. Once his eyes connected with Eiagan's, his grin grew, then he turned back to Emora.

"No, not anymore."

"I heard tales that Noxious was in love with you. Was it true?" Ari asked, pressing further.

"A lot of questions today, Ari." Eiagan dragged her eyes away from Porvarth and back to Ari. "There were times I wondered if it was love or dependency with Porvarth, but I know that it's love. I would not be the same without him. I don't doubt my love for him. And what you heard was true, Noxious was once in love with me."

217

"And?" Ari asked, worse than the elderly ladies gossiping around the wells.

"I loved him, but I could never be with him. He was descended from my brother-in-law, and as such he bore a shocking resemblance to my late husband. I never could stop seeing that, seeing Zero in him. It wasn't fair to Nox, but it was not something I could control."

"And yet, he is one of your dearest friends now. How?" Ari held his breath, seeking some grain of wisdom that might aid him in moving past his own visions and hesitancy.

Until then, Eiagan had not realized how her relationship with Nox had grown. She *had* known they were close, but when had the vision of Zero faded? When was the first time she looked upon Nox and saw him, not her beloved Zero?

"I cannot say. It merely changed in time, and I am glad for it. Perhaps the same will be true for you, should you decide you love my sister enough to fight against those visions that tell you she was not yours all that time."

Ari ran his fingers over his lips, his gaze lost in the void as his mind focused on something else entirely. Perhaps he thought of her kisses, those before Nessa had taken her from him. Perhaps it was something else entirely, but once his gaze refocused, he swallowed.

"Was she?" Ari's voice trembled, his lower lip wavering with each stolen breath. He was a man on the verge of a spiral, one that Eiagan knew well.

Eiagan gripped his arm to ground him, then said, "I think she was. I think, in those times that she was lost and alone, she thought of you. I believe that is how she survived it all. Everything that happened to her... *everything, Ari*... I believe you were the one thing she might think of to hold on until I returned."

Ari swallowed again and licked his lips. Eiagan knew the sick feeling in his stomach too, the one that made him keep swallowing the bile and licking his lips like a sick dog. "Porvarth nearly went out of his mind while you were gone. He did, truly, and I think I might have been the only one who really understood how he felt."

"Life does not promise to be fair, Ari. You are only promised that you will live, with no guarantee of the sort of life you will have. I think what we do now, how we approach our lives with Emora and Porvarth, that will be the true test of our strength."

Ari nodded. "I agree with you, but am I strong enough for it?"

Eiagan chuckled. "I think of anyone in our family, you are the most equipped to survive it. You have thus far. Now, let us head back to camp before it gets too dark to see our hands in front of our faces."

"Or to see a sneak attack," Ari said, then tackled Eiagan to the ground.

Eiagan fell face-first into the dirt but came to her senses fast enough to roll and pin Ari with his face in the mud—a fitting turn of events for such a dastardly move. He wiggled for a moment before Eiagan removed her knee from his shoulder and let him up. With a smirk, she shoved him and headed toward the wagon to gather a change of clothing.

"That was cruel," Ari called behind her.

"Yet necessary to ensure you know your place." Eiagan reached the wagon just as Emora was wrapping up her conversation with Porvarth. She smiled and stepped down from the wagon while Porvarth leaned over the edge, resting his head on his arm.

"How are you feeling?" he asked, his bright blue eyes filled with something akin to happiness.

"Improved. How is Emora?" Eiagan sipped from her water canteen, desperate to quench her thirst but sure she might vomit if she drank too fast.

Porvarth sat straighter and sighed. "Also improved I think, but it will be some time before she can fully recover. She fears Ari no longer cares for her as he once did."

"I believe he does but it will take them both time to recover from what Nessa did to them." Eiagan climbed into the wagon and accepted the meat Porvarth offered.

"If I could kill Nessa a thousand times over, I am not sure it would ever be enough." Porvarth spat the bitter words then bit into a chunk of meat. "I think I might enjoy watching you skin her bit by bit, all while she is awake to feel it."

Eiagan's eyes widened, shocked for likely the first time in her life, at the words that spilled from the kind-hearted man's mouth. She swallowed her bite then took Porvarth's hand, earning his full attention. His shoulder softened and his face took a somber expression. Eiagan's words were not necessary. He'd realized the cruelty of his own statement.

"I know. We must never become like her, but the things she did to your sister were abominable. I am not at liberty to share Emora's trauma, but it is vast and cannot be easily remedied."

Eiagan blinked, releasing a tear she had fought hard to hold back. Knowing what Emora went through, to think of it made Eiagan's entire body ache. A chill shot up her spine thinking of her time in the dungeon when Keirnor had taken liberty against her by kissing her. It had been a shock, and for a moment Eiagan was unable to process thought well enough to fight back. She had only escaped her grave the day before, but even so, the vile assault should have sparked a violent response—something more than biting his lip.

"What are you thinking about?"

Eiagan shook her head and nibbled her meat again, but Porvarth would not be put off so easily. He turned her to face him, his eyes scanning her face as he searched for any sign she might be in pain, lost, confused... anything *but* alright.

"What did he do to you?" he asked, his teeth clenched as he forced each word through. His cheeks flushed, and his eyes sparked with anger.

"It is over, and Ari and Tend were there to help me through it. I do not wish to —"

Porvarth's nostrils flared, and the telltale signs of a shift exhibited themselves.

Eiagan pulled him closer and held his biceps in either hand, then pressed her forehead against his. "Breathe, Porvarth. Breathe and calm yourself. There is no need to let the dragon take over. I will tell you what happened."

Porvarth sucked in air, gasping like a fish on the shores. "I... cannot... breathe." His skin burned and his body trembled. He pulled away from her and scrambled from the wagon. "I... I need to fly."

The loxmore shifted and shot into the sky in one fluid motion, then circled above them, screeching until the trees shook. Erdravac stepped beside Eiagan, followed by Ari.

"What happened?" Ari asked, shifting his gaze toward Eiagan.

"He knows something happened in the dungeon... with Keirnor." Eiagan stared into the sky, now black and filled with twinkling stars around a crescent moon. "He has never been so angry, at least, not as a dragon."

"He could not control it?" Erdravac asked.

"He might have but… but perhaps it is better to release the anger than to hold it in." Eiagan realized in that moment, that split-second of clarity, that perhaps that was also her situation. Perhaps, if she let the anger take her and focused it on something she could not harm, then it might clear her mind. She needed more than training sessions with Ari. She needed something to fight, something physical in front of her to take her blows.

"Porvarth, come back!"

Porvarth screeched one last time, then darted toward the forest floor. He shifted mid-landing and landed on two feet before shaking off the last of his scales. Ari tossed him a pair of pants and a tunic, then grasped Erdravac by the arm to lead him away. It was a private matter, and one Eiagan was sure would not be easy to discuss.

"What is the matter with you? You suspect something happened and rather than listen to me, you behave like a fledgling dragon? You are better than that, Porvarth." Eiagan pressed her lips together, biting off more words at the sight of his glare.

"Do not tell me how I should react to the very idea that disgusting man did something to you!" Porvarth leaned in so the rest of the camp couldn't overhear. "Emora told me things, the things he did to her when she *was* in her right mind and couldn't stop him. How do you think Ari would react if he knew that?"

Eiagan turned on her heel and buckled over before purging what little she'd eaten. Emora hadn't even shared that with her, and likely would never tell Ari. The pain in her stomach, like the twist of a knife each time she considered what Emora must have felt during that time all because *she* had died. Eiagan was not there to protect her. She was not there when Astrid died, not there to ensure Nessa did not steal Emora, she just… wasn't there.

In an instant, Porvarth flipped from seething to understanding as he held her hair away from her face and gently stroked her cheek. Eiagan wiped her mouth and accepted the water Porvarth offered her. After a few sips, she handed it back and climbed back into the wagon. Emora eyed her from a distance, as did most of the caravan, but Porvarth pulled her back into their own private conversation when he sat between Eiagan and their stares.

"Tell me, please, what he did. What happened?"

Eiagan licked her lips. "He only kissed me. He forced me against the wall in my cell, then kissed me. When I came to my senses, thanks to Tend, Ari, and Borgard, I bit him. I almost killed him, but the guards stopped me before I got my hands on him well enough."

"You swear that there is no more? That is the full truth?"

Eiagan let her eyes meet his. "Would you disown me if there had been more?" She hated how her voice cracked, how it betrayed her weakness even with Porvarth. To be wanted and needed and loved by him was everything to her, but to show her own weakness in this way, after feeling violated and abused, it was like salt in her wounds.

"Is that all you think of me? That my love is so easily tainted by the actions of another, that I would turn my back against you?" His eyes searched Eiagan's, hurt and worried. When she did not answer, he said, "I would never, no matter what he did, turn away from you. I would not even if he'd had you a thousand times, because I am the one who holds your heart. I do, though, wish he were alive so that I could carve out his heart and feed it to him for supper."

Tears slipped over the apples of both cheeks, stinging Eiagan's eyes. She sniffled. "Here I am, whining about a kiss when Emora... God in Heaven, what she must be going through."

"We went through different things, but our wounds are the same," Emora said, surprising Eiagan when she settled beside her on the wagon bench. Eiagan almost chastised herself for not hearing her approach, but she was tired—tired of being alert, tired of chastising herself when she was not. Just tired.

The others climbed into the back of the wagon—Ari, Borgard, Erdravac, Gael, and Catia—all packed like a basket of salted fish, each with indecipherable expressions upon their faces.

"We were talking amongst ourselves, and we came to a conclusion," Emora said. "We each have our traumas, yet instead of leaning on one another and allowing our wounds to heal, we try to hide them and remain strong in front of one another. I suggest that we stop hiding what harms us and share it now."

Eiagan's throat seized, and her lips parted. Porvarth tensed beside her. "What do you mean," he asked.

"That we speak now. We speak and we help each other, and we promise that nothing said here leaves this space." Erdravac's pleading gaze reached Eiagan, just as her sister's insistent tugging at her sleeve.

"I suppose it cannot hurt." Porvarth shifted his weight so that he could see over the bench.

"Let us sit by the fire. It will be warmer, and perhaps we might find courage staring into the flames," Ari said, rising so that he might lead the way.

Eiagan followed, but deep in her gut she wondered if their tales of woe and pain would aid her recovery, or only make her wish she might smite all those who hurt her beloved family. As they encircled the fire, Eiagan sorted through five centuries of pain and want and need, finding it difficult to pinpoint exact moments that needed attention. And it was then, in that very moment, Eiagan realized her entire life had been little more than a series of traumas sprinkled with a dozen moments of happiness. Should she share her life story and spend all eternity at that fire, or bite her tongue and suffer as she had since the day she was born? Her question was left in the air when Erdravac offered to speak first.

TWENTY-FOUR

Reven Allurigard

Reven took each step with hesitation and a sense that his hope would only lead to heartache, but he pressed on toward the mysterious door all the same. There was no sign of Nessa save the chill that took the air whenever she left a room. Rather, when her projection left the room, leaving Reven wondering if he had *ever* seen the woman in her true form, in flesh and bone. How powerful was she in her true form if her projection could do so much?

He closed his eyes and centered himself with a deep breath before pulling the door open. Inside was a fully furnished quarters—a lush bed with a chest at the foot, an armoire and chest of drawers, beautiful tapestries that opened to... not a *window*, but a large painting of a meadow. Reven's gaze swept over the room several times before landing on a petite woman staring at him with wide, brown eyes.

She was clean, hair neatly kept, and her clothing was well mended. Though thin, she was in no way undernourished. Her cheeks were pink and full, but those lips… they parted in awe as her eyes swept over him again.

"Reeve?" she croaked, her fingers tightening on the paintbrush she held. Beside her was an easel with a stretched canvas, hardly covered with paint. Splatters of darkness dotted her face as it did the canvas, but Reven hardly noticed them. Instead, he matched her shock.

He blinked, finally, breaking their stare. "No. No, not… not Reeve." His throat constricted, holding back every tear he'd held in since the news of his mother's death had reached his ears. His chest grew heavy, his feet, his hands. He could not move. "It is me, Mother. Reven."

Astrid dropped the paintbrush and gasped, then shook her head. "No. You are a vision."

Reven shook his head. "No, not a vision. Nessa, she sent me here."

His heart dropped. A vision. This woman was not his mother, not the beloved Astrid everyone had missed as much as they had missed Hazel. It was a trick put on by Nessa to drive him to insanity. It would not work. He wouldn't let her use his mother's memory to push him over the edge, to a state where he might do her bidding without question. Reven turned away, his hand on the door.

She grasped his other hand.

She was real… flesh… his mother's touch.

"You are real," she whispered.

Reven swallowed. "I am. Are… are *you?*"

227

Astrid huffed and smiled. "I have been waiting for this day forever. Have you come to rescue me, my son?"

Confusion flooded Reven, filling his mind with more questions than he might ever ask, but he would not leave the prison without her. Whatever Nessa's plans might be, he would not allow her to use his mother to fulfill them. But then… had she intended to allow Astrid to leave with him?

"What is her plan, Mother? Everyone believes you are dead. How am I looking at you now?"

Astrid swallowed. Her dark eyes swept the room, then settled on him again. "I woke here after she attacked me in the forest with Emora." Her eyes widened. "Emora! Is she —"

"Safe, Mother. And Eiagan is alive, risen from her place in the Bleak as Simorana had planned all along."

Her face paled then, all color drained starch as the canvas behind her. "Eiagan is alive? And Emora is free?"

Reven tugged his mother closer, a protective urge overwhelming him.

"Indeed. Mother, what is happening?" Reven's anxiety peaked, and adrenaline surged through his body, ready to fight to the death to ensure his mother, Darby, and the children escaped this Hell even if he had to die to ensure it.

Astrid smiled. "It's time, my son. It's time."

"Time for what, Mother?" He gripped his mother's shoulders still uncertain he could trust this sudden change. "This room is beautiful. Almost as if she took care of you. Everything is so normal and pretty."

"She did, but only because she wanted a family, Reven. All of this, it was to buy me, to pull me away from those I loved most. To punish those she thinks took everything from her. Your aunts."

Reven ran a hand through his black hair and groaned. If only someone would offer information that made *sense* to him. Of course, Nessa's past was riddled with agonizing pain, but neither Eiagan nor Emora were to blame. In fact, they had endured many of the same circumstances, even come close to following the same dark path that Nessa had. However, taking Astrid and then Noxious, taking the children, and taking him *did* serve to punish Eiagan and Emora. But to what end?

"What is her plan? How does she want this to end?" Reven asked.

"With her in their place, of course." Astrid snickered at the foolish words. "It's as if she believes she can eliminate them and simply step into their place, family intact."

Reven met her chuckle and asked, "How does she intend to sway the minds of those left behind? Porvarth? Ari? They will never—"

"She'll kill them, Reven. She will kill any who do not bend to her will, and those who do will be caged like me. Make no mistake, she will bring more here and keep us—"

"Wait, wait... Noxious is here. She made an arrangement with him. We are to be released, Mother."

Astrid's eyes clouded and she lowered her gaze. "What?"

"She will release us tomorrow." Wouldn't she? Or was it a ruse to inspire him to be grateful he had his mother back and not question his imprisonment.

"I do not know what to think of it," Astrid admitted.

"Come, let's take you back to our room. Surely, Noxious will know what to do."

She did not fight him, but her confusion was great. She seemed half-lost, no longer the epitome of clarity she had been only moments before. She blinked and narrowed her eyes but followed him all the same. Reven only prayed his friend would know what

229

to do, for if he did not, Reven feared they might all live through this Hell every day until they died... if they *ever* died.

Astrid's confusion remained as they wandered from her room — where she hesitated at the exit but followed with a gentle tug on her arm — and down the hallway. Whatever she thought about Nessa was clouded by years spent captive. A chill spread over Reven. Was she even right, or was her mind distorted beyond saving? He clenched his jaw and continued toward the tower room where Darby and Nox awaited, praying one of them could help her.

He wanted his family back, but even with his mother standing beside him, Reven felt empty. He should find himself in the middle of a joyous reunion, yet all he could do was ponder how this played into Nessa's plans. A reunion with his dead mother... the mage even ruined that moment. But as sure as he breathed, he would find his happy ending if he had to kill Nessa himself to have it.

TWENTY-FIVE

Noxious "The Savage" Skjoldsson

Violet played in the corner with her friends seemingly happy, though she was quite ready to go home. Nox hadn't grown the courage to tell her they might never go home. An aching took his chest then, wondering if the child would have a better life if he allowed Darby to take Violet with her rather than live trapped in Nessa's world with him. In his heart, he knew the answer. He merely needed to ask the princess for this favor but doing so ripped his heart to shreds. How would he survive without his beloved Violet?

Nox licked his lips and brushed his fingers over Darby's shoulder. She sat over a book anxiously awaiting Reven's return, so she startled when he touched her.

"Apologies, princess. I did not mean to startle you."

231

"No, I'm sorry," she said. "I'm so jumpy when Reven is out of my sight. Why do you suppose he has been gone for so long?" She closed the book but would receive no reply, nor could Nox ask her to provide for Violet. Nessa opened the door, distracting them both.

She entered the room wearing a dress, something Nox had not seen before. Her usual leather pants and tunic were indicators she was ever ready for a fight, but now she looked more the part of a princess. The only thing that dampened her beauty was that dreadful, devilish smile.

"Noxious, might I have your audience, please?" Nessa asked.

"Please? Since when do you request anything of me so kindly?" Even so, Nox left Darby and went to the door, where Nessa waited for him to follow her politely phrased command.

"Papa?" Violet ran across the room and grasped her father's leg.

"It will be alright, darling. Play with your friends, and I will return soon."

Violet's gaze shifted to Nessa, and she scowled but said nothing. She hugged Nox and ran back to her friends but did not take her eyes off them until Nox closed the door behind him. He followed Nessa, her green dress skirts trailing behind her like an unraveling carpet down the corridor. She took him to a sparsely furnished room and closed the door before taking a seat in a chair near the fire. Had this been where she brought Reven? Where was the young prince?

"Where is Reven?" Nox sat in the vacant chair near Nessa, poised for unwelcome news.

"He is safe if that is what you mean to ask. Reuniting with his mother, I would assume." She folded her hands on her lap while waves of blonde hair fell over her shoulders.

Was she trying to entice him? Surely, she knew — then her words fell on his ears, and he processed them, picked them apart. "His *mother?*"

"Indeed, she is alive. They are likely having a grand reunion now, possibly plotting my death." Nessa shrugged, and that feisty spark in her dimmed. Something had changed, though determining what it might be was an impossible task. And not one Nox cared to undertake.

"Dare I ask *how* she is alive?"

She shrugged again. "I needed Emora. Astrid and Lucifer were in the way, so I merely created an illusion and transported them here. Lucifer escaped, the blasted horse, but Astrid has been here all along, safe and sound."

"Perhaps safe but I would think not sound if she has been locked away all this time." Nox scoffed, unable to determine whether he believed her or not. Even so, after everything he had seen, he was hard-pressed *not* to believe in the impossible. After all, Eiagan had risen from the grave. Why not Astrid? Why not...

Nessa shook her head. "I'm afraid not."

"What?" Nox narrowed his eyes on her and scowled.

"I see the question in your eyes, but Hazel is gone. I have destroyed my brain trying to find a way to bring her back, but alas, I can only do so much." She stared into the fire, still not revealing her reason for bringing him to this private room.

"You expect me to believe you have tried to bring my wife back to me? For what reason?"

She shifted her gaze back to him. "I am not a monster like you believe me to be. Perhaps I am cold and calculating, but no more so than your beloved Eiagan. I have done no more and no less than she has, yet you see me as the enemy. Why?"

Nox almost choked on his own spit. "Why? You sit there knowing all you have done and ask me why?"

"I do. Just because I have killed people you love does not mean I am worse than a woman who killed other people. Simply because she killed those who had no meaning to you, you offer her forgiveness over me." She leaned forward as if sharing a secret. "In case you didn't know, those she killed had families who loved them, too."

"That is far from true." Nox ground his teeth. Eiagan had only killed for necessity. Robbers, thieves, murderers, rapists... those were among her sum of lives taken. Not innocent blood.

"Do not sit there and assume you know everything about her. I have lived longer than even she has, and I know the things she has done. She has killed as many innocent people as I have, perhaps more, all in the name of keeping that throne. Your life is but a blink of time compared to hers, so do not assume you know her well enough to know all the things she has done." Nessa stood and paced, her dress swirling around her with each turn. "All she had to do was walk away. Give up the crown, and she might have been happy. But did she? No. No, she went on killing sprees to eliminate those who hated her."

"She didn't kill children."

"Didn't she? Do you think no one froze to death during her winter? Poor, innocent, sick children died every day thanks to the things she did."

"She didn't take joy in it the way you do, I am sure," Nox said, ignoring the way her words fell on him. Had Eiagan known children would die? Would she have changed anything she'd done if she had known what would happen to innocent people?

234

Nessa sighed. Minutes ticked by before she stood and began her pacing again. "I am no fool. I know there must be some end to this dance I have initiated with her but do not play me for a simpleton. I know the moment you find a way, you will escape and run back to her like you always do."

"I am a man of my word. You promised me the children would go free and in exchange, I will stay."

"And they will go tomorrow. I wanted to reunite Reven with his mother first." She sat again and settled her gaze on Nox... pale gray, almost white... she hadn't truly let him see it until now. She blinked, but they remained the same. She licked her lips. "I never killed a child on purpose, though I know my actions killed them regardless. I will honor my promise to you and release them all tomorrow."

"Not only release them but ensure their safety. I will not have you twisting my words and dropping them in the middle of The Banished Lands." Nox crossed his arms, trying to hide that he shook at the very thought Violet might be dropped in the frozen land to die.

"I had not considered such a thing. They will be returned to Goranin in a safe place." She shifted in her chair, moving herself a bit farther from his gaze. "Would you find Sudyak Meadow suitable?" She arched an eyebrow.

Those eyes... For a moment, he almost offered her the same forgiveness he had given Eiagan a thousand times... a million times... as many times as she needed it. But he hardened his heart for Hazel's sake, for the sake of all those he loved who had died, thanks to her insatiable desire to take what did not belong to her. She merely stared at him. He knew that sort of stare and had seen it in the eyes of many women who had looked upon him, but hers was *different* in some way. She longed for him, yes, but in her eyes, there was also acceptance, knowing he would never be hers. She'd already considered it, known how it would end, and dismissed it without a fight.

Nox swallowed and looked away, back into the fire. The dragon scraped along his mind, asking him permission to rip her throat out. She was only a projection. It would do no good to try, so he scolded the beast back into its place.

"That is suitable but close to Vidkun, where my family might find them, please."

"Reven, Darby, and Astrid will be with them. They will be safe anywhere in the meadows."

He glanced at her, not quite doubting her statement but unable to fathom she might *actually* let them go. "Near the castle, please."

"As you wish," she whispered, still staring at him as if he might disappear if she blinked.

"Why did you bring me here?"

"To this room? To this castle?" she asked, her tone shifting toward whimsical.

"Both." Nox's grumble put her right back into a defensive stance. Her moment of whimsy was gone, and in its place, a calculating and cold woman once again.

"I brought you to my castle so you might have peace. You do not see it now, but soon you will. You only needed to be away from her for a while to know the truth. She does not appreciate you as she should, but I will even if you never care about me enough to bid me a good morning. As for this room, it will be yours tomorrow. I will prepare it for you and the one next door for Violet."

Nox never knew what to say to this woman. She was more confusing than any he had ever met before, and as such, he concluded she must be entirely insane. Even Nessa did not know what she truly wanted, or it was something so unreasonable, so impossible that she would never truly achieve it. She would die trying, though, without question, and she would take anyone she pleased along with her on her path to Hell.

He scowled lest she mistake his confusion for giving in. "Fine."

"So that you know, I will never break a promise I make to you." It was a whisper, the kind that likely slipped from its speaker's mouth by accident, but once it had entered the air it could not be retrieved. She inhaled slowly and licked her lips. "I only want honesty between us even if you do not see that."

"Then why do you tell lies?"

Her gaze snapped to his again, indignant, then accepting. "It is true I have in the past, but that was before, and now I want something different."

"Something different? Are you telling me you no longer want the throne of Goranin? Of Varrow and all the surrounding kingdoms for your own?"

She chuckled. "Oh no, I still want those, and I will take them, but my reason has shifted from one of pure revenge and hatred to one of... shall we say... a selfish need."

"Revenge and hatred are selfish needs, but I will humor you. What has brought on this desire for change?" Nox did not believe a word that slipped from her tongue, but he was intrigued all the same. He would relay this information to Darby so she might share it with Eiagan and the others. Perhaps there was enough in her claims to formulate a plan against her.

"Many things can bring about a change of heart, though I suppose I have not truly *changed* my heart. I will take what I want and kill anyone who stands in my way, but I will not destroy the lands in the name of Asantaval as I had planned. I will bring it to

237

life again under my rule. But those desires pale in comparison to one that has taken my mind entirely."

Bile churned in Nox's stomach, but he asked anyway. "What?"

Nessa's pale face flushed pink, and she lowered her face and gaze to her lap. "I want a family."

Nox laughed, a roar that startled her so much she jumped. "You want a family? After everything you have done to the people of these lands, you expect them to allow you to apologize and have a family? You must understand the *meaning* of family before you can claim one, Nessa."

She stood again, unprovoked by his outburst.

"Have you ever considered how incredibly sad it is that I do not know the meaning, Noxious?"

He stood, meeting her wavering gaze. She could not keep his eye contact, and this was her undoing. She told the truth, finally, and it revealed her weakest point. Noxious almost felt sorry for her knowing how well he would use her emotions against her, how he would twist her world inside out before yanking away the very thing she wanted most. But then, as if she knew his heart and mind, she stepped away from him.

"I did not mean with you." She turned her back to him and stood straight. "Or with any of them."

Them. Them, his family, the people he loved most. Would she kill them all? Was releasing the children all a ruse to earn his trust?

"Oh, you did not? Then why, pray tell, am I here?"

"To listen. To understand. And perhaps... perhaps to..." She choked on the words, leaving them open.

"To forgive?"

"Even if I succeeded in bringing you Hazel back, you would not forgive me for the same reason you could never *fully* love her.

238

Eiagan will always have that hold over you and no matter what another woman does, she would never distract you from that single-minded desire."

"I *loved* my wife!" Nox's roar echoed through the room, but she did not flinch again.

Instead, she squared her shoulders and met his fury. "I know that you did! But you could never let go of that last small spark you held for Eiagan. You know that it is true, Noxious. Do not lie to yourself."

How the woman saw right into his soul was beyond him, but it was true. He loved Hazel desperately, but that everlasting spark for Eiagan would never, ever disappear. He would never act upon it, never pay it a single moment of attention ever again, but it did exist. It always had. Nox shifted her attention from something she might use against him to something that would blow her world, her desire apart.

"You know, you might have had everything you desire if you had only thought about your choices."

"Eiagan took everything from me!" She huffed now, heated and angry, her eyes blazing with fury.

"You might have shared it with her! Did you ever, even once, think of what might have been if you'd only approached her? You might have saved Reeve. Might have aided her in killing Icluedian and ruling Goranin. Instead, she did it alone. Perhaps with Zero, yes, but what she truly needed all her life was—"

"Stop!" Nessa held her hand up, cutting him off midsentence. "S... stop... please."

Nox observed while the full weight of his words fell over her. He had meant it as a distraction, but it was true. If Nessa had approached Eiagan, offered her proof of her identity and all the things Icluedian had done to her, Eiagan's story... *Nessa's* story...

and even Emora's might have been different. All those truths crashed around her, swallowed her whole, and brought her to her knees.

Nessa sobbed.

Nox swallowed a lump in his throat, not one that was forced there by fear or worry, but because now — *now* — she was human. This woman, this insanity in human flesh, had become human before his eyes. She was ruthless, a murderer, darkness and death enveloped in a beautiful package. But she was also broken. As broken as Eiagan, and by the same man, the same life, the same *everything*. What little empathy Nox had for this broken thing had, somehow, shifted. Despite every instinct to kick her while she was down, to douse her wounds with flame, Noxious instead kneeled beside her.

"Perhaps you were correct in your assessment, but not wholly," he said.

She ignored him and continued to sob. It was not for show, not an act to draw him in. It was raw and true, the sobs of a woman so tired from life, so beaten and bruised, so twisted around by her circumstances that there was nothing left for her but this — the final decision. Would she give up and give in to loss, or let her vengeance push her right into the grave?

"I do see your pain, Nessa. I see it, and I feel it as I do Eiagan's. The reality is that it is the same as mine, the same as many. I am only sorry we have met this way and not another. No matter what you've done, and no matter how I hate you for it, the truth remains. You deserved better. You both did."

Shock coursed through him, not at Nessa's actions, but because he meant what he said. Heaven help him, he felt sorry for her. He'd known Icluedian only through the history books, through his family's tales, and from Eiagan's own stories, but he couldn't imagine meeting the man face-to-face would surprise him in the least. Nox knew the man well enough to know that this woman had been tortured in ways that would make even the strongest of men wail. Sickened to his core by his own sympathy, Nox closed his eyes and prayed for the right thing to say… to do… anything that would end this war before more innocent life was taken.

TWENTY-SIX

Nessa Callanan

The brutality of this moment weighted on Nessa's shoulders so heavily, she came undone. What had she done? Could it truly have been that easy? Noxious spoke, but Nessa hardly heard his words. They were likely more hurtful, angry words of no use to her while her entire life shattered before her. Icluedian was the enemy. He had *always* been the enemy, and he was common among them... among Eiagan and Emora and Reeve and... her. Nessa knew the truth but until that moment, until she saw that flash in his eyes that said he might have been hers in another life, she hadn't truly considered what she might have gained if she'd done everything differently.

A brush over her shoulder froze her in place. He would kill her. Noxious would know her form was real, no projection this time. She

242

had come here in flesh and blood and bone, risking everything to be true to her promise. She could not very well be honest with him if she appeared as a projection, and as such she had convinced herself he would not know the difference and she would be safe. But he touched her now. *He touched her.*

For a blink, Nessa imagined he touched her in kindness, that his fingers brushing over her shoulder meant something more than testing her reality. But that moment passed with a breath.

"You are real? You are here in body?" he asked, his breath catching.

In a fluid motion, Nessa sprung to her feet and distanced herself from him. Nox stayed in place, eyes wide and mouth agape.

"Keep that dragon in its place or I swear, I will—"

"I will," he whispered. He licked his lips and motioned toward the chair. "I'm sitting."

He sat but kept his gaze on Nessa. Her heart went wild, but she couldn't escape, not without using her magic. Doing so would weaken her to the point she could not project for days. She needed her projections. Eiagan and the others would not hesitate to put a sword through her skull if she appeared in person.

"I have to leave. Will you allow me or—"

Nox sprang from his seat, thought better of it, and sat again. "Wait. Wait, do not leave yet. I need to know more. Heaven help my foolish mind, I need to know what turned you into this. Thus far, Reven's visions have told us nothing more than the story of an abandoned child with a bright future. Perhaps your father was a bit daft and your mother conniving, but those hardly account for what you have become."

It was a trick to keep her there, she knew, but when he looked at her that way, she could deny him nothing. Against her judgment

243

and that screaming voice in her head that told her to run, she sat. If this was to be her last day upon earth, she would prefer it spent with him anyway.

"Asantaval had no seasons, at least, none that might be marked by the usual signs like blooming flowers, a leaf's change of color, a fresh snowfall, but by the chill in the air, my father was sure the dead of winter had befallen our family. He sat across from the Council, the very one that would determine the fate of the Callanan family and its reign, while Mother and I took our places in the chairs behind him. When the chief elder settled his steel gaze on Father's face, he knew they had already made their decision, that he would not be able to plead for our family, that we would — at best — be run out of Astantaval."

"For what?" Nox asked though not impatiently as before.

"I will get to that part. This is important." When he did not ask *why* it was important, Nessa went on. "Father sat straighter, a lackluster attempt at commanding a room filled with men who would sooner he drop dead than rule for another day. My Uncle Bribadge was not a part of the meeting, but if and when my father found himself unseated, it would be within reason to suspect his brother and his family would also be ejected from their home — or killed, if luck did not shine on them that day. Dall, the Chief Elder, pointed that long, gnarly finger at my father and said, 'It has come to our attention that Princess Ellenessia has no control over her ability, and as such, she is a danger to the people of Asantaval. Your failure to disclose that your wife, Queen Lureah, maintained magical ability in her ancestral line, is a direct assault against our code of laws, as you well know. We have no other choice but to relieve you of your position, and to immediately expel you from Asantaval.'" Nessa snickered. "I could not forget his words if I wanted to. They were like a death sentence before the sentencing even began."

"So, they usurped the throne because of magic?" Nox shifted so he faced her fully, inclined so he seemed interested in the story. Perhaps he was, but Nessa's hackles still stood on end.

"Yes, but I was not willing to walk away without a fight. I screamed at them, yelled that they could not do that to my father. I bolted from my chair and balled my fists at my sides in a failed attempt to seem intimidating. I was seething, practically shaking with anger, but my mother ordered me to sit. Unfortunately, my outburst only added fuel to an already uncontrolled fire. The tantrum was only further proof I was unable to control myself. They banished us, but not before Dall offered a condescending glare to my mother and said, 'I suggest you gain control of your daughter before she loses *all* control.'"

"I assume that did not go well. I know what Hazel would have done in such an—"

Nessa couldn't help but laugh, interrupting Nox's comment. Hazel would never have done what her mother did, never. "Your Hazel was a force, but I assure you that she and my mother were nothing alike. My mother reminded him that I had merely killed an animal. I did not slaughter a village. They were convinced I might kill a human next. They insisted I had created problem after problem, and despite their patience with my family, my parents still could not see what was best for Asantaval. According to the Council, it was clear his selfish desire to remain king was all that drove him, when it should have been the well-being of this kingdom that forced him from his bed each morning."

Nox narrowed his eyes and sat back in his seat. "So, they expected your father to... what? Eliminate you? Banish you from the kingdom because of your ability?"

Nessa ran a hand through her blonde hair, nervous when he gazed at her that way. The man saw right through her, every fear as if it were written on her face. Blasted man. "I suppose. But... I ruined everything. My anger took control, and I screamed. I had not anticipated what a scream could do, the power it holds when one is untrained and raw in magic. It unleashed my fury in physical form, and waves of pure, raw energy crossed the room, narrowly avoiding my father. The Council members, however, were in the direct path of the energy. As such, they were dealt a blow so punishing, their eyes and ears bled, their tongues wagged as they worked to breathe around the invisible, tightening fists around their necks, and their skin sagged over their bones."

"You killed them? By screaming at them?"

Nessa bit her lip, staving off the instinct to defend herself. Not with him. With him, she would be honest even if it killed her. "I did not mean to. My mother screamed at me to stop, but it was impossible. I was lost in it. She shook me — violent shake after shake that did little to dissuade me from killing everyone in the room. And so, I did. I peeled skin from bone, cracked the bones and sailed them into the walls already sprayed with blood. I utterly destroyed the bodies of every Council member that had been in attendance, save one."

"One? He ran?"

"He hid, but I left him alive to serve a purpose."

Nox scoffed. "I thought you said you did not kill them on purpose?"

"At first, I didn't, but then I couldn't stop. It was like another person took over. I sent him away to tell the others that I had seen their wicked ways, their thirst for power, and I would be the one who brought them to their knees. My mother dragged me backward while my father stared at me as if he had never seen me before in his life. Mother's hands illuminated over me as she pressed her palms against my cheeks. Though light in color, the energy was dark and demanding, and it sucked the anger right from my body until I slumped forward in Mother's arms."

Nessa glanced at Nox, but his expression had not changed. Even so, she couldn't read exactly *what* emotion he presented, so she went on.

"Father was in shock. Blood, bone, skin... it littered the floor and the walls while cloaks and jewels—the signature dress of the Council—crumpled in piles. Dall's signet ring, still wrapped around a single finger, glinted in the light as a warning to them all. Mother insisted we leave right away, so she snatched Father's hand. In a blink, we were freefalling through a tunnel of darkness—pure, unadulterated Hell that had been, by my father's understanding, crafted by his own wife. He was green with nausea, but the velocity of our fall did not allow him to purge what little food he'd eaten over the previous days. Instead, all he could manage was a string of curse words as he flailed.

"Below us, the tunnel opened to reveal a meadow filled to bursting with flowers and tall grass. A cottage appeared, and then our plumet slowed until we stood on our own feet at the front of the cottage. A woman—dark skinned with waves of black hair, threw open the front door and stormed across the porch, her hands poised to deliver a crushing blow. She was angry, fuming."

"I know this part of the story. You arrived at Simorana's house."

"Indeed. She screamed at my mother, reminded her that she had told her *never* to return. I was dizzy from the fall, but she continued yelling at my mother. Reminded her of a warning to stay away from dark magic, that it would cost her everything one day. Evidently, my mother had refused to heed those warnings."

"Yes, well, magic often forces people to make the wrong choices, does it not?" He leaned forward, resting his elbows on his knees. Arrogant dragon.

"I vomited on the grass. Only then did my father notice how blood-stained I was. I had *murdered* half of the Council of Asantaval. His child, his *beloved* daughter, had slaughtered a room of men with little more than a wave of anger, and I stood before him covered with the evidence. I was sick with myself, but he stumbled and stepped backward, distracting Simorana from her verbal assault on my mother. Simorana asked what I had done, but mother wouldn't answer. Instead, she begged her for help. Begged her to hide me and my father, protect us from harm."

"If I know anything about Simorana, I would assume this was not an acceptable answer."

Nessa could not help but chuckle. "You would assume correctly. She insisted, but my father was the one to admit... well... he was in shock and mumbled that I had murdered everyone... all of them... I knew then that I had lost my father. He would never see me as his daughter again, and why should he? I *wasn't*, and we both know I am much more like my birth father anyway."

Nox said nothing but stared into the fire. A shadow passed over his face and he closed his eyes, then shook his head and said, "What happened?"

"My mother's pleas were lost on my father. He had shut us both out, but even so, he begged Simorana to set us up in a safe house until we could move north. Simorana taunted him, asked if he would desire a meeting with the King of Goranin, given there was nothing north but his wicked castle and a court filled with hatred and anger. Father anticipated we would go farther, past Goranin altogether... by ship, I suppose. Simorana had other plans, namely, a safe house she used near the borders. She allowed us safe passage with the promise we would never show our faces at her home again. She had children staying at her home."

"Astrid and Emora?"

Nessa nodded. "Yes. She swore to kill us all if we harmed either of them."

"Lucky for you then that Simorana died in the battle against Moriarian." Nox crossed his arms, putting space between them. It was not unexpected, so Nessa tried not to feel so slighted by it. Even so, she longed for him to stay open to her, to just listen. Understand. The way he understood Eiagan.

"Perhaps." Nessa shrugged and shifted her weight again. "If she had not protected Eiagan with that spell, she might have survived the battle. She was a formidable woman, and I was sure she would kill us all as she'd promised if we did not evacuate her property. My father though, his mind was already stretched to its limit. He'd fallen in love with my mother young and had never seen that side of her. She had been sent away many times for training, but my grandfather never told him what *sort* of training she'd received on the surface. But he mistrusted her now, and with good reason. Simorana's last words to him did not help our cause. I could never forget it. She said, 'I warn you, fallen king, your wife comes from a long line of mages with ill intentions and deadly, spiteful hearts. She might be your love, but I can promise you that she seeks more than that in return from you.'"

"She was an intelligent woman." Nox scoffed but uncrossed his arms. "So, you went with your family to the safehouse. Then what? How did you end up here?"

"Much more than I might explain right now." Nessa rose but Nox met her, grasped her upper arms with a gentle touch she had not expected, so it froze her in place. Would he slip those hands higher and strangle her to death? Would she stop him? *No.* Nessa would do many things, but she would not kill this man, not even if he tried to put her in her grave.

Nox released her almost as soon as he realized he'd taken hold of her. "I would like to hear more. Despite every fiber of my soul telling me to run away from you, I find myself wanting to know what brought you here to this moment."

"A glutton for punishment, then?" she asked, her heart kicking so hard against her chest she worried she might lose consciousness.

"A seeker of truth. Sit. Tell me more."

Nessa's pale eyes scanned the room… the door… back to him. He sat again, waiting.

"I'm not foolish enough to test you, mage. Sit and speak to me, tell me what you so desperately need me to hear that you would bring me here, take me prisoner, and —"

Nessa gasped and her mouth opened. "That is not… I do not want you to be a prisoner here, Noxious. I will give you quarters and free movement throughout the castle."

"But I cannot *leave* it, and as such, I am a prisoner, Nessa."

Her prisoner. Nessa squeezed her eyes shut until her eyelids ached. There were decisions to be made she was wholly unprepared to analyze let alone execute, and this man only made those decisions more difficult. Why did she bring him here? She opened her eyes, let her gaze fall on him, waiting, anticipating her words. She knew why she brought him. She would lose this war, she knew. She had for some time, but before she died, she hoped, *prayed* he might offer her a moment of peace. Just one. Just a chance to tell her side of the story before her darkness was extinguished forever.

Nessa sat and gathered her dress away from the fire and inhaled. "Alright. I will stay."

TWENTY-SEVEN

3731, THE YEAR OF RECKONING
OUTSIDE THE MINER'S VILLAGE
SMOLZARK TERRITORY, GORANIN

Eiagan Allurigard

Eiagan hesitated when Gael sat among her family at the fire. Would sharing stories of woe offer fuel for the man should he decide to turn against them, or would it solidify a new bond built on real trust? Erdravac watched Eiagan, waiting patiently for her to decide whether this confessional would indeed take place, or whether it would disperse before it even began. Eiagan sat between Porvarth and Emora and nodded toward Erdravac.

The young king stared into the fire, a common trait amongst the group when admitting their true emotions. Soon enough, he took a deep breath and began.

"Keirnor was the eldest and had always been my father's favored son. I was too weak, too kind to our people for our father to ever believe I might be a good king. In hindsight, it appears the people might also believe the same, but I had hoped they might see to reason. I had hoped that I could take that desolate, traumatized land and make it into something grand again." Erdravac wiped his hands on his pants, then cleared his throat.

"Father used to send me into the forest to hunt, or so he said, then he would send his huntsman after me. Sometimes I spent weeks evading them, but often, one would injure me enough to call the hunt complete. They didn't enjoy it, but if they did not... Well, you can imagine."

Eiagan could not contain her scoff. In that way, Moriarian was no different from Icluedian. In fact, that her father had not sent his children into the forest to be hunted for sprot was a shock. Erdravac's eye contact with Eiagan said everything — *I know your pain and more.*

"There were so many things he did, but right now, at this moment, I feel more betrayed by my people who preferred a sociopathic queen over me. What more can I offer but peace and freedom?" he asked — rhetorically, yet Porvarth felt the need to reply.

"Perhaps it is not you who possesses the problem, but them? You are kind and merciful and loyal, but those qualities are not admirable to jealous and selfish people. And so, I say it is your people who must change, and not you." Porvarth's eyes twinkled in the firelight, offering — for the first time — a word of encouragement and praise toward Erdravac. "When this war is won, I dare say your people could use a swift kick in their seat, and then a proper scolding before they should enjoy the fruits of our labors."

Erdravac chuckled. "And here I thought you despised me and all I stood for."

"I do not despise you. I don't particularly *like* you, but I do not bear you ill will." Porvarth's lips curved into a grin, the same impish expression that managed to keep him in Eiagan's good graces when he behaved badly.

Erdravac shook his head, then asked, "And what would be your advice to one who has killed his own brother and cannot seem to ignore the guilt of it?"

Porvarth tensed beside Eiagan, but it was fleeting. "I would say that your brother made his choice, whether right or wrong, and you should not bear his death as a sin on your shoulders." It was as much a statement to Eiagan as it was to Erdravac. "Guilt is part of healing, but it should not eat you alive. The choice was not yours, but his."

Erdravac lowered his gaze to the fire again, lost in thought. He licked his lips and sighed. "Well, that seems like a very small list of complaints now that they are out in the open, yet I cannot shake this feeling of... of..." He motioned his hands, searching for the correct words.

"Being lost while the whole world keeps spinning around you as if you are not even there?" Emora offered. Erdravac nodded and relaxed. "I know it well. But your worries are not small, Erdravac. Your pain and suffering should not be pushed aside as if they never happened."

Eiagan spied Gael from the corner of her eye, but the man only sat upon a log, listening intently as Erdravac and Emora conversed for a short time. Ari was speaking when Eiagan turned her attention back to the conversation, reminiscing over his time in the dungeon.

"I could not understand how Emora could love me with such ferocity, and then hate me equally as well within a day." Ari glanced at Emora, who mimicked Erdravac's stare into the depths of the fire.

He shifted his gaze to his feet. "I never was good for much of anything except fishing and behaving like a scoundrel, but she changed that. From the moment I saw her, she stole my heart, then she gave hers to Gregor. I could no more blame her for it than I could blame the sun for rising each morning. He had always been a better man than me, and as he was my dearest friend, I bade him no ill will."

Emora's tension radiated from her body, making Eiagan feel the same.

"I never knew that. You never said anything to me before I met Gregor," Emora said.

"What could I say? I didn't deserve you. And when Gregor died, I wanted to heal your heart, but I... I only..."

"You did, Ari. You did, and I did love you. I *do* love you," Emora said.

"I know that you do. But there are things in my memory that haunt me, and I wonder if I will ever be able to move past them long enough to make new memories."

"Bah," Borgard said with a humph. "The woman suffered Hell at the hands of Nessa and that pathetic excuse for a prince, Keirnor. Your time in a dungeon was no match for *her* time in one. I have seen what Varrowan men do to women, and I say if you love her, then heal her. You heal her, and your healing will follow. She'll ensure it. It is a man's duty, after all, to do such things for his wife, or in this case, a woman who should already be your wife."

Porvarth blinked several times, then pivoted his head to watch Emora.

She licked her lips and took Ari's hand. "I adore you, Ari, but I will not force you to keep a promise you made to me all those years ago. If you wish for me to release you from this situation, I will do so without animosity or regret for the time we had together."

"That isn't what I want," Ari said. His breaths grew heavy, weighted with all the words he needed to say but could not. "I don't know how to convey how I feel or what I fear."

"I believe you fear what you do not know, and so I will tell you now. I will say what happened to me those years, and then I might begin to see those wounds scar if not heal cleanly."

Eiagan tensed now. To assume what had happened to Emora was far different from hearing it from her own lips.

"At first, Nessa remained in my body almost all the time, but the magic made her weak. Eventually, she would retreat for hours at a time to rest, leaving me to my own devices. I never could go far, for Keirnor lurked about every corner. I knew, though, that she had relations with him while I was locked away from my body. I... *felt* it. Later, when he had lost all favor with her, I think it disgusted her to be with him, so sometimes..." Emora's lower lip quivered, then she said, "Sometimes I would return to my body in the midst of it, and though I fought him, Keirnor did not care that I was no longer Nessa."

Ari stood straight up and ran his hands through his hair while clenching his jaw. Eiagan breathed deeply, reminding herself that Keirnor was dead and there was no more to be done to the man.

"I should have stabbed him beyond recognition," Erdravac said. "I had no idea, Emora. I am... I am so terribly sorry that I showed remorse for killing my brother after what he did to you."

"It is no fault of yours, Erdravac. It just... is." Emora clutched her hands in her lap. "He would hit me sometimes, especially if Nessa had been gone for some time and he was bored. Other times, I would think of leaping from the highest tower, but I knew I could not. Eiagan would return, and she would make every suffering worth it. I only had to hold on long enough."

"Bloody bastard," Borgard said.

Ari grasped Emora's hand and pulled her to her feet gently but insistently. "We need to speak in private. Excuse us," he said, then led Emora to one of the tents.

Porvarth's gaze instantly shifted toward Eiagan, who shook her head. "It will be well. It is a long overdue conversation."

"I wish he were still alive so that I might hunt him down and kill him all over again," Erdravac said, much to Borgard's amusement.

The man laughed, then dove headlong into his own story. "A Varrowan killed my wife. I ended his life, but it still feels hollow in my chest. I spent so much time hunting him, and now that he is dead..." Borgard shrugged.

"You are stuck with us fighting a war you never asked for," Porvarth said.

"No one asked for it," the Balconian said. "But it is better than stewing in my own anger and hatred toward a man who is dead."

"Your child?" Eiagan asked.

"In Isadore with my wife's family. I never was a good father, and with my wife gone, it seemed better to leave her there while I killed the man who took her mother. In hindsight, it was a miserable thing to do."

"We can find your child, if you wish," Eiagan said, longing for her own departed son. She always missed Iric, but now, when emotions ran high, she felt that gaping hole deep in her chest.

Borgard merely grumbled and stood, then stumbled toward the other tent.

"Isn't he a pleasant one?" Catia asked, watching Borgard's back as he entered the tent. "Though I understand his grief in some ways. I lost a child."

Eiagan's gaze fluttered toward Catia, suddenly pulled to another level of understanding the woman's desire to hide in the shadows, and her lack of care if she should die during their mission. Catia's eyes locked with Eiagan's, and while no words were spoken, there was a charge between them that even Porvarth felt. He slipped his arm around Eiagan's waist, supporting her whether she needed it or not.

"He was a babe, less than a year old when a fever took him. There were no real physicians within a day's ride, and though I tried to reach one in time, he died on the way." Catia's stare hazed, and her mind wandered back to that moment. "He is buried along the road, somewhere."

At least Iric had a grave, a place where Eiagan could go and feel close to him. Catia's child was buried in a hole along the side of some road, and all because she was unable to control the happenings in her own kingdom. This was not lost on Eiagan. The pain each of her people felt sat atop her shoulders, because she was the one tasked with protecting them. It had been *her* duty after killing her father, yet she spent so much time trying to control everything, she'd forgotten the most important part of being a queen.

"I should have been here. Instead of chasing after the crooked tax collectors and thieves, I should have been here," Eiagan said.

"Who would have protected the kingdom, then?" Porvarth asked.

"I could have sent the armies or created a council to control them, but instead, I refused to trust anyone. I created this strife, all of it, every bit that spans Goranin and every surrounding kingdom." Eiagan stood, unable to hear more and still remain in one piece. She had heard her sister's pain, heard that of her friends, and if she should hear more—from Porvarth—then she might not ever see past the shadows that reminded her she was not good enough.

Gael stood in her path before Eiagan even realized she was wandering toward her tent. Her pale eyes narrowed as her nostrils flared, but the man was not intimidated.

"I must speak with you and Emora… in private," he said. "At first light, once you have slept and had some time to process all you have heard, we must speak for the better of your people. There are things you must know before we arrive in Eathevall."

"Such as?" Eiagan asked.

Gael looked around the fire at the faces staring back at him, then said, "I ask for secrecy for your sake, Highness, not for mine. The secrets I must tell you should not be commonly known unless you choose for them to be made so. If you do, then you may tell them in your own way."

"We will meet you at first light, but if you offer us more rubbish and lies, I can promise you will not live to regret it," Eiagan said, then urged Porvarth toward their tent. The others continued to talk around the fire, but Eiagan was quite ready for sleep, so she settled quickly beside Porvarth.

"Are you comfortable?" Porvarth shifted beside Eiagan, his legs tangled with hers so that he might be as close as possible. He brushed hair from her face when she tucked her head against his chest.

"I am. I am exhausted but each time I close my eyes, I wonder what might happen next on our way home."

"It does seem fate has turned against us."

"I think it is the opposite. To return to Vidkun must be the right decision considering everything Nessa has done to keep us away, including opening old wounds," Eiagan said.

"You think she is the one creating the earthquakes as well?"

Eiagan shrugged. "I would never underestimate her given all she has already done. It would seem such things as manipulating the earth might be easy for someone so gifted with magic." Eiagan shifted to face Porvarth and drew his face to hers. She kissed him, drawing his line of questioning to an end — or so she had hoped, but it seemed the loxmore's inquisitive mind would not be satisfied so easily.

Porvarth drew away for a moment, then peppered Eiagan's face with small kisses. "I love you, and I pray that your training sessions with Ari will give both of you what I cannot."

Guilt washed over Eiagan, prickling her face with sweat. "Porvarth, I—"

"Shh, do not make apologies to me. If Ari helps you heal a part of yourself that I cannot, and if you can help him in the same way, then I am pleased he is our friend. I feel no jealousy where that is concerned, though I must say I do wish Erdravac had someone to talk to."

Eiagan narrowed her eyes and leaned up on her elbow. It was unusual for Porvarth to show any interest in Erdravac other than to offer slight jabs and judging glares, so his sudden concern with the unseated king's well-being was intriguing. "What do you mean?"

"He seems..." Porvarth hesitated, then said, "desperate. He fought and won his throne, only to lose it again within months. I imagine it is a stinging loss, especially accompanied with..." He motioned toward Eiagan, reminding her that there had been more than one man who'd had his eyes upon her. "And now that I have heard what his father did for sport, it seems a little familiar, wouldn't you say?"

Eiagan scoffed over part of his statement. "He is quite over me. It is the feeling of betrayal he despises. The idea that his people prefer a lunatic tyrant as their leader over a kind, dutiful king. And it does feel a bit familiar, to be quite honest. Including his father's hunts."

Porvarth chuckled. "You were a *tad* tyrannical, my love. That said, I suppose you are right. That would be enough to sour anyone's mood." He pulled Eiagan close again and tucked her against his chest. He buried his face in her hair, tickling her face with each breath.

Eiagan thought for a moment about Porvarth's concerns. After some time, she decided she would speak with Erdravac again in the morning, after seeing Gael, to ensure his thoughts were on the same path as hers, if only to ensure their mutual kingdoms did not fall fully into Nessa's grip. But truth be told, Eiagan *did* care about the man and his well-being despite being of Varrowan blood. He'd given as much as anyone in their fight, and his mind must be sharp for what lie ahead.

Eiagan opened her mouth to inform Porvarth of her plans, but his steady breaths gave her pause. The loxmore was asleep, tucked behind her with his arms wrapped around her as if she might float away during the night. Rather than wake him, she closed her eyes and let her mind drift toward the prospect of happier times — times when she might sleep in her own bed again, when she might look upon her family without fearing for their lives or wondering where their minds were. Perhaps even a time when she might feel safe enough to consider *growing* her family.

Among the quiet chatter outside, Vey's dulcet tone and Quix's familiar voice joined the rest of her family. They had rejoined them, ready to accompany them the rest of the way to Vidkun. Her party was whole again, so she might rest.

She inhaled and released her breath slowly, then drifted to sleep.

TWENTY-EIGHT

Noxious "The Savage" Skjoldsson

"I'm afraid I don't truly understand what pushed you to murder those men. To lose a kingdom is painful, yes, but why did you obliterate them?" Noxious gazed upon her with inquisitive eyes. He knew spending this much time with her, pulling information from her with gentle words and kind gestures, would only lead to pain in the end, but as long as she was conversing with him, she was not killing people he loved.

"I did not kill them because of what they did. It pushed me over the edge, yes, but those men were not upstanding citizens by any stretch of the imagination. They, too, had murdered people, abused women and children, and stolen from the people to line their own pockets. They were despicable, yet they stood there judging my father as if they were perfect. I will remind you I am not the only woman who reacted poorly to the loss of her kingdom."

"Yes, well, Eiagan had not… Well, I suppose she *did* kill unruly people, but she…" Nox was at a loss for words. His heart twinged because it was discontented with the conclusion in his mind. Were Nessa and Eiagan all that different? Yes. Eiagan did not torture Emora, Ari, Tend, and others in their camp. Nessa had killed — or at least pretended to kill — Astrid and Lucifer. She had sent a plague that killed Hazel, then kidnapped children from all corners of the kingdoms. "You are a far sight worse, I'd say. What you did to Emora was malicious beyond need."

"Perhaps, but she is no innocent lamb. She tried to kill me when we were younger. Centuries ago." Nessa rolled her shoulders back and lifted her chin.

"You were as conniving then as you are now. She had good reason to kill you."

"That may be so, but she was no sweet thing back then. She had the same darkness, and you know it to be true. You know who I am, Noxious. You know, in your heart, I am not that different from them."

She wasn't. Nox swallowed the stone in his throat because Lord help him, she was right. Whatever dastardly things Nessa had done could be equally matched by things Eiagan and Emora had done. None of the women was sinless, none innocent. All were malevolent when they wanted to be. And bless his soul, the only reason he held her to a harsher standard *was* because she'd done those things to people he loved and not to strangers. Did that make *him* any better?

Nessa smirked. "You see it, don't you? I am no different. We were all cut from the same cloth, like it or not."

"Then why do you hate them so? They might be the only people alive who would understand you."

Nessa's smirk widened. "Oh, yes, well, we have not reached the best parts yet. I am sure you will understand once I explain my relationship with Zero and how your beloved Eiagan stole him right from beneath me."

"From what I was told, Zero had no other women in his life when he fell in love with Eiagan." Noxious was sure his family's history was accurate. His distant grandfather had been quite careful to notate everything in his brother's life since it was his actions that offered their family eternal favor with the Winter Queen.

"Mmm... Well, Akeel and Zero were not always as close as they were under your Eiagan's early reign. In fact, they had been separated at birth, different mothers and all, and had not even met one another until I arranged it."

Nox's stomach bottomed out again. There were notes about the separation, but Nox had only deemed it unnecessary information. If Nessa knew about the time before Akeel and Zero were reunited, then perhaps some of what she said was true.

"Tell me about that time." His brow broke with sweat. He both wanted to know and despised the idea of it.

"Why? I am quite sure it is not something that concerns you. My broken heart and eternal pain are of no worry whatsoever to you and yours." She crossed her arms, closing him out. Not yet. He needed her open and talking so he might find the root of her evil, the thing that twisted that pretty mind until it shattered. He needed to know, if only to ensure the same didn't happen to Eiagan or Emora. And then he would use it against her, put an end to this once and for all.

Nox sighed. "Despite my aversion toward you, I find I do want to know. I would like to understand so I won't take hatred to the grave with me."

Pale eyes met his again. She sighed and waved her hand. "Fine. I'll begin with the first time I met him, but first, I must release the children as I promised. It's morning."

TWENTY-NINE

Nessa Callanan

The children were huddled around the Nelaravorian princess as usual, lost in her story when Nessa entered the room. Little eyes focused on her, then their bodies trembled as they awaited her demands. Nessa's heart lurched. What had she done? These children were no part of her war against Goranin and the Allurigard sisters, yet she had allowed her uncontrolled anger to dictate her actions again. She swallowed bile and lifted her chin. It was no wonder Noxious couldn't see she was no different from his beloved Eiagan. Even if he did, Eiagan's behavior was often indefensible as well.

"Noxious has bargained your release. You are free to go." She palmed the door handle and clenched her teeth. There was more to be said, but issuing an apology would only make her appear weaker. So, she waited.

"And how do you suppose we should leave?" Reven asked, always with his sarcastic undertone. Astrid clenched his hand as if she might be left behind if she were not physically attached to her son.

Nessa lifted her hand and pressed it palm down on the stone wall. It melted beneath her touch until a vision of Sudyak Meadow appeared clear as if they were standing in the gardens themselves. The castle was an hour walk from where they would be released, as was Nox's request. Reven peered through it with undisguised concern.

"It is there and real as the floor you stand upon. A deal is a deal, and I have no need of children any longer." Nessa waved her hand, encouraging them to get moving. She had no intention of keeping Nox waiting lest he change his mind about hearing her side of the story.

"Why the sudden—"

"Just go!" Nessa yelled, practically shoving the prince through the portal opening. Astrid, still attached, fell through with him. The Nelaravorian princess gasped, then held a child's hand. Violet stood in the corner, trembling. Nessa softened her features if only for Violet's benefit and nodded. "He is perfectly fine, see?"

They peered through the opening and relaxed. Reven stood brushing the dirt from his pants, searching for a portal he would never find until another person slipped through it. Astrid spun in place, immediately recognizing where they had landed. Her adoptive mother's ravaged home was nearby.

"Alright, you all first then I will follow. Hurry now." The children did as Darby instructed, each leaping in turn through the portal. Reven helped each up and cleaned them off before waiting for the next to drop through. Finally, the princess wiped her brow and narrowed her eyes at Nessa.

"You cannot hope to win this war, Nessa. Why not come through and turn yourself in. I will testify that you did not lay a hand on the children, and perhaps you will not be sentenced to death?"

Nessa chuckled. "Oh, Princess Darby, I'll hang for what I've done, rest assured, but not before I inflict pain upon your people the likes of which they have never experienced. Send the message to your parents if you would." Nessa shoved the princess through the portal and removed her hand from the wall. A good wipe over her dress skirts cleaned it while she tried, with great effort and little success, to rein in her grief. She would not attack Nelaravore. Only a fool would do such a thing, but for anyone to see her weakened was a death sentence she was not quite ready to suffer.

With a deep inhale, she returned to Nox.

He sat by the fire where she had left him, lost in thought. His head rested in his hands, elbows on his knees. Nessa cleared her throat.

"Where were we?" she asked and sat across from him again.

"You released the children? And Violet?"

Drat. In her frustration, she had not taken note of the child after she'd pushed Darby through the portal. Her mouth fell open, then she closed it and stood. Noxious bolted upright and met her at the door.

"If you put a hand upon my daughter, I will kill you with my bare hands. No magic will save you from my wrath, woman." Those golden eyes flamed, reminding her he was as formidable a dragon as any.

269

"I did not. I merely… she is in the room waiting." She lowered her eyes, ashamed to have forgotten the child. She would have been a horrible mother, not that she had a good example in either her birth mother or her adoptive one.

"Take me to her. Now."

Nessa didn't pause to make excuses. Instead, she took the man to his daughter. Inside, Violet's tears slipped over her cheeks in waves, punching Nessa right in the gut. Not even Darby had noticed the child remained in the corner, but Nox would have her head for this. There would be no changing that, and she would deserve it, too.

"You *left* her here and sent the others back?" His tone was terse but he worked to control his reaction.

"I… was… distracted. Come, let's take her to her room and we can talk there. I think she will like it."

Nox shook his head and picked up his child. "You cannot correct mistakes like this with pretty things, Nessa. She needs a parent, one who loves her and cares for her. Since you took her mother, I am all she has. We'll take her to the room so she can sleep, but that is the only reason I am not…" He glanced at his child, then lowered his voice. "She is the only reason I am not forcing consequences upon you at this moment."

Nessa licked her lips and led them to Violet's quarters. She had spared no coin where decorating was concerned and had filled it with so many dolls it was mildly off putting, but she hoped it might satisfy the child enough to satiate her father's lust for blood.

Nox slipped into the room with Violet but blocked Nessa's entry. "I will meet you by the fire. I want to comfort my daughter alone, please."

He couldn't escape the castle, so Nessa nodded and returned to the fire.

Half an hour passed before the dragon returned to her, but she assumed the child was well rattled after what she had witnessed and then left behind to fend for herself. Nessa stood to greet him, but the moment he closed the door behind himself, he turned on her with bloodthirsty rage. He crossed the room in a flash, gripped her around the neck, and pinned her to the wall.

"My patience with you is down to meager specks, woman. If you ever harm my child in any way again, I will shred you into strips even the crows would turn away." He released her, gasping for air as her vision blurred.

She wouldn't fight him if he tried to killed her, but blasted, it hurt.

Nessa stumbled into her chair as he took his, but the conversation would not be the same. She had lost whatever part of him understood her plight, whatever part might have, if even a little, felt sorry for her.

He wiped his hands on his pants and grumbled.

"Go on, tell me of your life with Zero, though I doubt he could have loved you more than he loved Eiagan. The man changed into this for her," he said, motioning over himself — the dragon. "And considering your inability to empathize with even a child's fears, I doubt there was ever a time you were innocent enough to *deserve* his love."

Nessa's gaze fell to the floor. Her throat ached, not only because he'd nearly strangled her, but there was also that rock of sadness she tried to swallow. It burned, and she hated it. She should be stronger after everything she'd already been through, but this man seemed to bring forth her weakest parts, those still left unhealed.

Might Zero have done that for her? Transformed himself into something else? There was no way to know, not really. The boy had

271

never truly seen her for what she was, always hearing but never *listening* when she spoke. Zero was in love with the idea of love, to be sure, but that didn't mean losing him did not cut deeper than any knife.

"My...my parents argued a lot then. Often, I had to cover my ears to drown the screaming and duck flying objects that smashed against the walls. Once, they fought so fiercely that I couldn't think straight. I wandered from the house, much farther than I was permitted to, and found myself at a stream. I drank a while, then settled against a tree. I fell asleep there but was awakened by a rustling in the trees."

"It was Zero?" Nox asked.

"Mmm, yes. I stood quickly, thinking it was a bear or wolf, and nearly lost my head. An arrow sped past, barely missing me before lodging into a tree. I remember blinking so many times my eyes hurt, but I couldn't believe what was right before my eyes. I turned my head, finally, and my gaze settled on the owner of the arrow that had nearly taken my life. A boy, a bit older than me, stood with his mouth agape as I slowly wrapped my mind around what happened — or *nearly* happened."

"He might have saved us all a few bad days if he had killed you." Nox clenched his teeth, grinding them until they flexed his entire jaw. Nessa's heart cracked again, once more the villain in his eyes. He would never see the things his beloved Eiagan had done, all the ways she ruined him that were so much worse than anything Nessa had done. Even so, she went on with her story.

"'Land's sakes, girl, I nearly killed you.' Those were the first words the greatest love of my life ever said to me. Locks of his hair fell over his forehead, plastered with sweat and mud. His ruddy cheeks were smeared with dirt, distracting me momentarily. He asked what I was doing in the forest dressed in a doeskin cloak, then accused me of being an imbecile."

Nessa paused, knowing well Nox would have something to add. He remained silent.

"A tickle on my cheek distracted me from the conversation, so I brushed my hand over it. He had nicked me. He tried to check my wound, but everything caught up then. I yelled at him, scolded him, and reminded him to look before he shot the next time. His cheeks flushed, and he frowned. He kept apologizing until I couldn't stand it any longer and let him tend to the wound. He patted it with a handkerchief. It was…"

Nessa faded, lost in the memory.

"It was?"

"I… I can't do this. I thought I could tell you all of this, let you see inside my life, but I can't." Nessa stood, but Nox stopped her again. "Please, let me pass."

"And if I don't?" He taunted her and pushed her to see what she would do. Nothing… and he knew it.

"I will leave you with an image of that time, but I cannot bear reliving it myself. Please, do not make me relive that moment and hear you taunt and tease me over it. It's all I have."

Golden eyes softened a little, as did his brusque stance. "Fine. I want to see everything."

Nessa nodded, waved her hand over the room, then ran.

Behind her, the wall shimmered and twisted until the image appeared, leaving Noxious alone to see the rest of the story, the day his ancestor brought his lineage face-to-face with the woman who wanted nothing more than to destroy them all. Zero, as a young boy, stood facing Nessa. She was beautiful despite Nox's efforts to pretend she wasn't, but he saw, too, what Eiagan had always seen.

273

The resemblance was uncanny. He was identical to his ancestor in every feasible way, and that made everything clearer. He sat and watched the wall as if a live play took place in front of him. But an odd sensation took over, leading him to not only see and hear the story but to… *feel* it. To feel what she felt. To understand Nessa's deepest thoughts all while they happened in front of him.

"Put pressure on it. Here, take my handkerchief." Zero handed Nessa a wrinkled square cloth, but Nessa only stared at it. "Well, will you take it or keep looking at me as if I am a monster? It was an accident, and I mean you no harm." His eyes sparkled — a bit of mischief, to be sure — as his lips turned into a frown. Finally, he lowered his arm.

"It will be fine. Who are you? Where are you from?" Nessa asked, glancing over her shoulder.

"Zero Skjoldsson," he said and wiped his hand on his pants. "I live here in Eathevall with my father. And you are?"

"Nessa," she said, hardly able to control the ache in her cheeks. For whatever ridiculous reason, she wanted to smile at him, but that was foolish. She could never entertain even the idea of making a friend, especially not a Goraninite, likely a hunter's son with little promise for a bright future. Even so, he was pleasant, and it was nice to talk to someone who knew nothing of her or her past.

"Well, since you will not accept my help, will you accept half of my lunch? I have turkey and an apple, though I'm afraid it might be a bit mealy. It is rather old." Zero rummaged through his leather satchel and retrieved something else. "I have this, too. I was saving it for a special day but… but you can have it." He extended his hand and dropped a sugar cube into Nessa's palm.

Nessa hadn't realized she'd extended her hand in return until the sugar landed in it. Sugar was scarce in Goranin, Nessa had learned, and that he had a cube of it at all was no small surprise. Perhaps his father wasn't a hunter. Or perhaps he was simply good at it and made well for his family.

Zero blushed. "I saved my coin for a solid month to buy that, but you look like you could use a bright spot in your day."

Nessa swallowed. No one had ever offered her so much kindness. Of course, the villagers in Asantaval spoiled her early on when she was small, but that was always to win favor with their king, not because they were kind. This boy, though, gave her the sugar without a moment of hesitation, knowing nothing of her identity save her name. He smiled at her as she stood staring at the lump. She turned it in her hand and gave it back to him.

"It is a kind gesture, to be sure, but I would prefer your company over the sugar. You should eat it since you worked to buy it."

He took the lump and split it in half, then gave half back to her. "A compromise," he said, then popped his half into his mouth. "What would you like to do?"

"Do you need to hunt?"

Zero shook his head. "You are the only breathing thing I've found all day. My father will be angry, but I cannot find what does not exist. King Icluedian has ravaged this land."

"Mmm... I have heard he is nothing but a devil in human skin."

"You have heard? Where did you say you came from?" Zero's eyes took her in again as if he might discover her heritage if he stared at her long enough. He never would, of course – born in Goranin, raised in Asantaval, and now a fugitive from her own people – so she let him look her over and make his guesses.

"Let me guess... Isadore?"

Nessa giggled. "How did you guess?" Absolutely wrong, but Nessa let him draw his own conclusions. She knew well that letting others paint their own picture of the truth was always easier than making up her own lies. People tended to swallow their own assumptions much better anyway.

"Your fair hair and skin are much like the princess there, and you seem delicate. When did you arrive in Goranin, and why, for all the money in the land, would you ever come to Goranin in the first place?" Zero kicked a pinecone and watched it hop along the forest floor while Nessa considered her reply.

"My father found work here, and my mother is Goraninite." Only a partial lie, but he believed it enough that he did not question her further.

"Well, our king is insufferable, but if you stay out of his way, you might survive to adulthood. I would wager you would at least outlive his children."

Nessa froze. His children… more children?

Zero paused and looked over his shoulder. "Are you well? You look as if you saw a ghost."

Nessa shook her head and smiled. "I am. I was only thinking of those poor children, that is all. Do you suppose anyone will ever kill the wretched king?"

He chuckled and said, "My father says only the devil himself can smite that abomination, but I think one day someone might find a way to take his immortality and kill him. What a day of celebration that would become. I doubt that will be during my lifetime, but one might hope."

Nessa followed him in silence, listening to his quiet footsteps over the black dirt. Everything was different on the surface, even the sound of footsteps and the way her voice never echoed, not like it did beneath the land. The sunshine filtered through the trees and fell upon her face, illuminating and warming it, unlike the false lighting in Asantaval. The pine and wet leaves and dirt mixed to create an earthy smell, another novelty Nessa catalogued for further exploration.

"Would you like to see a place I like to go?" Zero pointed ahead with a small smile. "Only around the bend a little."

Nessa shrugged and continued following him, only then realizing she had no idea where she was or how to return to the cottage. She had trusted *this boy without question and allowed him to lead her deep into the forest. For a moment, her heart hammered her ribs as her body prepared for flight. She had been so enamored by the sights and sounds and smells she had forgotten that she was a foreigner in a land she did not know, with a bloodthirsty king and any number of disenfranchised villagers who would kill her merely for the cloak she wore.*

Zero stopped after another dozen steps, then turned. "Are you coming? You can see it from here." He nodded toward the curve in the path.

Nessa swallowed her fear — if the need arose, she would use her magical ability — and went to his side. Ahead, a waterfall poured between two boulders, ending in a small pool. Her lips curled into a smile as all fear drained from her body.

"Race you!" Zero shouted, then darted toward the pool with Nessa on his heels.

Her smile grew, and a sliver of something exploded to life in her heart. What it was, she could never say, but trailing behind Zero, she decided it did not need a name. Whatever it was, it pleased her. And when he reached the waterfall and slowed to let her win the race, that explosion spread through the rest of her body.

Zero was kind. It was not a requirement because she was his princess, not a show put on in front of a stranger, not a trick so that he could hurt her or steal from her. He was simply kind, and it seemed that was all Nessa really needed to feel like herself again.

THIRTY

Eiagan Allurigard

Morning brought a certain clarity that other times of day failed to present when Eiagan had a decision to make. It was as if the decision came to her when she slept and waited patiently until she opened her eyes, though that didn't mean the decision was enjoyable. No matter what Gael said, she would think of her people first, leaving her nephew to the wolves if it meant saving the lives of many. Eiagan swallowed the horrific taste that came to her mouth at that thought, dressed, and headed to Gael's tent.

She didn't need to request permission. The flap was already open, inviting her in. Emora slipped from her tent a blink later, her gaze connecting with Eiagan's. Somehow, both women knew they would change once they met with Gael. Whatever Gael told them

278

would alter not only the course of this war but also their lives forever.

Eiagan nodded and stepped inside with Emora as her shadow.

"Good morning, ladies. Let's get down to it, shall we?" Gael was not his usual self but instead was solemn and quiet. It was quite a change from the boisterous greetings they had become accustomed to.

The women sat upon a plaid woven blanket covering Gael's small chest of belongings.

"I assume you have questions first, or shall I relay the information that will change everything?" Gael's gaze darted between Eiagan and Emora, but neither could decide which was more pressing. Eiagan finally settled on the immediate threat.

"What happened in Asantaval? Is it dead or alive? Do you truly have an army or are you exaggerating your ability?"

Gael shifted his weight and let out a deep breath. "It is alive but weak and small. The original war devastated most of the people. Famine and plagues killed many beneath the ground in the centuries since, and when Ellenessia and her parents were banished, what remained of the council took over. Many died under suspicion of working with the former king."

"And now? What remains?"

"A small village of about a thousand highly skilled mages and crafters able to create projections so real, a body can feel them." Gael's eyes met Eiagan's alone. "The warriors you saw rising from beneath the earth were mostly phantoms with our bravest warriors amongst them, hiding throughout so that none might be picked out from the phantoms."

"Why did you lie all this time?" Eiagan asked. "Did you fear I would not do as you asked and return your land?"

279

Gael shrugged. "As you are an Allurigard, it was not a chance we wanted to take, but we do intend to keep up our end of the bargain. We will grow, and when we do, we will do our part to pull our weight among the alliances formed after this fight."

"And why do you call my sister the savior?" Emora asked.

"Because we believe she is the only one who might kill Nessa. Others have tried and failed, even you, Princess. And I believe she is because she killed Icluedian. I saw her once when she was young, shortly after you were sent away, Princess Emora. I'd been sent to the surface to scout and overheard a conversation between Eiagan and Reeve." His gaze shifted to Eiagan. "You were so young then, just a wee thing, but I knew. I knew you were the one to end your father's tyrannical rule."

Gael's gaze took a certain reminiscent quality that almost made Eiagan sick. Anyone might have heard her speaking with Reeve, and they *had*. They were lucky it had only been Gael and not one of Icluedian's many spies.

"When you entered our lands and stole the plant to attempt to save Hazel, we knew your heart was pure once more. At least, we knew it was time to move forward with our plans to return to the surface and reclaim our lands."

Eiagan scoffed. "Pure is debatable."

"Your intention when you entered the cavern for Hazel's cure was pure and honorable. Your actions thus far have only been to protect your people with no thought of personal gain. The point is Nessa believes there is an army of great size, and we can use that against her. The projections feel as real as a person standing beside you, and they are deadly, just like Nessa's. We can fool her enough to corner her, then you might do with her as you wish."

Eiagan considered telling Gael of her plan to do just that, but using her grandmother's ability to project an army ten times the size of Nessa's. If they could only convince the Varrowans to shift back to their side, they could tip the scales fully against Nessa. That was unlikely, though, considering they seemed to prefer Nessa.

Gael cleared his throat, bringing Eiagan back from her planning.

"How are you still alive?" Emora asked.

Gael scratched his red beard and sighed. "You could say I betrayed my brother in a way. I took an elixir after my wife died, something my son had earned from a mage in Drumire where we had gone after my family was run out of Asantaval. They had no desire to stay with my brother, and I agreed."

"Everlasting life, then?" Emora asked, nodding. Once again, it seemed no one ever wished to die, which baffled Eiagan more than anything. Why would anyone *choose* such suffering for all eternity?

"Not everlasting as yours, but it did offer many centuries of longevity. My sons are among those fighting for Asantaval, commanding the phantoms."

"But you left your kingdom when your brother was banished, as you said? How did you ever return? Why did you take the elixir behind his back?" Emora had taken charge of the interrogation, it seemed, but Eiagan allowed it since her sister had pulled more from Gael in ten minutes than she had managed in days.

"I took the elixir because my brother was losing. He lost his way, his mind, his wife, and his child. He couldn't see what was right in front of him though I tried to show him. It was my fault Nessa was in Asantaval, but it was his fault things got so far out of hand. He never saw what his wife was doing right under his nose. I had to do something to ensure Asantaval didn't remain in the corrupt

281

council's hands for long, so…" He shrugged and shook his head. "I did what I did, and here we are.

"As for why they accepted my return, well, it took much convincing, a few murders where illegitimate councilmen were concerned, but eventually, those remaining grew to trust me again, especially after my brother and sister-in-law were murdered by your father. I took my sons underground again and have done all I can to ensure our longevity, but now…" He sighed. "We have grown tired of the darkness after so many centuries. We want a treaty with Goranin, of that you can be sure, but Nessa will stop at nothing to destroy us all. She wants it for herself, and I fear she might win if we do not calculate our moves tens steps ahead of her."

"She seems to believe Astantaval will forgive her, I would assume, since she wants to claim everything in your kingdom's name," Eiagan said.

Gael snickered. "She might wish that, but it will never happen. She has deluded herself."

Eiagan assessed him, his stature and intent, and found she believed him. "What information will change our future, this secret you are so sure will change everything?"

"It is something I hesitate to tell you but you will figure it out on your own soon enough. Killing her might be more difficult than you think, especially once you know who she truly is, my friends." Gael's tone took a sympathetic turn that piqued Eiagan's senses. Whatever he said wouldn't be good, even if she disagreed over her reaction to it.

Emora huffed and crossed her arms, her dark hair frizzing around the frame of her face. "I won't hesitate to cut her head from her shoulders no matter who she is."

"Imagine if Eiagan had felt the same of you not so long ago. In fact, it would be the same." Gael's eyes widened slightly as if to say *there is your answer.*

Eiagan caught the slight uptick in his tone, the way he held his breath to see if either of them picked up on his cryptic statement, but she was at a loss. As Emora said, there was little the woman could do to spare her life if Eiagan ever got her hands on her flesh and not a projection. Though she was weary of death, so tired of killing when it seemed new enemies emerged with each kill, she would do so again if it was the only way.

"Eiagan, Emora... you know well that your father lived many centuries. He had wives before Serecala and many children with those wives. He had other children *with* Serecala before you." Gael led them down a path Eiagan was sure ended with nothing but darkness, a void willing to swallow her whole if she set foot on that path. But she had no choice.

"Icluedian killed them all or led them to their own demise as he did Reeve," Emora said.

Eiagan's mind burned. No. This was preposterous, and she would have none of it.

"What you imply is impossible. If Icluedian had..." Eiagan paused to consider the facts, to calculate the likelihood Gael's words rang true. She swallowed, sick to her stomach at the thought of it, but it *was* possible. Icluedian had admitted as much himself all those centuries ago.

"Are you certain?" Eiagan asked.

"I am more sure of this truth than I am of my own birthday." He offered his hand, palm up, as a peace offering. "I know that our trust is strained, but know the people of Asantaval only want back what was theirs and nothing more. We will support your cause and be your strongest ally. If allowed to grow, we will replenish our lands and strive to become trade partners, friends, and protectors of the kingdoms surrounding us."

Emora shook her head. "Perhaps I am dull this early in the morning, but do you mean to imply that monster is our *sister?*"

Gael nodded slightly with soft eyes and a relaxed stature. "Nessa is your sister, princess. Born of Serecala a handful of years before your birth, left in the loxmore community, and adopted by happenstance into Asantaval. The history is written and well documented, available for you should you want to study it."

Emora blinked and swayed, then reached for Eiagan. Eiagan steadied her sister though her own mind was blurred, working to anchor in reality. Eiagan licked her lips and stood, helping Emora to her feet.

"I need to think." She did, but in her heart, Eiagan knew what he said was true. It made so little sense that it made *all* the sense in the world, and Gael was right. This… this *connection* to Nessa changed things. Oh, she would still kill the woman for all she had done, but now… *now* it would be another death that would haunt her. She would murder another sibling. How could she? She was so *tired* of killing, and to kill another sibling? Her sister?

Eiagan Allurigard, slayer of her own blood.

She left the tent, unaware she had even done so before she stumbled over a tree root. The ground met her face, its dampness smearing across her cheek.

"Eiagan?" Quix bent to help her up, but she was already pushing up on all fours, stumbling over her own feet as he watched her. She wandered all the way back to her tent where Porvarth was dressing. He had just tied the laces of his tunic when she slipped into the tent and fell, knees first, onto their makeshift bed. Erdravac sat upon a bedroll midway through a discussion with Porvarth, but he froze when Eiagan fell into the tent.

"Eiagan? Darling, are you —"

"She's my sister," Eiagan whispered.

Porvarth blinked. "Come again? Is Emora alright? Has something —"

Eiagan grasped his hands and stared up into those endless blue eyes. He would understand. Porvarth always, *always* understood how she felt. He would help her place her emotions, and organize them into manageable bits, so she didn't fall apart, didn't turn into the maniacal monster she was so accustomed to when things went all wrong.

"*Nessa* is my sister, Porvarth. I must... I must kill another one of them."

Porvarth's face went white as his bedroll, and Erdravac gasped. Porvarth inhaled slowly, methodically, until the words were processed. "That is... inconvenient and alarming, but it does not change who she truly is at the core. She is a demon, Eiagan, and we must eliminate her."

"My sister, Porvarth."

Eiagan had forgotten Emora completely, but she reinstated herself into Eiagan's thoughts when she, too, stumbled into the tent with Ari. The women locked gazes, both lost and alone yet surrounded by loved ones. Would anyone truly understand them? Could anyone know what it meant that this woman, the devil they had been so ready to slaughter with glee, was their sister?

Emora nodded. There was a spark there, something that passed between them that no one saw, but they felt. *They* knew. *They* understood each other. The plan had to change. They could not kill her because if they did, it would ruin them so wholly they would never come back from it.

"She is your sister?" Erdravac whispered, staring at the ground as if he couldn't quite make himself believe such a thing.

Ari's arms wrapped around Emora, supporting her while Porvarth put both hands on Eiagan's cheeks, keeping her focused on him alone.

"What can I do? What do you need from me?"

Eiagan shook her head. "We... we *cannot*, Porvarth. I haven't a clue what we might do, but I cannot kill another of my siblings."

"She's murdered with glee, Eiagan. Surely, you understand..." Erdravac's statement faded with the breeze, and his chest rose and fell with a sigh. He, too, knew the toll it would take on them if they killed their sister no matter how horrible she was, no matter what she had done to them or anyone else. "What shall we do?"

Eiagan squeezed her eyes shut. For the first time in her entire life, the Winter Queen did not know what to do. Porvarth's thumbs caressed under her eyes, soothing her.

"Iditania's prison," he said, confident and determined. "You will put her there and think no more of her. She cannot escape it, not if Iditania enacts the same spell on it that kept her imprisoned all those centuries. Perhaps Iditania can also bind her magic. If not, we will find someone who can."

Eiagan's eyelids fluttered open, connecting with him, reading him, knowing this was the only way. He was right. She could not kill her, but she could never let her go free. Iditania's eternal prison was the only way. Eiagan's gaze shifted to Emora, their pale eyes connecting. Their blood had cursed them all their lives, and it seemed Nessa was equally as cursed. Even so, she could not enact this plan without Emora's consent. After all, she had been as ruined by Nessa as anyone.

Emora nodded, her lips quivering. "I do not know how to feel, but I will support your choice. Imprison her, bind her magic, take everything from her... but do not... do not kill her." She sucked in a breath, her cheeks red and tear-stained. "We can be better than her."

"The others won't like this, but as insane as it sounds, I believe I agree with you." Erdravac stood and brushed dirt from his pants. He licked his lips and glanced between the couples. Eiagan was meant to talk with him, to seek some way she might help him through this difficult time, but how could she do such a thing now? She hardly knew her own senses and would be of no use to him.

"Shall I inform the camp of our change in plans?" Erdravac asked, hesitating at the entry.

Eiagan shook her head, forcing herself from her haze back into the present. "No. I... I will do it. Fetch me a squawk, would you? I must tell Nox of this development."

With that, Erdravac exited the tent, leaving Eiagan and Emora to digest this new torment.

THIRTY-ONE

Reven Allurigard

"I didn't expect her to release us if I am honest," Reven said, ruffling his hair as he often did when presented with something that boggled his mind so thoroughly, he needed an outlet for his frustration. Dropped into the middle of Sudyak Meadow, he couldn't figure out how to transport all the children to the castle where they would begin the task of reuniting them with their families.

"I expected her to release us, but I assumed it would be our..." Darby leaned close and whispered, "bodies."

"I never thought I would see anything but her castle walls again," Astrid admitted, already seeming healthier with each passing minute. "Simorana's home was over there, so Vidkun is north just that way. We'll see the castle when we crest the hill. We should

288

move along so the children can eat and rest. We'll reunite them with their families as soon as possible."

Reven offered his hand to one child, then realized Violet was not among them. This was not unexpected. "I do hope Violet is well."

Darby smoothed her blonde hair and smiled, but it was forced and false. "I am sure her father will protect her, and Nessa seems unwilling to cross him. Did you notice how she fawned over him? So strange."

"Not when you consider that she is a raving lunatic," Reven said.

"She is in love with him," Astrid said with a wave of her hand. "He looks like Zero, who was at some point dear to her. I never heard the entire story, only bits and pieces I picked up while locked away for all these years. But Emora and I both know the striking resemblance he and Zero have. We've known them both." She licked her lips, pale but pinking with each breath.

How odd that his mother had known both men in some measure. Reven tried to wrap his mind around how much that might pain both Eiagan *and* Nessa, but found he only had sympathy for one of his aunts.

"Are Eiagan and Emora truly alive? Are they well?" Astrid asked.

"Yes, Mother, the sisters are alive and as well as they can be, all things considered. They will be thrilled to have you back and ready to end this war once and for all." Reven looked upon his mother, finally allowing himself to feel something akin to happiness. She was here, alive, and though her mind might take time to heal, even with Darby's aid, she *would* heal.

Her gaze lowered to her shoes. She wrung her fingers and sighed. "I wish my mind was a bit more settled, but I am sure once I see them and the rest of our family, things will improve. I know I sound a bit off, but I have seen and heard so many things, most of which make little sense. I am trying to sort through it all, I promise, my darling."

Reven placed a hand on his mother's shoulder and kissed her forehead. "I know, Mother, and I am sure seeing your family will increase your clarity. Darby might help you relax and heal with her ability as well."

Reven thought it odd she didn't mention her husband, Ballan, so he brought it up. It would be a shock for him to see his wife, but perhaps more of a shock if his mother had entirely forgotten she had a husband that was not Reeve Allurigard.

"Mother, do you remember Ballan?" he asked, glancing at Darby. She swallowed and let her gaze shift toward Astrid.

"Of course. I'm no simpleton, but he…" Astrid narrowed her eyes and stopped walking. "He… died? Or… my memory is failing me, but I cannot say whether my husband is alive or dead." Sadness took her eyes and her sullen expression spread to her shoulders and body, slumping her like an old lady.

"Alive, mother. At least, he was before we were taken months ago."

She brightened and smiled, growing an inch with his words. "He's alive?"

Reven nodded.

She shook her head and laughed. "Perhaps there will be even more good news when we arrive at the castle. Let's hurry!" Astrid picked up her pace, nearly dragging the children along toward Vidkun Castle.

Reven didn't dare tell her anything else. He didn't know what she remembered or didn't, and most of what had happened in her absence wasn't truly his story to tell — Emora's entrapment, for one.

Instead, he shared another look with Darby, kissed her cheek, and motioned north.

"Home, we go. Lead the way, Mother."

THIRTY-TWO

Eiagan Allurigard

Eiagan's group traveled the remaining distance to Vidkun castle in silence. Lucifer seemed the only one in a good mood as he trotted along, bobbing his head to some melody unheard by anyone but him. Eiagan had spent the previous five marticks of travel working through what she might say to Erdravac, but words continued to fail her. It was not often she was left without them, but it seemed learning Nessa was her sister had robbed her of most thought processes.

Fortunately, good weather, early rising, determination, and no surprise attacks had shaved significant time from their travels. Still, Eiagan could not find anything to be happy about.

"Perhaps I am not good with reading people, but I would wager by the way you continue to glance my way, there is something you'd

292

like to say but cannot bear to hear your own voice?" Erdravac positioned his horse closer to Eiagan so he might whisper.

"I cannot bear the sound of anyone's but I suppose I must speak eventually. I was only considering your story, the one you told last night."

Porvarth cleared his throat and urged his horse forward, leaving the two alone to talk.

"That can only mean one thing," Erdravac said. "I harbor no feelings for you, Eiagan. At least, none that might concern you."

"I only wish to ensure that you have *someone* to hear your woes, Erdravac. They are deep and cutting, and I am a willing ear if needed. Whatever did or did not happen between us is of no consequence to our friendship."

He nodded, his dark hair breaking from the somewhat haphazard way he had combed it. He was handsome, that much she could admit, and any number of women would be blessed to have him. Only, she was double blessed with the man who'd stolen her heart and she would never leave his side, even if death took them at the same time because of it.

"I know. I am merely seeing my problems another way, and that requires some rumination. I swear by my crown that I will consult with you if there is need for concern. So, you can tell Porvarth that I am well enough and he can stow his worry."

Eiagan chuckled. "He is still a loxmore at heart, young king."

"And he is a good healer, a good man, and will make a good husband and king. I am licking my wounds, but I will survive them."

"Let us move on, then," she said.

When they crested the hill, Vidkun castle soared above them, tickling the clouds. It called to her, a cold and demanding temptress, but it was home no matter how many horrific memories it housed. Eiagan urged Lucifer forward and guided her people the rest of the way home.

Once inside the small courtyard, Eiagan spied the Pit. Her stomach churned remembering the last time she'd seen it, when her sister's limp body lay sprawled on the pathway leading to it. She wished nothing more than to see it filled and sealed, but that was work for another day. When her caravan passed the shopkeepers and barterers, she paused at the entrance. Tend met them there, a smile upon his face however misplaced it might be.

"Eiagan, you are home, my queen." He offered a hand and helped her from her horse while the others dismounted and exited the one cart that managed to stay intact on the trip. She embraced Tend, absorbed his warmth and familiarity, before nearly dropping to her knees. Behind him, the spitting image of her brother stood staring back at her.

"Reven?" Eiagan sidestepped Tend and hurried to her nephew, who stood with that infernal grin upon his face. Beside him, Darby, cheeks smeared with dirt, smiled meekly.

"Aunt, she released us. We only just returned with the children." He accepted her embrace, then spread his other arm wide to accept Emora, who sniffled and sobbed into his shoulder. "I will be fine, aunts. She never harmed any of us, not truly. But there is much to discuss. We should hurry into the confines of the war room so our secrets are not laid bare in front of traitorous ears, should they exist."

"We missed you so, Reven," Emora said. "Let us take you in and revel in this moment."

"I know. I missed you, and I love you both, but we must remain steadfast in our mission. We need to talk," he insisted. "There are things you need to know immediately."

Eiagan did not appreciate the tone he used since it almost surely meant there was news she did not wish to hear, but instead of questioning her nephew, she nodded toward the castle. Those in her innermost circle knew who was invited while Gael stood in place, unsure where he might be expected to wait. He'd offered the truth, as far as Eiagan knew, and now was no time to keep secrets. As much as she still worried he might be a spy in disguise, Gael was needed during the planning. Only he knew what his kingdom was truly capable of, and overplanning their part in the recapture of Varrow and the defeat of Nessa could have devastating consequences.

"Come, Gael, join us as we hear the news and plan our offense." Eiagan motioned inside again, but Reven grasped her upper arm.

"Perhaps before we go in, I should warn you. It will come as a shock but... Mother... *my mother,* is still alive. Nessa had her imprisoned and she sent her back with us. Her mind is a bit confused, but otherwise I think she is well."

"Astrid is alive?" Emora gasped, then smiled, her deepest wish a reality. There was no stopping the princess then. She darted around the group and ran inside to fetch her adoptive sister, one who had been closer to her than Eiagan could hope to be.

Truly, Eiagan wanted to run to Astrid as well, but to do such a thing in front of her people might startle them, and only Heaven knew they didn't need any additional stress. Instead, Eiagan grasped Porvarth's hand, pulled him from his shock, and headed toward the castle war room. The others trailed behind, including Catia who had also never set foot inside Vidkun, or Eathevall for that matter, and eyed it as if the very walls might swallow her up. There was every reason to believe they might.

The moment Emora shoved through the heavy wooden door, Astrid gasped and clutched Ballan's shirt front. Eiagan's heart stuttered for a moment as if she had seen a woman come back from the dead. In some way, she had. Ballan soothed her and wrapped a protective arm around his wife, reminding Eiagan of how much everyone had lost. She was so tired of this war, but it would end soon. *Soon.*

Once Emora's face became clear to Astrid, she pushed off of her husband and fell into Emora, sobbing. The room hushed. Eiagan allowed it for several minutes before clearing her throat. The longing in her heart surged forward, stung her throat and eyes, but Reven was right. There would be time for reunion and affection later. Now was time to plan as Nessa's end game circled them.

"I could not be happier, truly, but Reven was right. We should not slow our advancements where defeating Nessa is concerned. In fact, I think having both Astrid and Lucifer back from the grave should only spur us on."

Astrid offered her a slight nod and a smile, then wiped her eyes. "Lucifer is alive, too? He'd escaped, and I worried he had been killed."

"He's alive and strong as ever," Eiagan said, slowly relaxing.

"I'm so pleased, but Eiagan is right. We should plan, then once we have eliminated our foe, we will have a grand ball. Assuming that is permitted?" Astrid's eyes connected with Eiagan's again, begging her to allow them this one thing. Eiagan nodded, then took her seat.

Her pale eyes scanned the room as her people found their seats—save one.

"Where is Noxious?" Eiagan asked. "He should be here, of course."

Many pairs of eyes landed on her, but none spoke. Tend leaned across the table, grasped Eiagan's hands in his. "We have much to discuss, my queen. Our brother has been taken, willingly, in a trade for the children. He... he is with Nessa as her captor."

Eiagan shot from the chair as if she'd been skewered through with a spear. "What?" Her shout echoed through the small room, forcing a shiver down more than one spine. That Allurigard heat bubbled close to the surface, and it showed on her face, she was sure. "What do you mean he was taken?"

"He's safe," Reven added. "We spoke with him several times before we were sent away, and Darby can speak with him as she did with Ellaro. It's a cunning plan, truly, but we have only just arrived and not tested how it might work over long distances."

Eiagan's chest constricted further, aching with loss as she thought about her favored dragon, her dearest friend in the clutches of such a woman.

Erdravac shifted in his chair. "You say you can communicate with him as you did your dragon, Ellaro? Through your mind?" he asked.

"Indeed," Darby said. "As Reven said, I have not tested it long distances. She dropped us in Sudyak Meadow through a magical portal, so we have no way to know where she is in physical form. However, if our mind speaking works, we might use a locator spell to discover the whereabouts of Nessa's castle... prison... I am not entirely sure what it was, but if we can locate it then I would think we might also find a way in. I believe that is where she houses her body when she uses her projections."

"This is an interesting development," Gael added.

"Truly, especially considering our plan," Ari said.

Eiagan felt a tug at her wrist and glanced down. Porvarth, cheeky grin and all, peered up at her with his brilliant blue eyes, reminding her that she was standing in a room of seated people, still seething beneath her weak control of her emotions. "I can be your favored dragon just this once. You know well that Nox is strong enough to survive this."

"Ha," Catia said. "He might be strong enough to physically survive, but I'd bet my last coin that woman has him so turned around in his britches he cannot even see straight. Betting odds are high, she even has him doubting who the bad guy is." She crossed her arms, but she wasn't entirely wrong. Nox had a habit of falling for women who were not healthy for him—save Hazel—but that was hardly the first problem on Eiagan's mind.

The door creaked open, and Iditania stepped into the room. The last time Eiagan had laid eyes on her grandmother, she had been practically hysterical. She had regained her senses, it seemed, and was prepared to work through the kinks in their plan. As much as Eiagan hated knowing Nox was with Nessa, there was a war to win.

"Grandmother," Eiagan said and motioned to her to sit. There was no time for a happy family reunion with her either, only time for business.

Iditania took her chair and crossed her hands on her lap. "I have considered your plan and find that it will be difficult, but I believe it will work. I will need ample rest between now and then, but it is possible."

"Am I allowed to hear the plan now?" Gael asked, his reddish eyebrow cocked.

Eiagan sighed. She had no choice. "My grandmother is capable of projecting armies just as your people can. We will advance on

Nessa with our ghost armies after we take back Varrow. Assuming Princess Darby can locate her physical form, that is. I would like to keep losses minimal. Would your people provide their own phantom ranks?"

"I see no reason why not. Will you take your regular army to Varrow?"

"I believe it will be necessary, yes. Varrowans are mighty fighters and would know a phantom when they see it," Eiagan said. "Even so, we can intimidate them with a larger army filled in with projections."

"Are you absolutely sure of your final decision, Eiagan," Iditania asked, keeping Eiagan's decision to lock Nessa in her grandmother's old prison between them. Eiagan could not decide whether telling the others was the right thing or not, so she kept her mouth shut and nodded. She would tell them when the time was right. Besides, only the Lord knew whether her choice would bear fruit or drag her to Hell with it.

Iditania frowned and nodded. All at once Eiagan remembered Nessa was also Iditania's granddaughter, which lent an whole other set of pains to their plan. It seemed everyone in the room had been affected by the mage in some way.

"She is your blood, too, Grandmother," Emora said, voicing Eiagan's thoughts. "Should it be to much for you, we would understand."

Once again, the room fell silent as gazes fell upon Iditania.

She licked her lips. "She is my blood, but she is not my family. I will follow Eiagan in all things where this is concerned."

"I must admit, I was shocked when Astrid told us the truth of Nessa's lineage. Dare I ask how the two of you are managing?" Tend asked, glancing between Eiagan and Emora.

Eiagan's silent stare offered him every answer he required, so he merely nodded and fell silent gain.

Eiagan sighed. "Darby, what reason do we have to trust a locator spell will work through your connection when no other location enchantments have worked before?"

"The bond is a whole different sort of connection. It's soul to soul rather than physical object to the owner. It's stronger, like a kinship. Through it, we will find him." Darby was determined, a trait Eiagan admired.

"Fine. Now is the time to test your connection with Noxious. I must meet with Zanaka to determine our ranks and our plan where Varrow is concerned. Erdravac, would you join me?"

Darby rose, followed by Reven, ready to do her work. Erdravac stood and crossed the room, prepared to take back his kingdom. Everyone else looked toward Eiagan for clarification. *What shall we do* their eyes demanded.

"Rest. Eat. Prepare yourselves for what comes next." Her eyes landed on Astrid. "Reunite and spend time with those you love. Connect with those who are strangers in this room, for they will have your back in war. You should know them better than yourself."

With that, Eiagan shifted her gaze to Porvarth, letting that connection between them speak for her. *I love you… I need a moment to do what I do best… I will return to you as I am now and not as I once was.*

He nodded and turned his attention to Astrid and Emora.

"Shall we?" Erdravac offered, opening the door for her. With so little time left before the end — at least, what felt like the end — Eiagan couldn't help but think of her father. He had said once that he had protected his children from one who came before them. Had he meant Nessa? What might have happened if Nessa had only come to her sooner, professed her name, and offered her allegiance? Eiagan shook her head. There was no sense in speculating what might have been, not when reality was so pressing it nearly suffocated her.

She stepped through the door with Erdravac on her heels, stepping into her role was the feared Winter Queen once more. She only hoped she could shirk it again after the war was won.

THIRTY-THREE

Noxious "The Savage" Skjoldsson

Violet was quiet and happy enough with her dolls, so Noxious released his anger toward Nessa for leaving her alone after sending the others away. It would do no good to hold on to that anger, and it would likely only turn him into a grouchy, unbearable man. The dragon tickled its talons across his mind, begging to be released, to simply end this farse and be on with life. But Noxious had patience where his beast did not. He needed to understand, to know how this happened before dispatching of the woman who had ruined everything. Perhaps then he could ensure the boiling Allurigard blood didn't taint future generations.

"Father will return soon, my darling. Will you be alright?" Noxious brushed her hair away from her face and kissed her cheek.

"Yes, Papa, but I miss my friends." She glanced up at him with her sweet eyes — all her mother's — then turned back to her dolls.

"I know. We won't be here forever, I promise. As soon as Father understands, we will escape. I won't be long."

Noxious crossed the room and blew her a kiss, then closed the door and wandered toward Nessa's quarters. He had no idea whether the woman had returned from whatever business she had, but he intended to squeeze more information from her no matter how long it took or what he had to do. The history of his family had always been riddled with holes, just enough missing information that no one questioned it too much, but he couldn't pretend it didn't matter anymore. Those missing pieces might have changed everything.

He entered the room and found Nessa sitting by the fire again, this time with a book. Her gaze lifted, then fluttered back to the book. She closed it and placed it on a small table, one that had not been there before. Did she have nothing better to do than rearrange the furniture?

"You returned," she said, more a question that a statement, but Nox only nodded and made his way to his usual seat.

"You will tell me more? What happened between you and my ancestor?"

She chuckled. "You can hardly stand the sight of me, but if you want more, then I will show it to you as I did the last memory." Her hair was different, too, braided and tied up as if prepared for battle. She'd changed her clothing. No longer a dress, it was leather and slim-fitting, useful in battle. Nessa was ready to fight again. Time ran short.

"What will you do now, Nessa? Walk into a den of hungry dragons? Slaughter half the world to achieve your goals?" He leaned back in the chair and propped his leg on one knee before tugging his boot higher. His stomach growled, but he covered it with a sigh. "Do you mean to wage war without an army?"

"I have an army in Varrow. It's impressive, even if I must say so myself. They unseated that puny little Erdravac just to get a taste of what I offer. Suffice it to say, after Moriarian's death, they want a bit of revenge against Goranin and your precious Eiagan." The words burned her, tainted her system like venom, but it slowly began to make sense to the dragon.

"What would you do if I promised to not only stay, but try to turn my heart toward you if you only gave up your mission?" He leaned forward, earnest in his offer — mostly. He hadn't considered it until then, but if he could change her mind enough to keep her from going on a slaughtering spree, perhaps in time he might find a way to eliminate her *before* she could shed more innocent blood.

Her eyes softened if only for a moment, then she met him halfway, her spine stiff as a sword. "I'm no fool, dragon. You could never love me, and as such, I will not waste time contemplating an offer that leaves me with nothing much but a man who hates me and his daughter living in my castle. My bed would still be cold, and I would have no kingdom to rule besides that."

His golden eyes narrowed. The dragon rumbled inside, vying with his stomach to be heard. The beast wanted her blood so badly he could taste it on his human tongue.

"I *would* try. You are not much different from Eiagan. That is true. Your tales have shown me your life was no easy stroll, and in time I might see past the things you have done as I did with her. You are…" He paused. What was she? Certainly, he had no interest in this woman, but he did *understand* what made her turn madder than a wolf with the fever.

304

Her eyebrows arched and she grinned. "Well, out with it. I am a monster. Abominable. A mistake of nature worth nothing, but your pity will make you love me in time?" She laughed.

"You're human. I feel..." He raised a hand, palm up as if holding the answer in his hand. "I feel... I don't feel pity, but some sort of understanding that comes from seeing the same brutality you suffered forced on others. I have seen it more than any man should. I have *done* it in her name, as you said. In time, I would not hate you. In time, I might even tolerate your company."

Nessa swallowed and lowered her gaze. "Time is the one thing I'm afraid I don't have. I'm sorry, Noxious. I cannot give you what you ask." She stood and turned, waving her hand over the wall as she did. "You won't like what you see here, but know I did it for the love of my life. And I *did* love him, Noxious. I would have done anything for him."

She slammed the door, leaving Nox alone with another vision that played on the wall as if he were there. But something gnawed in his mind... not the scraping of his dragon, but something else. It requested access, lingered to see if he would allow it to flow into his mind... *Darby*.

It took some time to relax, to let her flow into his thoughts without struggling. He had to remind the dragon that Princess Darby was their ally, but as soon as the beast shrank into its corner, her kind voice crept in.

Nox, can you hear me?

"Yes, I can—" Nox stopped midsentence. She would never hear spoken word, so he thought it toward her as best as he could. *I hear you.*

Good. Listen to me... keep your mind open. We all arrived at the castle safely. Eiagan and the others are here. They know Nessa is their sister, and Eiagan has a plan, one that Nessa will never expect.

305

Noxious sent his understanding back down that pathway between them, then waited for her to relay the plan.

I will relay the plan, but first we must find her. Listen closely, dragon, and try not to flinch. We are using an ancient locator spell through the link, but it might hurt. Focus on something beautiful.

There was little in Nox's life that was beautiful, save Violet, and he would never want to associate his daughter with painful memories. Instead, he ignored Darby and focused on the story playing in front of him. Though it would bring him no comfort in his pain, it would distract him. And if he were lucky, it would bring him one step closer to the final goodbye.

In the year since they first met, it was not the first time Zero had gotten into mischief and angered his father, but this time it seemed Zero's horrible father would take everything the entire world had ever done wrong out on his son's back. Lash after lash whipped across his back as Zero struggled to free himself from the binds his father had wrapped around his wrists and ankles. He would kill the boy, and no one would say a thing about it in this desperate land.

Zero had forced Nessa to promise she would never follow him home. It was such a strange request, but she granted it without thought until he appeared in the forest one afternoon with two black eyes and a busted lip. No one could possibly trip over the threshold of their home and injure themselves so badly. It was a lie, and he never lied to her. Whatever secrets he kept, she needed to know. And so, she followed him.

The first time she watched his father harm him, it was just a smack across the face. Nessa winced but didn't interfere. The second time was a punch and a kick, but she bit her tongue and remained hidden in the forest. She plotted and planned how she might rescue him from this fate, but nothing came to her. The quarrels at her own home had become so violent she rarely went home herself.

But now, watching his father beat him within an inch of his life, Nessa was sure she would rather live in the forest than ever let him suffer again. She burst from the trees and put herself between Zero and his father's whip.

"Leave him alone!"

It was too late. The whip cut across Nessa's face so fast she didn't feel the sting until seconds later. Then the trickle of blood and the searing pain of torn flesh.

Zero launched at his father, but it did no good. A swift backhand brought him down again, rolling as he finally freed his ankles.

"Keep your hands off of him!" Nessa's scream shuddered the earth, forcing Zero to his knees again. He scrambled to avoid his father's blows, to protect Nessa from them as his attention turned toward her once more.

Nessa grasped Zero's arm and helped him to his feet while his father shifted his stance to avoid falling.

"Go, hurry, while the earth shakes!" Zero urged Nessa to go, never once assuming such a shift in the earth might be caused by his dearest friend. The two broke into a run, dodging trees and limbs as they crashed around them. Finally, they escaped the strip of forest that separated Zero's farm from Sudyak Meadow. They ran across it, past where Nessa knew the mage Simorana lived, and back into the depths of the forest until they reached a small cave that overlooked their waterfall.

Inside, Zero bent over and huffed to catch his breath. He could never go back, not now, not after what Nessa did. His father would kill him. His shirt, torn and bloodstained, barely hung from his shoulders in strips.

"I told you... never... to follow me. Why did you?"

Nessa shook her head. "You lied to me, and I wanted to know why."

Nessa went down to the river and manifested a bucket, which she filled to the brim with water. Upon returning to the cave, she found Zero had removed what little remained of his shirt and dabbed at the wounds he could reach.

"Here, let me. You'll only make them worse." Nessa took the remnants of the shirt and cleaned them in the water, then dabbed the blood of each wound until it was clean. In the far corner, she had stowed her favorite bag in case they ever needed anything while they were exploring. Nessa retrieved the bag and emptied its contents onto the cave floor. Zero did not question her. He was in too much pain.

Nessa applied ointments to the wounds, aiding their healing. She did wish her magical ability were beneficial, that it healed instead of causing destruction, but no matter how hard she tried, it seemed her magic would forever be a force of destruction. She could not heal Zero with it, but she could ensure no one ever hurt him again – and she would. Nessa would not let his father or any man lay a hand upon him again, and if one ever did, she would cut it off.

Zero let out a breath before relaxing. The ointment was working, slowly easing his pain and healing the wounds, but it would take some time before they were healed entirely.

"I wish I could run away and never return to this place," he said.

Fear struck Nessa so hard she gasped. "No, no, you… you cannot just leave me here. I have no friends besides you, and you are… you just cannot leave!"

Zero turned so that he could see Nessa's face. "You are the only reason I have stayed so long. If I stay, he will kill me. I have nowhere to hide from him, not even here. He will find me eventually, and when he does, if you are with me…" Zero shuddered. "I cannot imagine what he might do to you. The only reason he did not hurt you today was because of the earthquake."

"Take me with you. Do not leave me here to suffer alone without you." Nessa clutched a bloodied strip of his shirt, willing her emotions to stay put while she worked through this problem with him.

His crystalline green eyes caught hers, only for a moment before they darted back to the cave floor. "What would you have me do, Nessa? Build us a home in the middle of some forest somewhere? Hunt and fish so that we might stay alive?"

"Why not?" she asked, a bit of edge to her tone. "You are capable, and I can help you."

"There is nowhere I can hide that he will not find me, Nessa. My father is the cruelest man in the land, save the king himself." Zero sighed again and took Nessa's hand. "But I will stay for you so that you do not suffer alone in your darkness."

The moment he said those words, the ones she so desperately wanted to hear, she knew they were his death sentence. He was right. He could not stay and live, and she could not protect him every moment of the day. There was only one thing that would solve both problems.

"I will make sure he never touches you again, Zero. I will." She squeezed his hand even as he chuckled, his eyes gleaming.

"While I appreciate your tenacity, I cannot see how you might keep that promise. Father will hurt you, Nessa, and not in ways that can ever be mended. I should be the one to protect you by leaving this place."

Nessa stiffened, but Zero shook his head.

"I won't leave you. I give you my word that I will never leave here without you, but you must not try to confront my father. He would never kill you and risk a death sentence, but he will ruin you, Nessa. He will ruin you so that no man would ever want you, and I cannot let that happen."

Finally, Nessa understood his meaning. His father was a lowlife scoundrel who would do more to a woman than hit her. For a moment, she lost control of her emotions, let her anger surge forward just thinking of the things the man had done to her dear friend, notwithstanding what he might have done to others. The earth rattled again, but only for a moment before Nessa capped her anger and shoved it deep inside.

Zero had pulled her closer, protecting her from falling bits of debris inside the cave. Nessa had not considered telling Zero about her abilities. Not once since they met had she entertained the idea, but as he sat with his arms around her, she could not think of any reason not to tell him. How any boy – any man – might be so kind and gentle with no guide to show him, no real father to teach him, was an anomaly Nessa was sure she might never understand. To be fathered by such a cruel, heartless man, and yet become the best man Nessa believed walked upon the earth was a miracle.

She thought of her own biological parents... even thought of her adoptive parents... and realized she, too, had been purged from the very same Hell as Zero, yet her magic was angry and heated, nothing kind and gentle like Zero. He was, she decided, a man unlike any other.

"I promise you that one day you will forget this pain, that you will be a king and all the world will know that you are most deserving of everything good that comes to you," Nessa said, barely a whisper, but the shudder of Zero's chest said he'd heard her.

"That is a lovely dream, but it cannot – "

Nessa pushed off him. "It can. It will, and I can make it so."

Zero's lips spread into his usual grin, but behind it was a shield, one that he used to ensure nothing hopeful ever entered his mind. No hope, no longing, and certainly no belief that his lot might improve. And it was that shield, the protective barrier that kept him from ever wondering what more might exist for him.

"Nessa – "

"Zero. Listen to me," she said, her hands settled on his shoulders. "Just for a moment, let me speak unhindered." He nodded. "I have kept a secret from you, one that might scare you but I swear that I will never hurt you, and that I will always protect you."

"Nessa, what are – "

"Ah, ah... Let me speak. I can make sure no one ever hurts you again, and I can give you all the things I said, but you must never tell anyone about me. Breathe not a single word about my ability to anyone or risk my death."

"How... how can you protect me, Nessa? You are but a peasant girl, just like my family."

Nessa shook her head. "No, Zero. No, I am not... at least, I used to be something more. Have you ever heard of the long-dead land of Asantaval?"

"Once, when my father was raving drunk."

Nessa's smile spread as she told Zero her story, about the life she'd lived from the moment Bribadge brought her beneath the earth to that moment with him. He never balked or scoffed, never laughed at her. He listened intently until her story had finished, and then he swallowed the lump in his throat, his eyes taking her in as if she were different yet the same, as if he had always known her yet never met her at all.

"To think all this time, I have been in the company of royalty so grand as you, and not once did I ever feel inferior."

"Because you are not inferior, Zero. You are good and kind and you deserve such things in return. And I swear to you, with my very last breath upon this earth, I will give you all of this land, every mixlin that has been ravaged by men less honorable than you. I promise you, one day I will sit upon a throne so grand that even the old gods will be jealous."

Zero studied her, took in every feature as if memorizing the way she looked in that moment. He brushed his thumb over her cheek, so gentle to have been fathered by such a harsh man. "And what will happen to me when you take that throne?"

Nessa felt her cheeks flame, but she would not look away. No, they were young, merely children now, but there was no reason why she could not look to her future and see him there with her, ruling the lands that her mother had promised her long ago when she first learned her identity. If she could plan to take over half the world at her age, then there was certainly no reason she could not plan who might be at her side when she did.

"You will sit upon the throne beside me, of course."

For the first time since she met him, Zero looked at her as more than his friend, more than the girl who had spoiled his hunts more than once. He gazed upon her as his future, the girl who would, one day, stand by his side when everything that had ever been wrong finally healed.

"I think I would like that very much," he said, then kissed the top of her head.

Nessa's heart finally eased. "Until then, I will ensure your father is well managed." She stood and brushed the dirt from her dress, then offered her hand. "Come, let me show you something."

Outside, Nessa scoured the ground for a quartz rock large enough to perform her magic. By the river, she found one with a faint pinkness that would serve her well. Though her abilities were destructive, she had managed to control the destruction, to hone it until she could use it to create some beauty even through the destruction.

She palmed the quartz and pressed her hands together, allowing her magic to flow into it, to destroy it and remake it into something different. Then she opened her hand and offered the quartz to Zero.

"How... how did you do that?" He gazed down at the stone, now shaped as a perfect heart with intricately carved scrollwork that looped and swirled around both sides.

"Magic," Nessa teased, then urged him to keep it. "It is yours. Keep it, and when you feel lonely, you can look at it and be reminded that we have a future. And however long it might take to get there, remember that it is ours."

Nessa crept along the forest quiet as a predator, not far from the truth given her intent that night. She had ensured Zero was asleep before leaving the serenity of their cave, lost in dreams of their future. Now, more than ever, Nessa was determined to go against her parents' wishes that she remain *quiet and hidden. No, she would not fade into memory without taking back what was hers — all of it. She was the rightful heir of all that she could see in Goranin, and by her last breath she would have it and then some. Zero would have it all.*

There was only one thing standing in the way... one thing that might foil her plan before it even got started. His father.

The drunkard stumbled through the forest, a far sight from the right path home, and so Nessa took it as an opportunity. No one would question the death of a drunken man who wandered too close to a bear's den. Of course, bears were scarce in Goranin, but Nessa knew well enough what their markings looked like. Magic or not, she would ensure the people who found him believed it had been a bear... or a wolf... or any number of horrific creatures that one might find in the darkest parts of the forest.

She waited behind a tree until his path crossed hers, then she stepped behind him.

"You," she said, earning his attention.

He turned, tripped, but caught himself as he watched her. His grin, sickening and wide, cut his face in half as he took her in top to bottom.

"Well, now, look what I found." He lunged toward her, ready to take her without her consent, but that first rip had him howling louder than the wolves.

Nessa merely thought it, and it happened. A slice across his chest... then his abdomen until his innards spilled out... his face... legs...

Without laying a hand on him, she shredded him into an unrecognizable pile of flesh and bone and blood.

"There now, isn't that better?" she whispered, then went back to the cave to see Zero.

THIRTY-FOUR

Noxious "The Savage" Skjoldsson

Nox wiped his mouth and tossed the soiled rag over the puddle of vomit. He'd seen more than his fair share of rot in his lifetime, but Nessa's murders twisted his stomach in more ways than one. She hadn't been *wrong* necessarily to protect Zero, but her ability to melt a man in his boots with little more effort than it took to squash a nobwood fruit sent shivers down his spine. Eiagan was a formidable woman, to be sure, but Nessa's power radiated through the room though she was nowhere to be found. Couple what he'd seen with the pain of Darby's intrusion into his mind with that blasted locator spell, and he could hardly stand.

The quartz heart… Nox shoved his hand into his pants pocket and rubbed his finger over the family heirloom. No one knew where it had come from, only that it had served his family well for

314

centuries. Zero never told a soul where he had obtained it, but it was a beloved treasure passed from eldest son to eldest son — or in Nox's case, from his father to him, the only son who cared at all about family tradition. His elder brothers had left long ago, and Nox had not seen them in the better part of fifteen years.

Nox rolled the smooth stone over in his palm, unsure whether to toss it in the fire or guard it with his life.

The door handle clicked so he shoved the quartz back into his pocket. The door creaked open but no person entered, so Nox lowered his gaze. A red snake slithered over the floorboards until it reached him, then it transformed. She stood in front of him in the same clothing, though a bit wrinkled.

"Have you completed whatever monstrous deeds you've put on your list today?" he asked, swallowing bile that rose in his throat again.

Nessa's eyes shifted to the puddle of vomit then back to him. Lest his eyes deceive him, he thought she shuddered and swallowed. In an instant, though, her composure stiffened along with her spine. She lifted her chin.

"He was cruel and you would not exist today if I had not ended Zero's torment. He would have killed Akeel and Zero both in his drunken rage. Perhaps some gratitude is in order, or is it simply more fun to judge me while you hold murder in your own heart as well?" She'd added some form of armoring to her leathers, more prepared for battle than before. Blood — or at least, something like it — smeared over her forehead and cheeks and chin in a pattern of lines. What they meant was anyone's guess, but one thing was clear — it was warpaint, and she was enacting her final plan.

But she was not wrong.

"I've done my share, yes." He pointed to the purged food. "It was... unexpected."

Nessa's eyes softened but he didn't give her a chance to soften his heart to her mission. She was evil incarnate, and he would do well to remember that when she looked this way. But dragon's breath, though it made him sick to admit it, she was beautiful. He knew what Zero saw when he looked upon her all those centuries ago, but whoever she was then had died and left behind a shell. No... not a shell, exactly, but a hollowed-out woman whose heart had been replaced by anger and pain and hatred nothing would stamp out. Her soul had been lost long ago, and that was the difference between Nessa and Eiagan... Nessa and Emora. They had changed, found a better path to follow, but Nessa would never stop until her revenge mission had been fulfilled or she was dead.

"I need some time to process and be with my daughter. Will you allow it?"

Her eyes narrowed. "I said I wouldn't keep you from her. I'll send food. What would you like?"

"I'll eat anything but Violet likes venison stew with peas. Bread if you can." Placing a dining order with a former princess... a homicidal maniac... as if it were just another day spent at the tavern unnerved Nox more than the scene he'd just witnessed.

"Very well. I'll send it to you along with something sweet for her." She lowered her gaze to his chest. "Despite what you believe, I do regret leaving her alone. It was not my intention. I suppose I am not good with children."

Nox huffed. It was laughable that anyone might think she *was* a good influence for children, a proper caretaker, or in some way apt to handle the needs of such vulnerable humans. Anger followed by pain flashed through her eyes when they met his gaze again. Nox did not back down, but kept his gaze locked with hers. What was in that head of hers? What games… what tricks… what dastardly plots awaited him? God forbid she succeed in killing Eiagan and Emora, what then?

"I wouldn't know how to be a parent," she admitted. "But that is no excuse. I *am* sorry. I wish you would know that and accept it before…" She faded, leaving her thought unsaid.

Moments passed between them that way, simply staring into one another's eyes while all manner of emotion passed through each of them until they settled on something knowing, something understanding. This was the final stand, the last moments before all Hell broke and only one of them would be left standing. It had to be Eiagan, but for a breath Nox worried his friend might not be strong enough, that she wouldn't know how cunning and untethered her opponent was.

Nessa blinked and lowered her gaze again.

"Is there anything you wish to say?" she asked. "You look as though you would like to release a mountain's worth of curses upon me, and if it is what you wish, I will hear them."

As if burning a hole through his pocket, the stone called to him. He couldn't stop himself or the call to present it to her, leading to a thousand questions that were still unanswered. Nox slipped his hand into his pocket and retrieved the stone heart. Warm in his hand, he turned his palm upright, forcing a gasp from Nessa.

Seemingly without thought, she reached for it, then yanked her hand back. Eyes once again connecting with his, they held a question. Nox nodded and handed the quartz to her. Once in her hands, tears slipped over her cheeks and fell on the dark leather vest she wore, staining it still further. What else stained that vest? How much blood?

317

Captivated by the heart, Nessa turned it over in her hand again and again, her gaze lost somewhere in the past until she couldn't stand it another moment. She cradled it in her palm and extended her arm back to Nox, impatient as ever.

"It's yours," Noxious said, stepping away from her. Taking it back felt like more than accepting a family heirloom and more like accepting the same promise she'd made Zero. It held so much more history now than it had only hours ago, and keeping it would mean more than he was willing to accept.

Nessa stared at her own outstretched arm, hand open, presenting the quartz to Nox. "It was always his and now it's yours." Her fingers trembled, so Nox plucked the stone from her palm, careful not to touch her. His dragon, though, shuddered at the closeness and retreated deeper into his mind. Had she truly intimidated such a beast? A chill went down Nox's spine again.

Nessa sighed as a sliver of regret passed over her expression. It was gone before Nox could speak of it.

"I find myself surprised that he even kept it." She crossed her arms, closing herself off.

"It meant a lot to him. At least, that was the story we were told. He never said where it came from, so we assumed..." Nox's voice faded. Speaking her name aloud would only anger Nessa, but she was wise enough to read his thoughts.

She huffed. "Of course, his beloved Eiagan. You know, he loved me once, too. Maybe more than he loved her, but..." Nessa faded. She'd dropped her arms and lifted her hands palm up, almost as if begging Nox to believe her, that his ancestor had once loved her with such ferocity and intensity, that it warranted her present behavior.

Nox's jaw flexed until his teeth ground. Though he didn't want to, he understood her pain. Perhaps to never have love was better than to have it and lose it, but whether it was or not didn't matter. If Zero kept the stone, then his love for Nessa had been true. Whatever happened to tear them apart never changed that. It had merely opened his heart to someone else... to Eiagan.

"I know," he whispered, forcing himself to remember she was insane, a bloodthirsty murderer with no direction and no remorse, nothing like Eiagan.

He should destroy her here while she was present in her mortal form. He should shift and let his dragon rip her to shreds, assuming it could. It hid in the back of his mind, nary a nail scraping against his mind as it mingled in the shadows. But even if the beast were capable of destroying this centuries-old monster... could he? It wasn't his fight, not truly, and even if it were, Nox found himself unable to muster enough strength to do what he knew should be done. And Eiagan might never forgive him for going against her command to keep Nessa alive.

"I'll have the food sent," she said, then turned to open the door.

"Nessa?" Nox found himself reaching for her, then he dropped his hand before she turned back to him.

"Worry not, dragon. There is no meaning in that rock now. Those promises are long dead." She yanked the door open and disappeared, leaving Nox befuddled.

His shoulders slumped and he shoved the ridiculous stone in his pocket. There was no time to muddle through the inner workings of his confused mind. There were more pressing things, namely, working through the finer details of the mission with Darby who now tapped on his mind. Between the beast and the princess, Nox wondered if his mind would ever be his own.

THIRTY-FIVE

Eiagan Allurigard

Zanaka's warm eyes and wide smile brought a little more light to the day. Eiagan accepted his embrace and returned it with equal excitement. Months had felt like years apart from her friends and family, but soon enough she would set them all free from this darkness that hung over them.

"My queen, things seem to be coming together nicely, save the news, of course," Zanaka said.

Eiagan frowned but she could not change that Nessa was her sister. In truth, she couldn't say whether it would have made a difference given her desire to *stop* killing everything that crossed her path. If Nessa were anyone else, she might still offer imprisonment over death. She was tired of death.

"I've come to finalize the advancement on Varrow. Have you been informed of the plans to liberate the kingdom?"

"Yes, I have been thoroughly informed. Will the Asantavalian's join us in this mission?" Zanaka asked.

"Indeed. Our phantom armies will converge at the Varrowan border while our live ranks will follow soon after to secure the castle before we move on to Nessa, assuming Princess Darby might pinpoint her exact location with her connection to Noxious. Have you everything you need?"

"Yes, Highness." Zanaka bowed and offered Erdravac a grin. "I had not expected you, but it is good to see you. I am glad that wretched woman didn't take your head."

"Me too, brother, thank you," Erdravac said, meeting Zanaka's grin with his own boyish, roguish one.

"Eiagan!" Darby's voice rang from a tower window above the courtyard. "Come quick! I have some idea where they are, but Nox is unable to confirm since he is still locked inside."

Eiagan pursed her lips, a bit put off that the girl yelled her information across the entire courtyard for all the world to hear.

"Not much of warlord, is she?" Zanaka asked, chuckling.

"No. We had better return before she screams our entire plan to the whole of Goranin," Eiagan said, then turned foot and headed back to the war room with Erdravac. Zanaka stayed behind to continue his preparations, which pleased Eiagan.

Erdravac followed Eiagan wordlessly back to the planning room where Darby had, it seemed, made contact with Nox. She had wished her dearest friend had not sacrificed himself to the mage for their benefit, but she did see the brilliance in such a plan.

Along the table were maps of Goranin and Varrow long before they were split into two kingdoms, when the land had looked much different than it did then, including Havisham Forest which Reven studied with a magnifying glass.

Oh, Heavens. Not there.

Eiagan froze. The forest was as haunted as her dreams, and they would spend more time fighting spirits than sociopathic mages bent on destroying everything. She had never been there, of course, but Eiagan had heard the tales passed down from generation to generation. It was a place even Icluedian wouldn't dare venture, so whatever lived in that forest could stay there... alone.

Darby lifted her head toward Eiagan when she entered the room.

"Havisham?" Eiagan asked.

"I'm afraid so," Darby said. "I am told it is no happy place. It also explains the odd forest that surrounded the castle where we were imprisoned."

Eiagan sighed and pulled out her chair beside Porvarth. Emora, Ari and Tend sat at the table with her, while Gael and Erdravac paced. Catia fidgeted with her shirt but Eiagan knew she would not back down, not after everything she had seen.

"I am afraid it is a place even my father would not have ventured even if given free choice to do so. The castle there is the oldest known castle among the ancient kingdoms, a place thought haunted by a king so cruel, it would make Icluedian and Moriarian seem tame."

Porvarth chuckled, connecting the history. "Your ancestors have a penchant for hostility, darling."

Eiagan rolled her eyes. "It is true. He was one of the kings that came long before Goranin and Varrow were split in two, but I do know it holds a library." Eiagan realized her slip — that she nearly told everyone in the room Nessa planned to kill her in that library — and simply shrugged. "It likely contains volumes of history, not that it is relevant here." She connected gazes with Catia, who nodded. Emora shifted her weight in her seat, uncomfortable with the half-truth.

"Is it also possible that ancient dragons might also reside in the forest? Those we thought died out?" Ari asked.

Erdravac chewed his lip, seemingly a bit put off by the idea that his kingdom harbored not only the famous Havisham Forest, but perhaps an ancient breed of dragon no one dared cross—like Bracken. The dragon had killed Ellaro with ease, and Eiagan was sure he was invincible. At least, it would take magic the likes of which she had never seen to kill such a thing—or a ravenous dragon of larger size. They had never see him in human form, so her suspicion could be accurate.

"It would explain Bracken, yes, but I would think if there were many, then Nessa would take full advantage of them," Eiagan admitted. Screeching outside distracted everyone, but only briefly. Lucifer in bird form, flew through an open window and perched on Eiagan's shoulder, his frantic calls ceased.

Emora chuckled. "Do you ever wonder if he is even more than a magical shapeshifting horse?"

"Such as?" Tend asked, pausing to consider something besides Nessa for once.

Emora shrugged. "Oh, anything really. He has always been intuitive, and since he seems to see directly into my sister's soul, I do wonder if there is more behind his eyes than even we see."

"Perhaps, but we should not spend all our time contemplating such things. We should retire and rest before enacting our plans. Emora, Catia, would you join me for a meal?" Eiagan asked, pointedly *not* asking anyone else. Though she was sure the others wondered why they were not welcome to join, they did not question. People flooded from the room as if all the oxygen had been sucked right out of it—in truth, it felt the same to Eiagan, but she needed to discuss this new development with the only two souls who knew what Nessa had planned, what the future held.

No sooner had the door closed, the women were interrupted by a hollow, whistling call. A chill flooded the room, followed by a breeze that chilled even Eiagan. The three women stiffened while Eiagan drew her sword. Emora prepared to use her magic while Catia stood with a straight back and chin held high, quite ready to sass Nessa half to death if necessary. By Eiagan's estimation, she might succeed.

Nessa's tinkling giggle grew closer until her projection formed in front of Eiagan.

"Always ready with the sword," she said. "I have only come to discuss how we might end this with little bloodshed. There is a way, provided you are willing to sacrifice your pride and hand your kingdom over to me." Her hair was tied with braids and her face streaked with blood—a warrior ready for battle, just like the Astantavalian warriors.

"I will do no such thing, mage. I would sooner cut your tongue out and have it for dinner than turn over even a single grain of wheat to your hands. I know who you are, and I will not let another of us destroy this land." Eiagan offered a morsel then let Nessa decide whether to elaborate.

"Do you? How lovely. Shall we have a reunion?" Nessa checked her nails and smoothed her leather vest, then scoffed. "I would never be welcome at such an event, so let us not waste time. You know what I want."

"It can end differently, Nessa. It does not have to be this way, this all or nothing you seek. There is always some way to return from the things we have done wrong." Eiagan sheathed her sword. It would do no good against a phantom anyway, and shifted her position to one of argument rather than defense. Perhaps she might, at least, force the mage to listen to her. "My people have forgiven me, not all but most. I do not want to kill another..." Eiagan hesitated.

"Go on, say it." Nessa leaned forward, her nose a breath from Eiagan's. Like this, Eiagan wondered what else they might have in common besides those pale, soulless eyes.

"Sibling. My sister. I do not want to kill my sister."

"You were quite ready to kill Emora when you thought she had gone mad and taken everything. What changed?" Nessa's lip quivered into a snarl but Eiagan held her gaze, so close she smelled the blood smeared on the woman's face.

"I am tired of death. I want more for my people, more for my family. And there could be more for you, under certain circumstances, of course."

Nessa narrowed her eyes and stood straight as an arrow. "No, thank you. I have what I want, your *precious* Nox, and I do think he is one or two stories of woe away from understanding. And when he understands... Well, I cannot give away all the fun details, now can I?"

"I will destroy Asantaval and all you claim to love if so much as a scrape comes to Nox's skin," Eiagan said, seething with annoyance. To not want her sister dead was one thing, but to suffer her taunts in silence was something else altogether.

Nessa's expression shifted as quickly as the earth during the quakes. Her taunting grin and whimsical eyes saddened, and she swallowed. "I know. He is well, and so he will remain."

"I doubt that," Catia snapped, earning Nessa's attention. It was fleeting, so Catia stepped forward. "He has suffered enough at your hands. Do keep that in mind while playing your games with him."

Emora yanked Catia backward and shoved the woman behind her. Projection or not, she was still powerful enough to kill Catia with little more than a thought. Catia grumbled her displeasure with pursed lips, a stiff spine, and narrowed eyes. The woman had an air about her that caught Nessa's interest, but Eiagan distracted her before the mage had any ideas about kidnapping her as well.

"I will not hand my kingdom over and you will not yield. Where does this leave us?" Eiagan asked.

Nessa grinned. "I suppose we will meet on the battlefield, sister." Her projection faded and disappeared, leaving Eiagan, Emora, and Catia staring at a blank stone wall.

"What were you thinking, taunting her that way? She could have killed you!" Emora yanked Catia by the upper arm but the seamstress hissed an pulled away. "I'm sorry. I was only worried." Emora's tone softened but it didn't soften Catia's response.

"I'll do what I want when I want to do it, princess. If you think she is simply housing your friend for a time, feeding him biscuits and fine tea, you are both moronic. She will dig her claws in him until he believes she can be saved, perhaps even turn on you, and you will regret it when she does!" Catia's red hair billowed around her as she turned her head between them, catching each sister's gaze.

Eiagan relaxed her posture and approached Catia before gently placing a hand upon the woman's shoulder. It was panic, worry, fear... all those things mixed into some unbearable pit in her stomach that made her act out as she did. "I know my dragon, and I know he is the only man who might survive this. Perhaps he will unravel her ways, understand her and find sympathy, but he would not turn on us. Never."

Catia breathed a sigh of relief, but it was more than that. There was so much more Eiagan couldn't quite pinpoint, but she knew Catia's reaction was born of something complex and significant. As usual, there was no time to decipher it fully before action was required. There was also no time for rest now. It was time to take back Varrow for Erdravac, for her people, for the whole world.

"Do you truly think imprisonment will be enough, sister?" Emora asked.

"Not likely, but we must try. Nessa puts on a good show but I saw something different this time. She is a woman on a mission, of course, but beneath that is an exhausted woman. I know the look well." Eiagan brushed her black hair from her face and rubbed her hands over her eyes, on the brink of exhaustion herself.

"I pray you are right. God save the world if you are proven wrong, Winter Queen." Catia turned on her heel and slammed the door behind her.

Eiagan and Emora shared a glance. No words were exchanged but they knew. Catia had something worth losing even if she hadn't admitted it to them. The question was, would she fight with them to protect it or run?

THIRTY-SIX

Nessa Callanan

Nessa turned the carved pendant over in her hand several times. She hadn't meant to leave that in the armoire when she stored her captives in the west tower, but there it was all the same. The quick projection to taunt her sisters had taken its toll on her mortal body, and she was tired. But she had promised Nox the rest of the story, so she would tell him, but after she had recovered some of her energy.

Zero. Nessa sighed as she smoothed that pendant over and over again, a gift from him after she gave him the quartz heart. She might as well give it to Noxious for all the love it still held, but there was something soothing about touching it. It took her back to another time, one where she might have made different choices and suffered different consequences. Consequences that might not have been so awful.

Was it all a mistake? Of course, it was. She'd been a fool, cornered herself until there was no where to go, nothing to do but strike out. Perhaps there would be peace in that? To lose. To give in and finally find peace. Where would she go when she died? Would there be peace or would she burn in the pits of a never ending fury so hot she'd wish she'd never given up this fight? Only time would tell.

Nessa pocketed the pendant and stalked back to her quarters where Noxious waited. What good would restoring her energy do? He wouldn't kill her, and if he did, then she could think of no better way to die than by his hands. He would at least be merciful about it.

The warmth of her quarters drew her down the hallway but the soft murmur of Nox's voice gave her pause. She cracked the door and found him rocking his daughter back to sleep. She must have woken and wandered through the castle, but that would never do. If Bracken returned and found the small child unattended, he would swallow her whole for a snack, then Nessa would have to murder the only dragon she had on her side. Once upon a time, he had been part of her escape plan, but now she only wished she had never met the ancient relic of a time long since gone. Even the abandoned castle, sprawling over the lands nestled deep in Havisham Forest felt too cold and lonely now.

Nox's gaze shifted and settled on Nessa's face. Like that, so strong but gentle with a fragile child, he stole her heart further. He nodded and stood, so she stepped aside and allowed him to carry his daughter back to her room.

"I will only be a moment, and then I would prefer the tales from your lips rather than projections," he said, his golden eyes fixed on hers so fiercely, they pinned her to the wall.

She nodded and entered her quarters, quite cozy by anyone's standards. Nessa sighed. Everything might have been different if she had only chosen another path. This coziness might have been welcome even to the likes of Nox had she not become such a tyrant, a soulless demon who tortured and killed those he loved.

Nessa tossed another log onto the fire and sat. She assumed Nox's request for her to speak her own life story had more to do with stalling her than any real desire to understand her, but as long as he would listen, she would tell him what he wanted to know. If she died and fell straight into Hell, she would go knowing she had *this* peace first.

The door closed, bringing her back to reality after several moments staring into the fire.

"She had a bad dream, but she seems settled now. Is there a way she might contact me without wandering the castle?" Nox asked. His fatherly instinct was possibly the most attractive attribute Nessa had ever seen displayed in a man.

Nessa cleared her throat and stood, then brushed her hand over the wall. As her palm passed over the stone, a sort of portal-like mirror appeared.

"There. You will see her if she rouses and you can go to her." She closed the distance between them and sat again but Nox hesitated. "It is real, I assure you."

He shook his head and glanced at her. "It isn't that. I believe you. I only... Violet said..." He shook his head and sat. "It's nothing. Tell me, how did you reunite Akeel and Zero?"

She chuckled thinking back on that day. "It was simple really. I met Akeel in the forest just outside of Eathevall. I should say, I stalked him there when I heard his tales. He was a bastard son of a man who'd been murdered in a rather atrocious way," she said, slanting her eyes toward Nox. "I approached him and said I knew a man who had also been fathered by the heathen. He knew he had siblings since his father was quite wayward with women, and he was eager to meet Zero. They bonded almost immediately. Quite alike, they were."

Nox pursed his lips. No doubt, that was not part of the tales he'd heard. "Are you lying, Nessa?"

Nessa's head jerked against her will, but she was truly baffled. "Why on earth would I lie about that? It's such a trivial thing."

"What do you hope to accomplish here with me?"

"I was sure we discussed that already."

"Remind me," he snapped, then softened his features. "Please."

Nessa let out a long, slow sigh and waved her hand. "I'm not sure I know anymore. Let us get on with the story. One day while I was foraging for berries, I decided to see my parents. I had been with Zero for so long, I wanted to ensure they were still alive. Heaven knows, it was possible they would murder each other."

"Icluedian killed them. Emora told us."

"Did she tell you I hid under the bed while he slaughtered them? My father's head rolled across the floor while I just... *hid*."

"Why did you hide? You were powerful even then. You could have killed him and ended this entirely." Nox was on the edge of his seat, his fingers gripping the arms of his chair until they blanched.

Nessa laughed. "Of all the times for my magic to go silent, that was likely the worst. I tried. I *couldn't*. It was the first time I had ever

331

seen the man in flesh and bone, and I was terrified of him. He seemed so much more than an immortal man that day, almost like... as if he were..."

"Evil incarnate?" Nox offered.

Nessa shrugged. "I suppose. He seemed insurmountable, and so I hid. We both know I couldn't have done much, not with his invincibility, but I also think the wards he used to bind Serecala surrounded him, protected him from magic of all kinds. When he left I cried until my face was puffy and then I hid a while longer so Zero would never know I had been crying over my murdered parents."

Nox's gaze lowered and he released the arm rests. "I cannot imagine what that must have been like for you, so see your parents that way despite your disagreements with them."

Nessa chose to move on with her story so she would not spend precious moments blubbering over the death of a weak king and his traitorous wife. "I went to Simorana after they died, hoping she might help me but you well know how that turned out."

"Astrid offered to help while Emora was wary at first, then Emora learned magic from you. Then... Well, she thought she killed you. Where was Zero during this time? Did he not know?"

"I never told him Emora and Eiagan were my sisters. I should have, but... I never did. When Emora thought she killed me, I was weak from the projection and Zero found me unconscious. That was when we began drifting apart. I had lied to him and he knew it, but he never begged me to tell him the truth. Instead, he started to distance himself from me."

"More like you pushed him with your lies."

Nessa connected with him again, sorrow filling her entire body. "That is true."

"Why did you keep it all from him? He might have aided you as he eventually helped Eiagan." Nox's tone, almost begging, indicated some willingness to offer her leniency she did not deserve. There was no benefit of the doubt due to her. She had lied because it was her way, kept it all a secret because she could not imagine sharing it with him and ruining his image of her.

"In many ways I never thought he would understand. He knew I hated Icluedian but not that I was his daughter. Soon, my rage against my birth father and the things I was willing to do to taunt Icluedian worried Zero."

"Such as?"

Nessa chuckled. "Oh, so many things. Icluedian was a paranoid man, and all I needed to do was cause a little trouble here and there to make him lose control and slaughter half a community. Whenever he lowered his guard even a fraction, I spread a rumor that got him worked up again."

"What was the tipping point? Why did Zero leave? The conscription?"

"No, no," Nessa said, shaking her head. "It was me. He had grown weary of my vendetta. He wanted to settle and have a family, content to be a poor hunter his entire life so long as I was by his side, but that was not enough." Nessa dropped her hands in her lap. "Thanks to my upbringing, that would never be enough. Revenge tainted my blood, and I needed it like I needed air. Zero gave me a choice—end my vendetta against Icluedian and make a life with him, or continue on in my ways and lose him forever."

Nox's sympathetic gaze forced a stone in her throat. Why had she chosen as she had? Why? Why was revenge so much sweeter to her than Zero's kisses? His love? His offer of a happy family in a quiet corner of Goranin where Icluedian would never find them?

"And?" Nox asked though he knew her answer.

"I chose wrong."

THIRTY-SEVEN

Eiagan Allurigard

"It is time, my queen," Zanaka said, standing beside his horse as he offered Lucifer's reins to her. The black draft rumbled and connected his gaze with hers, stomping a few times to signify his willingness to follow her into battle again. Maybe this would be the last time. "Do you have all you need?"

"Indeed. Iditania is prepared and Gael has informed his people of the plans. Our phantom armies will converge on Varrow in a matter of hours, so we must hurry if we are to make them believe it is real." Eiagan mounted Lucifer—no saddle this time, the blasted things—and turned him east.

Porvarth shifted, ready for flight as her second mount. Between Lucifer and Porvarth, Eiagan was sure she was prepared to fight anything that came her way.

335

Eiagan looked over her shoulder at her people, those who would follow her to Varrow and into Havisham Forest, perhaps even into the depths of Hell if she asked them… maybe even if she didn't ask. Erdravac was more than ready to reclaim his rightful seat, and Eiagan had no doubt he would destroy the ancient castle once they had arrested Nessa. Borgard paced, ready to smash anything and everything he could get his hands on. Tend, Quix, and Vey circled with Porvarth, while Ari fidgeted with his favorite knives. Eiagan had insisted Ballan remain with Astrid, Reven, and Darby. Astrid's mind was still foggy despite Darby's help, and there was no reason to put her husband in danger. She needed him after everything that had happened to her. Catia, though, would hear no such nonsense. She was ready for a fight, and she refused to stay behind.

"Onward," Eiagan ordered, forgetting Iditania's ways. One step forward and she fell into a maze of swirling color, dropping like a dead dragon from the sky. Lucifer kicked and whinnied, but no thrashing would slow their descent. Eiagan gripped his mane while others fell around her, some upon horses while the dragons flapped to orient themselves. It was all useless.

Finally, her grandmother's portal slowed them and dropped them at the border with Varrow. Eiagan blinked, her mind still swirling while Lucifer padded over the ground to gain his footing. Between blinks, Eiagan scanned the area. There was no one. No army. No dragons. Nothing. Varrow was empty. At least, the border was void of people to protect it from her invasion.

"A trick, I am sure," Emora said, coming to a stop beside Eiagan, her horse balking at the very idea of moving after dropping through a magical gateway.

"What has she done with my people?" Erdravac asked, his eyes passing over the fields that separated Varrow from where they stood knee deep in the snow of The Banished Lands—technically the land of Asantaval. The wind whipped his short, dark hair, but his concern was evident.

"A trap or not, we must move onward. If Nessa is in Havisham Forest, we must move to arrive by nightfall," Eiagan said. Her people followed her across the border moments before a great rumbling followed them—the phantom army. Behind her, the projection of a vast army solidified. Some were dressed in the same furs and plaids as Gael, others wore Goraninite fighting armor and leather, while others appeared to be from Balcon, Arithropan, and other kingdoms. Iditania and Gael's people were master craftsman, to be sure, but Eiagan could only pray the projections were enough to fool the Varrowan army, wherever it was.

The deeper they moved into Nessa's territory, the darker it grew. The sun remained fixed in the sky, but a chill and sulkiness took over the land as if even it had grown weary of Nessa's hardened treatment and decided to spiral into depression. It would serve her right for destroying everything she laid her hands upon. This thought pushed another into Eiagan's mind. Had she destroyed Nox? Little Violet? A shudder took her spine, urging her to move faster to free her beloved friend.

At the crest of a great hill, Eiagan stopped again. Below, Varrow's castle stood. It was glorious in its own way, but without the eeriness Vidkun boasted. At the gate was the army, prepared to defend the official capital of Varrow, the very place that Erdravac should be seated ruling from his throne. Instead, they stood ready to defend it in Nessa's name.

Eiagan raised her arm as Zanaka raised the flag of Goranin. This was it, their declaration of intent to seize the land of Varrow and turn it back into the hands of its rightful heir. But as Zanaka raised

337

it, a sentry raised a flag from the tallest tower of the castle — the flag of Goranin.

"What?" Ari whispered.

Beside the first flag, another sentry raised a white flag. Eiagan sighed but only for a moment. Varrow would not be the first kingdom to proclaim surrender then turn into bloodthirsty heathens the second her army advanced for peace talks.

One lone soldier broke rank and galloped ahead, leaving the Varrowan army in formation, prepared but hesitant.

"Tend," Eiagan called, earning the dragon's attention. "Meet him halfway. Hear his claims and rip him to bits if he attempts to harm you."

A screech was his reply before he turned a half-circle in the air and darted toward the lone soldier dressed in typical Varrowan uniform. The soldier slowed and eventually stopped, waiting with uncertainty as Tend circled above, then landed with an earthshaking thump in front of him. The soldier dismounted his horse and bowed. Tend shifted, but even stark naked he commanded respect, and so the soldier kept his gaze on the ground as he spoke, relaying his message to Tend.

Eiagan and her people waited, most with tense shoulders and bated breath while Tend managed the affair at hand. Soon enough, Tend stepped back and shifted, leaving the soldier gape-mouthed as the mighty dragon darted back to his queen. Once by Eiagan's side, Tend shifted and dressed while relaying the message.

"They have anticipated an invasion from Goranin, and Varrow has been in civil war since Erdravac was unseated. This regiment killed the interim king and has pushed back Nessa's army so well, they scattered. He says they might regroup and attempt to take back the castle, but this regiment is loyal to King Erdravac and to

Goranin. He says, with all due respect, of course, that the Winter Queen terrifies them so that they would rather soil their pants like children then see her in battle."

Ari chuckled but Erdravac sighed. "So, we still may have a fight on our hands when we meet other regiments. I cannot decide if a civil war is any better than a war with Goranin."

"Perhaps, but he said the people are weary. They support Erdravac, but they feared Nessa's army. If we can offer them protection, I see no reason why they would want Nessa. Between the regular citizens and Erdravac's loyal army, I think we can manage." Tend, ever the optimistic one, buttoned the last button of his tunic and waited for Eiagan to make her choice.

She looked toward Zanaka. "Your thoughts, General?"

"Our informants have heard the rumblings, my queen. They are unhappy and only wish for peace, just as the people of Goranin have for some time. No one wants this war, least of all the citizens. Other informants have said the soldiers ranks are divided, but our armies are vast enough to eliminate Varrow entirely, never mind a split army."

"Yes, but we have no such army today, General," Ari added. "Our phantoms are fearsome, but not real."

"The Asantavalian's are real enough," Gael said, joining them. "We have enough behind our magic for a single battle, but I would hesitate to push beyond that. If the queen believes this regiment is earnest, I would suggest we take the castle and regroup, consider what we might need to infiltrate the remainder of the kingdom, then appropriate real, human soldiers as needed."

"He might be right, as much as I hate it. We cannot expect Grandmother to project soldiers all throughout the kingdom," Emora added. "To fight here is one thing, but to chase down half an army that still fights for Nessa is another. Besides, if they truly are spread over the kingdom, it would take days or weeks to find them. Have we that much time?"

"I would think not," Eiagan admitted. "Fine. We will take the castle for now, put Erdravac back upon his throne, then let him command his regiments as he sees fit, with a guard to ensure his safety, of course. Is that acceptable to all?" By all, of course, Eiagan meant those who sat upon thrones—Gael and soon, Erdravac.

"Yes, I agree," Gael said. "I will relay the information to our mages and we will adjust accordingly."

"Of course," Erdravac said. "The sooner I might prove myself, the better. I want to be a king they will love, and perhaps I might earn their trust in this."

"Onward, then," Eiagan said. "Tend, you can stay and ensure no one attempts to kill Erdravac. You are swift and fearsome, and so I believe he will be safest with you." She didn't wait for Tend to agree. She knew him well enough to know there was no argument.

Zanaka raised the flag of peace, leading them toward the castle on terms of peace rather than war. Eiagan's muscles burned, ready for a battle she had not yet entered, and she was unsure of each step ahead. Instinct told her it was too easy, too *bloodless* to be real, but if this regiment and others wished to align themselves with Goranin to return Varrow to its rightful king, then she must at least explore the option. Years ago, she might have ignored their white flag and charged ahead with her plan to eliminate them out of sheer spite, but now she truly *was* tired of killing everything to make her point.

Porvarth swooped low and kept a keen eye on his queen. Ahead, Zanaka performed his duties as general well enough that Eiagan's anxiety eased a fraction, though she was sure she would never fully relax for as long as she lived.

The gates were opened, allowing Eiagan and her people immediate access, though the phantom armies remained distant enough to attack if needed, but far enough that the ruse was not discovered. Inside, the main courtyard sprawled, empty of the usual activities that occurred on castle common grounds.

"Shall we discuss the terms of our surrender here in the open, or would you prefer an enclosed room?" the soldier's gaze locked with Eiagan. It was a question for her, not her general. At least the soldier knew who was most likely to snap if caged in for too long. Still, out in the open made her an easy target, so Eiagan nodded toward a corridor that led into the castle. It was secured on two sides, while leaving ample space for escape if necessary.

The soldier nodded, then said, "I am General Austavian, appointed by the regiment to lead them until our king is replaced on his throne." This time, his eyes shifted toward Erdravac for the first time, then they immediately lowered to his shoes. "We are ashamed we did not fight harder when he was there days ago. It will not happen again, sir."

Erdravac dismounted and handed his reins to Ari, who practically skinned the general alive with his assessing gaze. Eiagan smiled. Emora would always be safe with Ari, she knew, but this reinforcement pleased her.

"It is a matter for another day. Today, let us discuss how we might find the mage who took all from us and mount an attack against her." Erdravac took control immediately, pleasing Eiagan further.

"Majesty, her forces have dwindled. Those who support her are scattered and many would just as soon die than fight for her. They have been forced to take up arms by those who support her wholly."

"Conscripted, then?" Erdravac asked.

"Many sir, but not all. She believes her army is vast but they would turn on her in a blink if given the chance."

Erdravac licked his lips and considered his position for a moment. "Are your men willing to follow us into Havisham Forest?"

General Austavian's head snapped back so fast, Eiagan was sure he broke his own neck.

"Havisham, sir? What on earth would drive you to enter the haunted woods?"

"Havisham Castle, General. That is where Nessa keeps our friends prisoner, and that is where we will find her."

Eiagan was displeased Erdravac gave away so much information, but they *did* need men — real, flesh and bone men — to fight for them when they attacked Havisham. This, of course, assuming she had it guarded. Any number of scenarios might be possible — an army guarding the haunted castle, dragons, or nothing at all but the mage herself holding Noxious captive.

General Austavian swallowed, but nodded all the same. "It is a fearful mission, but the men are eager to prove their loyalty to you. Should you ask this of them, I believe they would follow you into the forest." Austavian's blonde hair peeked from under his leather cap, curly and unruly. He was young for a general, but perhaps older than Zanaka.

Eiagan's neck prickled, her innate sense for danger heightened. A split-second after, Lucifer whinnied and shifted his weight, tossing Eiagan to the ground. An arrow sped across the space and dove deep into the flesh of the horse's chest, eliciting a scream so deep it thundered in Eiagan's throat.

"Lucifer!" Emora screamed and dove toward him.

In a flash of glinting armor and brutal blows, surrounding soldiers caved in around the archer, capturing him before additional damage could be inflicted. Eiagan sprang to her feet, her sword drawn while her dragons circled and screeched, scattering the soldiers. Two remained, each holding up the traitorous archer by his arms.

"What is the meaning of this?" Austavian growled, crossing the distance to address the archer.

The archer spat on Austavian's shoe, hardly completing his smirk before Austavian came across his belly with a sword, ending him. The archer dropped in a heap on the stone, surrounded by an ever-growing puddle of his own blood.

The entire incident was over in the time it took Eiagan's anger to explode, and explode it did. While Emora and Catia tended Lucifer—hopefully to heal this fatal wound—Eiagan strode across the distance, daring anyone to whisper a breath let alone strike out at her. Austavian cowered, leaving Eiagan towering over him.

"We did not know, I swear it. The men have been—"

"Silence," Eiagan growled. "I have slit open many men in my time, General, but none who didn't deserve it to at least some degree. Certainly not before leeching every ounce of information from them I could! He is useless to me dead!"

Erdravac stood beside her, inching his way between them. Eiagan grumbled but allowed him to take the lead in his own kingdom—a feat considering every cell in her body screamed to skewer the idiotic general for eliminating the traitor before they could make good use of him.

"Go to Lucifer, Eiagan. I will manage this." He glanced at his cowering general, likely to be replaced momentarily, and sighed. "I will manage. The horse needs you."

Eiagan looked over her shoulder. The arrow lay broken on the stones beside Emora while she pressed her hands over the horse's chest. Lucifer's blood trailed through the cracks between rocks, traveling a scary distance from his body. The horse deserved more than this life, more than willingly taking an arrow for its rider. Eiagan went to him and kneeled beside him, stroking his ears while Emora whispered, draining what energy and magic she could from Catia as she did.

"It is alright, my friend. They will heal you. You need only relax," Eiagan whispered, soothing herself as well as the horse.

Porvarth landed beside them, far enough they might work, but close enough that he could shield them with his massive wingspan. If another traitor lay in hiding, Eiagan would skin him alive and make an example of him after prying every detail from him one broken bone at a time.

"I feel him healing. It is a deep wound, but it improves," Emora said, her brow slick with sweat.

Eiagan continued to stroke Lucifer's ears. "You have been more loyal a friend than anyone could ask for, sweet boy. You deserve to be free, to no longer fight in wars, to deliver messages as a bird, or to submit to the commands of a rider. You may take me to Nessa if you wish, but if you would rather not, I will send you back. You may be free, my friend. I set you free, as you have set me free so many times." Eiagan kissed Lucifer's forehead and patted his cheek, then went back to stroking his ears while Emora worked.

Lucifer's warm gaze connected with hers. Once again, Eiagan was sure the horse saw right into her soul. What did he see now? Had her soul healed? Was there some light where it had been so darkened before? Did he see the woman she wished to be, despite the hardened one she had been for so long?

344

Eiagan smiled and scratched his neck. "It is your choice, my friend, but whatever you choose to do, you are free."

Lucifer startled them all when he whinnied and thrust his neck forward, then scrambled to his feet. The women scattered, leaving space for the horse to rise, his thick muscles quivering as if he were prepared to shift into that winged Pegasus or even the raven, but he did not. Instead, heat radiated from him, warming Eiagan's face as she narrowed her eyes on the beast. Steam floated from him in all directions. Sweat frothed over his body.

"What is wrong with him?" Eiagan asked, her tone stressed and wavering. "Emora? Is he healed? Was it a poison?" She looked at her sister, who stared at the horse.

"I... I do not know!" Panicked, Emora reached for Lucifer but he darted away from her. Several paces apart from them, the horse padded the ground, each hoof print growing smaller until he couldn't stand any longer.

Lucifer fell on his side, screaming as if on fire. All those around them gaped, whispered, scattered as the horse rolled and bucked, screaming before falling again. He repeated this over and over until Eiagan was dizzy.

"Do something!" Eiagan yelled, tugging on her sister's sleeve. "He's dying!"

"What shall I do?" Emora screamed, wringing her hands.

"What is happening to him?" Ari asked, stepping aside so he might observe Lucifer without getting kicked in the head. Gael followed, tentatively drawing nearer Lucifer.

The horse groaned, now a misshapen mound of black flesh and fur, something wholly unhorse like, but unlike anything Eiagan had ever seen in her life. She had seen monstrous creatures, killed many of them, but this was a mystery.

345

Suddenly, like a baby bird escaping from an egg after a long struggle, Lucifer erupted. His flesh tore and fur peeled from skin in a splendid display of transformation until all that remained of their beloved horse was... a man.

Sprawled, naked and shivering on the ground, was a man.

Steam rolled over his body and sweat dripped over his skin. A thick wave of black hair topped his head. Muscle thickened his back, legs, and arms, but when he lifted his head and his eyes connected with Eiagan's, it stole her attention and she gasped.

"Lucifer?" she asked.

His lips parted but it was all she needed as confirmation.

"Someone get him a blanket! Hurry!" she shouted and drew nearer to him. She kneeled beside him, the heat still radiating from him like a fire. "What in the blazes of Hades are you?"

He let out a choked laugh and moved to cover himself. His brown eyes focused on her, blinking, then he said, "Lucifer is not my given name." His voice was broken, out of use, so he cleared his throat and swallowed. "I... hate... the name."

"Water, Ari, please!"

Ari darted away as Porvarth returned with a blanket. Once covered, Lucifer was determined to speak even before his weary, unused voice was ready.

"I am Luke. Lucifer was given to me by our captor," he croaked. "My people... cursed."

"Wait, have some water," Eiagan said. Ari returned and offered it, aiding Porvarth in lifting him to a seated position.

Luke took several swallows as if he had never had the benefit of a cool drink before in his life, then coughed, sputtering all over Eiagan.

"Apologies, my queen."

346

"It is no matter, Lucifer… Luke. Who… How…"

Luke chuckled again. "More than six hundred years I have been trapped in that body, and you set me free. It was all I ever needed, to have someone who truly cared for me to set me free."

All at once a flurry of emotion took Eiagan, but it was no time for sentimentality. In fact, it was no time for such an event at all, but there they were surrounding a horse turned man.

"Where have you come from?" Eiagan asked.

"My people are from Rucathea, but we were hunted for our abilities and eventually cursed. I will tell you everything, but I must… I must find them, my queen. Please allow me what you promised, my freedom to go to them."

"Of course, but I… What is this situation?" Eiagan asked, still several moments behind the present.

"Perhaps I should have mentioned my position, my queen," Luke said, his grin taking half of his face as he moved in front of her. "King Lukelvian Maelkovan of Rucathea, the last of the Maelkovan bloodline. We are a small tribe of peoples who possess abilities, some of which you have seen, but I must find my people."

Eiagan stood and offered her hand. "Let us go where we might discuss this. My kingdom will aid you in finding your people, but I must clear my head first, find Nessa, and imprison her before she ruins this land."

"If you can spare clothing, I will help you," Luke said. "I will follow you into this last battle before I search for my people, and I swear I will tell you everything along the way. We must hurry."

Eiagan blinked, not often shocked to silence. Surprised, yes, but to be shocked so greatly that her words blocked her throat was an anomaly to be sure. She licked her lips and grasped her sister's hand.

"Erdravac, we will need a meeting room, if you please. It seems the plan has changed for the moment."

THIRTY-EIGHT

Noxious "The Savage" Skjoldsson

Violet kissed Nox's cheek, seeming to understand without words that her father was on a mission that was unsafe for her. It wasn't the first time, but he hoped it would be the last for some time. He grew tired of walking away from those he loved most, but if these last few moments spent with Nessa provided him with enough information to finally end her reign of terror, then so be it. Violet would grow and thrive, and in the end, that was all that mattered.

"She misses you. Stay with her. The events of my life bear no weight any longer." Nessa's hand fell on the door handle, prepared to leave him alone with his daughter.

Nox shifted and stood, patting his daughter's head. "They bear weight with me as your prisoner. Violet needs rest, and she is quite happy with her…" He paused and glanced around the room. Stars, there were more frilly dolls, dresses, and toys than he'd ever seen in his life, but if Nessa thought buying Violet would win him over, she had another hard lesson to learn. "She's content for now. Tell me the rest. I need to know."

He motioned toward the door and Nessa obliged, though she did glance over her shoulder to ensure Violet was, indeed, content.

Noxious followed the blood-marked warrior all the way back to her rooms, then sat upon the chair he'd occupied frequently since becoming her prisoner, though he thought of himself as more of a permanent guest as of late. He simply could not work out the innermost parts of this woman's mind, and it nearly drove him to insanity. Even so, if Eiagan had her way — and there was no mistaking she would — Nessa would be either imprisoned or impaled over the Sword of Vidkun by the next day and he would be free.

Nessa fidgeted with the braids along the right side of her hair, keeping it from her face. Nox tried not to stare, even ordered the dragon to distract him, but the beast was exhausted from communicating with Darby and hid in the shadows. That, or this woman had finally terrified the lizard. But blasted, how could such a homicidal thing be so beautiful? Nox shook his head. Perhaps that was more *his* problem than reality. It seemed such women were his taste, after all. As good as she was, even Hazel had her moments.

"My choice haunted me for many nights, and once I even went to the little log cabin to beg him to run away with me. I would have left it all behind, but he'd been conscripted in that short time, drawn into Icluedian's army like another hunk of meat sent to do his bidding."

"I am sure that was a terrifying time, all things considered."

350

"I feared for his life daily and kept watch over him, but never contacted him again. I was the one who'd drawn him so close to this life, and I vowed I would keep him safe but keeping up with him proved difficult."

"He rose quickly through the ranks. I remember the stories," Nox said.

Nessa nodded. "Quite the soldier, it turned out. Before I knew it, he was Eiagan's general. They grew close, bonding over shared trauma. I suppose in that way I understand why she was drawn to him, but that did not change that he was *mine*."

Nessa's jaw clenched and that fire in her eyes roared to life. He'd better watch his step or lose his head. They were so close to the end of this misery, he couldn't afford missteps now. He would change the subject, dance around what made her lose her mind entirely.

"Were you there when Reeve was killed?"

Nessa lowered her gaze to the fire and swallowed. "Yes."

Nox's brows knitted together, surprised by the faintness of her voice, the way she flinched at the very mention of Reeve. "You saw everything?"

She inhaled slowly, measured. "For a moment, just a sliver of time mind you, I realized we were all the same. I both hated Eiagan for taking Zero but also felt connected to her for all Icluedian had done to her. He ruined her, broke her, made her the thing she is today whether you prefer to acknowledge it or not. The moment she ran her sword through our brother, I knew she was lost. I would have protected him. I *could* have if not for…"

Nox scooted forward. "For?"

"I'd used too much protecting Zero. I had no idea what might happen during that fight, so I used every ounce of strength I had to protect him. There was nothing left to heal with, not that I would

351

have been very good at such things anyway. I am made for destruction and darkness, though I might have tried if I had been able."

Fat tears slipped from her eyes again, streaking the blood lines that striped her face liked death.

"You lost something that day as well," he said, realizing that Reeve might have been the one to bring them all together, to heal all the wounds inflicted upon them by Icluedian, but it was too late.

"I think Reeve might have seen more in me than this." She motioned over her face, then darted her gaze back to the fire.

Nox stood, prompting her to prepare herself, but rather than strike at her, he kneeled beside her. Against his better judgment, he grasped her hand, chilled and smooth like the stone-hardened warrior she was, and squeezed it.

"Stop this now. This is your last chance to change everything, Nessa. It doesn't have to end with all of this bloodshed and hatred. You can change it. You can be better than your horrid father."

She pulled her hand back. "It can end no other way, Noxious. What must be will be."

Those icy eyes looked away from him, but they held no fear, only acceptance. This was not a woman ready for a fight. She was ready for the end... for death. This was her sentence, her chosen path, her end. She wanted to die.

"Nessa?"

She cleared her throat. "When they fell in love, my world shattered. I had lost everything I had ever wanted before I even realized I had it. Then he helped her kill Icluedian." She snickered. "I suppose all I ever had to do was ask him, and he might have murdered the man *with* me rather than leave me alone and heartbroken, but again, that was my fault. I never told him the truth."

Nox resigned to the chair again, knowing well she would not be dissuaded from marching right into her death.

"I thought once Icluedian was dead, I would feel whole again, but it only left a deeper hole in my gut. Perhaps if I had been the one to do it, it might have felt different, but I can never know."

"If you could change anything, what would you do differently?" Was there anything redeeming left in her? Anything he might grasp to avoid an all-consuming war before this was over?

For moments too long to measure, Nessa only stared at the flames licking the stone, sucking the air from the room. Eventually, she lifted those gray-white eyes to his again and offered the most pathetic, weak smile he had ever seen.

"Probably everything." She rose and strode across the room, then paused at the door. "I will return in a moment. I have something I want to give you and then I must go."

The second she left the room, Nox tickled Darby's mind. If there was any way to avoid what might come, now was the time to enact a plan. Since Eiagan was heading into Varrow that moment, there was little time to waste. Darby's mind opened and accepted Nox's haphazard and rambling thoughts as he explained everything he'd learned, including that sliver of Nessa he thought might be redeemable, if only enough to prevent bloodshed. Eiagan did not want to kill her sister, and the things Nox had learned about Nessa might aid in her mission.

Once Darby finished pilfering his brain, the dragon grunted. It wanted out, but now was not the time.

While he waited, Noxious considered Nessa. Was she truly different from them? From him? From Eiagan or Emora or any number of people he called his family? The things she did played over in his mind, reminding him she was not good. No, he would never see her as good, but he could not find it in himself any longer to hate her entirely. She was as broken as they were, only she found herself on the opposite side of the battlefield. Were there truly any sides, or were they all pawns in a meticulous game of strategy put on by malevolent forces?

Nox sighed and wiped his face with his hands. If a stranger heard his story, they would see him as a villain, too. He'd killed for Eiagan, even gleefully, and those deaths pained him now. He'd been so blinded by his love for Eiagan, he never considered her actions bordered on insanity. And now... Heaven help him further, he couldn't decide if he deserved any sort of peace after all he had done to push Goranin to what it had become before the people finally unseated Eiagan from her throne.

If this was Nessa's last stand, her death sentence, then she would be left wanting. Eiagan would not kill her, which meant Nessa would live for all eternity considering her life and all she had done. Something about that forced a twinge in his heart. To be left alone forever with nothing but his thoughts was terrifying, perhaps a fate worse than death, and it was in that realization that Noxious the Savage found pity for the woman.

Finally, Nessa returned to the room just as Nox's eyelids grew heavy. He had no inkling of the time—perhaps day, more likely night but what did it matter? She fidgeted with an item in her palm, something she worried over as she crossed the room and sat beside him again.

"He gave this to me long ago, and since you have the quartz, I thought it only right that you have this as well." She offered a pendant on a leather cord so he extended his hand. Nessa dropped it as if it burned her and turned her face away.

"Why?"

"I've no use for it, and perhaps your progeny might find your history more complete with it in your possession, should you choose to tell the entire story, of course." She folded her hands in her lap, prepared to speak again when Darby sent a message down their bond that almost gave him away when his eyes went wide.

We have taken Varrow and now we come for you. Hold tight my friend.

"I was thinking of my life just after you left and all the things I have done," Nox said, catching her attention.

Godawful screeching echoed through the room, startling Nessa before she replied. Though the woman was fearless, she still lurched forward and grasped her shirtfront just over her heart and gasped. Had she not expected another dragon? Bracken was her prized lizard, surely he arrived from time to time?

Nessa shot like lightning across the room and threw open the door, leaving it open as she went. Such a reaction intrigued Nox, primarily because she had been sure to close the doors whenever she left a room, save those times she had let him wander to go to Violet's room. Secondarily, she behaved as if the whole world had fallen apart and she must hurry to put it all back together before anyone else saw. Did she know Varrow had fallen? Did she suspect?

Unable to control his curiosity, Nox followed her out the door, keeping several paces behind so she wouldn't notice his company. The castle was a maze unlike any he had ever seen, but her flash of blonde hair offered enough direction for him to find his way outside. The castle was blackened and dreary, not unexpected, but

355

it still took Nox's breath away. He knew where they were now, without question, and he would confirm Darby's suspicion he was in Havisham Castle just as soon as he could, ensuring their travels were quick.

Black forest surrounded them, reaching toward the starry, moonlit sky. But the moon was shadowed by the flap of expansive wings, those dreadful and spiked appendages that struck fear in so many. Bracken was unlike any dragon Nox had ever seen before. Ancient and enormous, he took up more space than all of Eiagan's dragons together, and he killed the mighty Ellaro with ease. Where the dreadful thing had come from was anyone's guess, but it stirred the beast in Nox as it landed in front of Nessa and screeched again.

"Enough of that," she screamed up at the monster. "What news has brought you here? You were *never* to come here!"

The creature lowered its head until one eye, taller than Nessa, leveled with her. She didn't flinch, not even a breath out of place. Stars, the woman was *fearless*.

"Why are you here, beast?" She pressed against its snout and growled, but it only stepped back a fraction before raising its head and screaming into the darkness again. "What do you mean, Varrow is lost? The Winter Queen has managed to take even this from me?"

The dragon grunted and groaned, then its eyes shifted toward where Nox stood in the entryway, mouth agape. It lowered its steely gaze and growled, then flung Nessa aside and charged. Nox hardly had a breath before he shifted, gouging the stonework on either side of him as his body expanded and his wings erupted. The beast scraped along his mind then shoved its claws deep into his brain, taking control in every way possible. Nox barreled into the sky, narrowly avoiding Bracken's angry teeth.

He'd done it now. This was it, how he would die... in a battle... ripped apart by a horrific dragon that made even his beast tremble.

"Stop it! Stand down, you worthless lizard!" Nessa screamed, but her commands did nothing to slow Bracken's advance. They never would. The monster had wholly taken control, leaving Bracken little more than a predator who'd caught the scent of the most defenseless prey imaginable, and served up right before him, no less.

Nox did his best to dart this way and that, avoiding talons and teeth, but it was no way to win a fight. All those movements, swift and explosive, wore him down to nothing quickly, especially since he hadn't eaten well since he arrived at Nessa's makeshift home — an ancient castle hidden deep in the Havisham Forest of Varrow. He'd worry whether the tales of their haunting were true later, if he survived Bracken.

Nox glanced over his shoulder. If he tucked his wings and dove as fast as he could toward the castle, he might manage to slip inside and shift, then hide from the beast where it could not reach. It was cowardly, but at least he might live to see another day, to see his darling Violet again. Bracken, though, had other plans. He snatched Nox from the sky with a swift flick of his tail, connecting that barbed end with the fleshy part of Nox's chest.

Pain radiated from the wound, weakening him so that he fell from the sky, landing in a heap of broken wings and legs on the stone courtyard. Bracken drew his tail back again and slammed it onto Nox's soft belly, forcing bloody vomit from his mouth. Nessa's scream hardly registered as Bracken bombarded him with that dreadful, spiked tail. He would be nothing more than strips of meat by the time it was over. Would Nessa return Violet to Eiagan? Keep her safe? He lifted his head, wheezing as the dragon slipped in and out of his mind.

357

His gaze locked on Nessa.

Her eyes went wide. She panted quick breaths, her eyes darting between Bracken and Nox.

An explosion rocked the ground, forcing Nox's body to tremble and shift over the stone. Still in his dragon form, he let out a soft growl. Rain fell, washing his body as rivers of blood surrounded him. No, not rain... *blood.* Bracken's severed head landed an arm's length from Nox's face as bits of the dragon rained down over them.

Nox's gaze shifted to Nessa, his eyelids too heavy to keep open any longer.

Nessa, slick with blood and anger, kneeled beside him. Her hands fell on his snout, lifting his heavy head until she could look him in both eyes—a feat considering his size. Her gaze searched his and then she lay his head down again before assessing the damage inflicted upon him by her pet. He moaned, earning her attention again.

"Do not die, you insufferable lizard! What shall I do with a child?"

Noxious turned his darkened eyes toward her, taking in the mess around them as life drained from his body. She was different now, somehow. She blinked and huffed, her focus solely on him as her hands assessed every broken part, every bone-deep laceration. There it was, a small spark of kindness. Stars above, she might have been amazing if she had been born by anyone else, anywhere else, any *time* else.

"Noxious? I'm no healer! How shall I—" She cut her words short as his eyes closed, his life fading as the darkness overcame him.

His throat was always dry when the dragon left him. Nox had always assumed it was because of the fire, but now he wasn't so sure. The screeching. That might also lend itself as a good cause, but now all he thought of was how glorious only a sip of water might be.

But first... pry those eyes open and *find* water.

All at once everything fell on him and reality dawned like a new day. He should be dead, yet there he lay concerned about finding water to quench that stinging in his throat. Nox licked his lips and forced his eyes open, surrounded by piles of furs and soft cotton bedding. With no inkling of where he might be, the dragon shifter simply reveled in his life, that he still had one to enjoy such frivolous things as a comfortable bed. A sigh escaped his lips quite without his permission, earning the attention of another person in the room.

"You're awake." Nessa placed a pitcher on a small table and brought him a cup of water. "Here. Drink."

Her hand slipped behind his head and lifted him enough so that he might cool his burning throat.

"Violet is alright. I checked on her and told her you were resting but that you love her. I gave her food and more toys, but she did not seem to believe me. I cannot say I blame her, but I am sure seeing you might improve her mood. It was quite despondent when I—"

"Nessa." His voice was strained, harsh, but it stopped her incessant warbling. Was she nervous? "What happened?" Miraculously, he was able to sit unassisted. Was he fully healed? How?

"Bracken came to deliver a message. Eiagan took Varrow, but once he saw you I suppose his base instinct must have taken over. He tried to kill you and I... I couldn't have that, could I?" Her lower lip trembled.

359

Nox snickered. "I know all of that. One cannot forget a monster beating you to death, nor could I forget the explosion that macerated him. You killed your beast? For me?"

Nessa pursed her lips and put the cup on the table. "I killed him because he disobeyed."

She lied.

Nox smirked. Blast it all. He couldn't help it, nor could he unsee that small spark she'd had, that little river of kindness that saved his life. She ensured Violet would not become an orphan.

"I will pretend I believe you," he said, then inhaled. "Tell me the rest of the story, please. I fear we are running out of time."

"You still want to know? Aren't you in pain? My healing ability is hardly capable, and your scars are plenty." She motioned toward his abdomen but did not touch him. He lifted his shirt — not *his* shirt, but another clean one she must have put on him — and observed the scars that crossed over his abdomen and chest. He had died, he knew, but her power was beyond that of even Simorana. It was beyond even what *she* knew of her own ability. Nox swallowed, realizing he also wore pants. Devil's breath, she had dressed him after healing him. How did she get him into the bed?

He didn't want to know.

He dropped the shirt and sighed. "I will live, thank you. I'm quite used to pain after a fight. Tell me."

"I… I do not want to, Noxious." Her tumble of blonde waves was clean again, now tied into a braid that fell over her shoulder. How long had he been unconscious?

"Zero's death, did you —"

"Please, Nox," she whispered, her jaw tensed. Too far. He would not get her to utter a syllable about Zero's death, but that was a story he knew well.

"The plague that killed Iric?"

She nodded once. "In hindsight, it was a mistake. I should never have taken Eiagan's son. I wanted to push her over the edge, down into the darkest recesses of Hell with me."

"She spent centuries there, so you accomplished your task."

"You asked if I would change anything, and I told you probably everything, but if I could choose only one mistake to correct, that would be my choice. I would not take her son from her."

Nox stared at her. How curious. "The winter curse?"

"All for this, to arrive here where I might take everything I want, though it did take a bit longer than anticipated. She is a hearty one."

Nox snickered again and pushed his legs over the edge of the bed, dropping furs as he moved. He nodded toward the end of the bed, intending for her to sit with him, but instead, she sat on the floor and leaned against the bed.

"Do you regret any more of it? There is a difference between wishing you had done it all differently and regretting your actions altogether," Nox said, his body filled with pain despite her healing. She was right. She was made for darkness and destruction, but he was alive and would remain so for Violet, so he couldn't fault her weakness with healing magic. Even so, she had not only healed him but brought him *back*. He knew he saw the afterlife, touched its edges, but it disappeared just before he was conscious enough to want water.

"I regret all of it," she admitted, her elbows propped on her knees as she dropped her chin into her hands. Like this, she seemed like a child, helpless and hapless.

Nox sat fully and slid onto the floor beside her, his knee bumping into hers where she sat studying her boots. He might have liked her in another life. But not this one. In this one, she stole his Hazel and

361

hurt his beloved family. He could never forget what she'd done, but sakes alive, he didn't want her dead. "Do not go through with this, Nessa. I have given you my promise to stay here, and I will keep it always. Do not walk into this. Do not take more blood and —"

She snickered. She stretched her legs out and crossed them at the ankle, then crossed her arms, shutting him out. "We know how this will end, Nox. It's time. Though you are the only thing that makes me wish I had never done any of the things I have, even more than Zero."

His brown hair, still blood splattered and dirty, fell in his face, forcing a small smile from her.

"Why?" he asked.

This brought on a full smile. "I thought I loved Zero. I suppose, in many ways, I did. But I wasn't ready for him, not then. I think all this time what I really needed was you."

"I still don't understand. Why me?"

She brushed the hair from his face. He let her, if only to get to the root of this, to know what she would do when she walked out that door again. "You listened when no one else would. You have tried to understand even when every fiber of your being, including that dreadful dragon, only wants to rip me apart. Your heart is kind, Noxious. You are no savage, but a beautiful man who deserves so much more than what you have been given."

Nox shook his head, anger bubbling just beneath his skin. The dragon was still too tired to fight, but he wasn't.

"That is the problem, Nessa! Zero listened! It is you who refused to listen to those who loved you, and if you had, then perhaps now we would be somewhere else having an entirely different conversation!"

362

"Zero heard me, Nox, but he did not listen. Never truly. He loved what he thought I could be and so he made up what he wanted to hear instead of listening. He did the same to your Eiagan, but she never saw that. He was taken from her before she could realize that who she was did not compare to who he imagined she *might* be. He was more in love with her potential than with her. But not you. You see her and accept her, just as you see me. You don't accept me, but you have offered me more dignity than any man ever has, and for that I am grateful."

Nox's throat bobbed, his mind swirling with emotions that made no sense. What was she doing to him? How had she changed his mind about her in a matter of days? No, not changed his mind but made him... sympathize. His heart ached for her as it did for Eiagan, perhaps more.

"What will you do now? Walk into your slaughter?" Did she truly think she could take these lands against an army? Against Eiagan?

She tilted her head the slightest, allowing him insight into her deepest thoughts through those haunting eyes. For a moment, he could have convinced himself they were Eiagan's eyes.

"Retrieve your child. Go down the hallway, turn right at the end and follow it all the way to the wall. Press your hand over the stone. From there, you will find your way home through a portal I created while you slept. You won't have to traverse these woods."

Nox's back went rigid and he shifted his weight to fully view her, though his vision still swam. "What?"

"I want you to go. Take your Violet home where she might thrive among people who love her."

"I don't understand. Are you setting us free? Why?"

Nessa pressed her palm against his cheek and inclined toward him just enough that he might know what she said was no lie, but slipped from her lips with every ounce of her heart behind it. "Because I love you, so I will let you go."

His breath caught. He supposed he knew that, somehow, but hearing her say it aloud was quite different from assuming it based on her actions. Nox's entire body seized with anxiety, his stomach queasy with confusion and unchecked emotions.

"What?" he whispered.

Nessa lowered her gaze but did not remove her hand from his face. "Do not pretend as if you didn't know. I am not asking you to understand or even care that I love you, but... please... do not pretend it is not real."

He wouldn't see her again, he knew. Though he knew Eiagan would do everything she could imagine to capture Nessa instead of killing her, Nessa was on a mission to find her own end. As such, he saw no way either woman might escape the fate. It would eat Eiagan alive, but Nox prayed it would not be so, that she *would* find a way to imprison her sister instead of killing her.

Why must life be so confusing? How cruel it was to offer every opportunity on the day of birth, only to rip each one away day after day until all that remained was a hollow, empty soul covered with a beautiful face.

Nox did not shirk her hand, but squeezed his eyes shut for a moment to gather his words. "Eiagan will kill you, Nessa," he whispered. "If you give her no other choice, she will kill you to save her people."

Her other hand found his face, both palms pressed against his cheeks.

"I know. It's time."

He opened his eyes, connected with her gaze, shivered. "You accept this fate after all you have done to get here?"

She nodded.

"You wanted everything, and now nothing?"

She nodded again. "I'm tired."

"Then I tell you this, Ellenessia Allurigard, I pray you find peace in the afterlife. I understand you. I see that small sliver in you that I also see in Eiagan, and I... I *forgive* you for your wretched mistakes."

She swallowed and closed her eyes, letting his words wash over her. He slipped the quartz from his pocket, surprised to find it there, and pulled one hand from his face, startling her. She tensed, but only for a moment. Nox pressed the warm, smooth stone into her palm and closed her fingers over it. "Choose a different path, Nessa. Choose life over death. Choose a way that ends without more bloodshed, including your own."

A sob choked in her throat and tears slipped over her cheeks as she clutched the small stone. Her eyes met his again, questioning the intent behind every word. She was so broken, so ruined by everyone who had seen her as nothing more than power and magic and a thing to be used. And that magic, blast it straight to Hell, how it twisted her into this thing, this monster with no guidance. What she might have been if life had not taken more than it deserved from her.

He pressed his palms to her face, further smearing the blood stripes of her warrior kingdom. He could have slipped his hands a fraction lower, wrapped them around her slender neck, snapped life out of her in a blink... but it wasn't what he wanted. Not anymore.

"Choose life, Nessa."

She closed her eyes again, perhaps contemplating a world where she might choose her destiny for herself, perhaps pondering what options she *did* have. Whatever it was broke Nox's heart, that last part of him that could not fathom how he went from desiring nothing more than ripping her apart, to a man who knew she was only a girl destroyed by circumstances she never could have controlled.

He inclined toward her and pressed his lips to hers, eliciting a gasp. Her eyes flew open as his closed. Eiagan would kill her, though he knew it would be her last resort. If Nessa had decided this was her end, then it would be. He prayed again his lifelong friend would not end her sister's life so that she would not suffer yet another murder's consequences, but now he also prayed it for her, for Nessa. Eiagan… Emora… Nessa… all three women deserved more than what their father and the curse of eternal life had forced upon them, and Nox prayed that they might have peace one day.

Nessa whimpered and pressed harder, her tears salting their goodbye. Then she broke away and tried to escape, but Nox grasped her wrist.

"Wait. Please," he whispered.

Nessa huffed. "You are merely stalling the inevitable, Noxious. What will be, will be, and there is nothing you might do to stop this ending."

Nox tightened his grip on her wrist and stood. "There must be something. I cannot stand here and watch you and Eiagan and Emora do this any longer. Icluedian ruined you all, and it is unfair that any of you must pay for his mistakes."

She licked her lips, her eyes narrowed in contemplation. This was his moment, his one last opportunity to change the course of the future. Blasted woman, he couldn't even look at her with a clear mind despite all she had done.

"Nox—"

He yanked her closer and kissed her again, harder this time so she knew the first was no mistake. Heaven help him, this *was* a mistake, but he could no more stop it than he might stop the moon from rising each night. She pressed against him, nothing between them but a lifetime of pain and suffering, lost in this kiss as if it were the only thing she had ever wanted in her centuries of life.

Then she pushed away from him. And ran.

"Wait!" Nox chased her, unsure why he couldn't let her walk out the door. She had a choice to make, but he knew what it would be and found himself unable to accept it. She froze in place, her breaths heaving her shoulders as she contemplated her situation. For a blink, Nox thought he might change her mind, then her shoulders stiffened and she took that warrior pose again.

"Go home, Nox. Take Violet home and never think of me again," she whispered. "I am sorry I brought you here, that I forced you to see —"

"I don't regret it. Are you so angry you cannot see that?"

Nessa turned, confusion flooding her gaze. "You feel sorry for me now and it is easy to forget all I did to you, but that will not last. I love you, Nox. I *love* you, and that will get you killed."

"Is... is that why you choose this? To die? Because of me?" He didn't even recognize his own voice. A hiss filled the room, and then she was gone. The snake slipped through the door, but by the time Nox reached it, even that ruby red serpent was gone.

THIRTY-NINE

Eiagan Allurigard

"There is much to tell, but you are short on time, Queen of Goranin," Luke said.

Eiagan stared at the man, still caught somewhere in the mystery of what he was, as he explained why his story was of little consequence until they freed the ancient kingdoms from Nessa's grip. Eiagan was not one to instantly trust anyone, but Luke was not *just* anyone. He was Lucifer, the horse who had taken her to battle against Moriarian, delivered messages to her alone, stuck by her side when she was lost in her grief, saw into her soul as if he could read it. Human... horse... raven... it made no difference. Except that as a human, Eiagan couldn't help but sink into a self-conscious abyss. He knew as much of her soul as Porvarth did.

368

"I assure you, understanding your tale is of great importance to me," Eiagan said.

Luke frowned then took a steadying breath. "It was so long ago, but I remember it as if it were yesterday. There was strife among the villages in Rucathea, and my tribe was losing land by the day. I fear the story is quite long, but the short of it is simple, actually. It is no different from what Goranin faces, what Varrow faces, what any kingdom in the ancient lands has seen in its history. Fights grew fiercer, longer, and more blood was shed than necessary. And then magic made everything worse."

"It always does," Porvarth added.

Luke grinned. "He is not wrong, but the details of my story will slow you too much. Know that we were cursed by another tribe and forced to stay in animal form. My tribe had always been prideful and flaunted our abilities, I admit as much, but this curse has humbled me more than any rebuke. And now, I pray I can find the remainder of my tribe, save them from this wretched magic, and resume our lives as well as we might, all things considered."

Eiagan swallowed. Indeed, there was likely *much* more to the story, but they had to face Nessa… and soon.

She licked her lips and nodded. "I suppose the shortened version will have to do for now, but know that I am at your disposal. Anything you need, I will provide for your search."

Luke bowed his head. "Thank you, my friend. Let me help you as I have done from the beginning, and when your kingdom is secure, I will share the finer details of my story." Luke glanced around the room, taking in the befuddlement with kind eyes. "It isn't every day you see a horse turn into a man, it seems." He smiled, his cheeks pink-tinged, the shook his head. "I know it's odd, but is it really so odd you cannot believe it? You have men who turn into

369

dragons and do not question it. We must move back into position and finish what you started."

"He's right. As intriguing as his story is, we have a task," Erdravac said. "Eiagan, you have trusted him this long, so I see no reason why we cannot move forward with our original plan."

"Indeed, and I can help you. I know Havisham Castle well enough to know its secrets," Luke said.

"How convenient," Catia added, still hesitant.

Luke smiled at her but his charm was lost on the woman. Eiagan understood. Catia knew nothing of Lucifer before he appeared at their side merely a day earlier.

"When this is done, I will send a team of soldiers who might aid you in finding your lost people. I pray you will not only find them, but one day return with a happy ending to your story."

But now was not a time for tales. Now was a time for focus and determination.

"I thank you, Eiagan," he said. "Let us be on our way."

Eiagan arched an eyebrow, then said, "I'll need a horse, Erdravac."

Luke chuckled. "I can accommodate you. Transformation is one of my abilities. I was merely unable to transform *back* into a human."

As much as Eiagan adored the horse, knowing he was a man beneath it all made her blush. It was not the same as riding one of her dragons. She'd known from the beginning who they were and their abilities, but not Luke. He was as new as any soldier where his human form was concerned, but as a horse, he was unparalleled in battle. She *did* need him, and if he was willing, there was no reason for her to refuse.

She glanced at Porvarth. He nodded. "I trust him with you more than a skittish horse from the guard," he said.

Eiagan inhaled and ensured her sword was secure. "So be it, then. We have quite a haunting ride to our destination. Let us be gone."

The forest's darkness was unlike anything Eiagan had ever seen. There was the darkness held by night, but even when the stars and moon were blocked by clouds, there was a sliver of light that always led her way. But not here. This was all consuming, entire, man-eating darkness. Their torches hardly lit enough of the forest for them to navigate ahead.

Luke's footing was better than the others, but even still, he slipped and slid over the soft forest floor, almost as if it ate his hooves with each step. Flight with the dragons would be easier, but their element of surprise would be ruined.

Darkness surrounded Eiagan, washed over her, filled her up until it had nowhere to go but back out again. She had made a choice, one that the others still had not realized. They would not go with her into the castle. They would not even see blood. Only Iditania knew her true plan, one that left her with nothing to do now but enact it. The phantom armies along with they physical armies waited outside of the forest, prepared if Nessa should run or attempt a counterattack, but this, the final confrontation was for Eiagan and she wouldn't hear of anyone else putting themselves in danger.

Echoes closed in until they whispered in her ear, but the queen had heard worse in her long life, so she pushed on until the blackness opened and the castle appeared fully. No dragons, no soldiers, no one at all guarded the crumbling structure. Eiagan found it difficult to believe Nessa had hidden her true body there, but Darby's location spells were not wrong. She swallowed. How would she find Nox? Was he still alive? Violet?

Eiagan squeezed her eyes shut and took another breath. From her pocket, she pulled a vial of liquid her grandmother had given her, though she had tried to change her mind. There was no changing it. This was the right way, the proper agreement, just like the one she had made with Simorana years ago. If she was to die, then she would do it on her terms and protecting those she most loved. With that in mind, she tossed the vial into the air and sliced it open with her sword.

The liquid flashed.

"What is that?" Emora asked, watching as the liquid fell over her and the others. Her eyes grew heavy, drowsy. "Eiagan, you —"

She fell, asleep, on the forest floor before she could utter her curse against her sister. Catia fell next to her, offering a scowl as she went. Then the others one by one until all that remained was Porvarth. He stared at her with those big blue eyes, haunting betrayal filling them as his lids grew heavy.

"I'm sorry," Eiagan whispered.

Porvarth fell beside Ari, safe and asleep. Eiagan dismounted Luke. "I know your instinct is to go with me, but I need you to watch over them. Will you?"

His hoof pounds against the soft earth said two things... *I am furious with you... I will guard them with my life.*

Eiagan gave them one last look, then with her sword at her side, she pushed onward. It was not the first time she had planned to walk into the depths of Hell alone, but this time she was sure there was no one to save her if everything went wrong.

She entered the main courtyard and was accosted by the rancid smell of charred, rotting meat. Chunks of flesh littered the area —

scaled and black. Eiagan's heart stopped as she searched the area. Whatever dragon met his end here had done so recently despite the rot. Surely, this was not Noxious the Savage sprawled in pieces over the broken stone? She shook her head.

"No. Impossible." Eiagan refused to believe he could be ended so easily and entered the heavy wooden entrance to the castle. The door creaked, an obligatory sound in such a castle, Eiagan decided, but she gave it little thought once she was inside. The castle was equally as dismal inside.

Nothing in this area was familiar from Catia's visions, so Eiagan continued exploring. Still, no one stopped her. No one confronted her. If Nessa knew she had arrived, she certainly was patient. Not a dust mote stirred in the heavily tapestried hallway, likely magic, but it did unnerve the queen. It was too quiet, too still. Ahead, the hallway split. She took the right, guarding her back until she knew there was nothing behind her. She unsheathed her sword and blew a stray tendril of black hair from her face. She'd been sure to braid it and wear her finest leathers. This was no time to be modest but to ensure she was ready for this fight, the most daunting of her life.

At the end of the hall, something familiar caught her eye. A framed portrait of the former king lit by candlelight on a small table. This was the entrance to the library Catia and Emora had seen in their vision. Eiagan crossed the threshold and entered a room lit well by the fireplace and candles, though the musty scent of old books still overpowered the smoke.

"Finally, you've come." Nessa emerged from between two aisles of books, her blonde hair also braided away from her face, while her cheeks, forehead, and chin were marked with blood as they had been in her projection. Eiagan finally relaxed. The difficult part was over. She'd found Nessa.

Eiagan sheathed her sword.

"Confident. We have that in common," Nessa said.

"It seems we have much in common," Eiagan said, eyeing her elder sister.

Nessa flicked her wrist, but Eiagan easily deflected the flying stack of books.

"Come now, is that all? I am thoroughly insulted." Eiagan sighed. "I did hope we could have a civil discussion before the antics began."

Nessa chuckled. "I suppose that was a bit childish, but I do love toying with my victims before killing them. Don't you? I find it invigorating."

"You will not kill me, Nessa." Eiagan crossed her arms, comfortable in her element. "You will not give up without a fight, of course, but you will not kill me. Perhaps we should make this easy for both of us. Come with me. Allow me to imprison you, and I will not kill you. I will uphold my bargain with Gael and allow Asantaval to reclaim their land and rule it as they see fit."

Nessa cackled. "Gael. You mean my worthless Uncle Bribadge. He'll turn on you just as he did my family and then me, of that you can be sure."

"Perhaps, but my army is well capable and could easily destroy what little is left of Asantaval. I would rather not, but that is not the reason I came all the way to Varrow, deep into these dreadful haunted woods. I came to put an end to our situation, Nessa, and I think we should get on with it. Where is Noxious?"

Nessa flinched but Eiagan couldn't read into it before she smiled. "I released him. He should be halfway back to Eathevall by now."

Eiagan had not expected that. Perhaps he had contacted Darby after Eiagan left Vidkun?

"You do not trust me, but what I say is true. I have no quarrel with Noxious. It has always been with you." Nessa mimicked Eiagan's stance — arms crossed, cool, composed.

"Why me, Nessa? Why Emora? Why not our father? If I had known you, we might have a full family now and not this maniacal blood alone." Eiagan said. For a moment, a twinge of unfulfilled hope twisted her heart. If Nessa had only made herself known, they might have ended Icluedian together, brought Emora back from Simorana sooner, and perhaps Reeve would have lived. They would have been a family together forever. Iric would live, and the people might have loved their ruling family.

"You took Zero from me. He was mine, and he left me to go and help you do exactly what I wanted to do. If not for you, I would — " Nessa paused. She simply stopped speaking and squeezed her eyes shut as if refusing to see what was right in front of her — everything that had happened was by her own making, her design, and ruined just as she had wished.

"And you took my son. You could have saved Reeve, even saved Zero. None of this had to happen," Eiagan said, shifting her weight to take a step. Nessa raised her hand, stopping her advance. "I would have loved you as I do Emora and as I did Reeve."

"I did not need your pathetic love. I needed…" Nessa stopped again. She growled and lunged at Eiagan, dagger drawn.

Eiagan dodged Nessa's lunge and threw her body into Nessa's stomach, her shoulder connecting with such force Nessa flipped over herself and landed on her back. Eiagan repositioned and prepared for another attack. Nessa moved from the floor to the other side of Eiagan with little more than a blink of magic. Eiagan spun and raised her arms, protecting herself from Nessa's second attack.

The women tumbled to the floor, Eiagan contorting herself until she straddled Nessa. With another infuriating blink of her magic, Nessa moved to the other side of the room. This phantom was quicker than Eiagan could move, a step ahead of her with each maneuver. Still, Eiagan would fight until the bitter end.

"I will enjoy killing you, then ripping your loved ones limb from limb. I know you left them in the forest, alone and sleeping. Do you know what lurks in those woods, sister?" Nessa grinned, the blood stripes on her face smeared and faint now.

"I left them in capable hands, and my grandmother..." Eiagan chuckled. "I suppose *our* grandmother is stronger than you think. Her protection will last days, little princess." Eiagan smiled again, moving around a table as Nessa paced like a caged tiger. "That must sting. To know I, your little sister, am a queen while you live here in this haunted, abandoned castle without even the title of princess any longer."

Nessa's jaw clenched, then that grin took her face again. "It does sting, I will admit. I could have kept him here, you know, and he would have stayed willingly."

"Noxious?" Eiagan chuckled and flung a stack of books off the table, ready to leap over it to behead the woman if she said one ill word about Noxious again.

"You do not even know him. You know nothing of his heart or his desires, only what you see on the surface. Tell me, do you even know the things he likes? Colors, foods, the things he desires for his daughter?"

Eiagan froze, anger seeping from that place within, the one she shared with her foe. The Allurigard blood never took kindly to being taunted, especially where their prized possessions were concerned. Eiagan paused and blinked. It was true, though she hated with every fiber of her being to admit it, Nessa was not wrong. Even now, even with everything between them and all they had been through together, she still branded him as *hers*. Her favored dragon, her dearest friend, her most trusted ally. What of him? What was she to *him*?

This distraction blurred Eiagan's mind.

"You care for him, I know," Nessa said, but always with that taunting tone that tore its claws over Eiagan's mind. Nessa was more like their father than she knew. She even played his games, picked her mind as Icluedian did.

"Enough of this. It ends now. Either come with me or fight me, but close your mouth and choose." It had to end before it went too far, before Eiagan's plan was no longer her own but twisted to suit her sister's evil ways.

The mage's lips spread into a wicked grin, one that said Eiagan had just been made a fool of — and she had. Nessa blinked to her side and plunged a dagger deep into Eiagan's chest, so deep it sliced rib bone and stuck. Eiagan gasped and clutched the handle of the dagger, but Nessa plunged a second blade deep into her abdomen, thrusting her backward. Eiagan landed hard, forcing the breath from her lungs.

Nessa rose and stood over her and pressed her boot on the dagger protruding from Eiagan's abdomen. Nothing happened. Eiagan did not cry out, did not scream. She didn't even wince. Instead, she smiled.

Nessa's face contorted as confusion and doubt took her mind to places she dared not explore. "How… how are you… What is this?"

Eiagan shifted her position, releasing herself from beneath Nessa's boot. The mage stumbled back as Eiagan rose and tore the daggers from her chest and abdomen, tossed them on the floor with a clang.

"What magic is this?" Nessa demanded. "You have no magic of your own! You should be dead! How are you projecting?"

Eiagan touched her wounds, smoothed the slick blood between her fingers, then snapped. The blood was gone, her wounds healed, her body clean as if nothing had ever happened to it.

"I know my own blood, Nessa, and a warrior's weakest point is their own trick."

Nessa's gasp was the last thing Eiagan saw before her mind swirled. Blackness took her again, forcing her mind into a state of survival that she had to fight with every ounce of her consciousness. Soon, light emerged from the other side of this ruse, bringing Eiagan fully back into her body. She gasped when her projection returned to her, settled inside, and merged with the present moment. She stood over Nessa's sleeping form, her true flesh and blood and bone body resting upon a luxurious bed of furs.

Nessa's eyelids whipped open and she sucked in a breath. Her gaze darted to Eiagan, filled to bursting with the sort of fear a caged animal has when they know it's over. She tried to sit, but the toxin had already taken her.

"Do not try to move too much," Eiagan said. "It won't kill you, but you will not overpower it."

"What have you done?" Nessa asked, gasping for each breath, struggling to sit despite Eiagan's warnings.

"I played your game better than you did, sister. And now here we are, waiting." Eiagan's gaze crossed the room and settled on a chaise. She went to it and sat, waiting for the toxin to sedate Nessa enough that she could be moved to Iditania's prison on the mountain. It had been a feat to find Nessa's body before she

378

discovered Eiagan had entered the castle through one of Iditania's favored portals, but the moment she injected her sister with the sedative, she felt herself fade as a projection of her found its way to the library… for this… the end.

"Nox…" Nessa whispered. "He is… safe." Sweat dripped from her forehead, dotted her upper lip, seared the remnants of her bloody warpaint until it was almost gone. Like this, Eiagan saw her, the resemblance between them. "On his… way… home," she panted.

"So you said, and you better hope that is true or I will peel every bit of your skin from your bones before the toxin takes its effect."

Nessa growled. "Just kill me!"

"No," Eiagan said. "It would be too merciful, and you do not deserve such things. Besides, I have no desire to kill another sibling and ruin what is left of my soul. This is not ideal for me either, but it is what must happen."

Nessa's glare might have frozen less formidable women, but Eiagan did not even catch a chill. The mage redirected her gaze to the ceiling and relaxed, though Eiagan remained vigilant. Iditania assured her the toxin would work if Eiagan could inject it into Nessa, hence the final ruse — a projection of Eiagan in the library, the very place Catia saw Nessa kill her. And Nessa had killed her, in a sense. The vision did not claim Eiagan had been *there* in the flesh.

Nessa licked her lips and released a great sigh. She hadn't much fight left in her after all these centuries. Eiagan understood.

"Do you ever think that we were cursed from the moment Serecala gave us birth?" Nessa asked, her head lolling slightly to the right so she could see Eiagan fully. Like this, exhausted and beaten, she seemed like a normal woman.

Eiagan snickered. "Nearly every day."

"Icluedian was a monster, but I think it was she who ruined us most. She was no mother, not truly, and mine in Asantaval was no better. Despite it, you were a good mother." Nessa's eyes matched the color of Eiagan's, exhibiting the Allurigard genes in all of their destructive glory.

"I tried to be everything ours was not," Eiagan admitted though she was never really sure if she had been.

Nessa's eyes closed, but she yanked them open again, connecting with Eiagan. "I should not have… killed… your son." Tears slipped from her eyes, but Eiagan could not be sure it was not put on. It caused an ache in her heart, but not enough to forgive this woman for stealing the only thing she had ever done right in her long life. Instead, she only nodded.

Nessa swallowed. "Nox said…" She paused to breath. It wouldn't be long. "He said you might have loved me… showed me… all the ways I was wrong."

Eiagan chuckled again. "And you believed him? It only took centuries for you to see it."

She barely shook her head. "Some part of me always felt it." Another swallow, a quick huff of breath. "Perhaps I was… too afraid to accept it… but I wonder what might have been if I had only told you." She laughed, low and quiet. "We might have had… the grandest kingdom in all the world. I see that now but… I'm tired."

"It's the toxin. I will keep you safe until you are imprisoned. Worry not."

"No. It isn't that. I'm… *tired.* Exhausted with life. I wish you would end it. Just kill me, Eiagan."

Eiagan stood and crossed the room, stopped at Nessa's bedside, and kneeled. "I cannot."

Eternal life was Nessa's punishment. Caught in prison with nothing but her thoughts, her memories, her ruined plans... that was her punishment.

"Why? I killed your son. I killed... many you have loved." Her breaths were frantic, wheezing.

"For that I *want* to kill you, but I cannot kill forever without end, and I cannot bear the thought of killing another of my blood, one who has suffered as I have. I must end it somewhere, and it is with you. Here. Now."

"I have everlasting life, but I *can* die. Where will you imprison me?" Nessa followed Eiagan's gaze, kept eye contact. "I know of... only one place that might contain my power. You will take me there? To our grandmother's eternal prison?"

Our grandmother. It sent a chill down Eiagan's spine.

"Someone will be assigned to bring you food and water and clean things. It is a prison, Nessa, not a torturous death sentence."

She let her gaze burn into Eiagan's. "I will escape one day. This, you know."

Eiagan's gray-white eyes did not flinch. "I know."

"And you are not afraid?"

Eiagan lifted her chin a fraction, peered down at Nessa. "No."

Nessa's eyes fluttered again, her fight lost. When they closed, Eiagan checked her pulse. It was strong and true, steady... unlike the woman who wielded it. It would be so easy to end her here, to kill her, and none would be the wiser. She could say it did not go as planned, that the toxin did not work, but Eiagan found she did not have the heart or the constitution for it.

Nessa was her sister.

And now her prisoner.

Eiagan heard his footsteps before he entered, and his voice was welcome after so much worry.

"You didn't kill her," Noxious said. He crossed the room and let his hand fall on her shoulder, offering his support once again. Nessa's words echoed in her mind, reminding her that she still had a hold over Nox that was unfair to him. She had to let him go.

Silence fell over them for a long while as they stood by Nessa's beside, until finally, Eiagan could take no more.

"We must move her to the prison before the toxin wears off. I have no desire to fight her in the flesh," Eiagan said. She lifted her gaze to Nox, whose mind was a far sight worse for the journey. His golden eyes connected with hers, released a thousand years of worry onto her, then fluttered closed.

"I do not know who I am anymore," he admitted. "I couldn't leave here until I knew. I just…"

Eiagan swallowed. "I know. Let us go home, my friend. There is much to discuss."

FORTY

Eiagan Allurigard

Eiagan's stomach still hadn't settled despite Porvarth's insistence that this summit was the single best step forward anyone on the throne of Goranin might make. It established peace, settled old rifts, and made allies of powerful and influential leaders—those that were left, of course after Nessa slaughtered her way through the ancient kingdoms. Soon, she would be expected to address those rulers and offer solutions to those problems that remained, prayerfully keeping peace among them all for more than a few measly years. It had only been a day since Nessa's imprisonment, so Eiagan tried to reassure herself.

A knock on the door interrupted her pacing, but it was not unwelcome. Perhaps slipping away from her own worries, even for a moment, might offer clarity and peace. She pulled the door open and found both Porvarth and Nox awaiting entry. She stepped aside and allowed them into her private room, but the solemn expression on Nox's face did little to ease her worry. She glanced at Porvarth, but his was no better.

"What is the matter?" she asked.

Noxious shrugged. "Nothing the matter, only a little uneasy about a bit of unresolved tension."

"Between?" Eiagan shifted her glance between Porvarth and Nox, who shared their own tension-filled stare. "Well?"

Nox ran his hands through his hair then over his face before releasing a deep sigh. "I have unresolved feelings about my time with Nessa, and as such, I am clouded and confused. I need a mission, Eiagan, one that would be safe enough for Violet to accompany me."

Eiagan blinked several times, clearing the fog of confusion from her own mind. "Unresolved feelings such as?"

Porvarth brushed his palm over her cheek and cupped it gently, diverting her attention. "He just needs to clear his head, darling. Nessa was not... shall we say *unlike* you in many ways, and as such, those of us with foolish hearts and forgiving ways are often—"

"What?" Eiagan interrupted, her jaw falling open. She knew Nox felt sympathy for Nessa, even enough empathy to wish she had had a better life, but, Lord above, was there *more?*

"It is not as it seems, Eiagan," Nox said, issuing Porvarth a scathing glare. "I feel for her, and that is all. She was as ruined by your father as you and the others, and I saw more when I was with her than I could ever explain. Between missing my wife and learning so much about a woman who—well, I only need a little time, my friend. My family and yours are inextricably entwined, and for a while, I need that to not be so."

Odd as it was, Eiagan *did* have some understanding of Noxious and his problem. She swallowed the bile of disgust so she might support her dear friend. "The young prince of Isadore has requested an advisor to help him renew his kingdom and strengthen alliances until he is of age to do so on his own. If she is willing, I can send Iditania along with you. She might care for Violet when you work. Would this be a position to your liking?"

Noxious searched Eiagan's eyes, read her like a book. "You do not like the arrangement. You want me to stay."

She did, but it was for her own selfish ways. In that, Nessa was right. Nox needed more than trailing along beside her as her second for however many years they had left to live. He deserved more. She sighed and leaned into Porvarth's touch.

"I want my family together, Nox, but I also understand that you need something to occupy you while your heart and mind heal. You deserve a life led the way you see fit. We will see you, though not as often as I would like, and I will feel secure knowing my grandmother will be there to aid you with Violet."

"Your grandmother does seem to love her," Nox said with a small smile. Iditania hadn't let the child, among others, out of her sight since little Violet returned. There was much regret in Iditania, including her inability to protect them from Nessa.

"Violet might enjoy an adventure outside the borders of Goranin. I remember the Isadorian landscape well. It was quite an enjoyable time when Icluedian sent me there, and it was the only place that ever soothed me in any way."

"You trust her fully with my child?" Nox asked, hesitating after all poor Violet had been through in a matter of a few months.

"I do. She will care for her. Iditania will not be made a fool of again," Eiagan said.

Nox looked once more to Porvarth. "Isadore is a beautiful place," he added, sealing Nox's fate.

Nox nodded. "Alright then. I suppose we will leave once the summit has finished."

Porvarth gasped. "I should think you would stay for the wedding and recoronation of the true and rightful queen. I am offended you would leave before such frill and fanfare!"

"You are only annoyed I will not see you crowned king, loxmore," Nox teased.

"We must give the people what they want, lizard friend," Porvarth teased. He would be a good king, kind and merciful, reminding Eiagan that her position did not always require a blade edge to be successful.

"What will the others do?" Nox asked, curious since it seemed their family had more duties to perform before they might all be together.

Apart but together, still family, she reminded herself. Of them all, Eiagan was quite sure her heart would ache most for Reven, the young prince who had fallen so deeply in love with a princess from a foreign land he was willing to give up his birthright to follow her anywhere. In this case, it was all the way across the seas to her kingdom of Nelaravore.

"Reven seeks the hand of the Princess of Nelaravore, and so he must return with her in three days to speak with her parents. Our alliance will remain strong, especially if Reven is heir to the throne alongside his future wife. Ballan and Astrid will go along with them. Zanaka chose his position as general over leaving with them, but I suspect that did not come without sacrifice in his heart. He will want time to adjust, time to visit them as well." Eiagan thought about her family once again and how spread across the world they might be, but it was good. They would keep peace among the nations.

"Emora and Ari will marry. He asked her just this morning," Porvarth said, the hopeless romantic who never gave up on Eiagan despite every reason to turn away from her horrid ways.

"Yes, well, she wishes to marry soon, sure he might change his mind," Eiagan said.

Porvarth chuckled. "He would no sooner change his mind than… Well, anything. He loves her."

"Borgard leaves tonight. He wishes to see his daughter after all these years, though her family hesitates to move back to Balcon. Vey and his wife have joined in the rebuilding of Goranin, while Gael has declared he will bring Asantaval to the surface soon. He will return there after the summit, but we will keep a close eye on those developments." Eiagan still did not *fully* trust him, though she suspected that had more to do with Nessa than anything Gael had done.

Nox raised an eyebrow and watched Porvarth's reaction when he asked, "And Erdravac? When will the new king return to his bloody kingdom?"

Porvarth's nose turned up, but he said nothing. The men would not be friends, likely, but Porvarth respected Erdravac enough to wish him well.

"It will take time, but he will bring Varrow back into some semblance of glory just as we will Goranin. Our alliance might be the strongest it has been since before the kingdom was split. I have spoken with Tend, Quix, and Catia. They will go with him to ensure he is safe. I do not entirely trust their armies, but with the dragons and the prognosticator, he stands a chance," Eiagan said.

"If there is a problem, do you think Catia will see it before it happens?" Nox asked.

"I pray so," Eiagan said, her black hair billowing in the breeze. It drew her attention to the window, reminding her that Luke was out there somewhere, figuring out where his people had gone and what might become of him now that his curse had been absolved. When she'd returned to her people sleeping in the forest, Luke had disappeared into the darkness while she roused them. They had searched for him, but it seemed he'd chosen a different path for himself and his people, one that did not include her or her support.

"Are you thinking of Lucifer? Or Luke, I suppose I should say. How odd he did not stay even to seek our help," Porvarth said, his gaze following hers to the window. She nodded. Porvarth slid his fingers down her arm and clasped her hand. "I am sure he will contact you. You broke his curse, Eiagan, and a man never forgets that sort of thing. He will return one day, even if only to tell you what he discovered and why he left with no goodbye."

"I only wish things had not taken centuries to —"

"Shh… no, my love. Everything happened as it should, even the difficult and gut-wrenching parts brought us to where we are now."

Nox slipped from the room, leaving her alone with Porvarth.

"I know in my mind, but my heart still hurts," she admitted.

"Then I will remind you every day that it only means you are human and you *have* a heart, darling. I love you, and after all these centuries, you are mine. I would wait another five hundred years, suffer everything all over again, if it meant I would be by your side in the end."

Eiagan smiled, if small and weak. "You have been with me since the beginning, haven't you?"

He chuckled. "You mean when you barged into my cave and demanded I heal you, then forced me to go along on a deadly journey with you to reclaim your throne?" He brushed her black hair over her shoulder and kissed her cheek, her jaw, and her nose.

Eiagan gripped his upper arms and pulled him away slightly, forcing him to look her in the eyes — those white-gray orbs that were just like her father's, though they were the only part of him that remained in any way. "I meant from the beginning, Porvarth, from that first day when my father killed your family. You knew me then, and you did not fear me. Despite everything I did and the horrible person I became, you never gave up hope that I would become something more. For five centuries, you prayed for me."

His eyes, blue as sapphires, would never be red again, but this way, he seemed more like the boy he was then. He'd been handsome even when he was young and gangly, which had not been lost on the young princess when he sat upon her horse, biting back sobs of pain the day Icluedian killed his parents and every animal on his farm. He'd been brave, wanted to save her when Icluedian lashed her so many times she lost consciousness. He never stopped waiting for her to realize she was more than Eiagan Allurigard, the Winter Queen. She was Eiagan, a little girl trapped inside an invincible, immortal being who only needed someone to love her without reason or expectation.

Porvarth said nothing. Instead, he kissed her and wrapped her in his embrace, showing her he was that someone.

"I will love you forever, my queen," he murmured, filling her with the courage she needed to command the summit. "From that first day, I knew I could never forget you. The kindness in your eyes despite what your father had done was the only thing that kept me from walking off a cliff that day."

Eiagan kissed him, letting her mind slip free from the binds of her blood. Perhaps, one day, Emora would do the same.

In the bowels of Vidkun castle, the discussion from the meeting room echoed through the halls. It seemed pleasant enough, but she was prepared for anything and everything to go wrong. The tentative truces between long-warring countries were no longer needed, with Nessa imprisoned in Iditania's immortal cage, but Eiagan hoped they might realize how lovely peace could be and uphold the truce in perpetuity.

Noxious, beaming, met Porvarth and Eiagan at the entrance to the meeting room. His smile was the falsest she had ever seen, but she pretended for his sake that it was real. He had been quiet since his return, and now she knew why, but Eiagan and the rest of their family did not hold it against him.

"It seems jovial in there," Nox said, nodding toward the room.

"Let us see if we can maintain the feelings forever," Eiagan said and pushed through the door. Silence took the room as all eyes landed on the queen, their eternal ruler despite her flaws. Her people had chosen her again, supported her, and trusted her to run the summit, to rule Goranin, and to provide them with a proper heir who would grow up in a home filled with love, honor, and loyalty. Eiagan blushed, thinking of her future with Porvarth, but it was time. He had waited for her long enough, and she wanted to be his wife.

"What solemn faces," Eiagan said with a grin, likely something many of the leaders had never seen upon her face. "I come to offer peace and a lasting relationship between my kingdom and all of yours, assuming it is what you wish after all this time fighting?"

390

Eyes shifted, glanced around the room, then back to her.

"It is what I want most for Varrow, of course," Erdravac said, standing to get the summit moving. "We have discussed trade in private, but here in the presence of the others, I would like to extend our hand formally. We can provide multitudes of textiles to Goranin in exchange for grain, which you know is difficult to grow in our rocky lands."

"We accept the offer and hope to increase our agreements," Eiagan said. "We will provide military support to your kingdom in exchange for yours, as discussed." Erdravac nodded.

"My kingdom is prepared to increase its visibility, but it must be done slowly. We have remained hidden with our dragons for some time, and for a good reason, but we are willing to work with others to establish a peaceful trade and existence," Darby offered. The rough men of Balcon and Slovartark ate her up like a snack, but she didn't flinch. Instead, she lifted her chin and dared them to cross her.

Isadore's young prince stood, already taking control of his position. "I am pleased to accept your aid to my kingdom, Your Highness. I believe it will be most encouraging to my people as we rebuild. We haven't much to offer now, but I would like to keep communication open with our neighbors for the future."

The remainder of the summit went as well as the beginning save Gael and the Slovartark representative's constant bickering over the history of Asantaval. Eiagan merely rolled her eyes and understood that not *all* of the kingdoms were meant to work well together. They only needed peace, and if they kept up their end of the bargain, then there was no reason to believe they could not experience many centuries of happiness.

But she was no fool.

Eiagan knew men could not keep the peace for that long, but she did pray it would last long enough for the people to learn to hate war, to hate fighting, and to rise up when things slid downhill. Empowering her citizens was of the utmost importance, and she would do so if it was the last thing she did on her throne.

EPILOGUE

Eiagan Allurigard

Despite the centuries passed, Eiagan remembered the pain of childbirth as if it were only yesterday she had brought Iric into the world. She clenched her jaw and pushed one last time, heaved through the pain as a tiny, wiggling bundle of joy screamed out into the dead of night. Eiagan fell back onto the bed and sighed, her body ruined entirely. She had fought wars, died and returned from the Bleak, lived longer than any human deserved, and this brought her body to its limit. She could hardly move enough to breathe.

"Darling?" Porvarth brushed sweaty hair from his wife's face and kissed her cheek. "What can I do?"

Eiagan forced a weak smile and turned her face to kiss him. "I will be fine. I am only exhausted."

"A beautiful daughter," Lenora, the midwife, giggled and wiped the baby clean, then handed her to her parents. "What a gorgeous little princess," she added.

Lenora cleaned up the area and covered Eiagan, careful not to disturb the new family in their moment of joy.

Eiagan cradled her daughter—already with such dark sprigs of hair—and kissed her head. The child's eyes sparkled as blue as the ocean, and Eiagan could not help but thank God for that. Something about the Allurigard eyes, those pale gray orbs, invited the Allurigard blood to run wild in her, in Emora, in Nessa... even in sweet Reven from time to time. But this child was different. She was more. She would be more than her name, more than her destiny. She would change the Allurigard name from feared to beloved.

Porvarth wrapped a protective arm around his family, holding them close. He had proven himself a wise and worthy king, and the people of Goranin adored him. Though part of her would always love her first husband, Zero's memory had prepared her for this, a life with a man who was made just for her. Porvarth was her perfect compliment, the one who knew her best and loved her anyway.

"What shall we name her?" Porvarth whispered. "I thought perhaps we might name her Reeve."

Eiagan smiled and her heart warmed. "Thank you, my darling, but we have Reven and he is enough. He fulfills the need in my heart for my brother, and so I had another thought."

He raised his eyebrow and waited with a cheeky grin that used to give her some form of indigestion. Often, it meant he had a humorous comment or anecdote prepared, but not this time. Now, he only absorbed the moment with her, feeding on the happiness this new life would bring to their family.

"I never told you this," Eiagan said. "I never truly understood until later, but when I found your sister in the fields at the loxmore community, what little of my heart remained almost broke entirely. I had wanted to find her for you, had hoped she was alive for your sake. When I found her dead, I... I *hurt* for you. I suppose even then, my heart knew what my mind refused."

Porvarth swallowed. "That time with you in the beginning, just after Moriarian took everything from you, I couldn't help wanting to give it all back. I wanted more than anything to see that little girl inside of you again, to bring you back from the brink of insanity, to..." He shrugged and grinned wider. "I loved you even then, and I both hated and loved it."

"I know," she whispered. "Can we call her Malin? For your sister?"

Porvarth kissed Eiagan's forehead and settled deeper on the bed beside her. "I would adore it."

A knock startled the baby and elicited a great wail unlike any Eiagan had ever heard. She chuckled. "She certainly has my impatience."

Porvarth chuckled and went to the door, allowing Emora and Ari inside the birthing room.

"I am sorry. I simply *could not* wait any longer," Emora said, clasping her hands. Her swollen belly would bring forth another princess soon enough, but the light in her sister's face was thanks to her healthy, lovely niece. "Please, can I hold her?"

Eiagan sat in the bed and handed the wiggling child to her sister.

"Oh, how lovely. Her eyes are so blue." Ari peered over his wife's shoulder and gazed into his niece's eyes. "I sent word to our allies. All are pleased and send their best wishes."

A twinge of hurt took Eiagan, but only for a moment. Her family was spread wide but always in her heart, always a simple message away. She would see them all soon at the annual summit, but she missed them dearly. It didn't seem quite right that Astrid was not there to hold Malin, or that Noxious and the others were several day's journey away, but they were all happy and that was what mattered most to Eiagan.

A tear slipped free from her pale eyes and over her cheek.

Porvarth brushed it away and offered her a warm, loving smile. "We did it, my love."

Eiagan sighed. Finally, the Winter Queen knew true happiness.

THREE YEARS LATER

Nessa Callanan

The winter had been colder than usual, but deeper in the cavern, it was warm, especially if one considered the copious woolen and fur blankets Eiagan had included in the last delivery. Nessa pulled one of the furs tighter over her shoulders and shifted so she might read better in the dim lighting. She had no sooner immersed herself in the woes of another than the familiar flapping of Porvarth's wings pulled her from the foreign world again. She closed the book and placed it on the small table beside her bed, unable to ignore the giddiness that gurgled from her chest.

It had been eleven days since Eiagan's last visit, four days later than usual. Nessa licked her lips and ran her hands through her hair, then went to the front of the prison to meet her sister at the enchanted iron bars. The enchantment hardly mattered with her magic fully bound. The first year without it nearly drove her mad, but since then, a certain quiet had taken her mind. Without the constant hum of magical ability buzzing in her body, she found relaxation like she'd never known.

Once she arrived at the gate, Nessa spied three women upon the dragon's back. This was out of the ordinary. If Eiagan ever brought another soul with her, it was usually Ari, and sometimes, though rarely, it was Emora. Ari would shoulder the brunt of the delivery — food, water, clothing, and other items that would sustain Nessa for another week or so. Emora would come when she was feeling particularly charitable, but usually, it was Eiagan alone with her husband, who never stayed. He left her alone to converse with Nessa whether she wanted to or not.

The women — Eiagan, Emora, and Iditania — slipped from Porvarth's back. He lifted himself from the ledge and flew in a circular pattern, waiting. This was also unusual.

Nessa grasped the bars and plastered on her smile. Normally, they were real — at least, over the last year they had been — but this one was forced. Something was wrong, but if she smiled through it, perhaps it would change the future?

"You've brought more visitors. Will they join us for our study? I believe we chose to go over the book of Proverbs again, yes?" Nessa tried to hold her emotions, to stow away that rising urge to scream *what has happened?* Emora frowned and looked at Eiagan but said nothing.

Eiagan dropped a small parcel at her feet. "There will be no scripture study today, I'm afraid."

"No study? But we… I thought… it was important to you?" What had she thought? That Eiagan had somehow found something redeeming in her as she read from that foreign book? Nessa never could decide whether Eiagan read it to convince herself to give her flesh and blood another chance, or whether it was intended to impart some new way of looking at life in Nessa's mind.

"It is important, yes, but there is a pressing matter we must discuss," Eiagan said.

"You're late. What kept you?" Nessa asked. After all this time teaching her their new religion, would her sister change her mind and execute her? That was the expression upon her face, one of murder and mayhem, something uncommon on Eiagan's face nowadays. This new Eiagan held a certain serenity Nessa had watched grow over these years.

"We've been busy," Emora snapped, still cold toward Nessa. Understandable, after everything, but she *did* bring her extra food once. Something called chocolate that Nessa was sure Emora left by accident once she'd put it on her tongue.

Iditania wrung her hands as always. Of them all, Nessa was most uncomfortable with their grandmother's presence.

"We were in Isadore. We have a problem. One not easily solved." Eiagan stepped closer. "I have sent all of my best men on a mission, but I fear they have made no advancement. I would go myself, but I cannot leave the throne."

"Or your child. She is still so young, but what mission requires my knowledge?" Nessa's pale eyes scanned Eiagan's face, then skipped to Emora and Iditania. "I am no advisor to you. I'm merely your lost and forlorn sister whom you are determined will discover redemption before your Lord in time. For what reason have you come here to tell me of your woes?" The pit opened in her stomach. She knew. There was but one reason Eiagan would include her in the goings on of the kingdom.

399

"Noxious has been taken. Disappeared ten days ago, and no one can find him." The words slipped from Eiagan's lips as if they burned her very soul coming out. She wanted to leave the throne, take her husband, and find their dearest friend at any cost—but that cost would be too great now. A daughter too young for such things and a kingdom still in its infancy where reconstruction was concerned would not allow the queen to leap into action as she once did, despite her burning desire to do just that. Leaving now would open Goranin up for potential invasion.

Nessa swallowed. "You said once he enjoys days alone to keep the dragon tame. Perhaps he is only —"

"He left Violet behind, then?" Emora asked, her tone harsh.

"Emora, please," Eiagan said with a sigh. "How would she have known that?"

"He left Violet?" Nessa pressed her cheeks against the bars. Her heart raced. She hadn't seen Nox since the day she was imprisoned. Since… the kiss. Still, despite the time since she last saw him, she knew his tendency to protect his daughter would never change. "Why have you come here, Eiagan? To taunt me with this?"

Eiagan grasped the bars with both hands, her face mere breaths from Nessa's. Her eyes blazed with that heat, the Allurigard stare that all three sisters had perfected eons ago. Her porcelain skin flushed. Through a clenched jaw she said, "You will find him and bring him home to his daughter."

Nessa released the bars and retreated three steps. "Me?"

"I have petitioned his brothers, but neither will search for him. For reasons unknown to me, they harbor him ill will despite all he has done for this kingdom." Her eyes increased their intensity until they were the same ones Nessa had looked into on the battlefield

400

long ago, a time when they were on opposite sides. "You are the only one I know who would risk as much to find him as I would."

Nessa swallowed. Eiagan was not wrong, but searching for a single man among all of the ancient kingdoms was a fools errand.

Eiagan shoved a key into the lock and turned it, her gaze locked on Nessa. "I swear upon all I love, that if you so much as harm a hair on the heads of anyone in this kingdom, I will find you again. I will find you, and I will skin you inch by inch and put your hide on display in the main square. Am I clear?"

Well, perhaps she hadn't changed *that* much. But Nessa understood her anger.

"Why is she here if Violet is alone? Is she not her guardian?" Nessa asked, ramming her finger toward Iditania. She despised the woman, truthfully, for having spawned such a horrendous man as their father, but that was of little consequence now.

"Violet is safe at Vidkun. Do not make me regret this decision, Nessa. It is true that I know of no other person who will go to the ends of the earth to find Nox and bring him home, but if you betray me, it will be your last act of betrayal." Eiagan pulled the iron door open but blocked the escape with her body. "And if you harm Violet—"

Her words were cut short by Nessa's hands on her shoulders, her gaze connected with hers. "Of all the people in the world, Violet is the one I would never harm. Not again. I will find him." She let her hands slide from Eiagan's shoulders, surprised to have survived such an intimate invasion of her sister's privacy. "Somehow, I will find him."

Emora stepped forward. "I will unbind a fraction of your magic, but it—"

"No!" Nessa screeched and retreated farther into the cave. "No! No magic!"

"But how will you—"

"I said no! That dreadful magic tore apart what little of me was not destroyed by our father. It is dark and evil and I will have no part of it." Nessa's fire burned hotter now, threatening to lash out toward the first person who dared step closer. She swallowed again, biting back that hot blood that defined them all. No. She would not allow it to define her any longer.

"You are a mortal woman now, Nessa, without magic." Emora groaned her annoyance, but Eiagan clasped a hand over their sister's shoulder.

"I fear you will be killed before your mission is complete," Iditania said. "No one knows where he has been taken, but there is only one place in Isadore the inhabitants of the kingdom will never tread. If he is there, you will need magic to bring him back." She was still so meek for a woman who could never die, at least not by any means they knew.

"I... I can't." Nessa's throat burned.

"But—"

"Emora," Eiagan scolded. "I remind you of all I accomplished without magic."

"There were magical people who helped you." Emora put her hands on her hips and narrowed her eyes at Eiagan.

Eiagan sighed. "I meant before the revolt, Emora. For centuries I managed to rule this kingdom with a fist so hard no one dared go against me, save you who had ulterior motives. Nessa can manage."

"Eiagan, I—"

Eiagan shook her head and growled. "Enough! It is Noxious, Emora! If I were not tethered to the throne I would go myself, with or without magic. There would be nothing on earth and then some that would stop me from finding him and bringing him home, yet I love him as a sister loves her brother. If I loved him as she does…" Eiagan's voice faded. She closed her eyes and let that calm wash over her, bringing the serene aura back to her present. "If I loved him as Nessa does, there would be no stopping me."

Emora's voice softened as well. "That's what I'm afraid of, sister. Without magic to make it easier, she might resort to… to… less accommodating methods."

"You mean I might revert to the maniacal woman you still believe I am?" Nessa said.

Emora raised a dark eyebrow. "Would anyone blame me for the accusation?"

Nessa stepped forward again, this time her focus solely on Emora. "What I did to you was reprehensible. I know there are no words and no actions I might perform to make what I did right, but I regret it all down to my bones, Emora. Use a travel binding on me. Make it so that I cannot disappear. Make it so that you can find me always with any locator spell you choose, but do it quickly so that I might find him. Please," she said, her lower lip trembling now. The tears would come soon, those traitorous things that seemed to grace her eyes more days than not.

Emora's gray-white eyes matched hers in intensity. She nodded, slight but there, and stepped aside. "I have seen what I needed to see and heard what I needed to hear. Go. Find him, but hurry. If he is where Iditania believes, he won't last long."

Eiagan also stepped aside. "Porvarth will take you to the base of the mountain. There you will find a horse and a pack with enough supplies to get you to Isadore. Once there, the Isadorian council and the king will meet with you and tell you all they know. Do not let them keep anything from you. They will try, for they do not wish to have Nox's death hanging over their heads, and as such they will likely lead you to believe they had no way of knowing this might happen."

"They knew there was a danger?" Nessa asked, her blood already boiling again.

"It seems so. Disappearances are a habit in their kingdom," Eiagan said, practically growling again. "Our resources are at your disposal, but remember what I told you. Do not make me regret this decision." She stepped close, her breath visible in the cold just in front of Nessa's face. "And do not let him die."

Eiagan's eyes watered, reminding Nessa that while Nox was not Eiagan's true love, she did love him well.

"I would rather die myself," Nessa whispered.

"Porvarth!" Eiagan called her husband, who likely would not enjoy a single moment of carrying Nessa anywhere other than right into a tar pit.

The dragon screeched his annoyance and swooped low enough for Nessa to reach him, but had he not she was quite sure Eiagan's shove would have done the trick just as well. She fell with a huff onto the iridescent reptile's back, hardly righting herself before he darted toward the ground. Another screech of discontent and he tossed her on her hide onto the forest floor. There was no mistaking the dragon's intent, but Nessa ignored it in favor of seeking out the horse.

Tied to a pine only a few strides away, it pawed at the earth ready to run. Good. She'd need a horse as hearty as him to do what needed doing, for she intended to run it entirely ragged to reach Isadore by nightfall.

And when she arrived... Oh, when she arrived, she would turn that kingdom upside down until she found what she sought, and they had better pray Noxious the Savage was no worse for the wear.

WHAT'S NEXT?

You might think this is the end of the road… and it is in some ways. For Eiagan, this is her happy ending, but for everyone else the story goes on. We'll see Eiagan and her family pop in occasionally, but the next books in the series will focus on other characters.

So, what can we expect?

Well, up next is the obvious choice — Nessa on her hunt to find Nox. But I have other books planned too, most of which you probably guessed in the last two or three chapters. We have Erdravac and his claim to the throne of Varrow, which is still in the balance. We have Borgard heading to find his daughter. There's Reven and Darby in Nelaravore beginning their relationship in earnest, and last but not least, we have Luke (Lucifer) and his adventure.

But that's not all. I also have prequels and other side novels planned for this mega-series, so have a peek at the next page for information about my website and social media pages so you can stay in the know!

ABOUT THE AUTHOR

M. J. Padgett is first and foremost a mom. Her free-spirited daughter has quite the vivid imagination, and her antics sometimes find their way into her mommy's work. She is a lover of all things chocolate, a Grimm and Dickens addict, a self-proclaimed smarty-pants, and an introvert to the core.

Writing is her true passion (after raising her daughter, of course), and she writes as often as possible. One of her favorite things about writing is creating a world where people can escape reality for a little while, maybe even walk away feeling hopeful about the real world around them. When it comes to reading, she loves a book that can make her forget where she is no matter the genre. If she can get lost and feel like the characters are her real friends, she's a happy reader.

You can visit MJ's website for more information at
www.mjpadgettbooks.com

There, you can join her blog and/or VIP page for exclusive offers, information, and fun activities.

MJ is most active on Instagram here:
https://www.instagram.com/m.j.padgett/

You can also find an amazing interactive platform (coming in 2022) here: www.piratecatpub.com This joint venture with author Crystal Crawford is a fun new way for our readers to grab new books, interact with us as they are written, and get behind the scenes information!

CPSIA information can be obtained
at www.ICGtesting.com
Printed in the USA
BVHW032250271222
655035BV00021B/60

9 798215 260111